OPALS *and* OUTRAGE

OTHER BOOKS AND BOOKS ON CASSETTE
BY LYNN GARDNER

Emeralds and Espionage

Pearls and Peril

Diamonds and Danger

Turquoise and Terrorists

Sapphires and Smugglers

Amethysts and Arson

Jade and Jeopardy

OPALS and OUTRAGE

a novel

Lynn Gardner

Covenant Communications, Inc.

Cover image © copyright 2001 PhotoDisc, Inc.

Cover design copyrighted 2001 by Covenant Communications, Inc.

Published by Covenant Communications, Inc.
American Fork, Utah

Copyright © 2001 by Lynn Gardner
All rights reserved. No part of this book may be reproduced in any format or in any medium without the written permission of the publisher, Covenant Communications, Inc., P.O. Box 416, American Fork, UT 84003. The views expressed herein are the responsibility of the author and do not necessarily represent the position of Covenant Communications, Inc.

This is a work of fiction. The characters, names, incidents, places, and dialogue are products of the author's imagination, and are not to be construed as real.

Printed in the United States of America
First Printing: February 2001

08 07 06 05 04 03 02 01   10 9 8 7 6 5 4 3 2 1

ISBN 1-57734-799-4

This book is dedicated to all Americans, those who wear a uniform and those who do not, who sacrifice their time, energy, and too often their very lives preserving the precious freedoms we enjoy in this "land of promise, which was choice above all other lands, which the Lord God had preserved for a righteous people" (Ether 2:7).

As a child in Idaho during World War II, I remember air raid drills and the black velvet fabric draped over windows to prevent any light from shining through in case of a surprise attack by the enemy. During my third grade year, Mom moved us to the Naval base at Farragut to be near Dad, who was stationed there, when she delivered her fourth child. I loved the huge American flag, which flew proudly over the base, and I adored my father standing guard in that high tower. To me, he was the Great Protector of all things good.

For nearly twenty-five years as a military wife, I waited at home, seeing to our children's needs and the myriad household details, while my husband "sat alert" in a concrete bunker, through the years, waiting for the claxon to send aircrews scurrying to bombers loaded with destruction for an invading enemy, or flew training missions to the far side of the globe. I consoled widows burying their husbands, who were our friends and neighbors, ever grateful that my own husband had returned safely.

But never once did I question my husband's decision to serve his country nor resent his time away from us. The cold war was a very real war, the enemy's face familiar and his threat terrifying.

Today America's greatest enemy is apathy. But that threat is as dangerous and as real to the survival of our freedoms as any army bearing weapons against us. Our war is against those who would make of America a godless nation, and those who would rely on godless men to lead us through the perilous last days. All that's needed for them to succeed is "for good men to do nothing." The war against this enemy must be fought by voting for good, moral people with integrity, and by speaking up against wrongdoing everywhere, from our own communities to the halls of Congress, and especially the White House.

If not now, when? If not me, who?

> Behold, this is a choice land, and whatsoever nation shall possess it shall be free from bondage, and from captivity, and from all other nations under heaven, ***if they will but serve the God of the land, who is Jesus Christ.*** (Ether 2:12; italics added)

CHAPTER 1

I sat up in bed, poised for flight, my heart pounding in terror. I stared about the darkened room, searching for some familiar shape, some identifying smell or sound. Strange bed. Strange room. Awakened from a deep, unsettled sleep by a strange noise. It came again, frighteningly close.

I waited, heart throbbing, hands clammy, not daring to breathe, not daring to move. Had he found me? After chasing me for three thousand miles, had Raven finally found me?

A hand touched my leg. I shot out of bed in a jumble of pillows, sheets, and comforter, choking on the scream that caught in my throat.

He was here! The raven-haired man was in this room. And I was so wound up in bedding that I couldn't run. The strange noise recurred, this time directly under me.

On the other side of the bed, the clock crashed to the floor. Someone stumbled against the night stand in the dark. He would come around the bed, find me as I lay paralyzed with fear on the floor, and finish the job he'd been paid a million dollars to do.

Kill me.

I fought the covers, trying desperately to untangle my legs from the sheet, trying to get to my feet, to find the door, to run for my life.

"Princess?" A sleepy voice spoke out of the darkness. "Where's my cell phone? I can't find the light."

Pent-up breath escaped in a rush. Relief washed through me as pure, undiluted ecstasy when I realized my husband was the man in the room with me, not Raven, the assassin. Awareness returned of where we were and why. I even recognized the strange noise that had awakened me from my horrible, recurring nightmare. Picking up the noisy lump under my leg, I felt for the "on" button.

"Yes?" I mumbled into the end I hoped was the mouthpiece.

"Bunny, you sound out of breath. Did I catch you just coming in from a night on the town?"

I groaned. "No, Dad." As the frantic beating of my heart quieted, I collapsed into the bundle of bedding still twisted around me, and with a corner of the sheet wiped the perspiration from my face. "Actually, I was running for my life."

Bart found the switch on the bedside lamp, illuminating our hotel suite in New Orleans' French Quarter. I shivered again, comforted by the knowledge that the frightening nightmare was simply that—a nightmare.

"Sorry, Bunny," Dad said, his rich, deep voice as soothing as hot chocolate on a cold morning. "I know it's turned your life upside down. I wish that whole episode had never happened. That I could have protected you somehow. But you know, you need . . ."

"I know, Dad." I tried not to sound irritated. "I need to put it behind me, get it out of my system. I know all the right words—I know what I'm supposed to do. I just don't have control of my mind when I sleep."

We'd been through this conversation time and again in the four months since an assassin had stalked me across the continent, seeking to claim the bounty that international terrorists had offered for my death. I'd been low man on the totem pole, with a mere million-dollar price tag on my head. Much more than that had been offered for all other members of Anastasia, Interpol's anti-terrorist division. That none of us had been caught was a major miracle.

"Sorry to have to call this time of night. Where are you, Bunny?"

"New Orleans." I wiped my clammy hands on the sheet. "What time is it?" I couldn't see a clock. No light peeked through the drapes, a pretty good indication that morning hadn't yet arrived.

"Midnight here in California. That makes it two A.M. in the party city. Why aren't you two out partying? Never mind. Let me talk to Bart." In a single breath, in the midst of a thought, Dad switched from father mode to Interpol mode. All business. Serious business, from the sound of his voice.

Bart performed the same transformation when he picked up his watch. He rolled off the bed to the floor beside me, reaching for the phone even before Dad asked to speak to him. I cradled the instrument between us so we could both hear the conversation.

"You're intruding on our vacation, you know, boss man." Bart plumped a pillow, pulled the down-filled comforter over us, and we snuggled together to hear the bad news. "What's up?"

"The Jihad is coming to America." Dad's declaration reverberated through us like an earthquake. If we'd had any trace of sleep-induced fogginess, it dissipated immediately.

Islamic Jihad terrorists were the elite of the terrorist world, declaring holy war on America, Israel, or any individual or group undertaking activities they perceived as threatening their interests. Ruthless, highly trained, well-armed, they believed their calling in life was to serve Allah by destroying unbelievers who opposed their ideology. And they were true mercenaries, available for hire to destroy anyone or anything for the right amount of money.

"How do you know?" Bart stiffened, his voice as tense as his frame.

I turned my back, snuggling into Bart's arms spoon fashion, needing the additional warmth of his body, mine chilled to the bone by Dad's unwelcome declaration.

His deep voice boomed through the small cell phone near my ear. "I was on the phone to Buck McAffrey when he got a call from Barksdale AFB in Shreveport."

Bart interrupted. "Who's McAffrey?"

"FBI agent in charge of the East Texas/Louisiana area. We've been friends a long time—work together occasionally. When his case load got too heavy last month, I helped him out. Offered to help on this one, since it's right up our alley. Anastasia's better trained to ferret out and deal with terrorists than anyone else in the world. I've got an assignment for you."

"Wait a minute." I turned around so I could speak into the phone. "What about our vacation? You promised we could have a whole week alone together."

"Just a brief interruption, Bunny. Meet David Chen at the airport at seven A.M. He's in the Lear jet. By then, we'll have a destination for ninic cleaned out that last group of terrorists in Iraq, he ...umber here in the States. We're checking it out now."

...ught. If I were a gambler, I'd bet my inheritance this would not be just a brief interruption. Good-bye, good times. Hello, trouble.

As Bart reached for a pencil and paper from the nightstand, he moved the phone out of hearing range. I pulled the comforter around my chin and pictured my father, Jack Alexander, head of the handpicked, uniquely talented and trained agents who battled terrorism worldwide. My mother, Margaret, his right hand and second in command, worked undercover with him.

They had recruited Bart fresh out of college. After six years, my husband's heartbeat still accelerated at the mention of a new case, a new challenge, another opportunity to defeat terrorism. This dangerous work was his life's blood, his passion, and sometimes I thought he loved it more than he did me. I was wise enough, however, never to make him choose, no matter how terrified I was at the possibility of losing him to a terrorist's bullet.

A year ago I'd begged, pleaded, then tricked my father into sending me to Quantico to complete the formal training I needed to become an agent with Anastasia. I loved my husband passionately, never wanted to be separated from him, and thought fighting terrorism at his side would be *my* contribution to the world.

As Bart moved back beside me, I intertwined my freezing legs with his warm ones. I couldn't shake the chill. Not with this news. Not with the everlasting nightmares from our last case still plaguing me. Raven, the assassin who'd trailed me from Los Angeles to the East Coast, disrupted my sleep all too often. Between Raven approaching closer each night, and the recurring dream of a crying baby I could never find to console, sleep had become an enemy.

His conversation finished, Bart tossed the phone on the bed and snuggled under the comforter, cocooning his arms and legs around me. "We could get back in bed, you know," he said, nuzzling my ear. "This floor's not the most comfortable I've ever slept on."

"You sleep on a lot of floors, do you?"

"More than I like to, unless I've got you next to me." He brushed an errant long black curl from my forehead.

"Does that make the floor softer?"

His breath tickled my ear. "No, but I forget all else when you're this close."

I sighed. "Didn't the slave driver just order us to pack our bags and surrender our vacation for duty and country?"

"Mmm. You smell good."

I twisted to face my husband, nose to nose. "You're avoiding my question." His lips got in the way. I came up for air. "Our first vacation in months is hereby canceled, is it not?" He sidestepped the issue, bestowing tender kisses from my eyelids to my chin and down my neck.

"You're not playing fair," I protested breathlessly. "I'm trying to hold a serious conversation here."

"Not to worry. We'll get to it in time."

"In time for what? An early morning flight?" His lips interrupted me again. I gave up. Or gave in, or defected to the enemy, or whatever you call it. Sweet surrender.

We did get back to my question about six A.M., when that strange noise woke me again—that horrible, exasperating telephone ringing above my head. Bart reached up on the bed, groped for a minute, then settled back on the pillow with the offending instrument pressed against his ear. I could hear Dad's voice without even trying.

"This is your wake-up call. Time to check out and be at the airport when David arrives. Here's the meeting time and address in Shreveport. You'll meet an airman who has details he wouldn't reveal over the phone to McAffrey. He alluded to an incriminating piece of paper in his possession. Make sure you get it. Alli, are you there?"

Bart thrust the phone toward me while he jotted down the information Dad gave him, then struggled to his feet, heading for the shower. "Doesn't that man ever sleep?" he muttered as he turned on the water.

"I'm here, Dad. What's the matter?" I peeled the comforter off and stretched.

"Your mother informed me I'm worse than a scoundrel for interrupting your vacation. Sorry, Bunny." He did sound just the slightest bit sorry. "This is so important, and you're right in the area . . ."

"So is David Chen."

"Bunny . . ."

I interrupted him. "If David's here in New Orleans, he could handle this assignment. What's so important that we couldn't take the rest of our vacation?"

"You can, after you interview an airman in Shreveport. Do whatever you want after you report on that visit. I need you two on this one, Bunny. It's vital that we get this information as soon as possible."

"David has the info we need?" I asked in resignation.

"Yes. I'll be in the Control Center, waiting for your report."

"I love you dearly, father of mine, but you're pushing the envelope."

Dad's laughter rumbled through the earpiece. "Message received, Bunny. I'm taking flak from both ends, but I swear, if this wasn't so important, I wouldn't have called in the middle of the night and interrupted your first vacation in months. You've reminded me, your sweet mother has reminded me, and I seem to recall your husband even mentioned it. I'm duly chastened, but hurry up and don't keep David waiting. I need that information."

I sighed as I headed for the shower. I'd painstakingly arranged a special day today, concluding with a wonderful surprise for Bart tonight. Shreveport might be a wonderful city, but it wasn't New Orleans, it wasn't on the banks of the Mississippi River, and I was positive I'd never be able to duplicate the romantic setting and the unique dinner I'd planned.

This vacation was extremely important, and timing was everything. The doctor hoped we'd be able to relax, leave stress behind, and just enjoy each other—and that when we returned to California, we'd have been successful in conceiving the child we both wanted so much. It was the culmination of months of tests and innovative procedures as we dealt with my apparent infertility after a tubal pregnancy left me with only one badly damaged fallopian tube. To have it all interrupted at this point was maddening. Although the results of the last attempt weren't in yet, none of us felt certain it had been successful, so we were all planning, hoping, praying that this time together, this vacation now gone awry, would accomplish the "almost impossible," as one doctor had called it.

It didn't seem fair that every year in the United States alone, over two million unwanted babies were aborted, murdered in cold blood, sacrificed as surely as if they had been placed upon idolatrous altars, and I couldn't manage to conceive even one.

I dressed in the cool cotton emerald-green sweater and broomstick print skirt I'd planned to wear today in New Orleans—something I could have worn all day, then to dinner tonight if we hadn't had time to come back and change clothes. Even with my wonderful plans blown out of the water, I wasn't giving up easily. Just in case the opportunity presented itself elsewhere, I'd be ready to follow through.

An hour later, we met an exhausted-looking David Chen at New Orleans Lakefront Airport on the apron with Anastasia's Lear jet. Age thirty-five, quiet and contemplative, with the grace and body of a gymnast, David had piercing dark eyes that missed very little.

"So what does my father have up his sleeve this time, David?" I asked.

"Morning, Allison." David handed Bart an envelope. "What do you mean?"

"Why didn't Dad give you this assignment? You're here. You're available, right?"

"Here, but not available." He flashed an apologetic smile. "Just passing through from the Middle East. I'm tying up loose ends on that last case in Iraq. Need to get back to the Control Center to figure out what's going on. Jack diverted me last night to leave the Lear with you and made reservations for me to return commercial. Sorry about your vacation."

"What did you find there that tied in here?" Bart asked, glancing inside the envelope.

"Would you believe a map of Idaho?" David's tired voice betrayed a note of disbelief. "In fact, you hold the evidence in your hands."

"What's the connection between Idaho and terrorists in Iraq?" At the moment, a logical connection eluded me.

"We'd all like the answer to that. Dominic found indications that Iraqi terrorists have connections with supremacist groups in Idaho, but we haven't established yet just what those connections are, other than possibly training." David paused, running his hands over his red eyes and down his face as if wiping away the fatigue. "Unfortunately, that's a pretty volatile combination, which is why your dad's pulling Anastasia off of whatever they were working on to concentrate on this. And if the suspected military clue actually connects with those two, we've got big trouble."

He pointed at the envelope Bart held. "That map is the current focus of our investigation. I faxed copies to the Control Center so they could start working on it while I was en route."

I looked at Bart. "I don't like the vibes I'm getting from this."

"Ditto, Princess. We'd better move, or we'll be late for the Shreveport meeting. You can check the evidence on our way." Bart slapped David on the shoulder. "Sweet dreams. Let me know what you find out about the map. I'll call Jack as soon as we finish this mysterious interview."

"Watch your back, Bart. A couple of the Iraqis escaped when we captured the rest. If this is as big as Jack suspects, that map could be a pretty hot item."

"Wait a minute." I didn't like the way this was turning out. I was supposed to be on leave from bad guys who had a tendency to shoot first and ask questions later. "I thought this was to be a simple interview, and then we'd be happily on our way."

"You can always hope, but I sure wouldn't count on it." David picked up his duffle bag and headed for the terminal, then turned, and walking backward, delivered a message that chilled me to my bones. "In fact, I'd be very careful if I were you. The two who escaped will have to answer to Osama bin Laden for the loss of the map. If they survive that interview, the only thing that'll save them will be recovering it."

CHAPTER 2

Bart pulled me into his arms, kissed me with unexpected enthusiasm, then gave me a gentle shove toward the plane. "Time to take up the gauntlet, my love," he said cheerfully, scooping our bags off the tarmac and propelling me in front of him.

"Bartholomew James Allan, you don't have to be so happy about our plans being scrapped. You could at least pretend to be annoyed, pretend to be angry with Dad for thrusting you right back into combat with the world's most notorious terrorist."

My grinning husband tossed our bags into the plane before literally picking me up and carrying me aboard the sleek Lear jet.

"Would you like me to be dishonest?" Bart asked, settling his six-foot four-inch frame into the pilot's seat and beginning take-off procedures. "Lie to you and tell you I'm outraged that Jack pulled me away from the French Quarter and the Garden District and the thousand other tourist places on your list?"

"Yes." I plopped into the co-pilot's seat and buckled my seat belt. "Lie to me. Tell me it was wonderful spending time with your wife. Lie to me and tell me you'd rather do anything than throw yourself back into Osama bin Laden's gun sights. Make me believe you've chosen this line of work because of duty to country and fellow man, instead of the rush you get from danger. Convince me you believe it's a dirty job, but somebody's got to do it. Just don't be so blasted cheerful about all my weeks of planning being chucked in an instant."

My tirade stopped while Bart contacted the tower for permission and instructions to take off. I stewed in silence. A pox on all the terrorists in the world! Why did my life have to be so impacted by every thought that occurred in the twisted minds of people like bin Laden? Millions of people in the world—make that billions—had never even heard of the man, or those like him, whose agendas consisted of death and destruction for no other reasons than power and greed.

Why did my life have to revolve around these creatures? They even invaded my sleep, filling my dreams with unimaginable horror. I couldn't escape from their evil, far-reaching tentacles. I hated not feeling in control of my life and myself. The recurring nightmare had robbed me of that. Was it asking too much to be able to distance myself from the work for just one week? Fat chance. No chance.

Within minutes, Lake Pontchartrain gave way to the swamps and bayous of rural Louisiana. As the housing developments of Baton Rouge replaced the green and blue of trees and water beneath us, my fury abated. Idly watching the world speed by far below, I wondered if my life would ever have any semblance of normalcy. Though I truly hated the interaction with the less-than-desirable characters we were frequently involved with, I loved the perplexing puzzles they provided. Loved piecing together little bits of seemingly unrelated information and making sense out of them. Most of all, I loved being with Bart and knowing I'd contributed to Anastasia's efforts to eliminate terrorism in the world.

"What's your take on this?" I asked, watching cotton-ball clouds leapfrogging lazily across the deep blue horizon.

"Let's see what we're getting into before I venture a guess. Right now, I have an uneasy feeling in the pit of my stomach that has nothing to do with my lack of breakfast." Bart handed the smudged, plain white envelope across the aisle. I opened it and drew out the map of Idaho David had given us. "I'm depending on your unique ability to see what other people usually overlook, Sherlock. If you solve the mystery, we can get back to our original plans without messing everything up." Bart's teasing smile didn't quite mask the concern I saw in those azure blue eyes.

A little shiver of prescience sent goose bumps rippling down my arms. Not only wouldn't this be a quick, cut-and-dried case, but I had a premonition that it was going to be every bit as big and as bad as Dad feared. I tried to shake off the dismal feeling that descended over me, attributing it to lack of sleep and breakfast, and focused on the map in my hand.

"Tell me about the map," Bart said. "Anything out of the ordinary? Obscurely encrypted clues? Starting places? Answers?"

Holding up one hand to forestall his rapid-fire questions, I examined the colored photocopy of a map of Idaho. It had apparently been reduced from its original size to eight by ten inches. "Too small to tell much of anything. No obvious markings, nothing that's been added to it. What did Dad say about it?"

"They found it in the terrorists' hideout."

I studied the map. "Have you ever been to Idaho?" There was still so much I didn't know about this husband of mine. Though we'd been married over a year, we'd spent almost as much time apart as we had together. The five years before our marriage, when he'd totally disappeared from my life, contained blanks that hadn't yet been filled in completely.

Bart shook his head. "Nope. How about you?"

"No. Another of those mysterious localities in America that I know very little about. I always find it amazing that I'm more familiar with foreign countries than my own. The only places in America I've seen are those I visited with Mom when I was young and she was still studying native cultures, recording their stories and legends, their dances and songs. After college, I went straight to New York—then you happened back into my life. No fun side trips to explore points between the coasts." I returned to the map. "This is Lewis and Clark country, where Sacajawea came from. I do remember that."

Bart nodded. "I can tell you that Idaho has great potatoes, the Continental Divide forms part of the border between Montana and Idaho, it's got one of the last wilderness areas in the US of A—and Hell's Canyon has some of the best white water rafting around."

"Not bad for an architect major. I'm impressed. Where'd you pick up those little tidbits?"

"Dinner table for the potatoes, flight maps for the Divide, and a *National Geographic* special on TV." Bart put the plane on auto pilot and reached for the map. "What do terrorists from one side of the world want with a sparsely populated piece of ground on the opposite side of the world?"

"Maybe you've just broken the code." I leaned back in my seat and tried to relax, tried to shake off the dismal feeling of trouble ahead. "Maybe they're setting up a training compound in the wilderness area where there aren't so many government agents spying on them—or onlookers poking their noses into where they shouldn't be. Or maybe they've discovered a gold mine to finance their dastardly deeds."

"Hmm. Or all of the above. Unfortunately, the possibilities are just about endless." Bart tossed the map back to me. "There's a nuclear plant there—one of the first built in the United States." His forehead creased in concentration. While he descended into deep thinking mode, I studied the map again, running my finger down each section before moving on to examine the next.

My fingernail snagged a rough spot in the very center of the map. I held the paper up. A hole no bigger than a pinprick allowed a mini-spotlight of sun to stream through. I looked closer.

"Looks like a pinhole in this map. David did say this was the original and he'd faxed a copy to the Control Center, didn't he?" I handed it to Bart. He held it up to the light.

"Perfectly round. Man-made, not a paper flaw. But was it made when it was thumbtacked to a board, or was it purposely put here to mark something?" He handed it back to me. "The hole is right through Idaho Falls, the closest town of any size to the nuclear reactor location."

I shuddered. "If the terrorists are targeting the nuclear reactor . . ."

The grim set of Bart's jaw suggested that idea had already crossed his mind. "Guess we'll find out soon enough—if that's the topic of conversation when we meet our informer. Let's hope we're heading down the wrong track."

We landed at Shreveport Regional Airport on the west side of town, rented a car, then drove slowly through the inevitable construction that seems to clog traffic in every city. Crossing the winding Red River to Bossier City, we exited I-20 at Airline Road, per instructions given to Dad from our informant, and found Pierre Bossier Mall.

I checked my watch. "Stores aren't open yet, unless the mall accommodates walkers to exercise out of the heat and humidity." As Bart opened the car door, oppressive, breath-sucking heat melted me, a weather condition that extended well into fall in the South.

"We'll check it out. Our source said he'd be at Kay Bee Toys with a little blonde girl by the Barbie display." Bart draped his arm around my shoulders as we crossed the parking lot. "We may have to wait for him. Maybe the food court's open. That would improve my disposition, and probably my outlook on this whole thing."

"As long as it's air-conditioned, I won't mind waiting, especially if there's a Mrs. Powell's Cinnamon Rolls or a CinnaBon." My empty stomach reacted immediately at the thought of one of my favorite foods.

"I can't figure out why you aren't roly-poly instead of slim and trim. The way you eat, you shouldn't even have a waistline!" Bart's hand slid to my waist and pinched me. "There's no flab at all there!"

"How often do I actually get to eat those mouth-watering delicacies? I talk a lot of calories, but I never consume them. You keep me too busy dodging bad guys to indulge my taste buds."

As Bart opened the door to the mall, I savored the rush of cool air. I'd even forego a fresh, delicious cinnamon roll with cream cheese icing for air-conditioning. One I could live without. The other I couldn't—not in the South.

Half a dozen people power-walked past us, and we fell in behind them, looking for the toy store. A few solitary souls sipped coffee with their breakfast rolls and newspapers near a splashing fountain. I longed to stop, but breakfast would be a luxury indulged in after our meeting.

In front of the toy store, located at the far end of the mall, a little girl with curly blonde hair peeked in the windows, pointing to some Barbie dolls on display. The man behind her, presumably her father, appeared totally absorbed in the little girl's comments. Thirty-five-ish, he wore a neatly pressed blue Air Force uniform with a slew of stripes up the arm.

Bart approached him. "Saunders?"

He turned and looked us over. "That's me. Sergeant Mike Saunders. You're from McAffrey?"

Bart introduced us. "You have information you couldn't give over the phone?"

The man stuck out his hand. "Yes. Sorry. I didn't realize how soon you'd arrive when I set up the meeting, so I figured I'd better be here even if the place wasn't open yet. Cassie loves to window shop, like her mom, so we've been having a good time."

I introduced myself to Cassie and asked about her favorite toy. Bart and Mike immediately put their heads together in serious discussion. I'd keep Cassie occupied in case her dad didn't want her to hear the conversation. As my grandmother used to say, "Little teapots have big ears." I remembered, to my mother's horror, being able to repeat overheard conversations almost verbatim.

"Barbie's my favorite," Cassie said, her big brown eyes glowing.

"Any special Barbie?"

"The ones from different countries, 'cause my daddy says we get to travel to a lot of countries, and I can have one from everywhere we go. I've already been in ten states."

"You're a very well-traveled little girl."

While Cassie pointed out Barbie dolls she'd like to add to her collection, I watched the men's reflections in the store window. Mike slipped something to Bart which he glanced at and pocketed. They shook hands, and as Mike turned to us, he squared his shoulders as if to shrug off some heavy burden. Forcing the semblance of a smile, he gave me a congenial nod and took Cassie's hand. "Come on, sweet pea. We'll have to come back later when the store's open."

Cassie turned and waved good-bye, then skipped down the mall, a happy, contented child beside a distracted, distressed father.

I linked my arm through Bart's as we headed for the mall exit. "What did he have that was so important he couldn't talk about it over the phone?"

"Mmm," seemed all the answer I'd get.

Since my husband in Interpol mode would be oblivious to anything concerning physical comfort until he'd disengaged and returned to the real world, I steered him straight for the food court and snagged a couple of cinnamon rolls and milks to go. He didn't even notice.

"Earth to Bart. Come in, please. Am I not going to be privy to that information?" I asked, looking up into Bart's somber blue eyes as we left the mall.

"Oh, sorry. Just trying to thread some things together." He opened the car door for me, then hurried around to start the engine and crank up the air-conditioning. It would be a scorcher today.

Bart pulled across the parking lot and stopped under a shady tree with the air-conditioning blowing while he called Dad. I placed his cinnamon roll on the dash in front of him, along with his carton of milk. He never even saw them. I tried to slowly savor each bite of the freshly baked delicacy, but hunger prevailed and I devoured it greedily, along with every fascinating word of Bart's report.

"Jack, we just met with Sergeant Mike Saunders. Got the recorder ready? Here's the story: one of Mike's best buddies, John, decided after several months of outrage over all the political stuff going on in the military, that he was getting out. This bothered Mike. John had nineteen years of service—only one year to go and he could retire. Mike stopped by John's house the day his friend moved and asked for the real lowdown.

"John told him he'd found somebody who'd actually *do* something for people in the military, and for America—unlike leaders with no morals who'd sold our government and military secrets to the Chinese. He boasted he'd be part of a real man's army, instead of a politically correct bunch of wimps who downgraded physical fitness and military readiness so pregnant women could go into combat. John joined a militant white supremacist group that would be trained and armed by professionals from overseas—specialists in bringing governments to their knees, or at least to the bargaining table."

I could see where this was leading. Those professionals were Jihad terrorists who indeed were specialists in bringing governments and organizations to their knees—after they'd blown up embassies, ambassadors, prime ministers, and barracks full of soldiers, not to mention countless innocent civilian bystanders. I hoped I was wrong, but Bart's white-knuckled grip on the steering wheel told me we were traveling the same frightening mental path.

"While they were talking, John kept stabbing a piece of paper with his finger, emphasizing his points. When he went to the kitchen to get Cokes, Mike grabbed the paper: a wedged-shaped piece of map with Idaho National Engineering Laboratory printed across the center and the number five handwritten and circled at the edge. At this point, Mike decided his friend was talking treason. He memorized the boundaries and the phone number scribbled across the bottom. When he got home, Mike copied the Idaho page from his road atlas, cutting the same wedge shape John had, then called the FBI, hoping they'd bail his friend out before he got in too deep. End of story."

Bart paused, listening to Dad's reply. "Sure I'll wait. It's your nickel." He wasn't waiting patiently. His free hand ran through his short, white-blond hair, tapped the steering wheel in a sharp staccato, then tugged at the leg of his Dockers. Changing hands with the cell phone, he started the routine all over again.

The suspense was killing me. What took Dad so long?

Bart stopped fidgeting and sat up straight. "Are you sure we can get there fast enough? Isn't there someone closer?" Another pause. "Roger." Bart disconnected and tossed the phone at me.

"What was that all about?" I removed Bart's untouched breakfast from the dash in front of him as he put the car in gear and drove toward the street.

"Another assignment. The phone number on John's map is on Dyess AFB in Abilene, Texas."

Another Air Force base connected to this burgeoning catastrophe? "What else did Dad say?"

Bart merged into traffic on I-20. "This is more important than anything else in the world right now, and we're close enough—and free to check it out." From his pocket, he pulled out the paper Mike gave him. "Jack's one worried man right now. I can see his point. Look at this."

I unfolded the paper. Dominating the entire center section of the wedge-shaped map was a huge, purple-shaded area labeled "Idaho National Engineering Laboratory"—where all the nuclear reactor activity in the area occurred.

CHAPTER 3

Nuclear reactors and terrorists in the same small quadrant equaled trouble. A dozen different scenarios flashed through my mind, each ending in disaster. Including my vacation.

A handwritten number five was circled on the wide end of the wedge. "Hmm. Does this mean it's their number five target, or that this is just one piece—the fifth portion—of a circle, and there are seven other pieces somewhere?" I continued to study the map. Three mountain ranges containing national forests pointed like long, green fingers toward the nuclear site.

"Just when I begin thinking I know what you're capable of, you toss me another surprise, Princess."

I looked up from the map to see Bart staring at me in amusement. "If any other man said that, I'd suspect it was a sexist comment—surprise at a woman's ability to think. Coming from you, I know it wasn't. But what do you mean?"

Pleasure and pride tinged Bart's answer. "You glance at it for ten seconds and determine there are seven missing pieces, not five or three." As he slowed for a construction flagman in a bright orange shirt, he reached for my hand and squeezed it. "You have a great analytical mind. Glad you're on my team. You're not only the most beautiful agent I've ever worked with, but by far the most fun. Maybe even the brightest."

I squeezed his hand, thrilled at the compliment which I knew came straight from his heart. Bart didn't toss bouquets without reason, but neither was he stingy with sincere appreciation. An important quality contributing immensely to happy marriages.

"More than happy to be working with you, love, but there wasn't anything analytical about it. I just envisioned a pie. The piece wasn't wide enough to have been cut into sixths or fourths, so it had to be eighths, if divided evenly. It may not have been. Back to what Dad said."

"This is beginning to have a very nasty look."

I slumped back in my seat. Much as I enjoyed mysteries, I needed this vacation desperately. The doctor was doing all in his power to help us conceive a child after my tubal pregnancy and discovery that I might never be able to have children, but the long series of fertility tests and procedures had been physically, psychologically, and emotionally exhausting.

Add to that the stress and fatigue resulting from my horrible nightmares. No one else in Anastasia appeared to suffer such aftereffects of their flight from paid assassins. Why was I the only one who couldn't shake off the fear Raven had instilled in me?

Back to the nagging question—was I capable of being an Interpol agent? Did I have the attributes, physically, mentally, and every way necessary to meet the dangerous, taxing requirements? Did anyone else vow to quit at the end of each job, as I had? Did I have some inherent weakness that would show up at the wrong time, endangering not only me, but my partner and the mission?

"So, my love, we're off to Abilene." Bart's cheery tone resounded with false gaiety. "We'll pop in and see Uncle Joe and Aunt Emma. She's still worried over your losing the baby, so she'll be happy to see pink in your cheeks again."

I sighed. "Who are we meeting in Abilene?"

"All we have is an address. When we land, they'll give us names. Jack talked to McAffrey as we spoke, and McAffrey assigned one of his men to check the address and addressee."

"Why can't McAffrey's man make the Abilene call?"

"He's investigating by computer and telephone. He's not even in Abilene," Bart explained. "They're feeding us the info to make the personal contacts, as . . ."

I interrupted. "I know. Anastasia's better trained to handle this type of thing. If that's what it actually turns out to be."

Thoughtful silence reigned until we reached the airport, where we faxed Dad a copy of the map. As we returned the rental car and got under way to Abilene, I knew Bart's thoughts were centered on the ramifications of foreign terrorists combining with white supremacy groups. FBI shootouts had occurred in Idaho with what I assumed might be this same bunch. Bombings and trouble in other areas had erupted with neo-Nazi organizations. What would happen if the real troublemakers—foreign terrorists—infested these groups with their passionate hatred of all things American? And weapons? And training in their evil, insidious ways of attacking innocent people?

A shiver rippled through me, and I quickly left that to Bart and Anastasia. Anastasia. The sum total of my father's—and my mother's—lives for the past twenty-five years. While he was infiltrating a group of terrorists in Vietnam with the OSI, the car in which Dad and his partner were riding exploded. His partner died. Jack Alexander escaped. The OSI jumped on the opportunity and confirmed his death, which enabled Dad to join the terrorists under an assumed identity. A Greek version of the Phoenix rising from the ashes, Anastasia was born from Dad's supposed death and became the foremost anti-terrorist organization in the world, under the umbrella of Interpol.

Bart interrupted my musings. "Give Aunt Emma and Uncle Joe a heads-up that we're coming to Abilene." He checked his watch. "Our ETA should be about forty-five minutes from now. By that time Jack will have the information for us, and we can meet our contact. Then we'll spend the rest of the day with Aunt Emma and Uncle Joe."

I called Emma, the beloved identical twin sister of Bart's mother, Alma.

"Why, how did Bart know I just took a lemon meringue pie out of the oven?" Emma said.

I laughed. "He has a sixth sense, especially where good food is concerned."

"You will be staying the night, won't you?"

"We're not sure. Do you have plans we'd be interrupting if we could stay?"

"Heavens, no. And the guest room is always ready. We're delighted we'll get to see you, even if only briefly." Her perky tone became tender. "How are you feeling, dear?"

"Wonderful," I lied. Well, it wasn't really a lie. Physically, I felt okay. Emotionally was another story.

"Joe will meet you when you land."

"Tell him not to bother, Aunt Emma. We'll rent a car."

"Nonsense. Joe'll bring you here, and you can take my car. No point going to all that expense and trouble when mine's sitting right here."

"You're too good to us, Emma. See you in an hour."

Her take-charge, bubbling enthusiasm exhausted me. Or was it my lack of sleep? I couldn't remember the last time I'd had a night without Raven's insidious image in my dreams. With each nightmare, he came closer to catching me, closer to killing me. I awakened sweat-drenched, trembling with fright, and terrified to close my eyes again. I dreaded nightfall. And I despised my weakness—my inability to control my fears.

Bart reached out to stroke my cheek. "Why don't you lean back and catch a quick catnap before we get to Abilene?"

"Afraid my bloodshot eyes might rouse Emma's maternal instincts?"

Bart laughed and pulled my hand to his lips. "You do look a little Christmasy—lovely green eyes in a sea of red. And I don't want her all over me for not taking care of you."

"You do take good care of me, love." I squeezed his hand. "I'll let Emma know you have nothing to do with my bloodshot eyes."

"Go ahead. Nod off. What little sleep you got last night was interrupted."

It did feel good to close my eyes and relax, but I wouldn't go to sleep. I wouldn't invite the nightmare again by doing that. But just relaxing, putting the perplexing puzzles aside for a few minutes, would accomplish as much as sleeping. I cleared my mind of all thought and relaxed each muscle from my toes up.

Suddenly a horrible noise jolted me upright in my seat. Bart's cell phone again, in my lap. "You've got to change the ringer on that." I tossed it to him. "Otherwise, it goes out the window."

"Allan here. What have you got for me?" He paused. "I'll pass the phone to Alli so she can write down the info. Here she is." Bart gave the phone back as I dug a notepad and pen from my purse. Dad identified the name and address of our contact at Dyess AFB in Abilene.

"It's a woman?" I asked as I scribbled down the information.

"McAffrey said she's a widow. Her husband was killed on one of our 'peace-keeping' missions. Call as soon as you've talked to her, Bunny." Dad hung up.

"What have we got?" Bart asked.

"Military widow." I repeated what Dad told me.

"Well, if she's as disenchanted as our first contact, she certainly has motive. While you were nodding off, I checked our slice of map a little closer. Looks like it might have come from the same map we have, just enlarged. So Mike's friend's destination is Idaho." Bart drifted into thought.

"I hear it's a beautiful state." The comment fell on deaf ears. When Bart slips into Interpol mode pondering a problem, he can tune out an earthquake.

My thoughts turned to the surprise I'd planned for tonight in New Orleans—the lush, romantic surroundings, the fabulous dinner of Bart's favorite foods aboard the river boat, with the lights of the city reflecting off the water as a backdrop. And the emerald-green teddy folded carefully in the pocket of my bag.

As if tuned to my thoughts, he broke into my reverie. "Since your orchestrated scheme got pre-empted, tell me what you'd arranged."

"Sorry, Charlie. No can do. My plans were very special, so I'm just going to have to find another exotic location and start all over again."

"Any hints?" Bart's impish expression reminded me of a little boy begging to open a present early.

"You'll like it."

He raised one eyebrow. "Sure?"

"Positive."

"Not another tourist thing?" His voice was dubious.

"Absolutely not. I promise you'll love every minute."

"Another hint?"

"Nope. You'll just have to tough it out, big guy. Maybe that'll give you a little incentive to get us back on our vacation track."

Bart looked pained. "Princess, you know this wasn't my idea."

"Oh, and you didn't *jump* at the chance to leave New Orleans? Your heart beats for something besides *adventure?* For the adrenaline rush danger gives you? Tell me I'm wrong." I stopped. "No." I held up both hands. "On second thought, don't say a word."

Bart reached for my hand and pulled it to his lips. "How about three? I love you."

"I'll accept that."

The cell phone buzzed again in my lap. I picked it up, turned off the ringer, and tossed it to Bart. "I promise, if you don't change that horrible noise, I *will* throw it out the window."

"Allan here." He listened for an incredibly long interval while I got more and more curious. When he finally disconnected, I waited for his report.

"So?" I prompted.

"So what?"

"You know perfectly well 'so what'! Who was the long-winded person on the other end?"

"You know what they say . . . curiosity killed the cat."

"Well, this cat may do some killing of her own if you hold out on me."

My husband's azure-blue eyes no longer sparkled with teasing. "You don't want to know, Princess. You really don't want to know."

CHAPTER 4

Uncle Joe met us on the parking apron at Abilene Airport in his behemoth black Cadillac. A big man, taller than Bart, Joe easily weighed two hundred and ninety pounds. His brown eyes sparkled merrily above a trim salt-and-pepper beard. He smothered me in a bear hug, then pounded Bart affectionately on the back

"It does a body good, laying eyes on you two." Joe pecked my cheek affectionately. "You're sure looking better than the last time I saw you."

"Hospital white isn't my best color," I said wryly.

"Glad to see you on your feet and back in the fray." He scooped up our bags and propelled us toward the Cadillac.

"You can't keep a good man down." Bart winked as he opened the door for me. "Or woman." Joe tossed our bags into the massive trunk of the classic Caddy and cranked up the engine.

"I see the old bomb's still running." Bart patted the dash of the gleaming ancient automobile, Joe's pride and joy.

"She'll probably outlast me," Joe said.

"You probably take better care of her than you do yourself," I laughed.

"You hit the nail, little lady, smack on the head. I baby her some every day. All that love I lavish on her keeps her purrin' like a kitten."

I quickly buckled my seat belt, remembering Joe's wild driving habits. "Where's Emma?"

"At Carla's. She put a quilt on, and Emma couldn't wait to get her fingers all pricked up helping. As soon as we get home, she'll tie off."

"Uncle Joe, you sound just like a quilter," I teased.

He shook his head as he made a pass at a stop sign. In Santa Barbara, they're called "California stops"—when you just glance both ways and barrel right on through. Heaven help anyone who got in the way with Joe behind the wheel of this huge car he handled like a tank.

"Well, you know those two women. They think just 'cause I'm retired I don't have anything to do. Emma even had me put in a couple of stitches. Said it was a special quilt for Nikki's baby, and everybody would do their two cents' worth. I didn't last long. These big clumsy fingers couldn't handle that little needle."

"How's Jake and his broken leg?" Carla and her family lived next door to Emma and Joe. Their five-year-old Jake, with a little boy's exuberance and enthusiasm for jumping off everything he could climb on, had landed wrong and broken his leg while we were in Abilene in February.

"Healed fine. He's as daring as ever. I think he and that little friend of his, Nathan, try to outdo each other to see who can be the biggest daredevil." Joe shook his head. "Now, what brings you two back to Abilene? I know it isn't to visit a couple of old retired folks."

"Routine Anastasia business. We're interviewing a lady. Shouldn't take very long if we can catch her at home." Bart shifted gears. "Emma said she'd just baked a lemon meringue pie. Makes my mouth water thinking about it."

Joe glanced at Bart, nodded, and launched into a discourse on the extended hot weather and current drought conditions, which continued until we reached their home. He parked under a huge shady oak tree in the driveway of the attractive two-story red brick house. Velvet violet pansies of February had been replaced by bright orange and yellow marigolds, which better withstand the oppressive summer heat in Texas.

"I'll get Emma," Joe said, opening the car door.

"I'll go. I want to say hello to Jake and Hailey."

"Hurry, Princess. We need to talk to our contact as soon as possible."

"Won't be a minute!" I left the bags to the men and hurried through the little swinging gate between the properties. As I rang the bell, I could hear the buzz of happy voices inside. Hailey opened the door, a petite eight-year-old with her blue-eyed friend, Rachel, at her side. She stared at me for a minute, then exclaimed, "You're the lady who put the prince and princess in the tree!"

I laughed. "That's me. Can I come in?"

Hailey and Rachel grabbed my hands and pulled me into the living room, where their mothers and Aunt Emma chattered gaily over a brightly colored baby quilt in the middle of the room. Emma jumped up and rushed to hug me. Carla and Nikki waved from the quilt, and Jake and Nathan scrambled out from underneath it to see who'd arrived.

The excited little girls introduced Rachel's baby sister, beautiful Emily Nicole, and Nikki let me hold her. I ducked my head, pretending to be totally absorbed in the perfect little being snuggled contentedly in my arms, but I didn't want anyone to see my eyes suddenly fill with tears. How I longed to hold my own precious little one like this.

I felt a strong connection to these people I'd known so briefly but who had, nevertheless, touched me deeply. Carla had flown in and out of my life in five quick minutes when she'd crossed the lawn to get someone to tend Hailey while she rushed Jake to the hospital with his broken leg. I'd spent an anxious couple of hours with Hailey, nursing her high fever, discovered I knew nothing about kids, then agonized over whether I'd be better off devoting my life to Anastasia instead of having children.

Nikki, Rachel, and Nathan had rescued me, assuming nursing responsibilities when Bart and I needed to leave Abilene to catch a crazed arsonist. They had been characters crossing the stage, interacting momentarily, then returning to their assigned roles. But that brief interaction, when lives cross at pivotal moments, can forge strong relationships. I felt we were old and dear friends.

Emma gently touched my cheek. "Come on, dear. We'd better feed those men of ours before you have to take off again."

Reluctantly I nestled Emily back in her mother's arms, then pried four little pairs of arms from around my legs with the promise that I would return and recite again the story of the real prince and princess I'd hidden in a tree.

Emma linked her arm through mine as we crossed the grass back through the white swinging gate to her house. "I'm happy to see you're looking more like your old self again, dear."

"Yes, I'm totally recovered—from the bullet wound and the surgery." At least the exterior scars were healed. The interior scars might never heal completely. When I'd finally decided I did want the large family Bart always hoped for, I'd had emergency surgery for a tubal pregnancy and was informed that my chances of getting pregnant again ranged from very slim to next to nothing.

"Alma said you were undergoing some new kind of fertility procedures." Emma hesitated. "I don't mean to pry, but have you had any success?"

"We're not quite finished with the treatment or the tests. The doctor's hopeful, but I'm getting discouraged. Who'd have thought it would take so much work to have a baby, when people all over the world get pregnant without even thinking about it—or even wanting to? I'd planned a special evening tonight, hoping a relaxing atmosphere might be conducive to helping the plan along."

"And what was that?" Emma asked as she opened the back door.

"Moonlight cruise and dinner on a romantic old paddle-wheeler on the Mississippi, with New Orleans lights and live music as a backdrop, plus an enticing satin teddy. Now, tell me how I'm supposed to replicate that in Abilene!"

Emma laughed. "We are a little short on river boats here, but I'm sure you'll think of something." Then her azure eyes became serious as she patted my arm tenderly. "Don't give up, dear. And try not to be discouraged. All the best things in life seem to require time and patience."

Bart made noises like he wanted to escape immediately and do the interview before lunch, but Uncle Joe had other ideas. He'd already ransacked the refrigerator for sandwich makings so Aunt Emma could quickly assemble her specialty—a gourmet version of tuna salad. Over lunch, discussion topics steered clear of Anastasia's work, concentrating on updates on Bart's cousins and current events.

With Bart increasingly antsy, we excused ourselves immediately after eating, borrowed Emma's snazzy little red Chrysler LeBaron convertible that already had the top down, and departed for our rendezvous with the young widow, my hair blowing wildly about my face.

I glanced at Bart's grim expression. "You had a hard time concentrating on conversation. Guess I should have overridden Emma's enthusiastic hospitality and insisted that they eat without us. I didn't realize how uptight you were about this interview."

"I should have clued you in. Just so you have an idea of how important this is, I think your dad would place even you, his beloved only child, upon the sacrificial altar if it could keep the Jihad from spewing their hate in America." Bart clamped his mouth shut. I knew he was sorry he'd said it the instant it came out.

"That's what that phone call was about. What happened? What did Dad say when you talked to him the last time?"

Bart shook his head, keeping his eyes straight ahead on traffic. The look on his face sent ice coursing through my veins.

"Talk to me," I pleaded. "Tell me what he said." Those little shivers of prescience were tingling up my spine again. I never liked what they portended.

"Princess, don't ask." Bart reached for my hand and squeezed it, as if a show of his affection would stay my questions. "I promise you don't want to know. Leave it at that."

"Leave it? That's like waving a white chocolate macadamia nut cookie fresh from the oven under my nose and telling me I can't have any. You're committed now, Charlie, so out with it. And I don't want just a crumb. I want the entire cookie, no matter how sick it makes me."

Knowing I wouldn't relent until he'd shared the conversation, no matter how hurtful it might be, he began briefing me, slowly, carefully choosing his words. "Dominic's still in Iraq, watching the fallout from that last confrontation with bin Laden's terrorists—their capture of men and map." He paused for such a long time that I thought that was all I'd get. Finally, reluctantly, he dropped the bomb. "Osama bin Laden's dropped out of sight again."

"That's nothing new," I observed. "Authorities usually don't know where he is. Otherwise, he'd be arrested and tried for murder and terrorist acts in a dozen countries."

Bart didn't answer. I looked at him, at the tight muscles in his jaw, his white-knuckled grip on the steering wheel, and the disturbed—no, the distressed look on his face. As the horrible truth slowly dawned, outrage exploded inside me.

"He's here, isn't he? Here—in America. The most barbaric terrorist since Attila the Hun has come *here*." It took my breath away.

I squeezed my eyes shut, trying to dislodge the image of the bearded terrorist. It didn't work. I glared at Bart. "Actually, he makes Attila look like a saint. That brutal, fiendish creep, who has no qualms about blowing up thousands of people in one heartless blast, has actually come to the Land of the Free and the Home of the Brave to do his dirty work, hasn't he? And he wants this map. He wants his little pieces of paper back. He knows who has them, and he's come personally to collect them. Bart, do you know what that means? Do you have any idea what that means?"

Bart softly touched a finger to my lips to still my tirade, then tenderly kneaded my neck and shoulders with one hand. "I know what it means," he said quietly, keeping his eyes on the road as he drove. "Everyone who has a piece of that map is now a target."

I pushed his hand away and whirled on him with fire in my heart. "It means that Anastasia is the main target. It means that he's come for you, and Dad and Mom, and the rest." I felt my voice rising, felt hysteria bubbling out. I didn't care. I was so angry that I wanted to scream and stomp my feet and throw things. "It means the most elusive terrorist in history is in your backyard with a death warrant—with your name on it—which he means to sign with your blood. You didn't bat an eye when they told you on the phone. Do you have ice in your veins? Doesn't that news do anything to you?"

"Yeah, actually it scares the beejeebers out of me, babe. But what do you expect me to do—tuck my tail between my legs and hide? If you'll take a deep breath and think about it, you'll realize we're not as bad off as those poor dumb souls who have a piece of the map and think it'll solve their petty grievances with . . . whoever. *They're* the victims, the ones who don't have a snowball's chance in you-know-where of surviving the next twenty-four hours without help. And we—you and me—may be all that stands between them and bin Laden."

CHAPTER 5

The real truth of the matter slowly filtered through my anger and fear.

"Do you suppose bin Laden knows who holds pieces of the map, or was that handled by underlings?" I straightened up in my seat and brushed the hair out of my eyes. "How fast could he get to them? Actually, we're assuming a lot, aren't we? Or do you know more than I do? I guess when the map Mike gave you listed a phone number leading to Dyess, I imagined the contact here would also have a piece of map containing a phone number that would lead us to the next, and so on. Is that right, or am I way off base?"

"I think you're right on target, Princess. As usual. McAffrey's already moving Mike and his family out of sight for a while, and they'll get John and his family, too. We've got to convince this little widow that she may be in trouble—assuming she possesses a piece of the map."

"But if her phone number was on John's map, bin Laden would assume she'd know something. There has to be some connection between the two." I slumped back in my seat. Just when I thought I'd be free from these fanatics for a while, their tentacles reached out and entangled me, dragging me right back into the line of fire. So much for doctor's orders for a stress-free, idyllic rendezvous.

As we drove between fifty American flags whipping in the breeze at the entrance to Dyess Air Force Base, my throat filled with a king-sized lump. The American flag always stirred profound emotions within me. I couldn't listen to the "Star-Spangled Banner" without tears streaming down my face. My parents had instilled within me deep feelings of gratitude for the privilege of living in a democratic country, gratitude for those patriots who fought and died to keep America free.

And now one of America's greatest enemies had come to this sacred soil. I could imagine the Founding Fathers turning over in their graves. This fiend posed more of a threat to America today than Russia had during the cold war. The Russians had been kept in check by fear of retaliation. To Jihad terrorists, retaliation held no such fear. If they gave their lives for their cause—no matter that it was a warped and evil one to everyone else—they went straight to the arms of Allah. Thus there was no shortage of terrorists willing to volunteer for suicide missions, carrying armed bombs into buildings and blowing themselves up along with hundreds of innocent people.

I'd never understood Jihad's hatred of all things American. After all, we were supposed to be the good guys in the world. Never the oppressor, always the champion of the underdog, pouring billions of dollars into building up whatever nations we defeated because of their acts of aggression.

We stopped at the stone guard shack at the entrance to the base, and Bart flashed his Interpol ID at the Air Force security guard. Given permission to enter, Bart asked for directions to Washington Street. We proceeded through the gate down a street lined on one side with a static display of aircraft, two dozen or more, ranging from monstrous to minuscule in size, a veritable history of flight in the Air Force.

Bart stopped in front of a long, low brick duplex with brown siding. A multitude of once-beautiful rose bushes, apparently neglected through the occupant's personal crisis, withered along the drive and entryway to the open front door. Flattened empty cartons lined the porch outside, and boxes stacked five and six deep inside blocked the view to the room beyond.

"Looks like moving day. We may have just caught her." Bart came around and opened my door. I hesitated. Did I want to go in there? He reached for my hand and pulled me to my feet. "Let's get this over with."

As we approached the open door, voices raised in passion stopped us. Probably not a good time for an interview. Boxes piled high in front of the open, curtainless window blocked the speakers from our view, and concealed our presence from those inside.

"Kay, think about what you're doing," the voice of a young woman pleaded. "You're turning your back on everything Billy stood for, even died for. This won't make anything better."

Another voice answered in an angry, urgent rush. "It'll make *me* feel better. I'll be fighting back at those who sent my husband to die, maybe even get in a few punches where it'll hurt. At least I won't feel so helpless." She stopped. "Lisa, I have to do this. I'm so full of hate and outrage for these idiots who dumb down the military, then send them all over the world to fight bloody wars without enough training or equipment, I have to do something."

"Don't you think giving them all your savings is enough?" the first woman argued. "What would Billy think, knowing you haven't a cent in the world between you and starvation? These people are leeches. They hit you when you were at your very lowest emotionally. They didn't even wait until after the funeral. I saw that man talking to you by the casket. I watched your face. Even you couldn't believe he wouldn't wait until Billy was buried. Kay, they prey on weakness. Get out now. Go back to Ohio and live next door to your folks. Give Alyce a chance to know her grandparents and her aunts and uncles and cousins—and let them help you through this."

We were eavesdropping on something too private, too personal for strangers to hear. But I couldn't move. My heart, suddenly turned to lead, matched my leaden feet, which wanted to run, to escape from hearing this intimate, heart-wrenching conversation. But they wouldn't—or couldn't—move.

"Lisa, thanks for your help. I'd never have finished packing without you. Never have done any of this without you. You were heaven-sent." The voice now sounded simply resigned, tired. Too tired to continue this draining conversation. "But go home now, please. I've made up my mind, and I'm not going to change it. It's all I can do to give Billy's death some meaning. I've got to fight back at those who ordered my Billy to war to die." The tears began again, and the whole world seemed to pause while she regained control of herself. "Lisa, I have to do something, to act in some way, or I'll go crazy."

Heart-rending sobs punctuated her emotional explosion. I hated myself for listening, but I felt rooted to the sidewalk, connected to this tragedy by something that held me firmly in place and wouldn't allow me to move out of hearing distance. Bart, too, remained motionless, listening.

Through sniffles and half-contained sobs, she continued. "This way, I'll at least have the satisfaction of knowing those who demolished our military will pay for doing it."

"Kay, don't do anything rash. Please, go to your parents' place for a couple of weeks before you take this drastic step. What happens if you get out there and decide it's a mistake? Are they going to let you leave?"

There was a pregnant pause, so long that I thought the women must have moved into a different room. Then the voice, lifeless, emotionless, sounding near exhaustion now, answered. "They wouldn't hold me against my will. These are all volunteers—people who just can't take it anymore. People who have been dumped on too many times and have to fight back. This seems like the most effective way." She raised her voice. "Alyce, bring TJ and Josie and Jeremy. It's time for them to leave."

"Write to me and tell me how you are. Will you promise me that?" Lisa pleaded.

"When I get a chance. I'm assuming from the way they talked that I'll be out in the field training much of the time. I don't know how often I'll be able to mail a letter."

Children's voices interrupted the closing scenes of this emotionally charged drama on which we'd been shamelessly eavesdropping.

"Momma, do we have to go now? Please, can Alyce spend the night?" The child's pleading appeared to fall on deaf ears. No one spoke for an instant. I tried to visualize the scene inside. Two friends, saying good-bye, probably each knowing full well she'd never see the other again, one worried about a friend's life-altering decision and the other too filled with hatred and despair to make a rational decision. Finally they both spoke, almost at once.

"Not tonight, Josie." That must have been Lisa.

"Alyce, don't even ask. We have too much to do if we're going to be ready to leave in the morning. Lisa, I can't thank you enough for your help—for the meals—for just being here for me these past weeks. I couldn't have gotten through it without you."

"That's what friends are for. You know I'd do anything for you, help you any way I could. I did tell you, didn't I? Butch is getting out. We're moving, too. He's going to fly for the airlines."

"Well, maybe he'll be home more often from now on. When I first met you, I thought you were a widow, or divorced. You were always sitting in church with your children—alone. Like I am now." Her voice cracked, and she bit off her words with a deep breath.

I couldn't stand it another minute. I propelled myself forward, knocked on the open door, and saw two attractive young women standing in the midst of packing boxes with their arms around each other and tears streaming down their faces. Four small, wide-eyed children watched their mothers, not seeming quite sure what to make of the scene. A toddler wobbled forward and grasped a dark-haired, pony-tailed woman around the legs, his head tilted back, staring up to watch his mother crying.

I knocked swiftly again, standing just inside the doorway now. "I'm so sorry to interrupt. Kay Sterling? I'm Allison Allan. This is my husband, Bart."

They separated, wiping their faces with both hands, and turned to see who intruded on their privacy.

The taller of the two moved forward hesitantly, a puzzled expression on her wan face. "I'm Kay Sterling."

Bart stepped around me into the room. He held his hand out toward the too-slender woman, who appeared to be in her late twenties. Her clothes hung loosely on her, as though she'd recently lost a lot of weight. Somehow she wasn't what I'd pictured from the overheard conversation. Even with her eyes and nose red from crying, she was attractive enough to grace the cover of a national magazine. Thick blonde hair brushed her shoulders. Her eyes were deep blue, the color of Alma's delphiniums, and they held enough sadness—and fear—to break my heart.

"Listen, call me before you leave town," Lisa said, boosting the toddler to her hip. She took the little boy, probably about four years old, by the hand. "Come on, TJ. We need to get home. Josie, can you carry this for me?" She handed a diaper bag to the bright-eyed little girl with dark hair like her mother's, then turned again to Kay. "I mean it. Don't leave without stopping by or calling me. I have a goodie package for you to take in the car."

We stepped aside, and a sad-faced Alyce walked out beside an equally serious Josie, holding her hand. I guessed the two girls to be six or seven, not too young to be dear friends, and certainly old enough to realize this was good-bye. Not just good-bye until tomorrow or the next day, but maybe forever.

"I'm sorry to interrupt, Mrs. Sterling." Bart, with his ID open, moved quickly beside the young woman before she had time to recover from her friend's departure. "We're from Interpol. Do you have time to talk for a few minutes?"

"Interpol?" Her hand flew to her heart and she stepped back, bumping into the nearest stack of moving cartons.

"Mrs. Sterling, we have in our possession a piece of a map we received from someone who felt the security of the United States might be at risk. That piece of map led us to you. Do you have a section of the map, with a phone number written on it?"

"Interpol?" Kay Sterling repeated, blinking her eyes, her expression blank, as if she wasn't sure she'd heard correctly, or she couldn't remember from where she should know the term. Then her face paled, and one hand fluttered toward the boxes.

Afraid she was going to faint on the spot, I hurried to her side and slipped my arm around her waist, easing her toward a carton near her side. "Sit down, Mrs. Sterling." I knelt in front of her and looked up into deep blue eyes that continued to register shock. "We have information that foreign terrorists are training militant groups in Idaho and planning horrendous acts of terrorism against the United States. We need to stop them before they spread death and destruction in America or cause chaos with transportation or communication systems. Will you help us, please?"

She looked down at me, focusing those magnificent blue eyes on my face, as if really seeing me for the first time. She stared for a minute, then slowly raised her eyes to look at Bart. She seemed to be rousing from a trance, not fully aware of her surroundings, shaking off a heavy slumber from which she'd been awakened.

"Mrs. Sterling, we believe you have a pie-shaped wedge of a map of Idaho which contains a circled numeral and a telephone number."

Bart squatted in front of her so their eyes were level as he repeated his message with quiet urgency. "We need that piece of paper. It's vital to the security of the United States. I'm truly sorry about your husband's death. I'm sorry your little girl no longer has a father to love her. But I'm terribly proud of your husband."

Tears welled in Kay Sterling's eyes and spilled unchecked down her pale cheeks. Bart reached for her small white hand and held it between his two large tanned ones. "Mrs. Sterling, I'm grateful to you for the sacrifices you've made for this country as a military wife. Serving in the military isn't easy on anyone in the family. But hundreds of thousands of people have given their lives, just like your husband, so their families could enjoy living in a free country. Your husband made the ultimate sacrifice by placing his life on the altar of freedom. I'm asking you to pay tribute to that act, to honor your husband's memory by sacrificing your outrage at men not worthy to clean your shoes. Give me the paper. Let me stop these terrorists before they begin destroying the way of life your husband died to preserve."

No one moved. I didn't dare breathe for fear I'd break the spell Bart had woven with his words. I watched Kay's face, wondering if they would further inflame her or touch her heart as they'd touched mine. Did she have in her possession what we hoped to get from her, or were we completely off base with our assumptions and our search?

CHAPTER 6

Kay's eyes never left Bart's face. She took a deep breath, and seemed to return to this time and place from some far-off dimension. Her lips pressed together in a straight, thin line and she slowly, quite deliberately withdrew her hand from Bart's grasp.

I prepared for the worst: a vicious torrent of hateful words and being thrown out of her house. There wasn't much at hand she could physically throw at us, but from the look on her face, I had the feeling that if there was something handy, she'd probably start tossing.

Just then Alyce ran into the house, happily waving a book in the air. "Momma, look what Josie gave me. It's her favorite book, and she said I could take it with me to Idaho." Alyce slapped the book in her mother's lap and leaned into her face. "She said I could keep it forever. She's my very best friend."

I glanced at the book, then into Kay's face, my mind racing. I'd heard Kay tell Lisa she'd seen her sitting alone in church and thought she was widowed or divorced. If this was Josie's favorite book, they must be Mormons. Did that mean Kay was, too? Or had she just been visiting, investigating the Church?

"Kay, are you a member of The Church of Jesus Christ of Latter-day Saints?" Alyce had already interrupted the mood of the moment, had broken the spell Bart temporarily wove around us, and possibly postponed Kay's refusal to cooperate with our request. My curiosity wouldn't wait, especially in view of the possibility that we were about to be ejected empty-handed.

"That's my church. Do you go there, too?" Alyce said, her dark eyes shining with surprise and her little pixie face filled with excitement.

"Yes, we do. We were baptized a year ago. Have you been baptized yet?" I didn't dare look at Kay. I didn't know where this was going, but anything was better than being ousted before obtaining the map and phone number we needed.

"I'm not old enough yet. But when I do, Josie gets to be baptized at the same time. Our birthdays are on the same day." Her happy pronouncement seemed tempered by the sudden realization that she might never see Josie again. She looked up at her mother. "Will we still get to do that?"

Kay didn't answer, didn't seem to hear her question. Alyce put her little hand on her mother's cheek and turned her head so they were face to face, practically nose to nose. "Will we still get to be baptized at the same time, Momma? If we move to Idaho, and Josie's moving somewhere else . . ." Alyce's voice dropped off to nothing, and her sweet pixie face filled with uncertainty.

"We'll see, honey. When the time comes." Kay's absent-minded reply gave me hope. She was thinking. She hadn't thrown us out yet. Actually, she hadn't even answered us yet. We still didn't know what she had—or didn't have—that might aid our quest.

Somewhere a clock ticked relentlessly, one second after another disappearing, never to be retrieved. The sound echoed through boxes waiting to be loaded in a truck and transported to a new home. In what kind of home would they be unpacked? What did white supremacists live in while plotting to overthrow the government of their fatherland? A land which nurtured the freedoms allowing them the right to harbor such revolutionary, traitorous ideas—just not the right to carry them out.

Freedom of thought and speech were different from freedom to destroy someone else's property. I'd always been taught that my freedom ended where the other guy's chin began. Right now, somebody's chin looked to be in serious jeopardy.

"Mrs. Sterling?" Bart's quiet voice broke the strained silence. "May we please have your map?" He wasn't asking *if* she had it, thus giving her a chance to deny her possession. Bart simply, calmly asked that she hand it over.

"What makes you so sure I have such a thing?" Wispy blonde bangs bobbed as she tossed her head, raising her nose in the air to peer down the well-shaped length of it at Bart. He stood—an imposing view, all six feet four inches standing straight and tall in front of her.

Kay Sterling ran a hand nervously across her forehead, gave the *Children's Stories from the Book of Mormon* resting in her lap to Alyce, and stood, drawing herself up to her full height. She didn't quite reach Bart's chin.

"Your phone number's on the piece of map we have. And your map contains a phone number of someone else down the line." Bart's voice contained a certainty I wasn't sure I shared as he placed his hands lightly on the young widow's shoulders. "Whatever you do with your life and your daughter's from this moment is your own business. What you do with that map, however, will have a domino effect on the history of the country your husband loved enough to sacrifice his life for. Kay, I need that map. Please."

I'd give him anything I possessed if he used those pleading words and tones on me. But would Kay? The tension in the room had even little Alyce silently watching the two, her big dark eyes flashing from her mother to Bart and back again.

The tiniest shiver shook Kay's shoulders as she exhaled, surrendering the stiffness in her spine. Without a word, she retrieved her purse from the counter in the kitchen and extracted a folded piece of paper. She paused, looked at us, then at Alyce before retracing her steps to Bart. Silently she handed him the paper as she stretched her other hand toward the child. Alyce, still clutching the book, buried her face in Kay's faded cut-off jeans, wrapping both arms about the book and her mother's leg.

Bart unfolded the paper, glanced briefly at it, then took the still-extended hand. "Thank you. You may be . . ." He stopped, still holding her hand. "Needing some assistance for a little while," he finished quietly, glancing at me, then at Alyce.

I immediately got his message. "Alyce, will you show me your book? I don't think I've ever seen it."

Bart and Kay moved to the door as I knelt by the box recently vacated by Alyce's mother. Alyce pointed out her favorite stories while Bart spoke in quiet tones. From the frightened expression on Kay's face, I assumed he'd revealed the danger of remaining here even another hour.

Absently listening to Alyce, I watched emotions play across her mother's face. Bart could be so very charming and convincing; I hoped he was in top form now. If her friend Lisa hadn't been able to sway her, could a stranger? Kay struggled with the decision, searching first Bart's face as if seeking her answers there, then down the street as if watching for someone to come to her aid. To make this decision for her.

Suddenly she nodded, moved quickly to the back door and locked it, closed and locked the open kitchen windows, and hurried down the hall, slamming windows in each room.

While he secured the living room windows, Bart reported to Dad via cell phone at the Control Center in California. He finished his call as Kay returned moments later, depositing two suitcases at the front door. She had apparently packed earlier, and was ready to go. She grabbed her purse from the kitchen, and told Alyce to run to the bathroom before they left.

"Where are we going?" the child asked, looking up from her deep concentration on the book still open between us on the box.

"Mr. and Mrs. Allan are taking us for a ride." Kay's voice, strained and high, left no doubt that Bart's message had scared her to death. Alyce ran obediently down the hall, missing the quick but intense visual search her mother gave the living room and kitchen.

Kay followed Alyce, returning with jackets and a Raggedy Ann doll. Alyce quickly claimed possession of the doll.

"Have you ever ridden in a convertible with the top down?" I asked as the child frowned, realizing they were leaving the house and might not be back.

As Alyce looked at me, then out the front door at the candy-apple red convertible standing at the curb, excitement immediately displaced her worried look. She took my hand, and we hurried outside together. Bart loaded the suitcases while Kay locked the front door and the car parked under the carport. "This will be okay here, won't it?" she asked, nodding toward her car.

Bart assured her that Interpol had just arranged to have military police stationed at the house to protect her belongings. It would be an easy matter for terrorists to get on base by masquerading as military needing a ride home, or with help from a sympathizer like Kay Sterling who'd embraced their propaganda.

As we pulled away from the house, Bart explained what Jack had suggested. "You'll stay with my aunt and uncle until the FBI can put you in a safe location. Since the moving company picks up your household goods tomorrow, someone will be there to oversee it and sign the papers. The shipment will conveniently be misplaced until you're in a safe house where you can have your goods shipped."

As we left the base, the long line of flags billowing in the breeze did their usual number on me, bringing tears to my eyes and a tug at my heart. But this time, supreme satisfaction filled me at the way our system worked for its citizens when given the opportunity.

Bart watched to make sure we weren't being followed. It appeared, for the time being, that we were one step ahead of the terrorists.

With their usual overwhelming hospitality, Aunt Emma and Uncle Joe welcomed Kay and Alyce Sterling into their home and their hearts. Our bags were quietly replaced with their suitcases in the guest room, and while Aunt Emma took them on the get-acquainted-with-the-house tour, Bart briefed Joe on their situation, a very abbreviated version with only as many details as Joe had a need to know.

"The FBI could get here in an hour, or sometime tonight," Bart explained as he and Joe returned from putting our bags back in the trunk of the antique Cadillac. "McAffrey seems to move pretty fast. There may be an office in town with someone who can get them, but finding a place for them may cause some delay."

"You know we'll be glad to keep them as long as they need to stay," Joe said. "Don't rush things on our account. Emma loves having someone to fuss over, and now that she's being deprived of doing for you, she'll just be glad to do for them."

The three joined us at that moment from upstairs.

"Guess what!" Alyce jumped up and down in excitement.

"What?" I asked, bending toward the beaming child.

"Hailey lives next door!"

"How do you know Hailey?" I looked at Kay and Emma.

"Hailey and Josie and Rachel are my best friends." She whirled toward her mother. "Can I go see Hailey now?" she pleaded, tugging at her mother's shirttail. "Maybe Rachel is still there, too."

Kay looked at Bart, a question in her eyes. Bart nodded. "Aunt Emma can take her over." At that, Alyce grabbed Emma's hand and started for the door.

He turned to Kay. "You'd better stay here, so you don't have to answer questions. Princess, tell Emma what she needs to know. Then we have to be on our way."

I caught up with Emma at the back door, and while Alyce ran on through the swinging gate between the yards, I told Emma her guests would be picked up by the FBI and taken to a safe house for protection. "Tell Carla and Nikki you pressured Kay into staying overnight since her house is all packed to move. Don't explain how you know them. Say Kay is finalizing arrangements now and is exhausted. Discourage them from coming to your house if you can. Go after Alyce in an hour. Thanks, Emma. As usual, you're a lifesaver." I hugged Bart's petite aunt. "And tell Rachel, Nathan, Hailey, and Jake I'll have to take a rain check on the story."

Emma backed through the gate. "Your visit was much too short. I wanted to get you some of Vleta's chocolates before you left. And we wanted to take you out to Perini Ranch Steakhouse in Buffalo Gap for dinner. You'd love it. Oh, well. Next time. Be careful, dear. I do worry about you, you know, with your crazy lifestyle."

I blew her a kiss. "I know. I'm working on that. Thanks again." I hurried into the house and found Bart waiting in the front hall, talking to Kay Sterling.

"I know," she said as I joined them. "'Don't go to Idaho. Leave the hate behind.'" Her voice, quiet and tentative, expressed her uncertainty. "I'll have to think about that some more—Idaho. Not hate. I know I have to get rid of the hate, but it's hard to turn it off when it's been such a big part of me for a whole year. That's when Billy left for overseas."

I slipped my arm around her waist. "Give it to the Lord, and let Him carry the burden. He promised He would. It's too heavy for you. Alyce needs so much from you now. You need to be free to concentrate on her needs—and on your own new ones."

Joe shuffled noisily down the stairs. "Ready?"

Bart reached for my hand. "Yup. See, if you'd just let us rent a car, you wouldn't have to haul us back to the airport."

"And if I hadn't picked you up, I wouldn't have seen much of you, now would I?" He pulled the keys from his pocket and turned to Kay. "Emma will be right back. Make yourself at home. I won't be long."

Extracting my hand from Bart's, I waved the men through the open door. I worried about Kay being alone. Had she really changed her mind about going to Idaho and joining the group there? Would she have second thoughts and call someone to come and get her? Then I heard the back door. Emma could take it from here. She could love anyone into anything.

I touched Kay's arm. "You've made the right choice. Thank you for that decision. When you start to wonder, remember that you've saved countless lives by giving us this information." I turned and ran out the door before she could speak.

As we turned on Eleventh Street South heading for Abilene Regional Airport, a car flew past. The bumper sticker said it all about this lovely old town and its friendly inhabitants: "I wasn't born in Abilene, but I got here as fast as I could." Abilene's quality of life more than compensated for its lack of spectacular scenery.

I got the usual good-bye bear hug from Joe, but it wasn't one of those long, lingering, what-more-can-we-say-that-hasn't-already-been-said things, so I didn't mind. Bart had remembered, as was his custom, to have the plane fueled and readied while we were gone, so we took off immediately.

"Where to this time?" I asked, buckling my seat belt.

"Tucson." Bart busied himself with pilot things while I watched the dry landscape disappear below. The drought had left Abilene golden brown instead of green as it had been in February. Lytle and Kirby Lakes were soon far behind, along with Uncle Joe and Aunt Emma, and the Sterlings with their problems that wouldn't be solved just because she'd done the right thing. I said a prayer for her, hoping she'd turn to the Lord for help instead of the people who recruited her when she was emotionally unable to make wise decisions.

"How did you find out so fast that the phone number led to Tucson?" It occurred to me that while we were at Kay's house, Bart hadn't been on the phone to the Control Center very long.

Bart put the plane on auto pilot, then pulled the map from his pocket. "Jack had a list of area codes around military bases. Took him all of five seconds to match the phone number on Mrs. Sterling's map with Tucson."

"Another military base involved."

Bart nodded, his azure eyes dark with worry. "Davis Monthan Air Force Base. Princess, I don't like this. I wonder if all those politicians and bureaucrats who've never served in the military have any idea how they've undermined the security of their country by turning the services into politically correct social organizations."

I understood his concern. "Sacrifice for an ideal or principle is one thing, but . . ."

A pang of horror stabbed my heart and took my breath away with the sudden realization that I could relate intimately to Kay's situation. In his chosen profession of fighting terrorism, Bart could disappear permanently from my life at any time. Who would ever know except our close circle of friends and family? Or care? Would he have made a difference in the world? Would his sacrifice have been worth it? These were questions I couldn't contend with now. Questions I hoped I'd never have to answer.

I squeezed my eyes shut, trying to force unwanted images from my mind, and racked my brain for the last thread of conversation. "Do you have a name to go with the phone number in Tucson?"

My husband, lost in his own thoughts, had to be dragged back to the present to answer my question. "We will when we land. Let's see what we have, now that there are two pieces to the puzzle."

Bart leaned across the aisle, and we examined the map together. A penciled number six was circled at the edge of Kay's map. We found that it fit perfectly above the first piece, allowing the Targhee National Forest boundaries to merge and connecting the lines on Highway 22 and 33. Interstate 15 angled north toward the Montana border. The narrow end of the pie-shaped map pointed at Idaho Falls—as did the first map.

Just off I-15, between two little towns named Dubois and Spencer, an area marked "United States Sheep Experimental Station" vaulted from the page. We looked at each other, then back at the map, and one or both of us uttered the dreadful words aloud.

"Chemical and biological warfare."

CHAPTER 7

Neither of us spoke for the next several minutes. Horrible terms raced through my mind: anthrax, Hinta, Philo, Ebola Marburg, Ebola Zaire—all deadly viruses which, if unleashed on a population, could virtually wipe it out in a matter of weeks.

What kinds of experiments were conducted here by the United States? I looked at the map again. It comprised a huge area at the foot of the Centennial Mountains. Grazing land, with elevations ranging from over 5,100 feet at Dubois to above 5,800 feet at Spencer.

Were they working to develop a breed of sheep that could better withstand the weather at that altitude, or trying to eliminate diseases among sheep? Anthrax was an infectious, often fatal disease contracted by cattle and sheep that could easily spread to humans. It had been used in biological warfare before. Why not again?

Did the Jihad intend to take possession of the research station and convert it to their own experimentation and production of biological germs and viruses? With the right people in place, anything was possible.

I waved the map at Bart. "The only other thing of note on this section of the map is the Camas National Wildlife Refuge. That seems pretty benign. Any idea of the purpose of this Experimental Sheep Station, what they do there, or why it might interest Jihad terrorists?"

"None. I'm sure you've had the same thoughts I've had. But I'm stymied. The white supremacist group in northern Idaho moved from their compound. If the Jihad is connecting with that group, have they come here? Or do we have a separate group—or groups—in this corner of the state, too? Maybe we'll have an answer when we've gathered all the pieces of the map."

Bart's cell phone rang. Bless him! He'd changed that torturous ring to something merely aggravating.

"Allan here." Bart listened intently, motioned for the notepad and pen I carried in my purse, and scribbled notes. "Anything else? New info? Breakthroughs?"

He listened, jotting something occasionally, his expression darkening with each passing minute. My impatience and curiosity increased at the same rate. A very curious creature by nature, and, unfortunately, an equally impatient one, I didn't handle this type of situation well.

"Roger. We'll report as soon as we've made contact in Tucson. But if you have any other info, call. We'll be in the air for another ninety minutes." Bart punched off his phone and dropped it in his lap. He took the plane off auto pilot, fastidiously checking each gauge and dial in front of him.

Finally, I couldn't stand it another minute. "Well?"

"Well, what?" He even managed to keep a straight face when he said it.

"You delight in keeping me in suspense, don't you? You know I'm dying to hear what Dad told you, but will you volunteer any information? Of course not. I have to drag it out of you a syllable at a time. What did he say? Come on. Give."

Bart's impish grin was all the answer I got.

"This is cruel and uncalled-for treatment, buster, and you may not like the consequences." I unbuckled my seat belt.

"Okay. I'll tell you." Bart held up his hand as if to ward off whatever reprisal might be headed his way. "Do up that seat belt and forget the retaliation. I just can't pass up an opportunity to see that fire in your eyes."

"If you do that too often you may get burned," I warned. But I knew the warning fell on deaf ears. Both Bart and my father loved to yank my chain. And in all honesty, I had to admit I did some chain-pulling at every opportunity myself. "So give forth with the goods, love of my life. What tidbits of intelligence did my father drop in your lap this time?"

"The name and address of our contact in Tucson. Not at the base, however. Somewhere in town. We'll have to find it when we land. The Lear needs some new equipment. Like the GPS computer program where you type in the address you want, along with your point of departure, and it prints directions to get you there."

"Anastasia can certainly afford it. In fact, I'm surprised no one has thought to install it before. What else did Dad say? You did a whole lot more listening than talking."

"They think they've got a line on Osama bin Laden." That was all. A simple statement that hung in the air like a flight of mosquitos hovering over the next victim—seemingly innocuous until it landed.

"You can let the other shoe drop now. Where is he? Here?" I held my breath, wanting to know, yet *not* wanting to know, in case it was as bad as I feared.

"They think he flew into Montreal, then crossed the border at Plattsburgh, New York, in a van full of businessmen returning from a convention." Another one-sentence answer. At this rate, we'd be in Tucson before I'd pried all the information from my tight-lipped husband.

"Did they arrest him?"

"No."

"Why not? He's been indicted in United States courts. There are outstanding warrants for his arrest. If they know where he is, what on earth prevented them from taking him into custody?" I fluctuated between being absolutely appalled, indignantly irate, and totally terrified.

"Apparently they traced his movements after the fact, not while he was entering the country." Bart didn't look at me. That could only mean he knew a lot more bad news than he wanted to reveal.

I sighed, plopped the map on the floor between us, and leaned my head back against the seat. "You know what? I'm exhausted trying to drag this from you a bit at a time. If it's so terrible, maybe I don't want to hear it. There may not be enough sugar in the world to sweeten that bitter pill. So if there's anything else you want to tell me, I'd be glad to listen. Otherwise, I think I'll take a little nap. I'm suddenly more tired than I've been for a long time."

I glanced at Bart out of the corner of my eye. The muscles in his jaw twitched like he was gritting his teeth. Good. If I didn't play his little game, maybe he'd be more forthcoming with the information. Or it could mean he was trying to decide if I'd worry too much if he told me the truth. Maybe I really didn't want to know what Dad told him. Even being a natural optimist, there was only so much bad news one could handle at a time. I'd exceeded my limit already today.

I closed my eyes, slipped off my sandals, tensed my toes and relaxed them, then my calves, my knees, all the way up my body until I was completely relaxed. I wouldn't sleep; I wasn't exhausted enough, or foolish enough, to hazard the return of the nightmare, even in broad daylight and with Bart sitting two feet from me. But if my lack of interest was convincing, my tight-lipped husband might loosen up a little and either dispel the sense of foreboding crushing me, or drop the bomb that would ensure even more terrifying nightmares, if that was possible.

I waited. And waited. Bart remained silent. I zoned out, a step short of dozing, then sat up with a start when I felt the plane begin its descent.

"Put your shoes on, Princess. Tucson International's one minute ahead. While I rent a car, you can locate Labyrinth Drive on the map and find the fastest way to get there. We need to make this as quick as possible in case we have to make another stop today."

Another stop. Wherever we ended up, we'd be exhausted—if, in fact, we actually found a place to lay our heads. Too often in this kind of situation, there wasn't an opportunity to sleep, much less have a leisurely shower, dinner, and time to follow doctor's orders. A curse on all bad guys everywhere. Especially Osama bin Laden and his crew. If this opportunity passed and we had to re-do any of those torturous medical treatments, I'd make it a personal vendetta to track that scum down.

Bart taxied onto the apron at Tucson International and parked the Lear. When he opened its door, the blast of heat nearly seared my eyelashes. "I thought Shreveport was hot this morning," I said, hating to step onto the tarmac for fear I'd burn my feet right through the soles of my sandals. "I had no idea Tucson would be worse. You'd think it would be an easier heat to take—with Shreveport two hundred feet in elevation in the humid South, and Tucson over twenty-one hundred feet higher in the desert."

"It's also the middle of the afternoon, and this pavement has had all day long to soak up those rays." Bart grabbed my hand. "I'll race you inside."

"Right. How about if you just throw me over your shoulder and carry me instead? No! I didn't mean it! Put me down." I should have known better than to challenge my husband to do anything I didn't want him to take me up on. I imagined everyone in the tower and terminal watching the tall, blond athlete running effortlessly across the tarmac with me slung over his shoulder like a duffel bag, my broomstick skirt flying in the breeze. Very dignified entrance.

"Bart, please put me down. Oof! Your shoulder is introducing my navel to my spine. Please. Please," I begged between bounces.

Finally he stopped and dumped me on my feet. "Didn't want you to melt when you touched the pavement. You're so sweet that you might have, you know." He kissed the tip of my nose.

"Is that supposed to make up for my bruises?" I tugged my cotton sweater back into place and smoothed down my skirt.

I didn't see anyone snickering behind their hand or looking at us like we were a couple of looney characters, so maybe no one saw us after all. Thirty minutes later—a ridiculous amount of time to rent a car—we recovered from near heatstroke with the air-conditioner blasting full cold as we drove east on the Miracle Mile to the address of one Don Montana on Labyrinth Drive.

Unfortunately, Tucson traffic at four o'clock was akin to Los Angeles traffic at the same hour. Between that and construction delays, it was nearly five o'clock before we located the address on the northeast side of the city in a nice new subdivision.

No one answered at the white stucco Santa Fe-style house. Bart went around back in case someone was in the backyard, and I wandered toward the street to see if any neighbors were in view. A darling blond, blue-eyed boy rode past on a bicycle for the second time.

"Hi. What's your name?" I asked.

"Brock." He sped up and rode on by, then turned around and came back.

"Do you live around here, Brock?"

"Right over there." He pointed down the street to another attractive home built in the popular Southwest style, but he didn't stop to talk. I waited. He circled back and slowed down.

"Do you know the people who live here?" I felt like I was talking to a whirling dervish as he circled around me.

"Yes, but they moved this morning." He kept circling.

I looked back at the house. It didn't look empty. Window coverings were visible, and I'd seen furniture through the living room window. "Was it a sudden move, unexpected?"

"I guess. Matthew had to quit swimming lessons and soccer. He didn't want to go."

"Was Matthew your friend?"

Brock nodded, his big blue eyes solemn as he stopped his bicycle a few feet from me. "My best friend. He came before breakfast to say good-bye and tell me he couldn't have his birthday party today. They had to leave everything but their clothes—even his bike he got for his birthday."

"That's awful. Did Matthew say where they were going?" I forgot the triple-digit heat, the sun beating down mercilessly on me at the bit of information I was gleaning from this little boy with the beautiful sad eyes.

Brock shook his head. "Just that they had to hurry and leave before . . . I can't remember who he said was coming. When I saw you stop, I thought maybe you were the ones he meant."

"Matthew's family had to leave before someone came to their house?" I didn't like the feeling growing in the pit of my stomach. "No, Brock. They didn't leave because of us. We hoped to help them."

"Brock! Brock!" a little girl's voice called from down the street.

"That's Morgan, my sister. Gotta go. She'll be out in the street coming to get me if I don't hurry." Brock hopped on his bike and raced to meet the petite little girl standing with hands on her hips at the edge of the driveway waiting for her big brother. I glanced up and down the street. Nothing stirred in either direction. No other neighbors I could interview.

What was keeping Bart? I followed the round stepping-stone path through pastel-colored rocks to an empty backyard with an incredibly inviting pool. No sign of my missing husband.

My interview over with Brock, I once again noticed the heat. The intense, oppressive heat. I couldn't wait to get back to the California coast and the cool breezes blowing off the ocean. The end of the world would have arrived if it ever got this hot in Santa Barbara.

The back door stood slightly ajar. Was Bart guilty of breaking and entering? I poked my head inside. Not even the ticking of a clock broke the absolute silence. I opened my mouth to call to him, thought better of it, and slipped inside.

Matthew's family had indeed left in a hurry. Breakfast dishes were still on the table, milk curdled in the bottoms of the cereal bowls. I reached for the carton of milk to refrigerate it before I caught myself. In this heat, it had long since passed the point of being good for anything. Even the black and white cat that curled around my feet and rubbed against my legs probably wouldn't touch it.

I picked up the soft, sleek animal and scratched behind its ears. "Did they have to leave you behind, or couldn't they find you when it was time to go?" I asked softly. A deep purr was all the answer I got. "Guess we'd better see if Brock and Morgan can keep you—or find a home for you. You can't stay here by yourself. If you didn't starve, you'd suffocate in this heat."

I wandered through the immaculate but sweltering dining room and into the family room strewn with toys, magazines, and shoes and socks. Still no sign of Bart, and no other sound but the cat purring in my arms. Had he gone around the opposite side of the house and missed me? Then I heard the rattle of computer keys, and followed the telltale noise to a tiny study off the front foyer. My missing husband sat in the darkened room, beads of perspiration running down his face and neck, soaking the collar of his polo shirt.

"Guess they didn't want to waste air-conditioning on an empty house," I commented.

Bart started and whirled in his seat. "Don't do that, Princess! I didn't hear you come in."

"Find anything interesting?" I peered over his shoulder at the computer screen.

"As a matter of fact, I did. The computer was on. Somebody scanned some kind of document, so I thought I'd see if I could pull it up and print it out. I was just doing that when you scared the daylights out of me."

"Well, either you'll have to hurry, or I'll have to leave you to play with it alone. I can't stand the heat in here another minute." With the ample fabric in my long, loose-flowing skirt, I wiped the perspiration from my face and arms. Wasted effort. I could feel it trickling anew down my temples and back.

"Printing now," Bart said, clicking the print icon. "Find anything?"

I recounted my conversation with Brock.

Bart whistled. "I wonder who they expected, and how they found out someone was coming."

"Brock didn't know. In fact, he thought we might be the ones Matthew's family left in order to avoid. We don't need to stick around and find out."

We turned to the printer to watch the sheet emerge. The page seemed blank, then the small point of a map appeared and grew into the familiar pie-shaped wedge.

"Bingo." Bart's smile radiated success.

The telephone number interested me, if there was one. As the printer spit out the finished product, the numbers appeared in neat block letters, with a hand-printed and circled number seven. I reached to pull this third piece of the puzzle from the printer, then froze in mid-reach.

"I'll take that," demanded a male voice with a heavy foreign accent.

CHAPTER 8

We whirled toward the door of the tiny study. The ugly gun in the man's hand provided the first indication of trouble. The venomous look in his malevolent black eyes gave the second.

"Give it to me," he demanded. It sounded more like "Geeve eet toe me," but I got the drift. I glanced at Bart. The look he flashed told me to be careful and watch for an opening. It couldn't have been clearer if he'd spoken the words aloud before he turned with a slow, fluid motion to the computer to retrieve the sheet of paper from the printer.

I turned my attention to the man holding the gun. The long-sleeved black shirt buttoned at wrist and collar dramatized his stiff, uncompromising look. Coupled with the cruel black eyes and the gun pointing at me, I hardly noticed the pleasant proportions of his face until I focused on the man instead of the menace. He had an aristocratic nose and thick, shining black curls that just touched his strong, high forehead. When he spoke, he revealed yellowed, even teeth. But the most memorable thing about him was the strong aroma of his unpleasant aftershave lotion.

As Bart turned with the paper in his hand and carefully stretched it toward him, the man snatched it, glanced quickly at it, then back at us, the gun never wavering in his steady hand. Definitely a professional. Definitely dangerous.

He backed the two steps toward the door, his merciless black eyes narrowing in a look that I could only interpret as pure hatred. In that instant, I knew he would pull the trigger. He would kill us. My only thought was that all the work we'd done, all the tests, all the time we'd put into trying to conceive a baby—all of it was for naught. *Father, this just can't happen. This can't be Thy plan for us.*

Suddenly the doorbell rang. Not once, but again and again in short, quick, urgent chimes. Simultaneously, someone banged on the front door scarcely three feet from where the man stood. The black and white cat, nestled contentedly in my arms throughout this short ordeal, yowled and jumped free, fleeing between the legs of the startled man with the gun.

In that instant, with our captor's focus momentarily diverted, Bart dove across the room. The man's reflexes were incredible. He brought the gun down on Bart's head even as Bart tackled him and knocked him off his feet. I watched in horror as my husband crumpled to the floor and lay completely still.

I hadn't been idle myself in those action-packed seconds. As Bart moved, my hand connected with a heavy object on the desk behind me. I scooped it up and flung it at the man with all my strength. It missed the gun, but caught him on the wrist. I heard the splinter of bone connecting with marble as the heavy Aztec calendar disabled the man. The gun fell to the tile floor with a clatter, along with the green marble disk, and skittered down the hall out of reach.

Clutching the second object my fingers touched, I flew at the man before he retrieved the gun. The weapon in my hand turned out to be a gold letter opener, which I plunged without hesitation into his nearest body part. Later, I'd probably be glad it wasn't his heart. At the moment, I regretted it was only his thigh.

Again his incredible reflexes astounded me. He turned and raised his hand, smashing the back of it against my face. My head bounced off the wall, then my vision narrowed until I slipped into total darkness and oblivion.

* * * * *

My head hurt. Actually, hurt didn't describe it adequately. Ached, pounded, throbbed didn't either. When I got past the head, the rest of my body was suffering, too. Something weighed heavily on my chest, making breathing nearly impossible. I couldn't see in the darkness, couldn't move, had no idea where I was except probably in a sauna with the heat maxed.

I was afraid for a minute that I'd died and gone to my eternal reward—to burn in outer darkness. Then I remembered outer darkness would be freezing, not melting. I decided death must be more merciful than this, and I was still very much in this world. A small, cramped, crowded world.

Suddenly my claustrophobia kicked into overdrive. Frantically shoving at the mass on top of me, I fought to be free, to breathe, to find light and space and air and freedom and all those other precious things I desperately lacked at the moment.

The thing on top of me didn't budge. It was solid, heavy, but not inanimate. Bart. The memory of those last conscious moments flashed vividly before my eyes, and I felt anxiously for his arm, his neck, any pulse point that would reveal his condition. His head was crammed into one corner, his legs bent at angles in the opposite corner, leaving his body solidly across mine.

I felt his neck, panicked when there was no pulse, desperately explored farther. My probing fingers finally felt the weak but steady throb of my husband's heart beating in his chest. I murmured a quick thanks heavenward for this blessing, then another more fervent thank you when I realized how close we had come to leaving this existence forever.

Sauna though it may be, we were still alive. For the moment.

I felt the walls above and around me, seeking the door. There must be a door, and I had to find it quickly. Claustrophobia's a terrible thing. I didn't know whether anyone had ever died from it, but death seemed only the next step beyond the terror I now experienced.

My searching fingers finally touched a door casing. Now I needed to shift my husband's one hundred ninety pounds enough to reach the door handle. My head throbbing mightily with each strenuous movement, I reached as high as I thought a doorknob would be, but touched only warm, smooth wood. Of course it would be on the other side of the door, which I couldn't reach.

Desperate for air, for light and freedom, I eased myself, inch by inch, from under the dead weight of my still-unconscious husband.

Kneeling in the tiny cubicle where not a single sliver of light penetrated, I faced the door and ran my hands up the satiny surface until I touched the metal doorknob, burning hot. I jerked my finger away and popped it in my mouth.

Tucson may be hot, but not that hot.

Wrapping my voluminous skirt around the handle, I twisted and shoved. The door opened only a tiny crack—through which thick smoke curled immediately into the already unbearable torture chamber. Something heavy had been pushed against the door. I stood, swayed with dizziness, and pushed with all the strength I could muster. It moved only another inch or two. Smoke poured in, robbing the tiny space of all breathable air. I held my breath, put my back to the door, wedged my feet against the wall on the opposite side of the closet, and shoved with all my might, praying for heavenly help, for additional strength, for anything the Lord saw fit to grant me at this crucial moment.

I felt a shift on the other side of the door, heard scraping and grating on the tile floor, and suddenly the door gave way. I fell out, crashing to the hard tile with all the grace of a cow on a frozen pond. Smoke, so dark and thick I couldn't see anything, burned my eyes, my throat. Though I tried to keep my face to the floor and not breathe it, I coughed, inhaling the deadly fumes into my now bursting lungs.

I had to find the door. Had to get some air and get my husband out of that closet. I snaked along the hall, then suddenly panicked. What if I got out and couldn't get back to find Bart? Reversing direction, I felt my way blindly around the door and touched a shoe with a leg attached. I wrested Bart from the closet, depleting my strength and my breath. The heat and smoke were unbearable. The only element missing from this nightmare was flame licking at my exhausted flesh.

I had spoken too soon. With a loud whoosh, bright orange flames erupted behind me on the desk that had been shoved against the closet door, holding us in. At that moment, pounding commenced at the front door—in the opposite direction from where I'd been headed when I stopped to get Bart. Only a surge of adrenalin enabled me to find the doorknob. I burned my hand as I touched it.

I shouted for help, but my voice cracked and I didn't have enough wind to make myself heard. Pounding on the inside of the door with my fist, I wadded up a handful of skirt, found the deadbolt and turned it. The door flew open, banging into my forehead. Arms reached through the smoke and dragged me outside into the welcome fresh air of deepening twilight.

"My husband . . . inside." I collapsed on the cool grass, watching a slight form plunge back into the smoke billowing from the front door. For an instant she was silhouetted against the wildly dancing flames now raging out of control inside, consuming the desk and spreading to everything else flammable. Then she disappeared.

I rolled across the grass, afraid to get to my feet, afraid to inhale any more of that deadly smoke, and crawled on hands and knees toward the door. Smoke stung my eyes and tears rolled down my face, obscuring everything in front of me. I felt my way to the entrance and bumped into someone backing out. Together we dragged my unconscious husband to the grass near the street. I lay beside him gasping for air, coughing the smoke from my lungs, trying to feel his wrist for a pulse. My benefactor collapsed on the lawn beside us, hacking and coughing.

"Thank you," I wheezed.

My little blond friend on the bike screeched to a stop in the street next to us, his blue eyes wide and round as he watched the fire. "I called 911 like you said, Mom. The fire truck's coming."

I could hear the sirens even now. Fire trucks carry oxygen. Bart would need oxygen. I leaned up on one elbow and put my head on his chest. The slow tha-lump of his heart filled me with joy. Feeling his head, I discovered an oozing lump the size of an egg on one side.

"Brock, go home and stay with Morgan. Don't let her leave the house. I'll be there in a minute." Brock obediently, though reluctantly, mounted his bike and took off toward home.

People poured from houses up and down the street, some bringing water, one with blankets, totally unnecessary in this heat, some just standing, watching the flames devour the house of their former neighbors. As the fire trucks screeched to a halt in front of the house, a good-looking blond man pulled past them in his car and jumped out, leaving the door wide open. He ran to kneel beside my rescuer.

"JoDee, what happened? Are you okay?" He was apparently her husband and Brock's father. His resemblance to the little boy couldn't be missed. Wrapping his arms around the woman, he helped her to her feet. She buried her face in his shirt and clung to him. He pulled her out of the way and onto the neighbor's little area of grass as a tangle of fire hoses were dragged in place to play on the flames.

A couple of EMTs knelt at Bart's side with the precious oxygen and began administering it. Within a few seconds Bart groaned, stirred, and his eyes fluttered open. The cute female Hispanic technician held him down for a minute and gave him a few more whiffs of oxygen before he pushed it away and struggled to sit up. The male Anglo technician dabbed at the bump on Bart's head, making him wince as it was cleaned and dressed.

"How do you feel, besides having a splitting headache?" I asked, leaning against him to touch his face. The oxygen mask was thrust over my mouth and nose before I could continue.

Bart blinked as if to clear his vision, looked at me, then at the fire. He seemed to take in all the wrestling of hoses and work of containing the blaze, then looked back at me as he got another whiff of oxygen. Without his uttering a word, I read his thoughts quite clearly in those troubled eyes.

We were in a precarious position. We'd been inside—illegally—a house being destroyed by fire. We no longer had the map we'd come to get, and we had no idea what had happened to the people we hoped to warn of danger. We'd be detained and questioned—not a huge problem with Interpol ID and knowing we were innocent, but proving it might take time, and this was definitely an inconvenience. More troubling was the fact that the terrorists suddenly appeared to be one step ahead of us.

Could things get much worse? I should never ask.

CHAPTER 9

The media arrived. Television cameras, lights, microphones, and reporters would be pouring from the three vans that stopped just down the street. Police investigators would be right behind them, if they weren't here already. Maybe we could quietly slip away in the late evening twilight. Bart crawled slowly to his knees in anticipation of getting to his feet. I struggled to mine and helped him on one side while the cute Hispanic technician grabbed his other arm to steady him.

"Can you help us get to our car?" I asked. "We can talk to the police from there, but we don't need microphones thrust in our faces. I don't want my grandmother to see me on TV before I call and explain what happened. She has a heart condition, and might not be able to stand the shock of knowing what a close call we had."

I'd stretched the truth somewhat. My grandmother did have a heart condition—a tiny occasional irregular heartbeat the doctor said was nothing to worry about. But she lived in Greece, and the chances of her seeing this TV broadcast were next to non-existent. What was the old saw—desperate times require desperate measures? This qualified. One more thing of which to repent.

The technician helped me get Bart across the street and into the passenger seat of our rental car, reclined his seat back as far as it would go, opened all the doors to let the trapped over-heated air escape, and asked if there was anything else she could do. Fortunately my hair had fallen over my forehead, and neither of the medical personnel had seen the bump that tomorrow would be a lovely blue-and-green hue.

Bart signaled for me to go, then leaned his head back against the seat, his eyes closed. I knew we needed to leave immediately, but I had to say thank you one more time. I turned back and looked for Brock's mother. She and her husband had disappeared. They were probably at home, keeping their kids safe from the traffic congesting their once-quiet neighborhood.

We'd parked across the street with our car pointed in that direction, so I slid behind the wheel, started the car, and eased down the street without lights. With so much confusion going on, we wouldn't be missed for another minute or two. Just time to say thank you and escape.

I thought I remembered Morgan's driveway and stopped there, leaving the air-conditioner on full blast to make Bart more comfortable. As I ran to the door, I could see two little faces pressed against the window, watching the excitement.

The door opened before I rang the bell. A slender wisp of a woman stood silhouetted against the light from the foyer. I recognized the once-crisp, white shorts, now spotted with dark smudges.

"I came to thank you and Brock for saving our lives," I said. "We'd never have gotten out of that fire alive if you hadn't pulled us out when you did."

"I'm just glad Brock saw that man follow you in the back door. My son said he had to be the one the Montanas were afraid of, because he didn't think anyone could be afraid of a nice lady like you. We watched from the window. I came down and knocked on the door and rang the doorbell, but no one answered. I thought I heard noises inside, but I wasn't sure."

The Montanas' black and white cat curled about JoDee's ankles, and she reached down to pick him up, stroking him as he purred in her arms. I was glad he'd survived the fire.

JoDee continued. "Brock saw the man leave, but not you. We had to go to town, and when we got home, your car was still parked there. When Brock thought he saw smoke coming from the back door, I told him to call 911, and I ran to see what was going on."

"Thank you," I said. "And please thank Brock for me. He was a hero today. I think I owe you a bit of an explanation. Reporters and probably police will interview you, but I'd rather you didn't repeat this to them. Maybe you can find a way to tell Brock what a great job he did without revealing anything that would jeopardize the Montana family."

I glanced up the street. It was only a matter of minutes before we'd be missed. But what little could I say without saying too much?

"JoDee, we're with an international organization fighting terrorism. Don Montana had a lead for us. Apparently he discovered that someone besides us wanted that clue, and they fled before the danger reached them. Unfortunately, our timing wasn't as good. Just know that today you've provided a great service to your country. Please find a way to tell Brock that, without giving him bragging rights that will get back to the wrong parties."

With that I whirled away, leaving her speechless, still silhouetted in the doorway. I don't think I ever did see her face, but with a such a caring nature and darling son and daughter, she had to be a pretty special lady.

I drove in the opposite direction of the chaotic scene behind us, hoping no one had seen us leave or noted the license number, praying we'd be able to escape without the delay of interrogation. Without opening his eyes or moving his head, Bart held out his hand. I put mine in his and he squeezed it. "Fill in the missing chapters," he said. "What happened after I took a nap, compliments of Jihad?"

"I'm sort of guessing myself, since he did a similar number on me. I smacked his gun hand with a marble Aztec calendar—you know, those heavy, ornate things everyone gets as a souvenir from Mexico—and managed to poke a hole in his leg with a letter opener before he bounced me off the wall and knocked me out. When I came to, we were locked in a closet. I'm not sure why he didn't kill us right there, unless JoDee's banging on the door scared him off."

"JoDee?"

I glanced at Bart. He hadn't moved. Hadn't opened his eyes. That must be one serious ache in his head. I spotted a fast-food place at the next intersection and pulled into their drive-through lane. "I'm going to get you something so you can wash down a handful of aspirin," I said. "Want something to eat while we're here?" As I looked at the menu, I suddenly realized I was starving. When had we eaten last? Abilene? Was that today? Or yesterday? It seemed a lifetime ago.

Bart didn't bother to notice where we were or look at the colorful billboard menu outside my window. "Not sure I could keep anything down," he murmured. "Must have a bit of a concussion."

A bit of a concussion was probably a bit of an understatement, considering the size of the lump on his head and the length of time he'd remained out of it. If I insisted on taking him to a hospital, he'd be just as insistent that he didn't need to go. Accustomed to dealing with the aftereffects of such blows to the head, he certainly knew whether or not this was more serious than the others.

"Two double-bacon cheeseburgers, two large orders of fries, and two huge drinks, please." I hoped he'd be tempted by the smell and try to eat. Along with some aspirin, that might help as much as anything to restore the sparkle in his eye and normalcy to his system.

While I waited for our order, I retrieved the headache remedy from my purse, divided between us the remainder of pills in the nearly empty package, and put Bart's in his hand. I was definitely ready for mine. Though my headache might not be the magnitude of Bart's, it wasn't far behind.

Not daring to stop this close to the scene of the crime, I deposited our drinks in the cup holders between us, spread Bart's meal on his outstretched lap, unwrapped my sandwich, liberally spread my French fries with catsup, and pulled onto the busy Miracle Mile to make the trek back to the airport. Then I suddenly realized that flying might not be an option.

"You can't fly with a blinding headache," I said. "You might pass out again while we're in the air. What are we going to do, hole up and wait till morning, and see how you feel then?"

Bart roused from his lethargy and managed to swallow his aspirin with a long gulp of his drink before he fumbled in his pocket. "Princess, did you get a look at that phone number on the map before we relinquished it to bin Laden's emissary?"

I'd completely forgotten the map. "I did. Now I just have to remember the number. Give me a minute."

I wanted to close my eyes and recreate the scene—impossible while driving. Doubling my concentration, I pictured the tiny dark den, the little color printer spitting out a green and yellow pie-shaped wedge of map with the number seven circled. The phone number appeared in nicely printed block numerals in my mind as it had on the paper.

I repeated it aloud and glanced at Bart to see if he'd heard me, or was zoning on the other side of the car. He turned his head carefully, opened his eyes, and managed a weak smile. "Have I ever told you what an incredible creature you are?"

"Not lately." I flashed him an appreciative smile. "Any chance you have the strength to manage it now?" He held out his hand and I took it, a little connection to affirm our love for each other and our gratitude that we'd survived. I turned my attention back to traffic.

"Keep it in mind while I call Jack. He'll be berserk, wondering what's happened." Bart punched the speed dial on his cell phone, munching a fry while he waited for the connection.

Even over the hum of traffic, I could hear my father's voice raised in relief, and probably some anger at having to wait and worry, since he'd been anticipating this call for at least three hours.

"The number you want is . . ." Bart paused.

I recited it for him and he repeated the number, then added, "You'd better call someone to do cleanup quick. We left a mess of questions and a burning house. Don't know whether you want McAffrey's boys to handle it, or if you want to call the Tucson PD and explain what we were doing there before the media makes a major mystery of it."

Bart listened, stuffed a couple of fries in his mouth, and handed the phone to me. "Tell him what happened. I'm a bit blank in that area." It pleased me to see Bart immediately devour his cheeseburger.

"Hi, Dad. Bart's right. Someone needs to do some mop-up fast. I doubt anyone wants the real story to get out, though it might shake up some of America's apathy about terrorism if it did."

"What happened, Bunny? Are you okay? Did you talk to Don Montana? I assume he had the map if you got a phone number."

"Hang on a minute, Dad." I eased out of traffic and stopped in an empty bank parking lot. "Kind of hard to talk and drive in this traffic." Not to mention balance a meal in my lap. I recounted our findings in the Montana home and Bart's printing out the map. "Unfortunately, before we had a chance to examine it, we were relieved of it by someone who could only be Jihad, judging from the hatred in his eyes and the benevolent way he handled us."

Dad interrupted. "You haven't said if you're okay. Are you hurt?"

"Glad to be alive, thanks to divine intervention in the form of a caring neighbor and her inquisitive son. Our assailant could have killed us, but instead stuffed us in a closet and set a fire producing prodigious amounts of smoke before it actually flamed. I'm not sure what his intent was, but that and the persistent neighbors became our saving grace."

"Bunny, I get the feeling you're not telling me everything."

"You didn't ask for a catalogue of our injuries. We have one slight problem, though. Bart has a concussion . . ."

Bart relieved me of the phone. "I'm fine," he insisted to his boss. "You should have a fix on that phone number by now. Where do we go from here?"

"To bed," roared my father. He must have realized he'd raised his voice, as I heard nothing else from across the car.

"Jack, I'm fine. Where's the next stop? They're ahead of us now. No time to sit on our hands waiting for a little headache to disappear. Those people could be in danger—could be dead as we speak. We've got to keep on top of this."

I finished my cheeseburger and fries, undecided whether to pull back into traffic and head for the airport, wait for Dad's instructions, or start looking for a hotel for the night. The latter appealed intensely to me. I longed for a shower and clean, fresh sheets with a nice soft pillow on which to lay my aching head. Not to mention a quiet, peaceful, romantic interlude.

Hah! It would never happen. Even if Dad ordered us to spend the night, Bart would find some way to circumvent those orders. He worried about people. He knew the Jihad wouldn't check into a hotel and retire early. They'd be relentless in the pursuit of their objective, either from zeal for their cause or fear of Osama bin Laden.

I sighed and pulled back into traffic. Might as well get under way. The airport, fifteen minutes distant, would be our destination after Bart convinced Dad that he was alive, alert, and able to function. My opinion differed, of course, but what did I know? I was only his wife, and I was supposed to overlook his weaknesses—little things like dilated pupils, probably one reason Bart kept his eyes closed. From my own pounding head, I knew the price Bart paid by arguing with my father, when he'd probably prefer to lie back quietly and sleep it off.

Bart continued to sell Dad on his point of view, apparently with success. "Thanks, Jack. We'll check in when we land." He turned off the phone, leaned back, closed his eyes, and gingerly rubbed his forehead, as if that gentle massage could fend off the excruciating pain I knew he must be feeling.

"So, love of my life, what's our destination after Tucson International? I assume you finally convinced Dad you're fit to fly. You're not, you know."

Bart ignored my last comment. "The number was a Las Vegas exchange. Jack's sending Oz and Mai Li, since they're actually closer to Vegas in Santa Barbara than we are here. We'll go direct to Idaho Falls and start poking around there."

"Does 'direct' mean tonight or tomorrow?" One part of me desperately needed to be clean and rested. The other agreed with Bart. This urgent matter couldn't wait for my comfort.

"I hate to do it to you, Princess. I know you're exhausted, but we're going to Idaho tonight."

"What else did Dad say? What's going on, that he'd let you convince him to pursue this, knowing the physical state you're in?" Dad's chief concern was his agents' physical condition, knowing they'd never see a bullet coming if they were sick or exhausted.

"They think bin Laden left Newark on a red-eye flight to Denver last night. No further word, but that puts him within a couple of hours' flight to any of these points, including Idaho Falls."

I shuddered. Thoughts of a shower, bed, and rest fled, along with my peace of mind. I found it hard to visualize the forty-three-year-old terrorist leader, who headed the FBI's Ten Most Wanted list, here in the United States. How arrogant. How utterly contemptuous of American law enforcement he must be, to leave his hideout in Afghanistan and move openly around this country.

I looked at Bart, his eyes closed, hands folded over his belt. Better let him rest for the next few minutes. I had a feeling there would be no rest for either of us, or anyone in Anastasia, until this entire affair was resolved. It didn't take a fortune teller to see what was bound to turn up in those next deadly cards.

CHAPTER 10

I refrained from asking questions, allowing Bart what sleep he could get before we arrived at the airport. After we returned the rental car, he filed a flight plan to Fanning Field, Idaho Falls, Idaho, and we were airborne before the last glow of the sun completely faded from the western sky.

A zillion stars sparkled brilliantly in the midnight blue heavens, thanks to Tucson's ordinances which required downward-facing streetlights, thus protecting the incredible night sky for which the Southwest was famous. I couldn't remember when I'd seen such an array of heavenly light.

Bart pointed out the major constellations with which I was already familiar, and a dozen minor ones usually not visible to the naked eye. Then he put the plane on auto pilot, showed me what to monitor on the various instruments, and left the controls in my untrained hands. I think he was asleep before he stopped moving.

I remembered the first time he'd entrusted me with control of a Lear jet. We'd just snatched my mother from an assassin in the isles of Greece and were returning to Santa Barbara. Bart desperately needed sleep, and I did nothing more than monitor our course into Lajes Field on the Azores—where that same group of people blew our airplane right off the runway.

I fingered the emerald engagement ring nestled next to my wedding band. That had been the beginning and nearly the end of our engagement, not to mention our explosive wedding a few days later, when the wedding party had been fired upon and the mansion on the estate almost destroyed by firebombs. That extraordinary genesis had been a prelude to one incredible adventure after another during the last year. Most were unbelievable.

We'd arrive in Idaho Falls in two hours. Would that put us ahead of the terrorists, or were they already there? Had we been followed from the Montana residence? It would be too easy to check our flight plan and have someone waiting when we landed in Idaho, especially if the terrorists were already in place there.

Bart's habit of having the plane refueled each time we stopped served him well. There'd been no delay in taking off. My marvelous, methodical husband. He believed and lived by the premise that success was in the details, and he carefully attended to them.

I loved working with Bart. It was much nicer than fleeing across the country alone, watching every shadow that moved, left to my own devices to keep myself out of the gun sights of terrorist assassins. We were good together, a well-matched team. My wild imagination balanced his sometimes staid logic. His analytical disposition offset my inquisitive, intuitive nature. Oz compared us to a prancing Arabian show horse and a plodding work horse. One you couldn't keep in the harness, and the other you couldn't get out. Whatever. It worked. Our only problem was our innate fear that the other would be injured—or worse—during our confrontations with these diabolical men who valued life not a whit.

Bart's dilemma stemmed from wanting me next to him, yet desiring me safely at home, raising the children we hoped to have. I suffered my own dilemma. I wanted to work with Bart, wanted to be at his side doing what he loved most, feeling I was aiding and abetting in this valuable work that not everyone could or even wanted to do. At the same time I despised the criminal element, the lowlifes we were forced to encounter, hated being bruised and injured, exhausted and dirty, and unable to conveniently remedy that.

I longed for some normalcy in my life, but since terrorists don't keep bankers' hours, it was highly unlikely that my life would change—unless we were fortunate enough to have children, and I left tracking terrorism to Bart while I concentrated on tracking little hands and feet getting into mischief. That would be a hard decision to make. I'd miss being with Bart, miss the intellectual challenge of sorting and sifting through clues and evidence, examining possibilities, and puzzling through problems and predicaments caused by someone's lust for power and position.

Another facet of my problem was the haunting nightmare that threatened not only my health and sanity, but filled me with increasing doubts about my abilities as an effective agent. During the lonely flight, while Bart enjoyed what I hoped was a healing sleep, self-doubt crept into my psyche to grow and bloom there—never a good thing for an agent to indulge in, much less to allow to take root.

I checked the gauges again, then stared into the darkness. An hour and a half into the flight, and according to the flight maps, we'd already crossed the Colorado River cutting deeply through Glen Canyon. Somewhere in the darkness below, spectacular red rock formations of Bryce, Zion, Canyonlands, and Capitol Reef National Parks colored the land. Ahead, the lights of Salt Lake City glowed. Time to wake Bart.

I unbuckled my safety belt, knelt by his seat, and watched him for a minute in the glow of the instrument panel. How I loved this man who had been my big brother, champion, and protector throughout my childhood, my confidant and mentor through the triumphs and tragedies of my high school days while he was in college. My first and great love. No man knew me as well or loved me as deeply as this one—probably not even my own father, who had missed my growing-up years while he fought terrorism undercover in the nethermost parts of the world.

I leaned forward and kissed my husband gently. Would that I could land the plane and give him another thirty minutes of desperately needed sleep. Bart sat up, instantly awake, took in the instruments at a glance, and slipped his arms around me. "Nice way to wake up," he murmured. "I'll have to remember to return the favor." He held me tenderly for a minute, one hand pressing my head against his chest and the steady tha-lump of his heart, the other stroking my back. "Have I told you today how much I love you?" The words, spoken so quietly they were almost a whisper, warmed my soul.

"Probably. But I can never hear it enough." I tilted my head, touching the soft skin of his throat with my lips.

"Well, if I've already told you, I guess it's time to get back to the business of flying this airplane." Bart's voice filled with mock seriousness, his arms opened, and he gripped my forearms to push me away. I clamped my teeth playfully where a second ago I'd kissed him.

"Uncle. You win. I love you," he laughed, pulling me close again. "Your reflexes are too quick, you vixen."

"Your thought process was too slow, dulled no doubt by the nap I so lovingly allowed you to have. Never offer a woman love, then withhold it. That's a dangerous thing to do, especially if she's within arm's length."

Bart kissed me. "Or her teeth are within sinking distance. Lesson learned. Is it safe to let you go so we can get on with the flight?"

"Mmm. I'm not sure I like being told you love me under duress." I nibbled on his ear.

"Dressed, undressed, or duress, I love you, Princess. Thanks for loving me." Bart took my face in his hands and kissed my forehead, nose, and lips.

I slipped back into my seat and buckled my safety belt. "You're welcome. Usually it's the easiest, most natural thing in the world. Other times . . ." I let the rest of the sentence dangle unfinished.

"Remind me to bring up those 'other times' when we can discuss them in depth," Bart said, trying to appear seriously troubled.

"How long to Idaho Falls?"

"About forty-five minutes. Then you can have a good night's sleep."

"What's that?" I sighed, closing my eyes and leaning my head against the seat.

"What's what?" Bart sounded genuinely puzzled.

"A good night's sleep. It's been months since I've had one. I scarcely remember what it's like to sleep through the night without being haunted by Raven, or by that helpless baby crying out from somewhere beyond reach. I secretly wonder sometimes whether Raven will find me before I find the baby, and if so, what will happen? What does it mean?"

Bart reached for my hand and squeezed it in a sympathetic gesture.

I looked at him in the dim cabin light. "Is that the baby we lost, crying because it didn't get to come to us? Or is it another, waiting impatiently for its turn to come to earth?"

He turned to me. "Or?" How well he read me, my moods, my thoughts, the desires of my heart.

I took a deep breath. "Or is it someone else's child? Some unwanted, unloved baby, or one that someone must suffer the heartache of releasing for adoption because they can't keep it, or because they love it so unselfishly that they'd give it a chance for a better life?"

Bart was quiet, his breathing even and deep. No intake of breath when he heard it. No shallow breaths to recover from the surprise. "What do *you* think?" he asked softly. "Any intuitive thoughts or feelings on the subject?"

I shook my head. "No. I've thought about it a lot, lying in the dark at night after it wakes me. And even as I endured those fertility treatments, I wondered if they were all for naught, and the baby was trying to tell me not to worry, it was there waiting for me. I just had to find it. I don't know, love. I really don't know what to make of it."

"I'm sure you've prayed about it."

"Endlessly. Along with my plea for both nightmares to go away. Even after your blessing, they're still all too real, and they come all too often. Does that mean my faith isn't strong enough to banish them?"

"Princess, you know better than that. Only the Lord completely understands the workings of the subconscious. I certainly don't. But maybe it's just another of those trials and tribulations we're 'privileged' to experience during this mortal existence. And then . . ."

I interrupted. "I know. 'If thou endure it well, God shall exalt thee on high; thou shalt triumph over all thy foes.' But the Prophet Joseph Smith's foes were flesh and blood. Mine aren't."

Bart posed the question quietly, thoughtfully, as if he were trying to understand the answer himself. "Does that make it easier to endure? If someone is tarring and feathering you and tossing you in prison unjustly?"

"I'm sure it doesn't. But at least he could see his tormentors. He understood the reasoning behind his persecution. I'm not restoring the gospel of Jesus Christ to the earth like he did, nor opening a new dispensation. Of course Satan would stir up all sorts of opposition to that. But the fact is, I'm just not important enough to loose the powers of evil on. So why am I plagued night after night with nightmares that seem, on my small, inconsequential scale, as big to me as some of Joseph's opposition might have seemed to him?"

"First, you are important enough for Satan to concentrate on. And remember the verse before the one you quoted?"

I thought for a moment. "Refresh my memory."

"The Lord told him, 'Peace be unto thy soul; thine adversity and thine afflictions shall be but a small moment,' and then He promised what you quoted: 'If thou endure it well, God shall exalt thee on high; thou shalt triumph over all thy foes.'"

"Even the supernatural ones?"

"Maybe especially the ones that haunt our minds and our dreams and our goals. Remember, the Lord told Joseph that though he be cast into the hands of murderers, and the sentence of death passed upon him, and 'above all, if the very jaws of hell shall gape open the mouth wide after thee, know thou, my son, that all these things shall give thee experience, and shall be for thy good.'"

I couldn't answer for a minute. Relating scripture to personal situations was too up-close and personal this time.

"Are you okay?" Bart asked quietly as the moment extended to several.

I took a deep breath, trying to keep my voice calm and steady. "I've been there. Been in the hands of murderers with a sentence of death passed upon me. The jaws of death have gaped open wide after me." I shuddered. Memories I'd suppressed—or tried to—flooded back. "It's so hard to think any of that could be for my good. And, just for the sake of argument, if it actually was, I still don't understand the purpose of the nightmares and how they could possibly be for my good."

Bart sat quietly for a minute. "Ours is not to reason why," he paraphrased. "Ours is but to do or . . ." He stopped before completing the quote.

"Die," I finished for him. A feeling of foreboding sent chills shivering down my spine.

CHAPTER 11

Bart's attempts to lighten the moment and the mood failed miserably, and he fell silent, busying himself with landing the airplane. For good or ill, we'd arrived in Idaho Falls. I'd recognized one bright beacon as we landed: a white wedding cake-looking temple with a gold statue of the Angel Moroni gleaming on top, trumpeting his message to the world.

Compared to the enormous airport in Los Angeles, with its nonstop traffic and crowds of people coming and going at all hours of the day and night, the small terminal at Fanning Field felt almost intimate—especially in its near-deserted state at ten P.M. Not even any bad guys lurking in the shadows. Huge wooden crossbeams and glass partitioned the gates and waiting rooms, giving the long, narrow terminal a casual, rustic look, like something out of the Big Woods. Solitary customers for a car rental, we were on our way without delay.

We drove between rows of fully grown evergreen trees lining the airport road, and within minutes arrived at the Shilo Inn Resort Hotel and Conference Center, recommended by the rental reservationist. No cars followed us from the airport. The large, long, four-story blue and white edifice had huge stone pillars holding up the blue tiled roof of the entry—and there appeared to be no one in the parking lot waiting for us.

When we entered our fourth-floor room, I immediately threw open the curtains. Framed in the glass across the winding black expanse of the Snake River, the pristine white single spire of the temple pierced the darkness with a brilliance beyond landscaping lights. Possibly the spray from the famous falls below lent it the halo.

Or maybe it was something else—the heavenly glow of a heavenly place.

As I stepped onto the balcony, the smoothly flowing Snake River, the falls cascading frothy white down the river, and the temple shining like a lighthouse soothed my troubled soul. Below, on the grounds of the hotel, stone lamp posts topped by antique lights illuminated a bridge over a small stream paralleling the river, where couples strolled arm in arm.

Bart dropped our bags in the closet, turned off the interior light, and joined me on the balcony, sliding his arms around me from behind and resting his chin on my head. "Nice view," he murmured.

"It is," I agreed, leaning against him. "Almost makes that long flight worth it."

"Penny for your thoughts."

"Same thing I always think when I see a temple. Is this the one?"

"Do you want it to be?" Bart's breath tickled my ear as he leaned over and kissed my neck, sending delicious shivers down my arms.

"I don't know. This whole year, while we've been waiting to get our temple recommends so we could be sealed—become a 'forever family'—I've been trying to decide where we should have that very sacred ordinance performed. I know all temples are the same in terms of the ordinance performed there. But in another way, they're not really the same, because one will be more special to one person than another. Bishop O'Hare and Katie plan to be with us, and they assume we'll go to the Los Angeles Temple, because that's the closest." I paused, not quite sure how to explain what I felt.

"But . . ." Bart said, waiting for me to finish my thought.

"But to me, that's just another temple. For some reason, I don't feel an attachment to it like I thought I would for my special temple."

"Princess, you now have more than a hundred to choose from, so whichever temple you develop an attachment to, I'll take you there."

"When you say it that way, I feel selfish and ungrateful. The Los Angeles Temple is a three-hour freeway drive in air-conditioned comfort. Why would I ask for anything more than that? Some people save for years to be able to attend the temple closest to them, which might be hundreds of miles away. Forgive me for being such a spoiled brat?" I turned my face up to Bart.

"Not spoiled. You just want the most important step of our lives to be special. No one can argue with that." Bart kissed my cheek and held me tighter.

We stood silently listening to the river, watching the lights.

"Are you sorry we're not in New Orleans?" he asked softly.

I thought for a minute. "Probably not."

"I know you had something unique planned. Want to try to replicate it here?"

I turned in his arms and slid my hands up his chest. "Look me in the eye and tell me you're ready for a night on the town."

His eyes met mine. "Princess, I'll do anything you want. Absolutely anything."

I cocked my head and looked at him, trying to keep a straight face. "Anything?"

Bart took a deep breath and a hesitant step backwards, almost as if he'd been staggered by the implication that I'd want to do something after our exhausting day. Then, squaring his shoulders, he answered, "Yes. Anything."

"Good." I smiled up into his azure eyes and clasped my arms around his waist. "First, get out of those rumpled, smoky, smudged clothes, and I'll find you something suitable to wear."

I'll give him this: he was a good sport. Even with a concussion that must have left him with a pounding headache despite his short nap, the man would humor me and try to make up for our lost vacation. He loved me. What else could I say?

Leading him back inside the room, now lit only by moonlight, I unbuttoned his polo, unbuckled his belt, then reached for the button on his Dockers. He watched me silently, an amazed expression on his face. Dumbfounded was probably more accurate. Finally he came to life and took my hands. "I can do this, you know."

I smiled. "I know, but it's kind of fun. Besides, you were taking too long."

"That anxious to go, huh? Guess I'd better hurry. I'll finish while you change. Or do you need some help?"

"As a matter of fact, I do. Can you help me with this sweater?" I raised my arms.

My astute husband finally caught on. With a laugh, he picked me up and tossed me on the bed, then rolled beside me, leaned up on one elbow, and looked down into my eyes. "Did I ever tell you you're the biggest tease I've ever known?"

I laughed. "I did have you going for a minute there, didn't I?"

"Until I realized you couldn't have any more energy than I do, and the thing you'd want most of all is to shower, since you have such an aversion to being dirty, then snuggle into clean sheets and sleep the sleep of the innocent."

"You know me too well, lover. I'm going to have to become more unpredictable."

"Don't. It's all I can do to keep up with you as it is. You did notice the couple of minutes' lag behind your thought process. Ready to shed this grime?"

As we knelt beside the bed after a refreshing, relaxing shower, Bart invoked heaven's blessings on a good night's sleep and healing for our bodies. His prayer didn't go unanswered. When I woke the next morning, I realized I'd not only slept peacefully through the night without waking once, but I'd not had a single vestige of either nightmare. A minor miracle, to be sure.

I opened the drapes to a beautiful, golden September morning and found the sun well up on the horizon. The green belt between the hotel and the river teemed with walkers, joggers, strollers, cyclists, and skaters. Flocks of noisy ducks and geese thronged hungrily for a handout at the feet of a silver-haired couple generously tossing bags of broken bread to the brood.

"What's on our agenda this morning, fearless leader?" I inquired.

Bart flung back the covers, yawned and stretched. "Checking out the two sections of the map. I'll see if I can discover what might interest the Jihad in the Idaho National Engineering Laboratory, or what would intrigue supremacist groups. You take the other section and see what you can dig up on that Experimental Sheep Station."

I sat down on the edge of the bed and stroked Bart's unshaven cheek. "How's your head this morning?"

"Still lumpy. Every time I turned on that side of my head in the night, it woke me. But no headache, so guess I'll live."

"Glad to hear that. I'm planning on you living a very long time, buster, so don't do anything to disappoint me." I gingerly touched the lump. "At least you didn't require stitches. I can't believe you can take such incredible blows to the head without having it addle your brains."

He answered in a Rocky-type macho voice, "Yo. Us guys gotta be buff. Gotta take it," and reached to encircle me with his arms and pull me back into bed, but I slipped through his fingers and danced out of reach.

"Actually," I teased, "the Lord just gave men extra hard heads to help with the physical stuff, but you all let it carry over into the mental, too." I ducked into the bathroom and locked the door, knowing that my comment would get Bart out of bed in a flash. It did.

"Not fair to throw down the gauntlet and then take refuge behind a locked door," he said, rattling the knob.

"Go consult the phone book and find some numbers and addresses for us. Your turn in here in a minute."

When I emerged from my hasty retreat, Bart was making an appointment to meet with someone from the nuclear site. I'd visit the Chamber of Commerce and Visitors' Center to learn what might interest international terrorists. I had a hard time reconciling that element with what I'd perceived to be a pleasant, peaceful community.

When Bart tucked his gun under his belt in the small of his back and shrugged his jacket on to cover it, the illusion of pleasant and peaceful evaporated. I sighed and checked my purse to make sure I'd brought mine from the airplane, too. I hated carrying a gun. But I hated even more not having it when some lunatic suddenly started taking potshots at me.

During a brief exploratory drive around the hotel area, I spotted the Visitors' Center just before we pulled onto Broadway and saw Smitty's Breakfast and Steak House.

Breakfast at Smitty's became an information-gathering fest. A couple of bewhiskered old-timers in the booth behind me lamented the "good old days." As I listened with an outsider's ear, chills ran down my arms and little prickly hairs stood up on the back of my neck. I motioned for Bart to move from across the table and sit next to me so he could hear the fascinating conversation behind us.

We heard tales of bizarre happenings in the area above the Experimental Sheep Station. Strange lights, puzzling sheep killings, ground tremblings, cattle disappearing, a spotted animal like a jaguar or cheetah which had no business in those hills, and baffling noises back in the mountains to which no one could attribute a source. Then there was the usual talk of UFOs, as well as a lengthy, detailed discussion of whose houses or barns or other outbuildings had mysteriously burned with no apparent sign of arson.

The two regaled each other with stories of this ranch and that spread plagued with one or all of the strange goings-on in the "north country," as they called it, near the opal mines. Bart kept glancing at his watch, and finally announced he needed to leave or he'd be late for his appointment.

"Go ahead," I urged, not wanting to miss a word of the conversation behind me. "The Visitors' Center is just around the corner. When I finish with this delightful duo, and that stop, I'll walk back to the hotel." Bart nodded agreement and kissed my cheek as he scooped the bill off the table.

I resumed scribbling notes on what I was hearing. One man mentioned a mysterious piece of a map and the other laughed, reminding him that about every twenty years someone showed up with a map and resurrected the story of the lost treasure mine.

Suddenly one of them slapped the table. "Well, Clarence, gotta go. Good to see ya again. Don't let any of them UFOs haul ya off in the night and mess with yer head." He laughed a deep, throaty rumble. "Or anything else, ya old coot. Gotta get home and get ready. Think we're in for an early storm."

When he passed me, I slid out of my booth and turned toward Clarence, the man remaining at the table. Curly, collar-length salt and pepper hair matched the bristly beard covering most of his tanned, leathery face. Clear, intelligent, steel-gray eyes stared up at me as I hesitated before approaching him. "Do you have a few minutes to talk to me?" I asked, stepping toward his table.

As he looked me up and down, I became aware that my turquoise silk blouse and gauze skirt were conspicuous in a restaurant where jeans were the norm. I'd packed for sultry New Orleans, and hadn't given my attire a thought until those gray eyes began their appraisal.

"I'm Allison Allan. Yes, I'm from out of town," I acknowledged with a smile. "We flew in last night, and I overheard part of your conversation as we were eating. You seem knowledgeable about the area, and I thought you might tell me what to see while we're here."

Clarence started to get up, but I waved him back and slid into the seat opposite him. He watched me for a minute, making me feel like I'd just been examined and appraised. I wasn't sure I'd passed inspection. Finally he leaned forward, arms folded on the table in front of him, and asked, "What did you have in mind? Museums, libraries, art galleries?"

It must have been my clothes. I tried not to laugh. "Anything that's unique to this area. On the map, I saw the Idaho National Engineering Laboratory and the government's Experimental Sheep Station. I've never seen anything like that in any other part of the country. I heard you speak of some opal mines. I'm interested in what goes on in those places, and if the Laboratory, Station, or the mines are open to visitors."

His bushy eyebrows met in a quizzical expression. "Laboratory? You mean the INEL?"

Of course. Locals would have their own lingo and abbreviations. "Yes. Could we tour the place? And the other? Do you have a name for that?"

"The sheep station? No, ma'am. Just . . . the sheep station. You want to tour them? Guess you can. Look 'em up in the phone book and call." He seemed amused by my requests but too much of a gentleman to make fun of me.

"Were you born and raised here, or are you from somewhere else?" This man intrigued me. For all his rough, cowhand appearance, I'd bet a gentleman and scholar lurked beneath that rustic exterior. His faded plaid shirt was clean, though well-worn. Like the man inside it.

Clarence smiled a slow, lazy smile, his gray eyes crinkling at the edges in deep creases. He leaned back in the booth, waved at the waitress, and asked if I'd join him in a cup of Idaho's best.

"Thanks, no. I don't drink coffee and I just finished breakfast. But please, go ahead."

"You one of them Mormons?" He raised his expressive eyebrows and tilted his head.

"Yes. Are you?"

He laughed. "Probably. Was once. May still be. Don't know. Haven't checked lately, but no one's been out to see me for a while, so maybe they gave up on me."

A tall, slender redhead refilled the empty cup, asked if I'd like something, then disappeared.

Clarence ignored the steaming cup in front of him and nodded. "Yup, born and raised in Idaho. Lived all eighty-five years here, except for four years with Uncle Sam, fighting Nazis. Didn't see anything coming or going I liked any better, so I came back here and planted my roots a little deeper. Bought a place outside of town, and when the town came out to meet me, I bought another out farther. Don't think they'll get to me before I'm gone." He grinned, showing a set of teeth that were charmingly crooked, probably his originals.

"Where is this little place that's out farther?"

His gray eyes twinkled. "Up by Spencer."

"Spencer?" I pictured the pie-shaped piece of map. "Isn't that where the opal mines are?"

Clarence smiled and nodded, playing with the cup on the table in front of him.

"Up above the sheep station?"

He nodded again, that enigmatic smile still plastered across his weatherbeaten face.

"Tell me about it. And please don't be like my husband, making me work for every little tidbit. Tell me about Spencer, the mines—do you own one?—and about the sheep station. What do they do there? Are you a rancher? A cattleman or a sheepman? What do you—or did you—do for a living? Do you have a family? Wife and children?"

Clarence laughed so hard his coffee splashed out of the cup. "You're just like my baby. Asks a dozen questions without waiting for an answer." He fished a red bandana handkerchief from the back pocket of his faded jeans and swiped at his eyes. "She's older than you. Let's see; Betty must be about forty now. Twice your age," he guessed.

"Not quite. I'm twenty-five. How many children do you have?"

"Had two boys, two girls. Lost both boys in Vietnam." His gray eyes looked over my shoulder and probably through the wall behind me, not seeing, just remembering. "Both left a couple of kids, so I still have a part of them. Got a slew of grandkids, and some great-grandkids. Margie'd been real happy to see what we started all those years ago." His voice mellowed at her name.

"Your wife?"

The old man nodded. "Called home before she got to see any of those great-grandkids. They come out to see me every Sunday. 'Bout wear me out." He smiled, a contented look settling over his features.

"They all come every Sunday?"

"Nearly every one. 'Bout an hour after church, the whole danged clan descends, dinner in hand, to spend the afternoon. Five o'clock they pack up and go home, leavin' a tired but plenty happy ol' coot alone to recover from all that energy and noise."

As he paused, a pang shot through my heart and I wondered if, when we were Clarence's age, we'd have posterity to gather around us in a loving family. Or if we'd even live to reach his age.

He interrupted my painful musing. "But you wanted to know about the mines, didn't you?" Clarence was a natural-born storyteller, pulling me effortlessly into his narrative. I could have listened all day to that raspy, rather melodious voice with its slightly southern drawl.

"I also asked about you. Where did you get that southern drawl if you've lived here all your life?"

He leaned close, as if to tell me a secret. "I'm from southern Idaho." Sufficient explanation. "Done a little bit of everything. Farmin'. Ranchin'. Got the best-trained cow ponies this side of the Divide. Been offered a king's ransom for 'em, but wouldn't sell 'em for any amount."

Then he sat back in the booth and began. "About the mines—most famous is the Deer Hunt Mine. A couple of lost deer hunters stumbled across it about 1942. While they sat under a tree, waiting for the fog to lift—gets pretty foggy and misty up there in the fall—they found some rocks and stuffed them in their pockets. It took them another four or five years to find somebody to identify them, when they finally remembered to ask. Then they had to go back and find that tree and file a claim. Changed hands a couple of times, but it's now Spencer Opal Mine and been in the same family for a long time. Claudia runs it. She's worked it with her father since she was a girl. It's a family business. Gary and Marnie Dodson—that's Claudia's sister—run the Spencer Mercantile and sell the opals there."

The old man paused, a thoughtful look troubling his steel-gray eyes. "Somethin's going on up in those hills. Wish I could put my finger on it." He paused, gazing past me. "'Fraid it's big trouble. Big trouble," he repeated softly.

CHAPTER 12

"What kind of trouble?"

Clarence blinked at my question and looked at me in mild surprise. He seemed to have forgotten me.

I reached across the table and touched his leathery, blue-veined hand. "What do you think is going on up there, Clarence?"

The old man's eyes narrowed, evaluating me, or maybe reevaluating me. "Who are you, missy?"

Same old dilemma. Do I reveal who I really am, or string the nice old gentleman along until I'm sure I can safely identify us as Interpol? Intuitively I felt he could be trusted, that he might be the ally we needed, the insider who'd answer vital questions and steer us in the right direction, saving us precious time and energy in this investigation. But was my intuition correct?

I flashed what I hoped was a beguiling smile. "An impulsive, inquisitive, can't-mind-her-own-business Californian who's curious about Idaho."

Clarence sat stone-faced. "Ye-ah-es," he said slowly, stringing out the word to about three syllables. "I'm sure that's true. But there's something else. A purpose behind your questions. I see it in your eyes." He pulled at the corner of his moustache. "Are you some reporter looking for a story?"

I glanced quickly around the nearly deserted restaurant and took a deep breath. "No. Not a reporter. But I am looking for a story. And I think you're the person to tell it. I want to know about the lights, fires, animals, noises, everything you can tell me. I think you're right. There's big trouble coming, if it isn't here already."

I leaned forward, lowered my voice, and watched his expression as I said, "My husband and I are with an anti-terrorist organization. We've reason to believe that international terrorists are coming to Idaho, or they're already here, and we need to find out why and what they plan to do. Will you help me?"

A look of stunned disbelief crossed his tanned face, but his eyes never wavered from mine. He thought about it. I could almost see him going over every scenario he and his friend had discussed, trying to relate them to terrorists. His eyes narrowed again as he looked me over. I pulled my ID from my purse and slid it across the table in front of him.

He picked it up and studied it. "Interpol, huh?" he said after a thorough examination of both my ID and me. "You're an unlikely-looking agent. Would've pegged you for a yuppie, not a spy."

"That's because I'm not a spy. I solve puzzles. I take clues, pieces of information, and try to make sense out of them. Like what's happening in your neighborhood. Why? Who's behind it? We don't like terrorists. We don't like the things they do to our people and our country, or any people and country for that matter. Will you help us? Tell us all you know about the strange goings-on around here?"

The old man slid my ID across the table and reached for the cup in front of him. He was still thinking. He hadn't made up his mind. I wondered why. Because I didn't look like his perception of an agent? Or, like so many people today, because he didn't want to get involved? Was it fear? Apathy? Or maybe personal involvement? Had I just approached someone with an intimate knowledge of what was really going on in those hills? Maybe he was even behind some of it.

I waited, putting the burden of a reply on him while I watched that wrinkled face, purposely vacant of expression, those gray eyes that had watched nearly a century pass in this area. What experiences this man could tell, having lived through most of the great inventions of the modern world.

My heart quickened. We needed Clarence. We needed his expertise, his knowledge, his contacts, and his trust. And I needed to trust him. Did I? Could I—safely?

Clarence shoved the cup aside and straightened. "Guess I believe you. What do you want me to do?"

I smiled, hoping my extreme relief wasn't too obvious. "What's on your schedule today? Got a couple of free hours?"

He looked at his watch. "I will have. Doc's gonna check my ticker and blood pressure in about twenty minutes. Won't be long. Where will you be in a little over an hour?"

"How about the lobby of the Shilo Inn? I have an errand, too."

Clarence shook his head. "Not the hotel. Do you know Sportsman's Park? Right across the parking lot. You can't miss it."

I studied his face. Had I made an error? Why didn't he want to meet me at the hotel?

He reached for a battered, tan felt cowboy hat resting on the seat beside him and slid out, then unfolded himself slowly, as if creaking joints took time to straighten out after a long time sitting. I stood next to him, surprised at how much taller he was than I'd expected.

I offered my hand, which he gripped in his rough one and returned a strong, vigorous handshake. "Thanks for trusting me," I said. "I wasn't sure you were going to."

"I'll help what I can. Not sure I'll do you much good. But this is about as enclosed as I can stand." He nodded to indicate the restaurant. "Spent too much time outdoors. Small places and lots of people don't set too well with me. You okay with meeting at the park?"

I smiled. "Fine. Where will you be?"

"There's a bench on this side of the river where you can sit and watch the Falls. Right behind a Japanese temple-looking thing." He pulled a wadded-up five-dollar bill from his tight jeans pocket, tossed it on the table, and escorted me from the restaurant. Outside, he stopped, put his hat on, and adjusted it low over his eyes, nodded at me, and climbed into a battered old blue pickup.

No good-byes. No "Glad to meet you." No stiff city formalities. We'd completed our business, and he left. I liked him.

I paused in the shadow of the restaurant, watching traffic, checking parked cars for anyone watching me before hurrying across the street to the Visitors' Center on Lindsay Boulevard. I needed to discover everything I could about Idaho Falls, Idaho, and its environs. Especially those areas included in the two sections of the map used by the terrorists in Iraq. Some of whom were probably very close right now.

Bart needed to know about my upcoming meeting with Clarence. I missed my cell phone. We'd only brought Bart's, thinking we'd be together in New Orleans and wouldn't need two. We definitely hadn't prepared for this job. And I'd have to go shopping. Long, full gauze skirts and Idaho wind weren't compatible, I thought as I clutched at the yards of fabric that billowed out in front of me. I needed casual clothes, probably jeans and hiking boots, if I anticipated correctly what we'd be doing the next few days.

The Visitors' Center was a browser's dream. I collected material on more places and events than I'd imagined could be crammed into this little pocket of Idaho: museums, hot springs, outdoor adventures, sand dunes—I had to look at that twice. Mountains of sand six hundred feet high in the middle of farm country?

A huge table-top relief map displaying the area's elevations caught my eye. I studied Spencer and Dubois locations, the sheep station between, and the mountains where the strange things Clarence had talked about were happening. It helped to see the landscape from this perspective. The Snake River Plain was a huge smile across the bottom of the state, with the rest of the area predominantly mountainous.

I was still studying and gathering everything I could get my hands on when Bart appeared at my elbow. "You'll need two strong men to carry all that stuff," he said, unloading the burden from my arms to his.

"How was your appointment? Informative?" I inquired, adding another handful of brochures to the pile.

"Very. Sounds like an interesting place. What they're doing is engineering *and* environmentally related. Can you believe studying mussels' adhesive properties to learn how to make a better super glue? Not just studying, but developing methods to clone their genes through DNA technology."

I stopped pillaging the brochures on the wall and looked at Bart. "At a nuclear reactor site?"

He nodded. "There is one little item on their list of Research and Development projects that jumped out at me. For the Army, they've developed a state-of-the-art munitions assessment laboratory on wheels. It detects and assesses chemical and non-chemical warfare materials."

"Something terrorists or white supremacists could use?"

"It definitely warrants looking into. How did your eavesdropping session go?"

I laughed. "I prefer to call it investigating. It went very well. Hope I didn't make a mistake, but I told Clarence who we were. I felt he might be an invaluable source of information. He's meeting us by the Falls—I discovered they call it Falls with a capital F—to answer our questions." I glanced at my watch. "We've got about twenty minutes. I'm glad you came to find me. Thought I'd have to leave a message at the hotel. I miss my cell phone."

I stopped chattering when I saw the look on Bart's face. "Did I do something wrong?"

"How do you know he's just a harmless old man, and not involved in what's going on up there?" He bit his lip, turned silently and walked to the window, depositing his load of my accumulated treasures on a handy chair. I followed, speechless at his reaction, and waited until he turned back to face me. He wasn't finished. "How do you know you can trust him? This blows our cover much sooner than I'd planned." A strained patience filled his voice, but the irritation on his face had disappeared. I looked up into his puzzled blue eyes.

I reached for his arm. "I'm sorry if I blew it. I thought about it, wondered if I should, and then just felt we could trust him, that he would be one of the keys in getting to the bottom of this."

Bart looked at me without speaking. It probably seemed longer than it actually was before he took my hand and squeezed it, my husband's version of a hug in a public place. "Sorry, Princess. I should know better than to question your intuition. This is what you're best at, one of your unique and special talents as an agent. You're right. We do need inside information, and if you felt this man was trustworthy, I certainly should have faith in that unfailing discernment of yours. Where did you say you were meeting him?"

Relief washed through me. "Thanks for the vote of confidence." I blew him a kiss. "At the Falls, in about twenty minutes."

He thought about that, then nodded. "Be careful. We might have been followed from Tucson. Keep your eyes open, and try not to be so darned trusting, okay? I've got a solution to the cell phone problem, so I need to leave you alone to meet him, much as I hate the idea. But I'll hurry and be back as soon as I can. Where's the meeting place?"

I repeated the description Clarence gave me, then Bart took my freebies to the car while I stayed to see what other booty I could discover in this treasure trove of information. Southeastern Idaho was a gold mine of natural wonders, including the Craters of the Moon National Monument with its extinct volcanoes, cinder cones, and fantastically eerie landscape where the astronauts trained for their moon landing.

I opened a map of Idaho, spread it on the counter, and visualized the sections as I imagined they'd be if divided equally. Island Park, a corner of Yellowstone Park, and the Grand Teton National Park would be in sections seven and eight, which also included portions of Montana and Wyoming.

Suddenly, the scope of this overwhelmed me. If I'd eyeballed it correctly, the area would extend from Montana almost to the Utah border. I did some fast calculations. The circle should encompass everything within eighty-five miles of Idaho Falls. I borrowed a marker from the desk and marked the circle, dividing it into eight pie-shaped wedges.

One thought that occurred to me when I coupled the reactor site with terrorist tactics was the possibility that they'd try to steal a reactor and contaminate lakes and reservoirs with radioactive particles. Not being a scientist, or having any knowledge of the subject, I couldn't guess at the feasibility of such an act, but as I looked at the map, it didn't seem logical. This was sparsely populated country. The only town in section four was Atomic City, a tiny dot on the map. Why contaminate water for a population of less than what, two or three hundred thousand people in this southeastern section of the state? I'd just read that Idaho only had a total of 1,200,000 people for all of their 83,500 square miles, giving them the seventh lowest population density in the United States, though they were thirteenth in size.

Scratch the water pollution scenario.

Public land, mostly mountains, comprised over two-thirds of Idaho. That was probably why Randy Weaver chose Ruby Ridge and Richard Butler established his Aryan Nations compound up in the Panhandle. Few people. Fewer problems with neighbors.

Time to meet Clarence. Peering out the windows to check for loiterers or anyone in parked cars, I decided no one knew or cared I was here alone, and headed for the river. I liked river towns. San Antonio, Memphis, Chattanooga, Savannah, Charleston, New Orleans, New York—each was special because of its location on a river. Who'd have thought a little town in Idaho might qualify for that illustrious list of America's most beautiful and interesting cities? Time would tell.

The bench Clarence had described sat empty. I scanned traffic and parked cars. No one on foot or bicycle. I leaned on the wrought-iron railing and watched the swirling water cascade under the Broadway Street bridge, hoping this respite from bad guys would continue.

Huge volcanic boulders bordered the river, and some civic-minded soul, or group of souls, had fashioned a lovely park among the massive black rocks, with steps from one level of green oasis to another. Across the river, leaves of the white-barked quaking aspen shimmered brilliant gold against a pale-blue September sky streaked with wispy cirrus clouds.

A couple of tall evergreen trees and some twisted juniper, mirrored in the flowing blue-green water, stood as stark contrasts to the white cascading water and black rock. Upstream, the white spire of the temple stood loftily above the Falls. This wasn't a quiet place, with the roar of the Falls and traffic crossing the busy bridge a few feet away, but still, it was peaceful. And after the tumultuous events of yesterday and our too-close brush with death by fire or smoke inhalation, I needed an island of peace.

"Thought you'd enjoy the Falls. Everybody does."

I jumped at the voice directly behind me. Clarence joined me at the railing, leaning on it with both arms to peer down at the water rippling and rushing below us. I surveyed the area, remembering how paranoid an agent has to be to stay alive. Bart would call it careful.

"How's your ticker and blood pressure?" I asked.

"Good as can be expected for an organ that's been pumping steadily for eighty-five years without a rest. How's yours?"

I glanced up at the unexpected question. Clarence hadn't taken his eyes from the river, but a little tic at the edge of his mouth led me to believe he was having a hard time keeping a straight face. The man did have a sense of humor.

"Just fine, thank you. I fully expect that if I can dodge enough bullets and bad guys, I may live to be able to make that same claim."

This time Clarence looked at me. "You really tangle with those people?"

"All too often. Clarence, why would international terrorists be interested in your backyard? What's going on around here that they'd take notice of?"

The old man turned and planted himself with a sigh on the bench behind us. "Good question, missy."

"Allison," I prompted, scanning the area for danger before settling on the bench beside him. Either the terrorists hadn't caught up to us yet, or they were incredibly adept at staying out of sight.

He nodded. "You know about the Aryans up north?"

"Yes. Unfortunately, they may be a group the Jihad are planning to train."

Clarence looked up, his surprised gray eyes lighter than I remembered from the restaurant. "Jihad? In Idaho? You sure?"

"Seems unusual, doesn't it? I assume you're familiar with their dastardly operations."

He snorted. "I get CNN. The *Post Register* even prints international news."

"I wasn't implying that you're backwoods here. It just doesn't gel with their past history. They usually like to make statements by blowing up embassies or Manhattan's Twin Towers, for example. Things on a grand scale that will catch the public's attention and promote their ideology. That's why INEL and the sheep station piqued our interest. Maybe some of the work going on there would attract terrorists."

"Don't think I'll be too much help," Clarence said. "Those things happening in my neck of the woods don't smack of what you're talking about. But I'll be glad to show you around the area. Maybe you'll get a better feel for it when you see it firsthand."

Bart suddenly appeared, carrying a bright red and white sack marked KFC that smelled like a little bit of heaven. "When you said park bench on the river bank, I naturally thought of a picnic. That, and it's been nearly three hours since we had breakfast."

"Not possible." I looked at my watch. Well, close. "Clarence, my husband, Bartholomew James Allan. Provider of all the good things in my life, including lunch."

They shook hands, appraising each other silently for a fraction of a minute. "Glad to meet you, Mr. Allan. When I get to know you better, I'm going to ask you why in blazes you let this little wife of yours play around in the spy business."

My husband looked at me and laughed. "Call me Bart, Clarence, and when you get to know *her* better, you won't *have* to ask. Hope you didn't eat before you came. I got enough for the three of us and several more."

Bart opened the sack and handed out soft drinks, containers of fried chicken, and biscuits light enough to float away. Then he leaned against the railing, appearing to take in the pleasant surroundings. Apparently satisfied that no one had us under surveillance, he settled on the pavement at our feet, leaned back against the wrought-iron fence, and plunged into the small feast he'd brought.

He'd only taken two bites when his cell phone rang. "Allan here." Bart listened, sipped his drink, and kept listening, his face becoming cloudier by the minute. His total silence and dismal demeanor throughout the lengthy dissertation were all signs of extremely bad news.

As I mentally ran through the list of possibilities that such bad news could mean for us and this mission, my appetite left me abruptly.

CHAPTER 13

"Roger." Bart clicked off his cell phone with a simple one-word reply. "Where were we?" he asked, filling his mouth with what had looked like a succulent piece of chicken before this awful feeling descended on me. Food had suddenly lost its appeal.

"Clarence offered to take us on a get-acquainted tour of the area where all the strange things have been happening." I wanted desperately to ask about the mysterious call, but decided that if my husband wanted the almost-stranger to hear, he'd have told us.

"Don't know how much good it'll do, but it might give you an idea of what's going on up there. Maybe tie in with your investigation. Maybe not." Clarence shook his head. "Can't imagine the Jihad bein' interested in anything around here. We're small potatoes."

I spread the map of Idaho I'd acquired at the Visitors' Center on the bench between us to show the circle I'd drawn around Idaho Falls. "We think they're interested in something within this area."

"Or some combination of things," Bart added. "How valuable are the opals up there? Are there gold mines? Titanium? Any other precious metals that could provide financing for their expensive terrorist activities? I notice Idaho is called the Gem State. Is that literal or figurative?"

"Both. Gold in the beginning. Mined millions of dollars' worth. Then silver, zinc, copper, lead, antimony, and phosphate. We've got opals, garnets, particularly the star garnet, found nowhere else but here and India. Any Idahoan will tell you Idaho's gems are russet potatoes, or pine forests. A sports enthusiast will never finish his list."

"So what's up in those mountains, or anywhere else in this circle, that's attractive enough to bring terrorists here?"

Bart didn't get an immediate answer to his question. Clarence continued to thoughtfully munch his chicken, then concentrated on spreading honey over his twice-buttered biscuit.

I handed my chicken breast to Bart. The couple of bites I'd already had were churning in my stomach. Extreme fright sometimes caused me to lose my cookies, and right now, I was extremely frightened. No need to tempt fate.

Clarence finished his lunch in pensive silence. Bart's appetite didn't seem affected by his phone call, and he cleaned up my lunch as well as his. I sipped my soft drink, trying to quell the turbulence inside, my mind racing over all possible topics that could have caused Bart to look like the end of the world was imminent. If something had happened to anyone in Anastasia, there would be no reason for Bart not to tell me immediately, so I discounted that. It had to be something connected with this case. Had Osama bin Laden been successful in collecting his map sections and eliminating the holders of same? Was he in Idaho? That would be the worst news of all. Or right up there with the top ten things I could think of.

"Probably not enough opals or anything else in our mines to draw Jihad here," Clarence began slowly as he brushed his mouth and beard with a napkin, then cleaned each finger with the lemon-scented wet-wipe. "I doubt INEL or the sheep station have anything they'd come halfway around the world for, either. Just can't imagine those people bein' interested in anything 'round here—'cept maybe the land and the location."

"*And* the location, or *because* of the location?" Bart asked.

"Because of the location," the old man clarified, his gray eyes narrowing thoughtfully as he stared across the river. "If what you say is true, and they plan on a training operation, they'd need land, lots of it, that nobody else wants. Somebody's been makin' offers on some of the ranches up there. A couple of small property owners already sold out. We thought maybe Larsen wanted to expand, and he was quietly buying out anyone who wanted to sell."

"Larsen?" Had I read that name somewhere this morning?

"Rancher, potato processor, big man in these parts. You'll see his place on the way up to Spencer. Might as well get going, if you've a mind to see the area." He stood, brushed off his jeans, and settled his hat more firmly on his head.

Bart jumped agilely to his feet. "We'd like that."

"You folks want to follow me to my place in your car? Then I'll take you up the mountain in ol' Betsy."

"Clarence, I just picked up some new gadgets. Let's try them out." Bart grabbed a package from the front seat of our rental car and handed the old man a silver and black cell phone. "As long as we're within the same calling area, these have direct connect, like two-way radios. To talk, just press this button on the side, and let up when you're through. You can tell us what to look for along the way, or give us any ideas you come up with about what's going on."

Bart pressed the button on his phone and spoke into it. His voice was loud and clear. The old man smiled broadly, showing both rows of crooked teeth. A man who loved gadgets, and full of vitality for eighty-five years of age. No old-folks' home and rocking chair for him. Or endless hours in front of the TV set. This man would probably be active until the final day of his life.

"If we get separated at a light, we're going north on I-15," he said into his radio/phone, testing it, making sure he knew how it worked. "You can catch me on the highway." Clarence dipped his head in what I figured must be good-bye, or see you later, or whatever they say here, and climbed into his battered blue pickup with the radio in his hand.

We followed him west on Broadway, losing him as he gunned through a yellow light when we had to stop for the red. I was more concerned about the phone call than losing Clarence. "What was the bad news?" I asked as the blue pickup disappeared in traffic.

"Sure you want to hear?"

"Every single word. I assume Dad bore the bad tidings."

"Yes. And you're right; it was bad. Butler's Aryan Nation people who were kicked out of northern Idaho are congregating here with a new group of dissidents. The identity of the leader is still unknown, but apparently he's ex-military, fanatical, ruthless, smart bordering on genius, and recruiting cell leaders from all over, mostly disenchanted military men and women upset with the plethora of Perfumed Princes managing today's military."

"Perfumed Princes?"

"Probably a phrase Colonel David Hackworth coined. Sounds like something I've read in his column blasting the generals and upper-echelon guys who are afraid to stand up to those holding the military purse strings and overseeing promotions. Hackworth says he's hearing from Army, Navy, and Air Force personnel every day that they couldn't fight their way out of a retirement home right now if they had to."

"Wow. No wonder there's so much discontent in the military. These people must have a tremendous sense of patriotism to spend their careers serving their country, especially those who could make a lot more money on the outside. If their leaders are selling them down the river, cutting benefits, training, arms—yes, I can see there'd be a lot of outraged people."

"Think about the knowledge and experience they have. Then imagine what a fanatic could do if he fired them up and turned them against the government they believed had let them down." Bart shook his head, an angry scowl transforming his handsome face.

"They don't have any idea who he is?"

"Not yet. But they're going all out to discover his identity, his base of operations, and what his plans are. McAffrey's got all his spare men on it, and Jack's assigned everyone in Anastasia to do follow-up work. Dominic may be on to something, and Oz and Mai Li got a bit of information when they picked up the next map section at Nellis AFB in Las Vegas."

"They did get it, then?" I breathed a little sigh of relief. "I was afraid we'd missed the rest of the sections. Which one did they get?"

"Section eight. Your dad thought he'd spotted a pattern by that time and dispatched Lionel to Hill AFB in Ogden, Utah, to wait. He was right. Oz called Jack with the phone number on their section the minute it was in his hands, and Lion got on it before Oz and Mai Li finished their interview. They all found the same thing we did: disillusioned military people recruited to rebuild America's forces—with outside help. And taking with them whatever supplies they could spirit away from the base."

I shuddered. "Some help. Can't they see that what they're involved with is treason? What did Lion find?"

Lionel Brandt had been with Anastasia for exactly a year, along with David, Sky, Dominic, Oz, and Else. The Frenchman, nicknamed Lion for his mane of tousled blond hair and nervous energy and grace, seemed not to have a serious bone in his body, but his outrageous sense of humor hid a zealot's heart.

"Lion found section one, with a number at Mountain Home AFB in Boise, Idaho. Jack had already sent Dominic to Mountain Home, supposing that might be the next link. Dominic collected section two, and the FBI put that family into protective custody. Unfortunately, the guy at Nellis in Las Vegas wanted no part of protective custody. He was sold on the idea of a new, stronger military, and he was going to be part of it."

"What happened?"

"McAffrey had notified all local FBI offices and our people called them as soon as they'd made contact. They took him into custody, protective or otherwise. They may not get information out of him, but he'll be safe from bin Laden's boys, and there'll be one less nut loose, messing up the operation."

Clarence's blue pickup didn't waste any time getting to wherever we were going. I glanced at the speedometer. The old man pushed the seventy-five mile an hour speed limit. The engine must have been in a lot better shape than the body on his ancient vehicle.

I looked at Bart. Even his profile looked grim. "Whoever's behind this will know we're on to them, won't they?" I asked. "Even if we hadn't missed Don Montana in Tucson, when John didn't appear from Shreveport and Kay Sterling from Abilene came up missing, they'd know something was up. Any word on what happened to the Montana family?"

"Yes to your first question, no to the second. Too bad we haven't added any intelligence as we've collected the sections of the map. Your mom, Else, and Sky are working on the psychological stuff, trying to develop a profile from the bits of information collected so far."

Rip Schyler, nicknamed Sky, Anastasia's oldest member at sixty-one, held a doctorate in criminology, another in abnormal behavior. He profiled all our cases. The gray-haired Dutchman looked like a scholarly grandfather in horn-rimmed glasses and tweeds. If he could be considered the brains of the outfit, Else Elbert certainly qualified as the beauty. She was tall, blonde, Norwegian, and gorgeous, and her elegant manner and dress reflected her heritage as a cousin of British royalty. She was so gifted musically she could probably have made a living on stage, but her greatest talents in Anastasia were lightning reflexes, an extraordinary ability to read body language and intent, and her expertise in self-defense and personal protection. Her beautiful hands could be licensed as lethal weapons.

Bart's new phone beeped, and Clarence's voice filled the rental car. "Just passing the Larsen place on your right. Watch for signs along the road telling which division is doing highway cleanup duty, and you'll get an idea of how extensive his operations are."

Bart handed me the phone, and I pressed the talk button. "Thanks, Clarence. Keep filling us in so we'll know what we're seeing."

I began noticing the landscape: rainbows created as the sun glistened off gigantic sprays of water diffused from huge sprinkler irrigation pipes. We passed mile after mile of such water systems greening up land claimed from the sagebrush that still outlined some fields. Then I saw enormous silver silos with black lettering that spelled "Larsen Farms." The spread looked vast, and it just kept on going.

"Would somebody who already had so much pull a bunch of dirty tricks in order to scare off people and get their land?" I mused, thinking out loud. "I know it used to happen. I read about the cattlemen and sheep men who settled Idaho and the wars over grazing rights. Sheep could graze where cattle had been, but cattle couldn't follow sheep because the sheep grazed too close. That seems more like history, not something that would happen today."

"Ask Clarence," Bart said, nodding at the phone in my hand.

I pressed the talk button. "You'd speculated about Larsen buying up land. Could what's going on in your hills be caused by someone—Larsen, for example—wanting to acquire more property?"

Clarence didn't answer for a minute. Farmlands gave way to grasslands and some marshland. Finally Clarence's beep broke the silence. "Been thinkin' about that. Don't imagine Larsen has anything to do with it, or any of his people. Not his style. 'Course, I wouldn't put it past some of them Californians to do something like this."

I beeped him back immediately. "Are you serious, or are you pulling my chain, Clarence?" I turned to Bart while I waited for

Clarence's answer. "I read a tongue-in-cheek article about Idahoans' feelings for Californians who move here and try to fix what isn't broken in the government. If our state of origin is discovered, we may not be welcome poking our noses around."

"Jest pullin' your chain. Though it may warrant lookin' into." I heard the chuckle in Clarence's voice.

Huge rolled bales of hay littered flaxen hayfields, and silver green-leafed Russian olives lined the river banks. I checked the map, noting the little towns as we passed. Roberts, Hamer, Camas, Dubois. "The sheep station should be up there on the right in the hills."

"Bears a look-see. Maybe there'll be time to stop on the way back."

Looking like tiny black dots on the sage and gold hills, a few herds of range cattle roamed the rolling countryside. Every once in a while, a lone rider or a pair on horseback headed for one of the herds.

Clarence came on the radio. "Keep your eyes sharp. You might see antelope or deer around these parts."

I did see some antelope and pointed them out to Bart, two in one field, half a dozen others almost hidden in the sagebrush along a little creek, their white tails giving them away.

Suddenly we passed Spencer. I pointed at the sign. "That's where the opal mines are. For some reason, I thought Clarence lived below them instead of above them." We climbed steadily toward the Continental Divide for another five miles or so, before the turn signal on the blue pickup indicated Clarence's intention to exit the interstate.

"Looks like we've arrived," Bart said. He'd been watching in the rearview mirror, and as we turned off the road, his shoulders relaxed the slightest bit. No tail yet. *Yet,* I reminded myself. Sooner or later, there would be.

The blue pickup turned onto a gravel road, enveloping us in a cloud of dust as we followed.

I'd been watching for Clarence's place, but had seen nothing for several miles except open grazing land or silver sagebrush. "I don't see a house anywhere," I said. "Maybe 'arrived' is a bit premature."

As Bart lagged behind the pickup to stay out of the dust, I suddenly saw a column of smoke rise into the cornflower-blue sky from a cluster of trees more than halfway up the mountain.

Right in the direction we were headed.

CHAPTER 14

Clarence must have seen it, too. The old blue pickup fairly flew up the hill, bouncing from one side of the narrow gravel road to the other. Smoke now billowed thick and gray above the trees.

The road left the sagebrush behind and wound upward through an endless grove of golden-leafed quaking aspen, then into cool green Douglas fir. Bart slowed to a safe speed but the blue pickup raced ahead, threading through the trees like a race driver weaving through cars at the Indy 500.

Neither of us spoke. I held my breath, dreading what we'd find when we stopped. My stomach threatened to leave its appointed place, but that had nothing to do with the wild ride and everything to do with the trepidation tingling through my system. I felt like we were on a roller coaster heading for disaster.

At last the trees opened on a clearing, revealing the source of all the smoke. An outbuilding blazed out of control, totally consumed by wild orange flames leaping high into the air. Clarence, partially out of his truck, stood staring at the fire, sagging against the door as if he couldn't take that next step. Bart parked and we jumped out, running to the old man's side.

He shook his head sadly. "Too late to do anything but let it burn itself out."

"How could it have started?" I had to ask, though I didn't want to hear the answer. I had a terrible foreboding that this wouldn't be the last of the dear old man's problems, and would definitely be the beginning of ours. I tried to shake off the sense of impending doom that descended like a heavy, dark cloud, but it wouldn't go away.

Then a shudder shook me from head to toe. What if we'd brought these people to Clarence? What if the fire was a warning to him—or retribution—because he'd agreed to help us?

Clarence didn't answer at first, just watched the fire devour roof, walls, and everything that had been inside. Finally he turned and looked at me with moisture brimming in his steel-gray eyes. "Somebody set it," he said quietly. "The shed had no electricity. Nothing in it to cause spontaneous combustion. Arson, pure and simple."

"What was in there?" Bart asked. "Anything irreplaceable?"

"A lifetime's accumulation of tools and gear."

The roof caved in, sending a shower of sparks flaring up like a thousand Fourth of July sparklers.

I felt helpless. "Isn't there anything we can do? Hose it down?" In my heart I knew it was hopeless, but I couldn't just stand and watch. I needed to do something constructive, needed to salve my guilty conscience just in case we'd somehow brought this on Clarence.

Clarence shook his head. "Won't spread. I keep the grass and weeds trimmed so it's got nowhere to go. Might singe the trees behind it a little. Maybe not. Gotta check my animals and make sure they're okay."

"I'll go with you. Allison can keep an eye out here." Bart pulled his gun from his belt and fell into step beside the old man. I watched them walk away, Clarence hunch-shouldered and shuffling along the dusty path to a small barn almost hidden in the trees beyond the house. Less than an hour earlier, he had eagerly tried out a new gadget, looking fifteen years younger than his birth certificate indicated. Now, as his shoulders sagged, he looked every one of his eighty-five years.

I hadn't thought about the arsonist sticking around to admire his handiwork, but when Bart got his gun, I realized someone could be watching from the woods in any direction. My skin crawled to think that sick person might be so close. I pulled my purse from the car, hung it on my shoulder with my hand on the gun inside, then leaned against the pickup bed and stared into the trees, searching each section circling the clearing. No tingling warnings from my danger antennae, but I was grateful to have Bart and Clarence return within a few minutes. The barn and animals were untouched.

Bart watched the fire, anger flaming in his eyes. "Who'd do this, Clarence? And why?"

No answer. Clarence's lips were drawn tight in a thin line, almost hidden by his graying moustache. The old man didn't speak. Just resumed his position, leaning against the door of his old blue pickup, watching the fire.

I didn't know what to say, certainly didn't know what we could do. "Would you like us to leave? Would you rather be alone?" I put my hand gently on the old man's arm. "We don't want to be a bother, but if there is anything we can do, please let us help."

Finally he came to life. "You said this is a phone as well as a radio?"

Bart nodded and showed him how to use it. Clarence punched in the number with a gnarled finger, then put the phone to his ear. There was a long silence, then he yelled into the mouthpiece, "Cody? Clarence. Come up to my place as soon as you can. I need ya." He turned to Bart. "How do I shut it off?" Bart showed him the disconnect button, and when he'd hung up, he returned the phone to my husband.

"Cody? Is that someone who might be able to help?" I asked.

"Hope so," Clarence replied. "He's Indian, and mighty proud of his heritage. Seems like he's descended from Chief Joseph, or Sacagawea, or one of them famous people. Orphaned when he was little—raised by a family of whites that taught him all about his ancestors, then summers lived with his grandfather, who taught him Indian ways. Cody's the best darn tracker in the West."

"And you want him to see what he can find about the people who started your fire." Bart phrased it as a statement, not a question.

"If those sons o' blazes left any trace, Cody'll find it with his amazin' ability to sniff out human or animal. Almost supernatural. Makes the hair stand up on the back of your neck when you watch him. Like the trees wuz talking to him, or the wind."

"Can we do anything while we're waiting?" I asked, getting more antsy than I could handle with nothing constructive to do.

Clarence looked at Bart, then at me. "Do you have any of that spy stuff with you? You know, those bug detectors like they use on James Bond?"

Bart smiled. "We do. Do you want us to debug your house?"

The old man nodded solemnly. "Don't need to have them listening to my conversations, nor set fire to my house while I'm sleepin'. Can you check all that out and make sure no one's been foolin' around here?" He paused. "And see if they left any bombs or explosives behind?" Clarence was a worried man.

I realized I'd been so caught up in watching the fire that I hadn't looked at the house. Set away from the shed, nestled in a stand of tall Douglas fir that had been there a long time, the two-story log house looked hand-hewn, along with porch railings made of charmingly knotted and twisted cedar or juniper. Hunter-green shutters trimmed each window. The little balcony atop the front porch pointed to a gap in the trees and probably had a splendid view of the valley below.

"You built this yourself, didn't you?" I turned to Clarence with a new respect for the man standing next to me. "It's wonderful!"

He smiled and seemed embarrassed by my enthusiastic praise. "Put every log in place myself. Even cut most of 'em. Let's see if anybody's been inside."

The door wasn't locked. Apparently Clarence didn't feel the need, hidden up here in the trees. "This is the front room, kitchen's back there, bedrooms upstairs. I'll see if I can find something for us to drink while you find out if anyone's planted any of them things in here."

I began downstairs, and Bart disappeared upstairs. The living room, warmly furnished with Western-style well-lived-on furniture, occupied the entire front of the house. It was clean. No bugs.

Pictures of what looked like several generations of Clarence's family flanked a huge stone fireplace. His Margie had been a beautiful woman, and old Clarence had cut a handsome figure in his younger days. The girls looked like their mom with big, dark eyes and curly dark hair. The boys favored their father. The grandchildren were a mix of the two. At the top of the wall, above all the other pictures, hung a photograph of the Idaho Falls Temple with two people posing in front. I stood on a stool from beside the fireplace to identify the couple. Clarence and Margie.

As I entered the big country kitchen, which took up the entire back of the house, Clarence added water to frozen lemonade and stirred it vigorously. A stone fireplace shared one end wall with built-in shelves crammed with books. A long table and benches sat on a braided rug in the middle of the room. At the opposite end, where Clarence stood, was a cheery kitchen with pine cabinets and windows placed so the morning sun would probably reach them across the clearing. As he silently handed me a tumbler full of lemonade, he raised his eyebrows in question. I shook my head. I hadn't found anything yet.

Bart clattered down the stairs and joined us in the kitchen. I gave him a glass of lemonade and sipped my own while I finished "sweeping" the kitchen. The detector vibrated silently in my hand when it neared the telephone. I waved at Bart. Immediately dismantling the phone, he removed the recording device, and with a gleam in his eye and a smile on his lips, carried it outside and placed it as high up in the branches of a tree as he could reach.

Once the thing left the house, a surprising feeling of peace settled in. The gloom that had enveloped me on the wild ride up here dissipated as the afternoon sun peeked through the trees, splashing the logs with burnished gold. I heard birds' songs again, and the disaster that still smoldered seemed less tragic for the moment. Strange. Or was my imagination playing tricks on me?

"Who do you think is behind this?" I asked Clarence when we returned to the kitchen. "You must have some idea."

He sank into the big hunter-green plaid recliner by the fireplace, sipped his lemonade, and stared into the glass. "Didn't have any idea till you two came along. Even then, terrorists in Idaho didn't quite add up. But most folks leave this high country in the winter and move down where the snow isn't twelve feet deep from October to March. If they drove off or bought out everybody up here, they'd pretty much have the place to themselves year-round. Wouldn't have to worry about anybody seeing what they were doing, snooping around causing trouble." He leaned his head back and closed his eyes.

"If it isn't Jihad, somebody else is trying to scare people out of these hills," Bart said, staring out the window. "By bugging your phone, they show they need to know your response to the fire and the other incidents. Tell us about the noises."

"Sometimes you'd swear it was a helicopter, then before it disappears, you're convinced it ain't. We thought somebody was excavating with heavy equipment because of the ground tremors. But nobody can find any trace of that kind of activity."

I sat down on the bench near Clarence. "What about the lights?"

"Could have been airplane landing lights, but nobody's heard the plane's engines. That's when UFO stories surfaced." The old man shook his head.

"What's your best guess?" Bart turned from the window to join me on the bench at the table.

"Not sure I got one just yet." Clarence scratched at his beard. "Let me think on it a while, now that you clued me in on the terrorists. Sorry I can't show you around the area like I promised. Don't dare leave the place alone. Besides, I need to be here when Cody comes."

"Any idea when that will be?" Much as I enjoyed the old man's company, I felt we needed to be doing something constructive. Anxious to see the area and get a feel for what might be happening, I truly wanted to be up and moving.

"Could be any time," he drawled, glancing at the clock on the wall, "or might not be till tonight when he gets home and listens to his messages. Not sure where he's working today."

Bart drained the rest of his lemonade. "What kind of work does he do?"

"Spends most of his days digging around these parts, looking for artifacts and preserving Indian writing they've found in caves and rocks. He's an ark-ee-ologist. Lots of native stuff hereabouts. This whole country was inhabited by the Indians when Lewis and Clark came. We're celebrating the bicentennial of their excursion through these parts in the next year or so." He looked so pleased about it, you'd have thought he had something to do with it.

"Did they come through here? I looked at their route at the Visitors' Center, but I didn't pay much attention to where they actually entered Idaho."

Clarence leaned the recliner all the way back and folded his hands across his belt. The smile on his face reminded me of my cat when she'd just caught a mouse—totally pleased with herself. "If you believe history books, they entered at Lemhi Pass, then visited the Shoshone village, where they got horses to cross the Bitterroots before they went up to Missoula and over to Lewiston."

"And if you don't believe the history books? Where did they come in to Idaho?" All my attention centered on Clarence. The tone in his voice told me he knew something that wasn't common knowledge. Some little bit of information that pleased the old man mightily.

"Well, now . . ." He stopped, listened, and sat upright in his recliner. "Think I hear Cody comin'." He cleared the chair and headed out the front door before I could press for his answer.

CHAPTER 15

Clarence had pretty sharp hearing. I hadn't heard a thing except the birds calling to one another and the wind singing in the firs above us. But when we stepped onto the porch, the distinctive growl of a motorcycle climbing the hill grew steadily until it drowned out the quiet sounds of nature.

I'm not sure what I expected in the person of Cody, but the slender, jeans-clad, black-helmeted individual that screeched to a stop, sending a cloud of dust through the clearing, certainly wasn't it. His wide shoulders—apparently well-muscled from his digging—filled the pale-yellow polo shirt. He wore a tooled leather belt with turquoise stones set in the buckle, and boots. Old boots. Well-worn, dusty boots with holes in the bottoms.

The biggest surprise of all came when he removed his helmet, took in the still-smoldering fire at a single glance, and strode to the porch. Thick, glossy black hair with midnight-blue highlights gleamed in the sun, and his wide-set eyes, dark and probing, scanned the three of us on the porch as he came. All in all, with his classic features and tanned good looks, Cody could have been a poster person for the healthy Native American way of life. One incredible-looking specimen.

Bart stepped next to me and slipped his arm around my waist, gently pulling me closer to him, a very possessive move that endeared my husband to me more than ever.

"See you have a problem, old man."

"'Fraid so, Cody. This here's the Allans—Bart and Allison." Clarence stopped abruptly and looked at us, the question in his eyes unmistakable. Cody's dark eyes narrowed. He hadn't missed that look, that hesitation.

Bart stepped off the porch and stuck out his hand. "We're just in from California. We met Clarence over breakfast this morning, and he brought us up here to show us your beautiful country. Unfortunately, we found this."

Cody took the proffered hand and studied Bart, as if reading whether or not this tall, blond stranger told the truth. Apparently satisfied, he stepped back and looked up at me, nodded silently, then turned to give Clarence his full attention.

"See what you can find, will you, Cody? See if it's like the others. Can't believe anybody'd want to do this to me." Clarence shook his head as he ambled off the porch, leading the young man away from the house toward the smoldering heap.

"Have any of you been walking around here? You haven't obliterated any tracks?" He spoke quietly, enunciating clearly, very different from Clarence's slow drawl and habit of clipping off words and shortening phrases.

"Nice-looking guy," Bart said, drawing me into the porch swing with him and sliding his arm around my shoulders.

"Not my type. I go for tall, blond, blue-eyed California beach types. However, if he were my type . . ." I let the sentence dangle.

"What?" Bart prompted.

"I'm the one with the green eyes, remember. Yours are supposed to be blue." I turned to look up at him. "However, there's a tinge of green creeping in there. That azure color is fading fast."

Bart gave me a quick peck on the cheek. I slid my hand around his neck, pulled his head down, and kissed him with feeling. "Not to worry, love. What's the old saying? Just because you're on a diet doesn't mean you can't look in the bakery window. I can admire a sleek physique and handsome face without feeling anything more than admiration for one of God's creations. It's like when you look at Else." I stopped short, pulled away, and looked up into his face. "At least that's how I *hope* you feel. I'm continually amazed that you worked with her, turned down her propositions, and chose to marry me instead."

"Ah, Princess. You'd stolen my heart long before I met Else. She couldn't hold a candle to you." He pulled me against him and rested his chin on my head. "Yes, I can admire and appreciate her beauty, but there isn't a thing about her that makes my heart beat faster, or heats my blood like you do."

"You tell a great story, lover. If you tell it often enough, maybe you'll convince me it's true."

Clarence returned and joined us on the porch, settling into a wing-back pine chair next to the swing. "He's lookin'. Doesn't need me messing up his senses, he says. 'Bout gives you the creeps watching him. You just keep waiting for a hawk to swoop down, land on his outstretched hand, and tell him all he wants to know."

"Some people have a natural affinity with animals. Cody must be one of them." I leaned over to watch the young man examine the ground around the remains of the fire, then disappear into the trees, apparently following a trail of some kind. "He seems like an interesting character. How well do you know him? What does he do besides archeological work? Is he married? Does he live out here, too?"

"Whoa! There you go again, askin' questions like my Betty, without waiting for answers. I've known Cody since he was born, knew his folks before then. He's mostly consumed with his digging, so he's not married, lives alone in the mountains above Humphrey, and . . . well, that's about it. Guess you'll have to ask him if you want to know more."

"He's checked out each of the other fires up here?" Bart asked.

"After about the third or fourth one, when it didn't seem like a coincidence anymore. At first, no one could believe they'd been set on purpose. Just doesn't happen up here. Not like in California, where nobody respects anybody else's property." Clarence looked pointedly at us, then continued. "Out here, everybody sort of looks out for his neighbor. If you see something unusual, you keep an eye on it. Nobody's seen anything out of the ordinary, no strangers sniffing about. No strange vehicles in the hills. Almost like they swoop out of the midnight sky with the owls, do their dirty work, and leave with the raptors in the morning before the sun comes up."

"Raptors?" I envisioned the speedy little man-eating dinosaurs from *Jurassic Park*.

"Birds of prey," Clarence snorted. "Half a dozen different hawks around here. Then there's the falcons, bald and golden eagles, osprey, short-eared and great horned owls. To name a few," he finished.

Yes, I could see a falcon settling on Cody's arm, as easily as I imagined him being called "hawkeye." Those piercing dark eyes reminded me of bright-eyed predators I'd seen perched high atop bare tree limbs in aviaries.

I could also imagine him slinking through the trees with a gray wolf at his side. *Canis lupus.* The elusive, mysterious creature hunted to extinction in the early 1900s in America—before man came to his senses and reintroduced Canadian wolves into Idaho's Sawtooth Mountains. Thirty-five wolves were successfully relocated here, and recently litters of pups were born in Idaho for the first time in over eighty years.

First impressions were often wrong, and I hated to judge anyone by those perceptions formed in the first few minutes. But if I was right, Cody's natural tendencies leaned to the wild side rather than the civilized state. The wolf over the dog, mountain lion instead of a domestic cat. And definitely a raptor over a caged bird. I'd bet when he rode a horse, he didn't even use a saddle.

Suddenly I remembered Clarence mentioning Lewis and Clark meeting the Shoshone Indians, and his reference to history books. "You started to tell us something about Lewis and Clark coming into Idaho that the history books had wrong. What was it?"

The old man got that pleased-as-pie look on his face again. "As local legend has it, they made one exploratory trip they didn't enter into their journals. Or maybe those pages were never found."

Just then, Cody appeared quietly around the corner of the house. "Looks like it's the same person that set the others," he reported. "A small motorcycle ridden by one small man or woman. They used gas to douse the walls and interior, then probably tossed in a burning stick or rag. They went back the same way they came—over the hills—staying on the same track as much as possible. I'll follow the trail and see if I can find anything, but if it's like the others, they disappeared without a trace. Are you going to call the sheriff and report it?"

Clarence shook his head. "Cody, if you can't find out who did this, how on earth do you expect the police to find anything? No, I'm not goin' to call the sheriff. He's overworked, shorthanded, and couldn't do a thing you haven't already done."

"But I'm not the law, Clarence. The sheriff should be called." Cody glanced at us as if to say, if you're friends of this hard-headed old man, you'll convince him to report it. "I'd better get on that trail before it's too dark to see. I'm glad to meet you folks." He turned to go, then stopped and retraced his steps, offering a smile that I felt lacked sincerity, for all its flash of even white teeth. "Hope you enjoy your stay in Idaho. Are you here on business or pleasure?"

Bart stood and leaned against the rail. "A little of both. We came on business, but we intend to mix a whole lot of pleasure with it while we're here. Clarence tells us you're an archeologist and there are interesting hieroglyphs near here. Any chance you might have time to show us what you've uncovered?"

Cody glanced at me, as if to confirm this news, then his black eyes darted back to Bart. "How long will you be here?"

"It'll take at least a couple of weeks to conclude our business, longer if we intersperse it with a few side trips to see the area. How can we reach you?"

"Where are you staying? I'll call you when I have a few free hours after the storm."

"In Idaho Falls, at the Shilo Inn. Allan, in case you didn't catch the last name."

"I caught it." He glanced at me and dipped his head. "I'll be in touch." Then he turned and strode to his bike. No one spoke until the man, the bike, and the noise had disappeared into the trees.

Clarence seemed lost in thought, as did Bart. A few of those elusive things were running through my head, too. We hadn't learned a single thing from Cody. He asked questions in place of giving answers. There was something enigmatic about him. I wouldn't call him brooding, but neither would I have described him as happy-go-lucky. In fact, he didn't fit into any of the convenient cubbyholes in my mind. A completely different type, he utterly defied compartmentalization.

I looked at the sky. What did he mean, after the storm? There were no storm clouds in that beautiful September sky. Only chattering magpies swooping down, cockily parading their shining black and white feathers for us to admire.

"Will you be okay if we leave you up here alone tonight?" Bart asked, breaking the silence.

"Sure. I'll sleep with my shotgun handy. Might even bring in the dog and her pups from the barn. There isn't much that's more protective than a mother with new babies. She'll sound the alarm if anyone prowls outside."

Bart stood. "Clarence, we're going to drive back to Spencer and look around. Anything special you'd have shown us if we'd gone there?"

"Stop in at the Opal Country Café and meet Erin. Then go down the street to the Spencer Mercantile. Introduce yourselves to Gary and Marnie Dodson. They run the place. While you're there, pick me up a couple of those Mallo-Nut candy bars, a couple of Idaho Spud bars, and if Gary got in any of those cherry things, get me a couple of those, too. I stop in a couple of times a week to renew my candy supply, but don't know when I'll get down the hill again."

I stared at Clarence. "Are you planning to stay up here with your gun across your knees until these people are caught?"

"Yup. Don't need anybody burnin' down my house or my barn. Lost too much already."

"How's your food supply? Can we bring you anything else? Bread, milk, veggies?" I wanted to check his refrigerator to see what he needed, in case he'd be reluctant to have us go grocery shopping for him.

"Not this trip. Figure you'll be up here again real soon, so I'll make a list," he grinned widely, "as long as you're offering."

"If we hadn't offered, would you have asked?"

"Moot question, ain't it?" He tilted his head to the side a little and folded his hands across his belt. He had me there.

Bart held out his hand. "Can I have your notepad, Princess? I want to leave Clarence our cell phone numbers." As he wrote them, he instructed, "Call if anyone comes back, or even if you hear anything suspicious. I don't expect you'll be bothered tonight, but you'll let us know if anything happens, right?" Bart started down the steps and paused at the bottom to wait for Clarence's reply.

"Won't do any good to call. It'd take you an hour to get up here. I could be dead by then if they was of a mind to kill me and I hadn't got them first."

"Call anyway." Bart held out his hand to take mine.

"Please, promise you'll call if anything happens." I put my hand on Clarence's arm and looked down into his tired face.

"Sure. I'll call." He flashed a giving-in smile. "Don't forget the candy bars." His smile broadened and touched his eyes this time.

"Right."

As we walked hand in hand to the car, I savored the good feeling up here. Then I realized I'd felt it before Cody came and after he left, but while he was here, the air had crackled with tension. Why had his presence disrupted the tranquility? Because of the trauma of another fire? Because we were strangers and he didn't trust us? Because he incited jealousy in Bart? What disturbed me about that good-looking guy?

CHAPTER 16

As we started down the hill in silence, I remembered the story Clarence began twice and hadn't finished.

"I wanted to know what he meant when he said history books had the Lewis and Clark story wrong. Remind me to ask him when we come up next time." I looked at Bart, so deep in thought that he hadn't heard me. "Earth to Bart. Allison speaking. What far planet were you on?"

"Hmm. Just wondering about Cody."

"What did you think of him? No, not what you thought of him. What are your impressions of him?"

Bart glanced at me, a puzzled look on his face. "What's the difference?"

"I don't want your conclusions after you've been thinking about him. I want the fleeting impressions that crossed your mind when you first met him." As I watched a hawk swoop low over the sagebrush, drop out of sight, then ascend high into the open sky, I remembered my own impressions of Cody.

"Smart, well-educated, leery of strangers, compassionate, unafraid, self-confident. What was your impression?"

"I pictured a falconer, a man who runs with wolves, and . . ." I wasn't sure how to phrase the thought that just came to mind.

"And?" Bart prompted. The look on his face told me his eyes were greening again.

"A man with a secret. A very important secret he doesn't want to share."

Relief flickered quickly across Bart's face and disappeared. I reached across the console and patted his thigh. "You know you're my only love. I can't believe you think I'd look twice at him."

A sheepish smile crept across Bart's face. "Well, you have to admit he's a good-looking guy. I imagine women swoon over him wherever he goes."

"Probably. But unlike other women, I already have the best the world has to offer."

Bart pulled my hand to his lips and lightly kissed it. "You always say the right thing, Princess."

I flashed him an appreciative smile. "I have a great teacher. What are we doing in Spencer?"

"Like Clarence said, getting acquainted with the town's gentry. We need to know the players around here. And they need to get to feel comfortable with us. How do you like this countryside?"

We'd left the high ground, come down off the mountain, and were nearly back to the highway. I couldn't see a house or barn for miles in any direction. A few puffy white clouds chased each other across a clear cerulean sky that stretched forever. South of us in the distance, a couple of big blue buttes, old volcano cones, broke the long, straight horizon. To the west, high rolling hills escalated into higher mountain peaks.

"I like it," I said. "It's incredibly relaxing. When we drove up to Clarence's, with all that smoke pouring out of the woods, I felt a very real sense of impending disaster. It all but evaporated once the shock of the fire left me, and I was surprised at how peaceful it seemed, even knowing we're about to plunge into big trouble."

"Think anybody would have a problem with a couple more Californians buying a piece of property up here?"

"Are you serious?" I looked at my husband. "You are serious. Why? I mean, it certainly appeals to me, but tell me why it appeals to you."

"Call it a guy thing, but have you considered that I don't own a single piece of property? We live in the cottage on your parents' estate, which you will inherit someday along with untold millions of your mother's money. But a man likes to think he can support his wife instead of living off her good fortune. I'd like something for us that I contributed. And since your folks—and you—already own one of the choicest properties on the whole central California coast, I've been thinking of finding something different, something uniquely ours. Something I paid for with my own money."

I was stunned. I'd never given it a thought. Never considered for a moment that Bart might not feel he was providing for me.

"No comment?" He stopped at the highway and looked at me, waiting, I could tell, for my honest reaction. He needed immediate feedback on an issue I hadn't known existed. So much for great communication in our marriage.

"Actually, I'm speechless," I confessed. "I had no idea you felt this way. Every single new item in our cottage, you paid for. I figured that was sufficient. Since there's such an abundance, I never imagined you'd have qualms about sharing it with me." I reached across the console and stroked the back of his neck. "You know I don't care a fig about whether the money comes from your pocket or mine."

"I know *you* don't, Princess. But *I* do. I don't want to be supported like some gigolo. I want to be a good provider in every sense of the term, meeting our wants as well as our needs."

I thought of a clever comment about how our wants might overwhelm our budget if we didn't dip into my bank account, but decided this wasn't the time for comic relief. My husband had a serious, and, I had to admit, in his eyes, a valid concern.

"So you want to know if I'd like you to buy a little chunk of peace and quiet out here, where terrorists are probably trying to drive everyone out so they can secretly plot to overthrow the government of the United States? Sounds good to me. We'll definitely have interesting neighbors. Let's go see what we can find."

Bart pulled onto the highway without speaking. Whoops. I didn't handle that very well. Try again. "Seriously, are you thinking of buying property here to have a legitimate excuse for poking around the area, or are you really that much in love with the place?"

He tilted his head, raised a thoughtful eyebrow, and with a quirky little smile on his face said, "Maybe both. I've felt the difference in the atmosphere. The pace seems slower than in California. People appear to care about one another, if what Clarence says is true. Land's usually a good investment, and if we discover something here that's a real turnoff, we can always change our minds."

"Sounds good. I always wanted a little cabin hidden away in the mountains. On the other hand, although these rolling hills are nice, those ten-foot-high snow fences over there suggest that the wind blows a lot of snow across this road. And I'd like something with a few more trees—sort of like Clarence's place, maybe a trifle more accessible year-round. He did say they got twelve feet of snow up there in the winter, didn't he, and that most people rode out the winter somewhere else?"

"You don't miss a thing, do you?" He concentrated on the highway for a minute before he spoke again. "Thanks."

"For what?"

"For not calling me an idiot."

"Love of my life, why would I call you an idiot? I'm just sorry I hadn't picked up on that sooner. So, how do you feel now, Mr. About-To-Be-Property-Owner?"

He grinned that maddeningly charming grin that guarantees he can have anything he wants from me. "Like a kid anticipating the keys to the candy store."

"And how are you going to break the news to your boss that you're property shopping while you're supposed to be routing the Jihad from the area, Sherlock?"

"Elementary, my dear Watson. It's a cover, as you have so aptly pointed out already. We tell your father the truth: we're sniffing around for information about the area. We tell the locals the truth: we're looking for property to buy. Everybody hears the gospel truth."

Bart left the interstate at a sign that read, "Spencer, Opal Capitol of America." The map said population thirty-eight, elevation 5,884 feet. The paved road had no sidewalks or curbs. On the left, a huge sign proclaiming the "Old Trading Post" topped an ancient log building. They sold opals, and apparently a lot of other stuff. On the right, a big white teepee, or wigwam, also touted opals for sale.

The short block dead-ended on Main Street at the railroad tracks, with signs pointing in both directions to stores selling opals, and one pointing to the Opal Country Café. Bart turned right to investigate the two-story building on that end of town. It was another opal showroom, High Country Opal, run by Dennis and Jackie Hooper.

Clarence had mentioned the Spencer Mercantile, so Bart turned around and headed toward the showroom and gift shop. We passed the long, white building housing the café: neat, inviting, with several cars in the unpaved parking lot. Apparently a local favorite, since all the cars but one had Idaho plates.

It looked like we'd run out of town before we found the Merc, but we didn't. Two big, friendly dogs greeted us outside a two-story white frame building with a gas pump and ice machine in front and cheery yellow mums in boxes under the windows.

Inside, the dazzling opals displayed in glass cases caught my eye first, then big chunks of rocks with raw opals still in them. A couple of people were trying on rings and looking at pendants, so we browsed until the man behind the counter finished with them, then introduced ourselves, saying Clarence had sent us for candy bars and information.

Gary Dodson, with a dark moustache and a Don Johnson-like four-day growth of whiskers, gathered up the candy bars, asking why Clarence hadn't come for them himself.

"Somebody set fire to his shed, and he doesn't want to leave his place unguarded for a while," Bart said. "Have you had any problem with strange things going on around here?"

"Not down here," he responded. "But up at the mine, Claudia and A.J. have seen some weird lights and heard noises they couldn't identify. Even thought they felt an earthquake the other night, but the news didn't pick it up, so they didn't know what to make of it."

"Is the mine far from here?" I pointed to a couple of exquisite opal rings I wanted to try on. Gary obliged, adding a couple of his favorites. "About five miles out of town, then up the mountain two and a half miles. Here's an opal with a rainbow of color. This is a triplet."

"Triplet?" It looked like a pure oval opal to me.

"Most of the opal is found in thin, bright layers. When we layer them with other stones, they become opal doublets or triplets. A doublet is the opal with a clear layer of quartz laminated on it to provide protection and strength. A triplet has a layer of black basalt behind the opal in addition to the quartz cap. This darkens the gem and brings out the beautiful patterns of color."

"They started that in Australia, didn't they?" I remembered reading about the valuable black opal found there. "At first it was to pass off less valuable opals to tourists. Then they discovered it actually enhanced the layer of opal and protected it."

Gary nodded. "Opal is easily chipped, and strong detergents can damage the polished surface of the stone. So when the quartz cap is added, it requires little or no care."

"Any possibility we might see the mine?" Bart asked. "We don't want to do any mining. We'd just like to talk to Claudia and see the layout up there."

"Claudia and A.J. are getting ready to close up their place and come down for the winter. No way they can get up and down that mountain when it starts snowing and drifting. They feel like a storm's coming soon. I could call her if you want me to." Gary pulled out a star garnet and a couple of spectacular unset opals. "These are a couple of Claudia's favorites. They aren't for sale. She leaves them here just to show what we mine."

Bart leaned on the glass showcase to look at some of the other gems. "If they're getting ready to leave, maybe we should go as soon as possible. Would you mind calling her to see when it's convenient?"

"Sure. I'll call now." Gary put the rings back in the showcase and pointed to the back of the room, where displays filled the walls. "Might find something interesting there."

We wandered back while he called his sister-in-law. It would probably take half a day to examine everything of interest displayed in every corner of the room, and you'd definitely come away with new knowledge about mining gemstones in general, and opals in particular.

"Claudia says you can come now. They're closing up the place tomorrow."

"Tell her we'll leave immediately, if you'll give us directions." Bart pulled out his wallet to pay for the candy. I picked up one of Gary's cards and stuck it in my purse.

Finishing his conversation with Claudia, Gary rang up our purchase and drew a map. "Make sure you leave there before sunset. Anybody unfamiliar with that road doesn't want to be on it after dark." Gary walked us out and called Jester and Shadow, the two friendly greeter dogs that were showing great interest in our tires.

"Thanks, Gary. We'll be back later to see if you know of any property for sale around here. Clarence has such a sweet deal up on that mountain, we thought we'd try to find something similar." Bart slid behind the wheel and started the car, handing me the map. "Guide me."

We went south on Main Street, crossed what used to be very busy railroad tracks, according to pictures at the Merc, and wound around a mountain on a gravel road. We passed Rattlesnake Creek and Corral Creek, and at Three Mile Canyon we saw a moose back in the brush.

Five miles out of town, we opened the wide green gate that stretched across the dirt and gravel road, then started up the hill to the open pit mine slashed out of the side of the mountain. It became apparent why Gary warned us about driving this road after dark, and why Claudia and A.J. preferred to winter at a lower elevation. The road, filled with twists and hair-pin turns, wound upward through sagebrush heavy laden with yellow pollen and waist-high weeds, also topped by colorful pollen-filled blossoms.

I couldn't believe it when I saw a mobile home perched atop the mountain. "They must have air-lifted it in. I can't imagine driving it up that road with anything less than a bulldozer, and then I'm not sure how it made some of those turns."

We got out of the car, now parked by a warped and weathered picnic table under a huge evergreen tree, and turned to look back down the road. The view took my breath away. Golden wheat fields, green pastures, brown, ocher, and sage-colored hills, and patches of pine trees so dark they looked black spread out beneath us in a muted mosaic that stretched to the far horizon. Snow-covered jagged peaks to the left had to be the Grand Teton Mountains. Visible far to the south, the buttes were bumps on the skyline.

Claudia greeted us, collaring two big dogs, a Dalmation and a Rottweiller she called Buckwheat and Dino. A genial, sandy-blonde woman with a pleasing voice and skin tanned from working in the sun, she had a reserved air. As Bart quickly explained we were friends of Clarence, I felt a subtle relaxation in her demeanor. Was she afraid we were here to try to buy her out—or worse?

I picked up Bart's cue. "We're visiting from out of state. When I asked Clarence what we should be sure to see, he suggested the mine. He said you'd worked it nearly all your life."

"Since I was fifteen, except for two summers," she said. "To make a long story short, my dad, Mark Stetler, bought it from Charlie

Casper, who owned a sand and gravel outfit. Charlie bought it from the deer hunters who discovered it."

While Bart asked questions about how they dug the opals from the rock, I wandered around, close enough to hear the conversation but far enough to get a broad picture of this beautiful, isolated spot which would appeal to anyone planning treasonous activities and needing as little traffic as possible.

"Aren't you worried about someone coming up in the wintertime while you're gone and helping themselves to the opals?" I asked, turning back to hear Claudia's explanation.

"After it snows, the road isn't exactly accessible, and all this is usually covered with snow." She smiled at my ignorance of winter on the Continental Divide. I didn't bother to add that I'd thought they might come on snowmobiles. It wouldn't matter how they got up here if all this was buried under twelve feet of snow.

But that brought up another question. "Does everyone leave about this time of year for lower elevations?"

"Not necessarily. Since we can't mine the opal, we spend the winter cutting, polishing, and mounting it, and traveling to gem and mineral shows all over the country. There are a few die-hards who weather it out, but most of them aren't on top of the Divide, so they can get out easier."

I continued to visually search the area around their mobile home while Claudia explained how opal formed in gas pockets left by volcanic flow. The pockets filled with hot springs, suspending the opal in the hot water. As it cooled and the liquid evaporated, it solidified, and the opal or silica was left in the bottom of the pockets or geodes.

"Opal is the most colorful and mystifying of the major gemstones," she continued. "The colors produced in a single opal vary when the angle at which light strikes the piece is changed. Several different colors can be seen in a single place on an opal as it is moved around in the light." Claudia showed us some opal layered in a rock she picked up at random from where they'd been working. "When you find precious opal whose color is imposed on a milky translucent body, it's known as milk or white opal. Those with color patches on a dark-gray to black background are called black opals. No other stone besides the opal has such brilliant colors flashing from its surface."

I examined the smooth, milk-white rock with perfectly straight layers of pink running through it. "I've heard about fire opals. Do you find those here?"

"You need to be precise when you're talking about fire with relation to gemstones. In a diamond, fire refers to the dispersion of light and the spectral colors—the color sparkling from the stone in the light. But 'fire opal' is specific to the reddish or amber Mexican opal, which can be with or without color play. It's usually found in little knots in volcanic rock, therefore it appears in small stones."

She told Bart they were open to the public the three summer holiday weekends as well as the last week in August. People could come and dig out their own opals for a small fee, which I found fascinating. How would I know if I found an opal, since you had to chip them out of the mountain?

As I turned to ask that question, I spotted something almost hidden under a huge Douglas fir tree that made me bite my tongue to keep from speaking. I didn't turn around until I felt sure my face wouldn't reveal the turmoil going on inside me.

Surely she couldn't be involved.

Could she?

CHAPTER 17

When Bart had exhausted his list of questions, I smiled, thanked Claudia, and hurried to the car, my stomach doing flip-flops in my throat. I couldn't wait to be away from here, to tell Bart what I'd seen.

As Bart turned the car around, his cell phone rang. "Allan." He listened, gave a couple of "umhums" and "mmms," then said, "Shilo Inn. Do you want Alli to give you the number, or do you want us to make reservations for you?" Another pause. "Roger." He hung up.

"Dad?" I asked, gripping my seat as we started down the steep part of the hill, less concerned now about Claudia than Bart's latest news flash.

"Your mom. They're trying to get everyone out here as fast as they can, and want to make sure we all have rooms close together so we can coordinate our work. She'll make reservations for Anastasia, and pay for suites whether they actually arrive in time to use them or not. They're coming from various locations, so they'll be arriving not only at different times, but probably on different days."

"Have they discovered the identity of the new leader?"

"Margaret says they may have." Bart maneuvered around a particularly nasty spot in the road where erosion had cut a gully deep enough to get lost in. I wondered how often they had to repair the road. Probably after every heavy rain.

"When are Mom and Dad coming?" That would be something to look forward to. Possibly. To call my father a slave-driver wouldn't be an exaggeration. When he came on the scene, you looked neither to the right nor the left unless that would further the investigation.

"Anastasia acquired a new Lear jet. David Chen's picking it up this afternoon, and he'll fly them here first thing in the morning. Margaret and Else made some preliminary assignments, dividing up the eight sections on the map. Since we're already here and working on it, we got section six, the piece we picked up from Kay Sterling in Abilene. Guess I don't have to worry anymore about INEL and what's going on there."

"Who got that one? My guess would be Sky, unless Dad wanted to keep that for himself."

Bart nodded. "Your folks. Figures Jack would take the juicy one."

I breathed a sigh of relief when we reached the bottom of the hill and stopped at the green gate. I jumped out and opened it, waited while Bart drove through, and closed it behind us.

Bart continued as soon as I closed the car door. "Apparently Lion extracted some info from his contact when he picked up section one in Ogden, Utah, at Hill AFB, so they assigned him that area."

Dusk had fallen as we came down the hill from the mine, and the sun had long since disappeared behind the high mountains to the west. I turned on the interior light and opened the map with the divided circle, penciling in assignments as Bart recited them. Lionel Brandt's section one included Jackson Hole, Palisades Reservoir, and a lot of mountains. Section two went to Dominic Vicente, our cocky Spanish ex-bullfighter. It included more mountains, several small towns, Gray's Lake, and Blackfoot Reservoir.

"Rip Schyler has the section that could prove to be the most fascinating," I observed, studying the map. "Number three includes Blackfoot—interesting name for a town—Fort Hall Indian Reservation, Pocatello, American Falls with its huge reservoir, and Minidoka Dam. Don't you love these names? I read about the reservation and tribal powwow they have every year in August at the Fort Hall Reservation. Too bad we missed it. Did you know they had German prisoners of war incarcerated there during the Second World War?"

"You're just overflowing with interesting information. Did you get all that at the Visitors' Center?"

"That and a lot more. Are we going back to the Merc and talk to Gary, or to Clarence's with his candy bars?" I checked the time. "Actually, the Merc's probably closed by now."

Bart nodded. "I wanted to stop at the café and get acquainted with whoever hangs out there, and drive the fifteen miles or so to the Montana border, but there's not enough time. We need to get to know this country fast."

"How about a flight over it at first light in the Lear? Now that we have some idea of where things are, that might help with the broader picture."

"Good thinking, Princess. We'll do that before Anastasia arrives. David and your dad may think of it when they fly in tomorrow, but just in case, I'll mention it."

"When you call, ask Mom to bring me some other clothes. My New Orleans vacation wardrobe won't hack it here."

Bart turned off on the little road that led to Clarence's place. There were no lights visible up on the hill where I thought the house would be, but if he didn't have a light on upstairs in the bedroom, it might not show through the trees.

"I hope he's all right," I said. "He's such an interesting character. You don't suppose they'll come back and go for the barn or house, do you?" I worried about Clarence. I really liked the old man.

"I don't think they'll do anything until they let him know what they want. He'll probably have an offer to sell his place—unless he's already made it known that nothing will drive him from his home. Then he'd have something to worry about."

The winding drive through the trees seemed much less intimidating this trip than when we were racing toward the fire. "Is this Jihad? It seems too conservative for them, unless there really is a new leader who's containing them, keeping them from creating too big a mess up here and bringing the FBI down on them en masse."

Bart sighed. "Wish I knew, Princess. You're right; it doesn't seem violent enough for the way Jihad usually does business. But if they have a strong new local leader, and bin Laden's directed them to follow his instructions, anything is possible. Sooner or later, however, they're bound to break free from restraint and go back to business as usual, unless bin Laden expressly forbids it."

"Which I don't see happening. I'm sure he'd like nothing better than to turn his conscience-free men loose in America to wreak havoc and bloodshed."

We arrived at the clearing to find Clarence's pickup in the same spot he'd left it, with the door still open and the interior light on. I closed the door. There were no lights anywhere in the house, and once the pickup light went out, we were plunged into darkness. Even the embers of the fire had cooled and were black.

"Clarence, it's Bart and Allison," Bart called. I expected the dog to bark, but the only sounds were crickets chirping and the occasional hoot of an owl. I dug my penlight from my purse, and we hurried to the front porch guided by its tiny beam.

Please let him be all right, I prayed. *Don't let Osama bin Laden's evil touch him.*

As my light panned up the steps to the porch, it revealed a shoe with a foot in it, then a pant leg. I held my breath, hardly daring to shine the light all the way to his face. Clarence remained in the same chair as when we left, his arms folded neatly across his belt. His eyes were closed, and I couldn't hear him breathing.

Bart knelt beside him, felt for a pulse, and looked up at me, relief on his face. "I think he's just asleep. See if you can find a light."

I opened the screen door, brushed the inside wall, and a yellow porch light lit up the darkness as a lamp illuminated the interior of the front room.

"Clarence, wake up. It's Bart. Let's get you to bed." Bart shook the man a couple of times before he came out of his deep sleep and comprehended what was going on.

"We brought your candy bars from the Spencer Merc." I put the bag of requested goodies in his lap. "I'll bet you haven't had dinner yet, have you? Can I fix you something?"

Clarence smiled sleepily, grasped the sack, and closed his eyes again.

"Come on. You can't sleep out here." Bart took one arm while I held the other, and we raised the old man to his feet. He clung to the bag of candy bars, but allowed us to help him inside and up to his bedroom.

"Are you okay?" I asked as he sat down on the edge of his bed.

"Little tired. Guess I had more excitement today than usual."

"Can I get you something to eat?"

"I'll keep till mornin'. If I wake up hungry in the night, I've got a snack right here." He smiled a toothy, mischievous smile.

"I'll help him," Bart said. "Why don't you go to the barn and see if that mother dog will let you bring her and her pups into the house?" He slipped off Clarence's shoes, then started to undress him.

"I'd probably be frozen stiff in the mornin' if you hadn't come back. Thanks," I heard Clarence tell Bart as I went down the stairs. I believed it. When the sun went down, the heat disappeared, too.

I headed down the path I'd seen the men take this afternoon. The barn door stood open. Three horses whinnied when I approached. Shining my penlight along the door frame, I found a switch, flipped it, and the interior of the small barn lit up. The dog, a mixture of breeds I couldn't identify, jumped to her feet and stood between me and her puppies, growling softly.

I spoke to her gently while I checked the horses. Apparently Clarence hadn't fed them. I found some oats in a bin, dumped a scoop in each of their buckets, and made sure there was still water in their troughs. Then I approached the dog, stopping short of her corner. I sat down, held out my hand, and coaxed her to come to me. She did so hesitantly, but when I petted her and rubbed her head, she wagged her skinny tail and allowed me to pick up one of the puppies that had tumbled out of the basket. The litter followed, all five of them climbing into my lap.

"Come on, Mom. Let's get you into the house." I put the puppies in their basket, picked it up, and sweet-talked the dog into the house, struggling to keep the puppies from falling out. Bart rescued me at the stairs, relieving me of the heavy basket. I ran back to the barn, got their food and water dishes, turned off the light, and shut the door. Bart situated the dogs in a corner of the big country kitchen, then we filled their dishes and turned out the lights.

As we wound down the hill toward the highway, I leaned my head back and pondered the events of the day. We weren't any closer to unraveling the mystery we'd come to solve, and had, in fact, discovered additional factors that could only be placed in the question marks column.

Who was Cody? Was he a good guy or a bad guy? Whose side would he be on when and if this erupted into a war between the terrorists and the locals?

Then again, were terrorists actually involved in trying to drive people from their homes and take over this country, or was it some less dangerous group or individual? Thus far, it didn't really smack of terrorist tactics. Definitely not brutal enough.

"Penny for your thoughts," Bart said as he steered onto I-15 for the sixty-mile drive back to Idaho Falls.

"Pondering the possibilities. I didn't get to ask Clarence about the Lewis and Clark history mistake. I'm really curious about that. It's certainly a secret he enjoys knowing." Then I had another thought that brought me upright in my seat. "Bart, I forgot to tell you! Mom called as we got back in the car, and I totally forgot. Cody said the person who set those fires was a small man or woman who rode a small motorbike. I spotted one under a tree behind Claudia's mobile home. You don't suppose . . .? No. She seemed like too nice a lady to be involved in something like arson."

"What motive could she have?" Bart's puzzled expression showed in the dim glow of the dashboard lights.

"Mmm. Good question. Scratch that knee-jerk reaction. My muddled mind is too tired to think, anyway. I can't tell you how good that bed will feel. I do hope none of Anastasia have arrived, and we'll be able to collapse into bed without briefing anyone. By the way, fearless leader, have you mapped out a plan for tomorrow?"

"After a quick dawn flyover of the area up here, we'll go back to Clarence's. He offered to let us take his horses, and I'd like to check out a couple of things, including following that bike trail if we can find it. Then, if our day isn't too far gone, we'll go into Spencer and dine at the Opal Country Café and get acquainted with the locals. We need to check out all the other shops in town and visit the sheep station."

"You haven't mentioned looking at property," I reminded him.

"If I'm right, anybody who comes into the Merc and mentions selling will hear we're looking."

"You're letting Gary do your work for you."

Bart nodded. "With that RV park and convenience store, he gets a lot of business and likely has his finger on the pulse of the community."

"You're probably right." I glanced at the sky. "Look, the moon's finally coming up. If I can muster the energy, want to take a little moonlight stroll by the river before we go up to our room?"

"Whatever you want to do, Princess."

"Whatever?"

"Well, within reason." Bart smiled and reached for my hand. "I figure I'm fairly safe making a statement like that when you weren't sure you'd make it as far as the bed before collapsing."

The clock on the dash glowed ten P.M. as we turned into the parking lot. Bart did a quick drive-through to check out the surroundings, but there was nothing to arouse suspicion. I couldn't believe our good fortune in not having run into any of the bad guys thus far.

We walked through the quiet lobby, past a noisy room full of people finishing a dinner meeting, and out into the night on the other side of the hotel, where we were greeted by a silver moon rising over the temple and shimmering in the rippling black water of the Snake River.

Strolling arm in arm toward the river, we crossed the bridge between the stone lamp posts. As we stopped on the bridge, I turned toward Bart and slid my arms around his neck. A light bouncing around in a room on the fourth floor caught my eye. The two or three rooms on either side were fully lighted, their doors open onto their balconies.

Chills ran down my arms and I shuddered involuntarily.

"What's the matter, Princess?"

"Isn't that about where our room is?" I pointed at the darkened room, where a flashlight beam danced over walls and ceiling.

CHAPTER 18

Taking all of two seconds to decide it was our room, Bart pulled his gun, made sure I had mine, and told me to watch the balcony. He raced for the hotel door. I crept back across the bridge, stepped out of the light and into the shadows, keeping my eye on the flashlight still zipping intermittently across the ceiling.

Rats ran in packs. Where there was one, there might be two. Gun in hand, I scanned dark corners, watching for movement in shadows, listening for any sound in the night. If someone was out here, they were well hidden, knew I looked for them, and were not moving at all.

Suddenly I heard shouts from the fourth floor. Anticipating an attempted escape by way of the balcony, I started running toward the building, but got tangled in my long gauze skirt blowing in the wind and fell to the ground. I stripped it off, jumped to my feet, and raced to intercept the black form that leaped over the railing, then rappelled off the balcony toward the ground.

I tackled him as he hit the lawn, threw myself across his body, and hung on to his neck for dear life. I never saw the blow coming that felled me. Just stars shooting across the back of my eyes.

"Princess, are you hurt? Allison, speak to me." Bart picked me up and held me, running his fingers over my face, my hair, down my arms.

"Don't let them get away! I'm fine." I struggled to get loose. "Where did they go?"

"They? I only saw one."

"I only saw one, too. That's why I'm lying on the ground instead of still on top of the guy that came over the balcony. You must have come down the rope right behind him."

Bart pulled me gently to my feet. "Unfortunately, I was too slow. He heard the electronic key in the lock and went over the balcony as I opened the door. He'd left the sliding doors open for a fast escape."

"And I let him get away. I'm sorry. I figured there must be two of them, but I didn't hear or see the other one. Obviously he saw me." I put my fingers to the side of my head that hurt the most. "Ouch."

"Let's get you inside and check you over. What's this?" He held up my hand. A portion of a gold chain dangled from my tightly closed fist.

"I had hold of the guy's neck. I must have pulled it off. And speaking of off, I left my skirt out on the lawn in the dark somewhere. I need a different wardrobe for this work."

Bart jogged toward the bridge and came back holding the yards of gauze I'd discarded. "Let's go see to your head and our room."

On the elevator, I decided I'd been kicked. I remembered the sensation of a sharp blow to the head and flying bodily from atop the man who'd been in our room. I looked at the necklace still clutched in my hand. Probably a man's chain. Heavy gold links a woman wouldn't normally wear for everyday, or for burglarizing a hotel room. And the neck this came from would definitely bear evidence of it having been ripped off.

Then I remembered something else. The unforgettable aroma of cheap, strong aftershave lotion. Our man from Tucson.

If I hadn't had a splitting headache before I saw the mess in our room, it would have brought on a doozy all by itself. Every single item of clothing we had was strewn across the floor. To add insult to injury, the intruder had slashed all my clothes into worthless strips.

We stood speechless just inside the door. I wanted to cry, then I fought hysterical laughter bubbling up inside me. In the end, I just stood there woodenly, trying to make sense of the scene before me.

Bart picked up a piece of one of my skirts, strode to the glass doors, and using the skirt to preserve any fingerprints, shut and locked them. He called the desk and asked to have a manager sent immediately to our room, with a key to any one of the rooms Margaret Allan had reserved. If they had a problem with that, call Mrs. Allan for her permission, but get it done yesterday. He ordered the person on the phone to discuss it with no one but the manager.

Not a single other employee or anyone else would know anything about it. Did he have their solemn promise on that?

I stood in the same spot, not having moved an inch from when we entered the room, completely numbed by the scene before me and the throbbing in my head. A maverick thought moseyed across my mind, causing mourning for times past, when integrity meant something. How long would that person on the other end of the phone keep that promise not to tell anyone but the manager? Until they got home? Until a friendly employee came by? Until some personable stranger pried it out of them? Certainly unlike the days of the Old Testament or the Book of Mormon, when an oath or promise was sacred and kept, even under threat of death.

"Let's see your head," Bart said, dropping the phone in its cradle.

"I'm fine. No worse off than you were yesterday when you collided with that guy's gun. Was that yesterday? Seems like weeks ago."

"Sit down here, and let me take a look anyway." Bart fussed over me until the manager appeared, key in hand to a suite across the hall. Bless her heart, Mom had left instructions that all of us would have access to the rooms she'd reserved. That had cut red tape considerably in the past, and I was grateful she'd remembered to do it this time.

While Bart explained what happened and asked the manager to call the police, I grabbed my toiletry bag from the drawer in the bathroom. Unlike the break-in we'd experienced on our honeymoon at the Turtle Bay Hilton on Oahu, when everything had been dumped, the bathroom was still untouched.

I hoped Idaho Falls had a crack forensics team to gather and transmit fingerprints quickly to the FBI unit that collected and identified them. It would be nice to know, as quickly as possible, who we were dealing with here. Or who was dealing with us.

I didn't argue when Bart insisted that I take Mom's suite and go to bed. He'd wait for the police. My head needed to be placed gently on a pillow, directly after I'd swallowed the prescribed number of aspirin to quell the pain. Unfortunately, my brain didn't understand that it needed quiet time, too. It pondered the mysteries we'd encountered today, the events that would lead inextricably toward the next incidents, and the next, spiraling to what climax one could only guess.

Then the baby cried, the most plaintive sound I'd ever heard in my life. Hauntingly close, but I couldn't find her. I searched everywhere, her cries becoming more distressed the longer I looked, but she could not be found. I'd almost given up hope, fearing I'd be driven to madness by that lonely cry, when suddenly she appeared right in front of me, a tiny bundle dressed in white, wrapped in a white lace shawl.

As I hurried to pick her up, to hold and comfort her, I felt restrained from doing so. She wasn't mine yet. And in that moment, I knew that she might never be. My heart tore asunder, one half wrapping itself around that beautiful tiny bundle waiting for my arms to enfold her, and the other silently bleeding inside me. I felt the decision was mine: to have this baby, to love and raise her, or to turn away.

Turn away? Why would I turn from the dream I'd worked for, prayed for, wept over, enduring endless procedures and tests to bring her here?

Suddenly the scene darkened, and my baby faded from view, until even her plaintive cries were silent. Raven came instead, laughing, mocking, with deadly intent in his heart and mind. I cried out, but no one could hear me. I was alone. I ran, ran until I was exhausted, then hid until I heard him again, relentless, never stopping in his dogged determination to kill me.

Why? Why was I so important? The least of Anastasia's agents, I was hardly worth his time. Any day of the week he could collect many times over the bounty he'd receive for my head. Why did he continue to pursue me? *Please, leave me alone. Please, let me find my baby. You're keeping me from my baby.*

But he laughed at my pleas. Laughed until he caught me. Laughed as he brought the knife to my throat.

"Princess, wake up. Sweetheart, I'm here. It's okay." Bart lifted me in his arms, held me, rocking back and forth on the bed, kissing my face, wiping my forehead, whispering that I was safe. I clung to him in the dark, afraid to loosen my grip, fearing this was part of my nightmare and Raven would return to tear me from my husband's protecting arms. Eventually, the terror of the nightmare diminished.

"What are we going to do? You can't keep suffering these horrible nightmares." Bart dampened a washcloth and brought it to me. These torments in the night left me wringing wet, weak, and trembling from head to toe.

I wiped my face, neck, and hands, then lay back exhausted on the pillows he plumped for me. "I'm going home," I murmured.

"Home? To California?" Dumbfounded, Bart sat down on the side of the bed.

I nodded. "I saw her." Tears streamed down my face as I remembered her beautiful dark, curly hair, her deep blue eyes and lovely pink skin.

"Who?" Bart held one of my hands while he wiped at my tears with his other.

"Our baby. I found her, Bart. She's beautiful. She has my hair and your wonderful eyes." Then I remembered the rest of the nightmare. I touched Bart's face, stroked his cheek, ran my finger along his lower lip. I knew what I had to do. And now I knew why I had to do it. For some reason I had a hard time making my lips speak the words, as if to reveal the knowledge that was lodged securely, unflinchingly in my heart would somehow dispel the clarity I now had of the nightmare, the reason for it, and the solution.

"If I stay here, I'll lose her. I have to go home. If I don't do that for her, for us, I'll lose her." I didn't want to alarm Bart. I didn't want to sound dramatic. I just knew, with a surety that frightened me, what would be the result if I didn't.

I gently held Bart's face in my hands, looked into his eyes, and willed him to understand. "When—if—I lose this baby, I'll die."

CHAPTER 19

Bart lay beside me and gathered me into his arms. "I know you'd feel like dying if you lost another baby, but . . . ."

"No, Bart." I could speak calmly about it now. It was so clear. Why hadn't I seen it before, in all the months I'd suffered through the unimaginable horror of the nightly visitations of those two in my subconscious? "If I lose this baby, I'll lose my life at the same time."

Bart didn't speak. He just held me closer, stroking my hair. I could hear his heart pounding in his chest—not a quiet resting heartbeat, but thumping wildly, like mine when I woke from the nightmare.

"You sound certain," he said softly. "Want to tell me how you can be so sure all of a sudden?"

"I can't tell you. I just knew when I saw her in my dream—as if someone opened my mind and inserted the knowledge while I looked at her. Then she faded away, and Raven came. He caught me this time. Had his knife to my throat. Laughed because he'd finally succeeded. I knew then the choice was mine. I can continue with Anastasia, or I can go home, take care of myself, and have this baby."

"Are you carrying the baby now?"

The question startled me for a moment. I hadn't thought beyond the dream. Or nightmare. "I guess I ought to call Dr. Simon. We left before he told me the results of that last test. I figured since I didn't hear from him, the results were negative and we needed to keep trying. But if you want an unofficial opinion, simply from the intensity of that dream, mixed with a little intuition, I'd say yes. Your daughter is lying next to you, even as we speak."

That statement had the effect of an emotional double-whammy on both of us. Bart kissed me and held me close. I just felt an incredible sense of awe. We'd done it. We'd finally succeeded at what we'd worked so hard to accomplish—what so many others were able to do so effortlessly.

"We'll get you on the first flight back to California in the morning," he declared. "The rest of Anastasia should filter in tomorrow from about noon on, so there will be plenty of help and you won't feel like you're deserting me. And you'll have to promise that you'll go see Dr. Simon first thing."

"You sound like a nervous new father already," I teased.

"Promise me?" he insisted.

"Of course I promise. If you'll promise not to tell anyone until we have confirmation. I don't want to get our folks' hopes up, and they certainly don't need to be distracted from this problem. Speaking of the problem, we'd better get some sleep, or neither one of us will be worth shooting tomorrow. And we had a big day planned."

Bart drifted off to sleep as I lay in his arms. My mind refused to shut down. I replayed the nightmare, experienced again the exhausting emotional whirlpool, and as dawn began to light the sky, I finally succumbed to the welcome oblivion of sleep.

When I awoke, I was alone. A note on Bart's pillow informed me he'd gone to fly a grid over the area around Spencer. He had spoken with Mom earlier; she and Dad should arrive by noon. He'd installed the scrambler on the phone so it was secured, but hadn't called the airport for flight information. I tinkered with the thought of getting up and making my reservation, but my body didn't care much for the idea, so I snuggled back down and slept again, a deep, dreamless, restful sleep.

At noon, the phone woke me. Mom's frantic voice brought me upright in bed. "Thank heaven I found you. I despaired of ever reaching anyone up there. Why aren't you answering the cell phone?"

I racked my sleep-laden brain for the cause. "We bought some new high-tech phones, and we must have left the old one in the car. Sorry. Guess I figured Bart gave you our new numbers. What's up?"

"The new Lear jet David expected to pick up yesterday wasn't ready. We could rent a plane, but they promised it would be delivered tonight, so we'll wait and come then. Neither of us wanted to make that seventeen-hour drive from the coast to Idaho, and if we wait for the Lear, we'll get there just as fast. What's happening?"

"Bart updated you this morning when you talked?" I jumped out of bed and tossed the reams of Idaho information I'd collected yesterday where I'd been lying seconds before. There was something in that stack I'd meant to tell her about.

That's when I found the second note on the pillow next to mine. Bart had returned, found me still sleeping, and gone to Clarence's.

"Yes, but that was hours ago," she said. "Any progress? News?" I must have inherited my impatience from my mother. She couldn't stand to sit and wait either.

"Bart's in Spencer, investigating some things he saw from the air this morning."

"And you?"

"Going over a ton of information I picked up at the Visitors' Center. I'm dividing it by area to give each section leader a heads-up on anything in their sector that might interest terrorists. Although, from our experience already, there's nothing like being there in person and getting the straight scoop from those who know the area best."

"I take it you've had a breakthrough, then," Mom said as I sorted and separated, looking for the item I wanted to share. She sounded in the mood to talk, to glean all the information she could before she arrived, to be prepared to plunge in and make up for the time delay.

I told her about Clarence, Cody, the Dodsons and Claudia, Spencer, the opal mines, noises, animal deaths, arson, and repeated everything I imagined Bart had already told them. I couldn't feed her information fast enough to satisfy her. Dad would be in the same state: agitated, edgy, intensely impatient, and ready for action.

Since the INEL was basically the only thing in their area, I read to her, word for word, the brochure on it and suggested she might find something additional on the Internet. When I recited my now-abandoned hypothesis about nuclear contamination of water supplies, she thought that might be worth pursuing—not with regard to polluting Idaho's water, but a major city somewhere else.

Her attention increased when I mentioned the sheep station and my worry about biological warfare. A fourteen-year-old had died in

Idaho from the Hanta virus. Considering the number of deadly viruses in the world—Philo, Marburg, Ebola, Udine, and a host of others that as yet were regional—if the experiments at the sheep station with viruses, bacteria, and diseases were taken over by terrorists, it could be world-threatening.

"Now it's your turn, Mom. What's going on at the Control Center? You must have some word on bin Laden and his men. And how about the families that had the maps? Have they been protected? Did you retrieve all the sections of the map?"

"The Control Center is a madhouse—organized chaos," she reported. "I've lost track of people coming and going. Thank heaven for Alma and her quiet efficiency. She's the only sane person here at the moment. And definitely the only one actually keeping track of where everyone's headed. As for bin Laden, they're sure he's left Denver."

My hand froze as I reached for the brochure on Idaho's Oregon Trail. I tried to keep my voice calm, tried to quell the turmoil that erupted simultaneously in my head and my midsection. "Where do they think he's gone?"

Mom hesitated a fraction of a moment too long.

"He's coming to Idaho, isn't he? Please help me out here, Mom. I'm missing something. How come they know when he's gone and where he's probably going, but they can't pick him up while he's where they think he is?" I knew I was losing my cool, but I could not believe they could predict where he'd be, know when he left, and yet not apprehend the creep.

"Alli, are you okay? Honey, are you getting any sleep, or are you still having those horrible nightmares? You sound exhausted and almost hysterical."

"I'm not okay—because I'm not sleeping—because I'm plagued by Raven nightly; therefore, yes, I am exhausted. But I was fine until I thought again of the incompetence of whoever's after Osama bin Laden. I do tend to get hysterical when I realize that Bart and I are here, are known, and are probably right in the cross hairs of those two terrorists who escaped in Iraq. I assume their heads are still on the block if all the pieces of the map aren't returned to bin Laden, and I also assume that's why he's here in the flesh instead of still hiding out in Afghanistan. So maybe that's cause enough for a little hysteria. That, and I don't have a thing to wear. I'm sure Bart told you my clothes were shredded last night."

I stopped my tirade, remembered that I no longer needed the clothes, would probably be gone by the time they arrived, and was suddenly ashamed I'd unloaded on Mom. Of all people, she understood completely how I felt, having been in this same position for the last quarter-century.

"Actually, Bart omitted that little detail in his report." Mom's voice, more calm than when she'd called, remained quiet, but it now contained an edge. "What happened?"

"I'm assuming the men involved were the two terrorists who escaped from Iraq. They had the most to gain from finding the map sections we hold. Although it could easily be the Idaho contingent, if they're that organized, and frankly, I'd bet they are. These fires and other things going on up in those hills smack of scare tactics and sound like they were done by professionals."

"Allison," Mom interrupted, "tell me what happened."

"While we were exploring in the mountains, someone got into our room and shredded every last item of clothing I had."

"Just yours?"

"He tossed Bart's around. Maybe we got back too soon, and he didn't have time to take his knife to Bart's. Maybe Bart's pants were harder to shred than my skirts. I don't know why he only did mine." But chills ran down my arms as I thought of Raven. That would be so like him to shred only my clothes and leave Bart's. I shook off the thought. Raven was in prison. Supposedly.

"How did the intruder get into your room?" Mom's cool efficiency sounded a little less professional than before.

"Mom, you may not believe this, but at the time, I didn't care how he did. Just that he did. The headache I had sort of overrode all other considerations." Whoops. That slip would mean trouble.

"Headache? And what was the cause?"

"A boot to the side of my head when I tackled the guy after he rappelled off the balcony. Mom, I'm okay. My headache's gone this morning."

"And that's why Bart has gone without you? Because you're okay?"

She thought of everything. Still groggy from sleep, I was no match for her quick wit or her maternal instincts.

"I promise to take good care of your daughter, Mom. By the way, nights are cool here, even though the days are lovely and warm. So bring layers, and a warm coat."

Mom paused, as if trying to determine by the sound of my voice that I really was okay. "Bart said you needed me to bring some clothes. I've packed jeans, long-sleeved T-shirts, hiking boots, a couple of dressy outfits, and a jacket. Do you want me to bring your down-filled coat?"

"Umm. No. I won't be needing it." I couldn't tell her I'd probably pass her in the skies flying somewhere over the Mountain West. That would upset her, and I'd end up telling her why I had to return to California before I was ready to break the whole story. I hated not being totally honest and up-front with Mom, but my parents were overly concerned about my health, happiness, and general well-being. They didn't need to be worried about me when they had Osama bin Laden to worry about. That was a full kettle all by itself.

"Allison, call Bart and find out how they got into your room. Someone could repeat the process and walk in on you right now. Are you armed?"

"I have my gun right here." In fact, Bart had left it lying next to me, half in and half out of my purse. "Please don't worry. I'm fine. In fact, I think I've solved the mystery of the nightmares. I may never have another. I'll tell you about it when I see you. I've got to go. Talk to you later. Love you."

I hung up quickly and jumped in the shower so I couldn't hear the phone if it rang. Mother could be relentless in the pursuit of information as well as the pursuit of terrorists, and I didn't want to say any more than I already had. Besides, I needed the line open if Bart tried to call. Apparently he'd taken our new phones for him and Clarence to use. When I got out of the shower, I saw the old one next to my toiletry bag. My organized husband thought of everything, even leaving it turned off so no one could call and wake me.

I yearned to have access to my closet again. Even for a favorite outfit, two consecutive days in the turquoise silk blouse and gauze skirt was too much.

The next flight out of Idaho Falls didn't leave until four o'clock, so I organized the brochures into eight stacks and lined them up on the dresser. I labeled them to correspond with each map section and the agent assigned to that area, so there would be no question which belonged to whom—since I wouldn't be here to pass them out.

I suddenly discovered I was ravenous. Digging the new number from my purse, I called Bart from the old cell phone, just in case he and Clarence were about through and could join me for lunch.

"Nice to hear from you, Sleeping Beauty. I wanted to call and see how you felt this morning, but didn't, just in case you were still sleeping."

"I've been talking to Mom. Not much gets by her. When will you be back? Have you found anything?"

"As a matter of fact, we've run across some tracks that had to have been made by an airplane—a big one. Lots of horse and cattle tracks, too. Clarence thinks there might be rustling going on here."

"Rustling? What next? When will you be through?"

"We're hurrying to beat the storm Clarence predicts is coming, but don't wait for me. Go ahead and have lunch. Be careful, Princess. In fact, I'd rather you called for room service than go out alone. Those two could still be hanging around."

"I'll be fine, love. And I'll be careful. By the way, my flight leaves at four o'clock. Will you be back by then, or should I just take the shuttle to the airport?" I didn't add that I wanted to see him before I left town—he might feel obligated to return before they were finished.

"I'll be there by three. If you're ready, we'll make it to the airport in five minutes and you can check in, then we'll have an hour together."

"Thanks." This was going to be harder than I thought, leaving Bart behind, even if help was on the way. "See you in a couple of hours. You be careful out there with those rustlers."

I laughed to myself as I slung my purse over my shoulder, pulled the drapes to keep out the bright afternoon sun, leaving just a crack in the middle so I could find my way safely across the room, and headed for the door. Rustlers? Clarence had probably lived through the time when there really were rustlers, but today? Anything was possible. And it might logically answer some of those questions about happenings in the hills.

As I reached for the door handle, the lock suddenly buzzed. The handle turned slowly, deliberately, as if to prevent it from making noise, and the door inched open toward me. My heart leapt in my chest. No one from Anastasia should be in town yet. Maids usually knocked and announced themselves before they opened a door. Was this how the terrorists, or whoever those men were last night, got into our room? With a key?

CHAPTER 20

Quickly, quietly, I stepped into the darkened bathroom next to the entry and slipped my gun from my purse. The door creaked as it continued to open slowly. A man moved silently into the room, his footsteps cushioned by the carpet. Silhouetted against the slit of light at the window, I saw his tall, broad-shouldered form and the gun in his hand.

I hadn't heard the door close. Was the other man standing in the doorway, holding it open? Could I slip past him? Did I even dare try? Surprise made a powerful weapon. I said a quick prayer and eased around the bathroom door casing. The man inside the room, his back to me, headed for the pillows mounded on the bed, where I'd been stretched out sorting brochures.

The fingers of the second man were visible at my eye level, gripping the edge of the door. He had to be standing with his back against the door, half in and half out of the room, probably watching for hall traffic. Unless he was left-handed, he didn't have a gun ready. He did reek of aftershave lotion, the same overpowering and gag-producing aroma I'd smelled in Tucson. His weapon of choice? If this was the same man who'd tried to kill us to get the section of map, and I felt certain he was, he'd be twice as dangerous now that I'd injured him.

I visualized the space I'd have between the man and the doorframe, the number of steps it would take to clear the three feet in front of him, visualized every move I'd have to make to avoid being nabbed as I went by. Then, with my heart pounding and fighting raw terror in every fiber of my body, I darted around him.

His slow reaction time, probably because I'd startled him by bolting from the darkened room, allowed me to evade his grasp and almost reach the stairs before he followed in pursuit. I slid down the metal railing, hit the landing, and slid down the next portion to the third floor. If they took the elevator, they could reach the lobby before I did. I wouldn't go to the lobby.

With no car waiting, I'd have no possibility of escaping except on foot, and I was too obvious a target in my bright turquoise blouse. My yards of gauze skirt wouldn't help if I had to run for it. I needed a change of wardrobe immediately. Not to mention a change of venue.

The third-floor hall was empty in both directions. A plan had begun forming in my mind, but it required the help of maid service, which was noticeably absent. Planning on the men hitting the elevator, I scooped up the superfluous yards of my skirt in one arm and raced toward the end of the hall, praying for divine intervention, praying for help from some quarter, any quarter.

As I neared the end, the last door before the stairwell opened, and a maid backed from the room pulling a cleaning cart.

"Thank heaven I found you. I need your help. Can we go back in here and talk?"

The startled maid just stared at me.

I tried again in Spanish. This time she blinked her eyes and looked up and down the hall, as if looking for help, looking for someone to ask what she should do.

"I won't hurt you. Two men are after me, and I need your help to escape. Will you please go in there and listen to me?"

Hesitantly she pushed the cart back into the room, her big dark eyes wide with fear as she watched me close the door and lock it. Her beautiful complexion blanched white, and her slender hands quivered as she stuck them in her pockets.

"Do you speak English?" Knowing that when startled, some people don't immediately understand their second language, I thought maybe I'd frightened her, and she hadn't connected to what I'd said. I was right. She nodded but still didn't speak. Afraid she was too terrified to listen, I tried to put her at ease.

"I'm Allison Allan. What's your name?"

"Consuela, but I'm called Connie." She pulled her hands from her pockets and reached for a spray bottle of window cleaner.

"Where are you from, Connie?"

"California."

"So am I. I live just above Santa Barbara."

Success. She smiled and relaxed a bit. "I'm from San Diego. Actually, La Jolla."

"I know that area. There's a beautiful temple there."

Connie beamed. "Yes, I was married in that temple. It is most beautiful on the outside, but on the inside, too wonderful to describe."

"I'm a member of the Church, too, and hope to go there very soon. Connie, I'm hiding from two men who somehow obtained a key to my room. Last night they shredded my clothes, and today they came back. I need to disappear. I need different clothes, a way out of the hotel, and I have to rent a car. Can you help me?"

She looked thoughtful for a minute. "I brought some old clothes so I could help my sister clean her garage when I get off work this afternoon."

"Could I borrow them?" My hopes kited upward just a little.

"They are just old work clothes, but you are welcome to them. I have them in the linen closet." She put the spray bottle back on the cleaning cart and fished the keys from her pocket.

"Will you bring them here as quickly as you can, and watch for two men, one with strong, horrible-smelling aftershave. They're dangerous so try to avoid them." I stopped. Both times I'd encountered them, it had been dark. "I think they're Iraqi terrorists."

When the door closed, I checked the phone book and called the airport car rental agency on my cell phone. I told them who I was, and that we had already rented one car, but found we were going in separate directions and needed another. They had our driver's license numbers and credit card on file. Was there any way they could deliver a car to the Shilo Inn for me in the next fifteen minutes?

Bless helpful people and small towns. I couldn't imagine this would have been possible if I'd been in a hotel near LAX, or even near my home. They promised to deliver the car and the paperwork to the hotel in that time frame.

I didn't dare have them leave keys and paperwork at the desk. Someone there might have been bribed for keys to our rooms—unless electronic entry devices had been used to open the doors. That was always possible, but just in case, I couldn't afford to trust the desk personnel.

Connie returned with her work clothes: a pair of faded jeans and an old blue sweatshirt. My sandals would have to suffice for footwear, as our shoe size wasn't the same. While I changed, I asked her to intercept the car rental agent, bring the keys and paperwork to me, and make sure the front-desk people didn't see her do it. If the coast was clear, I'd follow, sign the paperwork, and be out of her hair immediately.

"Speaking of hair," she said, "I found this in the bottom of my bag. I bought several for my sister to use. She makes jeans quilts." It was a big red plaid square, a good old cowboy bandana like Clarence kept in his pocket. Perfect to cover my hair.

"Did you see the men?" I hoped they'd given up, searched our room for the maps, and weren't interested in me. Probably wishful thinking. After all, one of them could have a vendetta against me. I'd not only stabbed his thigh with the letter opener, I suspected I'd also broken his wrist with the marble Aztec calendar.

"I saw no one. I'll go first, open the service elevator, then you come." Connie took the cleaning cart and I watched her cover the length of the hall, stop at the elevator, then signal me to come. I raced to the elevator, ducked behind the cart as someone clattered up the stairs, and breathed again when the doors closed, sealing us inside.

I waited in the elevator with my finger on the hold button while Connie walked casually through the lobby. Within five minutes she returned, paperwork in hand. I signed it, and she retraced her steps to deliver it to the waiting rental agent. Then she reappeared with the keys.

"There is a group just checking in now, a whole busload, so the lobby is filled with people. This might be a good time to slip away. The car is parked right outside the door—a white sedan."

I hugged Connie and pressed a fifty-dollar bill into her hand in place of the keys I withdrew. "Thanks so much. You may have just saved my life. I'll remember you when we go to the San Diego Temple."

Before she could see what I'd given her and object, I hurried to the front door, one hand in my purse on my gun, the other holding the keys ready to open the lock before I reached it. You have to love electronic gadgets, especially at times like this.

As I cleared the glass entry, I smelled the odious aroma of the terrorist's aftershave. Without looking back, I quickly sidled between two women giving luggage instructions to a bellhop and slipped around the end of the car, unlocking the door with my electronic key.

As I started the car, out of the corner of my eye I saw a man leaning against the side of the building straighten, then take two steps toward me. I drove away. Fast. In the rearview mirror I saw him watching me, then he turned and entered the hotel.

Time to leave town.

I headed straight for the interstate. It would be two hours before Bart returned, but if I could get to Clarence's, I'd feel some measure of safety and could wait there for them. As I entered the freeway, I wondered what had changed the old man's mind about guarding his place. He'd seemed determined to stay put until the danger was over and he no longer felt threatened.

Speaking of threatened, the storm everyone foresaw now threatened to become a reality. I hadn't looked outside all morning, or I'd have seen the heavy clouds moving to obliterate the sun. Low and gray, they covered the mountains on all sides. Just what I needed, with bare toes sticking out of my sandals.

I watched the road behind me as I sped up the highway, making sure no one followed. I didn't need to lead those two to Clarence's isolated place, especially if I'd be there alone. Were they actually the two terrorists who had escaped Anastasia's net in Iraq? The one I'd glimpsed in the rearview mirror, the man who, thankfully, had botched our deaths in Tucson, looked the part. Or were they from the Idaho contingent of bin Laden's organization? Or local thugs not connected to the terrorists? Far too many bad guys to choose from.

I thought of calling Bart to tell him about the second break-in at the hotel, but I would have had to pull over and look up the number of his new cell phone. I figured I could be another ten miles down the road if I didn't, and he'd already said he wouldn't be back until three o'clock.

I pondered everything we'd encountered since Dad's phone call in New Orleans, trying to put the tiny clues we had in some logical order, trying to make sense out of what seemed to be a huge network of terrorist activities. But was it what it seemed?

Passing the sheep station, I noted its location off the highway and proximity to all the other strange things going on up here, and shuddered. What terrible things terrorists could do with a perfectly innocent setting and a legitimate enterprise. Or had they already?

As I flew past the Spencer exit, I thought fleetingly of stopping at the café for a bite to eat, but decided I could raid Clarence's cupboard. Even more than food, I craved the safety of that little clearing in the trees at the top of the hill.

Suddenly the cell phone in my purse rang, jangling my already rattled nerves.

Bart wasn't on the other end as I'd expected. Instead, Clarence's strained voice sent chills chasing up my arms and down my neck. "Mrs. Allan, we found 'em. Or they found us. We split up when they started shootin'. Bart headed for the high timber, but they got me. Can't reach Cody." He paused, as if to catch his breath. "Can you come to my place? Get the horse, follow the trail out of the clearing like you saw Cody do. I'm at the bottom of the hill."

"Who got you, Clarence? How bad are you hurt? I'm on my way to your place now, but I'll be another fifteen minutes, at least." I jammed the accelerator to the floor, disregarding the speed limit, hoping some highway patrolman would see me and I could take him along to help.

"I'll be here. Ain't goin' nowhere." His voice sounded far away.

"Clarence, is Bart okay?"

He didn't answer for a minute. Then, "Ain't sure. He was wearin' that horse right out climbin' that hill, but I didn't see him go down, so I think he made it." He fell silent, and I prayed with all my heart for Bart's safety.

"Miz Allan, I never told you 'bout Lewis and Clark. Need to do that." He took a raspy breath. "Sacagawea's brother, Chief Cameahwait, showed them a mine. Lode of gold a mile wide. Other stuff, too. Never put it in their journal. Didn't want anyone to know till they told Jefferson in person. Clark was killed for his map on the Natchez Trace . . . takin' it to Jefferson. Not suicide."

"Why are you telling me this now? Do you think it has something to do with what's going on up here?" I turned off the interstate onto the gravel road, kicking up a huge cloud of dust.

"Might be. Map was never recovered, but rumors been runnin' lately somebody had it and was trying to find the mine." Clarence coughed, a sound that scared me.

"Clarence, can't I drive to where you are?"

"No." He coughed again. "No road."

This time I drove up the winding lane between the quaking aspen as Clarence had—with the accelerator to the floor. I couldn't tell if the golden leaves on the trees really lacked luster or if my blurred vision caused the change. I swiped at the tears. *Please let me reach him in time.*

I hadn't seen or heard an ambulance. Surely he'd called 911.

"Clarence, did you call for an ambulance?"

No answer.

"Clarence, are you still with me? Talk to me, please."

CHAPTER 21

I slammed on the brakes, jumped from the car, and ran for the barn. The cold hit me about the time I reached the barn. It was freezing up here, and I had on bare-toed sandals. I was completely unprepared for this drastic change of climate and weather.

Then another thought hit me. I had reservations on a flight out of Idaho Falls at four o'clock. I had a baby to protect. What would riding a horse down a hill do to me? Or lifting an injured old man onto the horse? I'd have to think about that later. And Bart. When I'd taken care of Clarence, I could worry about Bart.

Extremely well-trained, the black and white pinto stood still as I bridled him, tossed on the blanket, then heaved on the saddle. It felt twice as heavy as the recreational saddles I'd used in New York's Central Park or in California. This was a real working saddle, like the ones I'd hoisted at Rancho Encantada in Santa Fe.

As I led the horse out of the stall, I saw Clarence's muck-cleaning clothes hanging on the wall by the door: a pair of filthy, manured-covered boots, leather gloves, and a tattered old sheepskin coat with hood that had certainly seen better days. But they looked heaven-sent to me. I stuck my feet, sandals and all, into the fleece-lined rubber boots. They'd work. The coat was definitely a blessing. My teeth were chattering already, and I'd only been up here five minutes.

Wrapping my purse around the saddle horn for easy access to both phone and gun, I pointed the horse toward the side of the clearing where Cody had followed the tracks into the trees. I pulled on one stiff leather glove, but stuffed the other one in my pocket. I couldn't use the phone or my gun with the bulky thing on.

"Clarence, I'm on my way. Can you hear me?" I said into the phone.

"I hear you. Where are you?" His voice was frighteningly weak.

"Just starting down the hill. I can see the motorcycle tracks. Will they lead me to you?"

No answer.

"Clarence, will the tracks lead me to you?"

"Yeah." It was more grunt than answer. I urged the horse a little faster, following the crushed grass. Cody's big, heavy motorcycle had left an easily followed trail. The pinto loped down the hill, following the tracks without guidance.

"Clarence, what's the pinto's name? He's one smart horse."

The phone remained silent for a minute, then Clarence's weak voice answered. "Old Toby. For the old Shoshone Indian who guided Lewis and Clark over the Bitterroots. Toby's my pride and joy."

"Toby, I hope you're as good a guide as that Shoshone," I said, leaning down to his ear. "I'm going to need all the help I can get."

We broke out of the trees into the sagebrush where the trail wasn't so easy to follow, but I gave Old Toby his head and watched the ground. He stuck to the motorcycle trail, and now and then I could see horse tracks alongside or atop the tire tracks.

"Clarence, we're down the hill. Where are you?"

"Stay on the trail. You'll run right into me." He coughed again. This time I could hear him just ahead as well as over the phone.

Old Toby leapt ahead with one nudge from my knee, and suddenly Clarence lay in front of us—in a pool of blood. Toby stopped inches from the old man and nuzzled him as I jumped off. I knelt and cradled Clarence in my arms. The ambulance would be too late—if, in fact, it was coming.

"I thought you were going to stay home and guard your place. What were you doing out with Bart?" I smoothed his gray hair away from his forehead.

"Couldn't do less than my sons." He coughed. "What they gave their life for is at risk. Got grandkids to think of. My boys' kids." He stopped. His breathing was ragged. "Country's been good to me. Time to give back." Clarence raised his hand, a finger pointing east at the mountain topped by a dark-green stand of trees, almost lost in the low-hanging clouds. "Up there."

His hand fell lifeless in his lap.

My tears mingled with the red stain across his shirt. "Clarence, you were a good man," I whispered in the ear that could no longer hear my words. "A rare breed."

The radio/phone in his hand beeped, and Bart spoke quietly. "Clarence, are you hanging in there?"

I took the small instrument, pressed the send button, and composed myself before I got out the words, "He didn't make it."

"Princess! What are you doing there?"

"I was on my way when he called. He couldn't reach Cody. He died in my arms, Bart." The tears began in earnest.

"Allison, listen to me. I can see your horse. Leave Clarence. Get on that horse and ride out of here." Bart whispered now, but the urgency in his voice was unmistakable.

"Where are you?"

"Don't talk. Listen. You're a sitting duck there. I can see you in my binoculars. They're all around. You've got to get out of here before they spot you."

A shot echoed across the valley. "Ugh!" Nothing more. Only the gasp of pain. Then Bart whispered, "Get out. Protect our baby. Go."

"Bart, what happened?" He didn't have to tell me. My husband had just been shot. Then I heard shouting, other voices over the phone. Bart still held the speaker button down. I couldn't talk to him, but I could hear everything being said around him. My heart sank. He'd not only been shot, he'd been captured.

The phone beeped off. The only sound in all the cold, gray world around me was the icy wind whistling down from that mountain. I didn't dare try to contact Bart. If they hadn't seen me yet, and didn't know I was here, I might have a chance to find him. If I pressed my speaker button, his phone would beep. I'd have to take a chance on tracking him without contacting him.

I gently slipped out from under Clarence's body, covered his face with his big cowboy hat, and picked up the binoculars he'd been using. I'd come back later for his body. He didn't need help anymore. Bart did. Old Toby hadn't moved since I'd jumped from the saddle, but he now seemed anxious to go. Did the smell of death have him pawing the ground, or was he psychic and ready for the hunt?

I mounted, then turned Toby toward the mountain and urged him to hurry. I couldn't let Bart die, too. Maybe if I'd gotten to Clarence sooner . . . No. That chest wound would have finished him even if the EMTs had made it right after he'd taken the bullet.

Toby galloped through the sagebrush, weaving around three- and four-foot-high bushes. When the sagebrush gave way to golden grass, he really opened up, but a rocky lava flow across our path stopped us. As he picked his way carefully around the huge black rocks, two voices hammered at each other in my head.

"Go home. Save the baby. Save yourself. What would Bart do if you died?"

"You can't go home. Bart needs you."

I shut both of them out of my mind and concentrated on one very fervent prayer.

Father, I'm in over my head. Please help me. And please protect Bart. I pray his wound is superficial, and I'll get to him before . . ."

I couldn't finish. I couldn't comprehend life without Bart. It simply wouldn't be worth living. If I didn't do everything in my power to find and save my husband, I couldn't live with myself even if the baby and I did survive.

Why does life have to be so hard? Haven't I been doing everything I could? Everything You asked? Please don't take Bart from me. And please, please, don't take this baby.

There was no decision to make. I had to help Bart, whatever the consequences. I let Toby find his way to the top of the mountain while I squeezed my eyes closed to hold back tears and shut my heart to the pain stabbing through me. We'd accomplished it once. Maybe we could work another miracle. Maybe. If either of us lived. But the dream haunted me.

I shook off the melancholy. I needed a plan. And I needed to stay out of sight of Bart's captors. I urged Toby toward the trees. I could call Gary Dodson to send someone for Clarence if I still had his number in my purse. Maybe Cody would get home and get Clarence's message. Did I trust Cody? Something about him bothered me, something secretive, mysterious.

I checked the battery in the radio/phone. Bart must have charged them last night. It still had a full charge. I tucked it in the pocket of my jeans. If I ended up off Toby for some reason, I had to make sure I had it with me. Then I checked the old one. Nearly out of charge. Bart hadn't planned on using it. Who could plan for something like this?

If I called for help, would the state police come in quietly, or with sirens and lights blaring? That would make matters worse; Bart's captors might kill him before we could get to him. Who were they? Terrorists? Rustlers? Or both?

Finding and connecting seemingly unrelated bits of information and solving puzzles was my forte. I hated the physical side of this work; I'd certainly never intended to take on a gang of cattle thieves or group of terrorists by myself. My blood suddenly chilled colder than the frigid wind whipping the trees I now entered.

Osama bin Laden.

Even with the heavy sheepskin coat buttoned snugly around me, I shuddered. And as if that most horrid of thoughts wasn't enough, snowflakes mixed with golden leaves blowing from the trees swirled through the air.

Could anything else happen? I suddenly felt like Job. *No. I'm sorry I said that. I know things could get worse, Father. I don't know how, but please don't throw them at me right now. I'm totally overwhelmed as it is.*

I stopped Toby and turned to look down the mountain. Where would Bart have been, that he could have seen me from up here? Through the slender white-barked trunks of the aspen, I could see the broad floor of the valley below, could see where I imagined Clarence would be. What happened to his horse?

If Bart had been just inside the tree line, where had the men come from who shot him? How had they sneaked up on him? Had he been too concerned about me and not careful enough about his own safety? That was exactly what I'd always feared would happen when we worked together. What he feared, too. If I hadn't come here, would he have eluded his captors? Not been shot?

I dismounted and examined the ground for some sign of struggle, for anything that would tell me someone had been here, for tracks to follow. Unfortunately, I wasn't a tracker. I led Toby farther into the trees, checking behind me to see how far I could go and still see the point in the valley where I'd been when Bart saw Toby. Had he been higher, above the aspen in the fir trees?

My only clue to his location on this entire mountain was that he could see me from somewhere up here. He could have been anywhere. I felt so hopeless I wanted to sit down and cry. But that wouldn't help Bart. What if he was bleeding to death on this stupid mountain? What if they hadn't taken him captive, but simply left him to die?

Father, Bart needs Thy help. Please protect him. Help me know what to do, and guide me to him. Please.

I re-mounted Toby and headed up the mountain, zigzagging back and forth in a wide path through the fir trees, hoping to see something that would tell me I was in the right area. Every two minutes I picked up the radio/phone, wanting to beep Bart, then put it back in my pocket again. I had to assume he was alive. I had to assume he'd been taken captive, or he would have called me. I had to assume I'd be led to him. A lot of assumptions. All I had. That—and faith that my prayers would be heard.

Gray clouds nestled in the tops of the Douglas fir. The higher up we went, the less visibility. I could no longer see the valley floor. The wind stopped and snowflakes fell thick and fluffy, lighting on my eyelashes, covering Toby's black mane in a blanket of white.

Clarence hadn't had a coat on. Bart wouldn't have one either, unless he'd worn his light jacket. He'd freeze in this weather. *Please help me find him before it's too late.*

As I prepared to make the turn and zig back, I saw an outcropping of rocks just ahead. I urged Toby toward them and dismounted.

This was it. This was where Bart had been when he'd contacted me on the radio. My heart lurched when I saw the dark stain on the rocks. Blood. Bart's precious blood. But he wasn't here, nor was his horse.

Two possibilities. I forced myself to face them. Either they'd killed him on the spot and taken him down from the mountain on his horse to dispose of the body somewhere else, or he was still alive and they'd taken him with them. Rustlers might just shoot him and dispose of the body. Would they keep a witness alive? The absence of a copious amount of blood buoyed my hopes.

Terrorists would want to know who he was, what he knew, who else knew. Then, when he'd answered their questions, and they had no more use for him . . .

I banished the thought and scoured the ground beyond the rocks for the direction in which they'd gone. Snow outlined the tracks of several horses headed down the north slope of the mountain, filling the indentations in the soft earth with a coating of solid white. But as soon as we started down the slope, I lost the trail. Heavy snowflakes coated everything. Soon it would be a whiteout, and I wouldn't be able to tell one direction from another. I gave Toby his head again, hoping some inner radar would enable him to follow where other horses had been minutes before.

Was it only minutes? I didn't have a watch, but it couldn't have been more than half an hour since Clarence pointed up the mountain and Bart called me. Since the shot rang out. Since I'd last heard from my husband.

With a prayer repeating over and over in my heart and my eyes on the ground, watching for any sign of the men and horses, I hadn't noticed that we'd come halfway down the mountain until Toby stopped. I looked up. We were out of the low clouds, the heavy snowflakes had abated, replaced by a gentle sifting of granular flakes, and I could see the valley, though I wouldn't be able to much longer. The gloom of heavy clouds brought an early twilight.

I shuddered to think how stupid and unobservant I'd been. I could have walked right into the waiting arms of the bad guys and never even seen them. I looked through Clarence's binoculars, scanning the area as far as I could see. No horses, no riders, no Bart.

Why had Toby stopped? I turned. Nothing behind me. Nothing moved on either side.

"Okay, boy. If you're trying to tell me something, I'm not getting the message. Pardon me for not speaking the language, but I haven't had much training in horse talk. Try again." I kneed him gently, to see if he really was determined to stop or if he'd just decided he wanted more direction and less freedom of choice. He ignored me.

"Toby, what am I supposed to see here?" I raised the glasses and did another scan from horizon to horizon. This time, I noticed a shadow at the foot of the mountain on the right. A small canyon. Toby gave a soft nicker.

"Is that what you're trying to tell me? Why didn't you just take me there?"

I laid the reins on his neck, and Toby obediently turned right, leaving the first invisible trail he'd chosen for another I couldn't see either. This time, I didn't bother to watch for tracks. I kept my head up, scanning with the binoculars frequently to make sure I was really alone out here in the wilds of Idaho.

Suddenly a shot rang out. Toby tossed his head and stopped.

CHAPTER 22

I couldn't remember a single thing from my training that covered a situation like this—nothing even remotely resembling these circumstances.

Okay, Father, what do I do now? Ride in like a posse to the rescue, or sneak up and catch them unaware? Some guidance here, please. I'm a babe in the woods and haven't a clue what I should do.

I had a long way to go before I could do any sneaking if the shot came from that little canyon, so I urged Toby forward. He responded immediately and loped through the silver sage, now dusted with a light layer of snow. As we neared the entrance to the canyon, I slowed him to a walk. Sounds carried a long distance in this clear mountain air, and I didn't need to announce our arrival.

Suddenly another shot rang out. Toby's ears pricked forward. I stopped him. Without the creaking of the leather saddle and the thudding of hooves, I could hear a faint cry. A woman's voice, calling for help.

I trained the binoculars on the opening. Perched atop a small rise halfway back up the canyon, a modest house nestled in a semicircle of slender trees, which appeared to be defending the dwelling against the wind that undoubtedly blew straight down the draw. A barn, shed, and some corrals spread below it. Someone lay in the dirt in the yard. No other human was visible in any direction. "Okay, Toby. Guess we'll ride in like the posse to the rescue. Go, boy." The horse leapt forward, and in scant minutes we entered the mouth of the box canyon.

An old woman lay on the ground between the barn and the house, a rifle in her hand, waving at me as we rode in. "Help me," she cried. "I can't get up." I jumped from the horse and knelt beside the woman. I could see that she was bone-thin, even with her baggy jeans and heavy parka.

"What're you doing on Clarence's horse?" she demanded before I could say a word.

"Riding to your rescue. What happened?"

"I was chasing that blasted wolverine away from my henhouse. Keeps digging underneath and killing my chickens. Killed my dog last week. No-good animal kills for the fun of it, and I thought he was going after me for a minute. Who're you?"

"Allison Allan. How can I help you?" The woman, probably in her late seventies, looked like she could handle a wolverine, fierce as it might be. Her ice-blue eyes, clear and unblinking, could undoubtedly even stare down a cat. A very big cat.

"Get me up off this blasted ground. I'm freezing to death. Twisted my leg when I went after that striped devil. Heard something snap. Probably broke it. Just my luck."

I'd guessed right about the wind blowing down the canyon. It whistled and whined through the trees, bringing snow flurries with it, thick and heavy like the ones at the top of the mountain. The poor woman *must* be freezing. I felt her leg through her jeans. It was warm, hard, and swollen. I put my hand underneath to feel the calf. Her pant leg was wet and sticky. I had blood on my hand when I pulled it away.

"You did more than just break it. I think you have a compound fracture. I'll have to stabilize it before I can move you." I stood and looked around for a small board. Snow covered everything right before my eyes.

"Never mind that. Go to those double doors in the side of the hill under the house. Got a Ski-Doo with a trailer. Bring it down here, and we can get me up to the house on that. You didn't tell me how you come to be riding Clarence's prize cow pony."

"Let me get you inside first." I ran up the dirt driveway that led to a basement carved out of the hillside and threw open wooden doors that had once been painted white. Neatly lined up facing the doors, barely visible in the twilight, were three snow machines, one with a five-foot-long sled-like trailer connected to it. The keys were in the ignition, and it started immediately.

I pulled the sled alongside the woman, who by now was nearly covered with snow. This would be painful for her, even though the sled was less than six inches high. "Let me wrap your leg first, so we won't damage it any more when we move it."

"Just get me off this ground. I'll be a blasted snowman if you don't hurry."

"What's your name? I can't just call you 'hey you.'" I wanted to call her a lot of things: stubborn, ornery, and brave. But I didn't.

"Hildegard Piggett. My friends call me Hildy. I'll let you know what you can call me once you get me in the house."

"Yes, ma'am." I considered a punch to the jaw to knock her out while I moved her, but decided she might just pass out from the pain, so I didn't bother. This would hurt her more than I cared to think. I took Clarence's thick sheepskin jacket off and slipped it under both her legs, then wrapped it around and buttoned it so neither leg would move, and hopefully there wouldn't be any tearing of the flesh.

"Now help me sit up, give me a minute to get my strength and grit my teeth, then lift my fanny onto the sled."

With my hands under her arms, I lifted her to a sitting position, waited for the signal, then slipped my arms around her chest and shifted her onto the conveyance. I think the coat weighed more than she did. I could probably have carried her in my arms. Maybe.

I gave her a minute to recover from that wave of pain, then swivelled her legs around onto the sled. She lay back, beads of perspiration covering her face, her arthritic knuckles white from gripping the sides of the sled. Afraid she'd go into shock, I drove the Ski-Doo up the wide path outlined with rocks to the front door, where I unhooked the sled and pulled it up the two wooden steps, then across the narrow wooden porch into the house.

The little wood-burning stove in the corner barely heated the tiny living room. Hildegard Piggett wasn't giving orders at the moment, so I opened the stove's glass door and tossed in a couple of split logs from the stack nearby. When I flipped the light switch, a single bare bulb lit the meager furnishings in the small room. Then I faced the formidable task of getting this woman settled until the ambulance arrived.

"Leave me be and get out there and take care of Old Toby," Mrs. Piggett directed. "Put him in the barn with my horses. There's an empty stall. Rub him down good and put a dry blanket on him. It's going to be a dang cold night. I didn't get my livestock fed, so while you're out there, take care of that, too. Be sure you close the barn door tight. This storm's going to be a bad one."

"Mrs. Piggett, I can't stay," I said evenly. "I'll get you comfortable and call the ambulance, but I've got to find my husband." I did need to take care of Toby, at least tie him to the corral while I helped this cantankerous old woman. I didn't need a wolf or coyote spooking him and scaring him off into the night.

"No phone out here, and an ambulance won't make it before we're snowed in. So forget it. It's just you and me. You aren't going anywhere, especially on a horse. Hear that?"

I listened to the wind, no longer just whistling through the trees, but working up to tempest proportions. I didn't stop to argue. Grabbing a pillow from the sofa, I carefully removed the coat and eased the pillow under her legs to raise them higher than her head. The bleeding had stopped. *Thank you, Father, for that blessing. Please help me remember how to do whatever I need to do for her.*

Covering her with a wool afghan from the sofa, I inched the sled closer to the stove so she'd stay warm, then I donned the heavy coat again and ran out the door. I could call the ambulance on Bart's old cell phone, leaving our radio/phones free in case Bart could get through. My heart ached at the delay. I didn't have a prayer of finding him in the dark. In the snow. But if I could get back to Clarence's . . . Clarence! I couldn't leave him lying out in the storm.

"Storm" was a misnomer. It was a full-blown blizzard. Snow fell so thick and fast that I could barely find the path we'd taken to the house only minutes before.

"Toby, where are you?" I hoped I was heading in the right direction. "Toby!" The horse snorted and found me. I followed the corral to the barn. It would be totally dark when I finished. I hoped I could find my way back to the house. I struggled to open the door in the wind, got Toby inside, then fought to close it behind us, leaving us in the pitch-black barn.

I fumbled for my purse, still secured to the saddle horn, found my little penlight, and explored the barn, putting Toby in the empty stall. Mrs. Piggett was right on all counts. I did have to brush Toby down. He was wet, and so was the saddle. While my hands were busy with the necessary tasks, my mind stayed busy with what-ifs. What if I couldn't find Bart? What if they'd discovered his phone and thrown it away? What if we were snowed in for days? What if Anastasia couldn't get here to help? The list went on and on, questions buzzing around in my head until I finished my chores and had to concentrate on getting back to the ranch house.

I followed the corral fence, then stumbled across the rocks lining the path to the house. They led me to the Ski-Doo parked across the front steps. I thought about putting it back in the storage cellar, then decided Mrs. Piggett had first priority.

The fire blazing cheerfully in the small wood-burning stove warmed the living room considerably. I shed the sheepskin coat and the manure-covered boots, then tossed in another couple of logs while Mrs. Piggett silently watched my every move. Her silence didn't bode well. I knew she'd be in a world of hurt, but she must also be in shock.

"Let me wash my hands and see what I can do for your leg." I headed into the back of the house to find a sink, mentally reviewing the extensive first-aid course I'd completed at Quantico last December. I had to be sure I did everything possible, since she'd be without any other medical help for a dangerously long time.

Suddenly the small radio/phone in my pocket beeped. I grabbed it, my heart pounding.

"Princess, where are you?" Beep. Bart waited for my answer.

I pressed my send button. "Are you okay? I'm at Hildegard Piggett's ranch."

"You missed your flight." At that simple statement, relief flooded through me from head to toe. My husband's calm voice sounded wonderful to my worried ears.

"There'll be another flight. Where are you?"

"I'm not sure. They blindfolded me. I managed to hide the phone under my belt. Thanks for not beeping me. I was sure you'd listen and figure out what was going on. I'll try to find out where I am and who these people are. They didn't let me hear or see anything until we got here. We've bedded down for the night in some sort of tunnel or cave in the mountain, but it's well-stocked and warm. By the way, I found the small bike in here. These people set the fires, not Claudia. They let me come to the john by the entrance. That's the only place the phone works. Looks like a storm outside."

"Storm is an understatement. Are you hurt? Were you shot?"

"Grazed. Turn off your phone for the night. Save the batteries. Turn it on in the morning, but don't call me. I'll contact you when I can. Get Anastasia working on this, and you get back to California. Take care of our baby. I love you, Princess."

The radio/phone beeped. Gone. Our conversation had lasted less than a minute.

I stood in the center of the dark kitchen, clutching the phone, loath to turn it off, yearning to talk through the night, to remain connected through this tiny miracle of modern technology.

Suddenly the phone feature of the device in my hand rang. I jumped, startled by the unexpected noise, the unexpected call. Who had this number? Only Clarence, as far as I knew. I punched the send/receive button and put the phone to my ear, speaking tentatively into the mouthpiece. "Hello?" I was almost afraid to know who was on the other end.

"Is this Mrs. Allan?"

"Yes." I'd heard that voice before. "Cody?"

His voice, icy as the wind that blew outside, didn't simply ask. It demanded. "What happened to Clarence?"

I squeezed my eyes to keep the tears from starting. The thought of the poor old man lying alone in the snow was more than I could handle right now. "Oh, Cody, he's dead."

"I know that. I also know Toby is missing. I know you were the last to see Clarence alive." He paused. "Did you kill him?"

CHAPTER 23

I couldn't utter a word. He'd literally knocked the wind and the words right out of me. Had Cody actually accused me of murder? Did he also think I'd stolen Clarence's prize pinto? In horse country, that was akin to stealing a man's wife, which ranked next to murder. I sank to the floor in a crumpled heap. He must think I was some kind of wacko.

Father, I said I was sorry about saying that things couldn't get much worse, remember? Please help me convince this man I'm innocent. How can I help Bart if I'm in jail?

Then I pictured Clarence, and the tears started all over again.

Cody's hostile voice intruded on my grief. "You have nothing to say before I turn you in to the police?"

"Actually, I have a lot to say, but I'm having a hard time talking about it because every time I think of that dear old man, I start to cry. Yes, I was the last person to see him. He died in my arms, Cody." I had to stop, control my emotions before I could finish. "Clarence called me when he couldn't get hold of you. He told me to get the horse from the barn and come and find him. He led me to him on my cell phone. I barely made it before he died. I did not kill him, and I did not steal Toby."

"If you didn't kill him, why did you leave him lying in the sagebrush?" Doubt and disbelief filled Cody's frigid voice.

"I was on the phone to Bart, telling him Clarence had died, when I heard my husband get shot. Clarence and Bart had gone into the valley behind Clarence's house—where you followed the motorbike. Someone shot at them. They got Clarence in the chest, then shot my husband and took him captive. I couldn't do any more for Clarence except mourn him, so I went searching for my husband, hoping to find him before he bled to death, too."

Cody didn't reply for a minute. "Where are you now?"

"At Hildegard Piggett's ranch. Cody, she fell and broke her leg, a compound fracture. I need to get her to a hospital, but I don't have any idea where the road is. She said the ambulance wouldn't be able to get in until after the storm, but I think she's in shock."

"Do you know what to do?" This time his tone was less hostile.

"I've got her wrapped in an afghan near the stove with her feet elevated. Her leg isn't bleeding anymore; in fact, there wasn't a lot of blood to begin with. Just a small amount on her jeans. I haven't disturbed it to look at it. I thought if it had coagulated and stuck to her jeans I'd better just leave it alone. I was about to put some ice on it to keep the swelling down."

"How did it happen?"

"She was chasing a wolverine that attacked her animals, and she fell. I heard her shots, saw her lying in the yard through the binoculars, and rode in to see what happened."

There was a deep silence on the other end of the cell phone.

"Cody, you do believe me, don't you? I didn't kill Clarence."

"Who are you? Why are you here?" The cold, caustic tone returned.

I felt certain Bart had secured our new phones, but felt just as sure that the one Cody called from wasn't secure. Anyone with the necessary equipment could listen to our exchange. If these were terrorists, and if they were as organized in Idaho as in other parts of the world, they'd have the equipment. "I need to ask you a question first," I said. "Where are you calling from?"

"Why?"

"Someone bugged Clarence's phone. I don't like my conversations overheard. Where are you calling from?" It was my turn to press for answers.

He didn't reply for a minute. "I'm at Clarence's house." He paused. "How did you find out about the bug?"

"Did you put it there, Cody? Were you spying on Clarence?" The tables were turned. He was on the hot seat now instead of me. I liked it much better this way.

"I just wanted to know how you knew it was there. How you came to find it. Why you even suspected anyone would do such a thing to Clarence."

"When we went home with him and found the fire, he was afraid whoever torched the shed would come back and burn the house, or harm him. He asked us to check his place for anything suspicious. We found that."

Cody was quiet again. Had he put the bug in Clarence's phone? The way he'd phrased the question led me to believe that he knew it was there. I found it easy to suspect a man who obviously carried a burdensome secret.

Since Cody hadn't replied, I proceeded. "How did you know Clarence was lying in the sagebrush?"

"He'd left a message on my answering machine. I came immediately, found a rental car in the driveway with your name on the receipt, and saw that the house and barn were empty. Then Bess came back to the barn with blood on her saddle, minus a rider. As I rode her down the hill, I saw you mount Toby and ride off like someone was after you. When I found Clarence, I figured you'd shot him and taken his horse."

"You didn't leave him there, did you?"

"Allison Allan, what are you doing in my kitchen? I need some help here." Mrs. Piggett had revived.

"No. I brought him home." Cody sounded indignant at my question.

"Thank you for that. Mrs. Piggett is calling me. Will you notify somebody to come and get her to the hospital as soon as possible? How long will this storm last?"

"I'll call. They'll have to helicopter her out. My guess is a day or two. Have you—"

"I can't talk anymore, Cody. I've got to save the batteries on my phone, and I need to see to Mrs. Piggett." I disconnected, got up off the cold kitchen floor, stuffed the phone back in my pocket, and hurried to check on Hildegard.

"Who ya talking to in there?" she demanded.

"Cody. Do you know him?"

"Everybody knows everybody in these hills. Don't neighbor much, but we depend on each other. What's Cody want?"

I suddenly felt dizzy. I sat on the floor next to Mrs. Piggett and put my head on my knees.

"What's the matter?"

"I just realized I haven't had anything to eat all day. I'm a little light-headed."

"Then get your body back in the kitchen and get something from the icebox. Can't have you passin' out on me. The shape I'm in, I need your help. How about heating some of that leftover soup? Bring me a cupful, too."

First-aid protocol specified not giving the patient anything to eat or drink, but since treatment wasn't imminent, some hot soup would probably be just the ticket. It would certainly hit the spot for me. I busied myself heating the soup, slicing some fresh homemade bread I found on the cabinet, and pouring glasses of milk for both of us.

When I returned to the living room, Mrs. Piggett had peeled the afghan down to her waist and was trying to wriggle out of the parka. "I'm too hot. Get me out of this coat," she demanded. Did this woman ever say please? Did she ever do anything but give orders in that harsh, curt voice?

"How about if I just scoot you away from the fire?" I suggested. "I don't want you to move any more than you have to. You might start bleeding again, or dislodge a piece of bone that could move around, causing major problems."

After pulling the sled back to the far corner of the room, I spoon-fed her some soup, then devoured mine. It tasted like a gourmet meal.

Hildegard watched me. "Why didn't you eat today?"

"I got busy and forgot, I guess."

She looked like she didn't believe me. "What did Cody want?"

Should I tell her? She'd find out as soon as she talked to anyone. "Clarence is dead." I couldn't even say the words without clouding up and crying.

Hildegard looked at me sharply. "You never did tell me what you was doin' on Toby."

What was with this woman? Didn't she have a heart or a sympathetic bone in her skinny body? She was so cold that ice wouldn't melt in her mouth. I sighed. "My husband and I were with Clarence yesterday when someone torched his shed. They started tracking the arsonist this morning, and someone shot Clarence. He called me, asked me to get Toby and find him. He died in my arms. They also shot my husband and took him captive. I was trailing them when I ran across you. Cody found Clarence, thought I'd killed him and stolen Toby, and was giving me an opportunity to defend myself before he called the sheriff and turned me in."

"Rustlers."

"Excuse me?"

"Rustlers. Responsible for all the strange noises up in these mountains, and the missing cattle, too. I suspect the slaughtered sheep are just a decoy to throw folks off their track."

"You really think there are rustlers in this modern day?" If both Clarence and Hildegard believed it, there must be something to the theory.

"Modern day, modern methods. They're using planes or helicopters, airlifting them out. They're sure not trucking them out." Hildegard's voice held no trace of doubt.

"My husband said they'd found tire tracks from a huge airplane, and lots of horse and cattle tracks," I said. "Do you really believe that's the cause of all the other weird goings-on up here?"

"What have you heard?" I swear this woman didn't know how to ask a civil question. Everything came out as a demand or an order.

I suddenly remembered one story I'd heard the two men tell in the café yesterday that I'd forgotten to ask Clarence about. Now I'd never have the chance. Maybe Hildegard had seen or heard of it.

"There have been sightings of a spotted animal, like a cheetah or jaguar. Do you suppose there's a mountain lion, or even a wolf or coyote with strange markings that they're confusing with a big cat?"

"They been smokin' something. Or it was a mountain lion they saw in the trees, and took the shadows for markings. What else you heard?"

I watched Hildegard's reaction while I recounted the entire list: ground vibrations, strange lights, strange noises, arson on many ranches and farms, the animal problems. Bingo. Mrs. Hildegard Piggett didn't like something in that list, or she knew something. But what?

She didn't say anything. Just closed her eyes and pursed her thin little lips into an even thinner line until they almost disappeared.

"What do you know about this, Mrs. Piggett? Do you think it's caused by the rustlers, either while they're doing their thing or as a cover-up? Or is someone else behind all the unusual things going on up here?"

"I got some painkillers in the medicine chest in the bathroom. Bring me the bottle."

More orders. Was she doing it to gain a reprieve from my questions? To evade giving answers? I carried our empty dishes to the kitchen. There were three doors beyond the kitchen; they opened into two small bedrooms and a bathroom. I found the painkillers, and as I started back with the bottle, I noticed a state-of-the-art computer in one of the bedrooms.

She wanted three tablets. As I held up her head, waiting as she took them one at a time, I asked, "What do you use your computer for? Genealogy?"

Hildegard took the last of her pills and handed me the glass. "Not mine. Belongs to my daughter."

That surprised me. I hadn't seen a picture in the entire house. Didn't people usually have pictures of family around? "Does your daughter live with you?"

"No. Uses this as a business office. Says she can write it off on her taxes and save some money. I've put the place in her name, and she comes here to do her books."

"What kind of books? Is she an accountant?" Why would anyone come clear out here to do books? How could she possibly save money with the price of gas so high? The line from *Alice in Wonderland* flitted through my mind. Curiouser and curiouser.

"She keeps books for several companies. She's a whiz with numbers. No social butterfly; don't think she ever had a date in her life. But she can make that computer hum when she's working. Her fingers just fly across the keys. She's a plain Jane. Nobody wanted her for her looks, but everybody wants her for her brains."

That long speech seemed to tire Hildegard. She closed her eyes and lay quiet. I went into the kitchen, washed the dishes, and left them in the drainer. Maybe when she was sleeping, I'd take a peek at the computer. I'd be interested in what kind of books the daughter kept that needed to be hidden away in the mountains.

The wind buffeted the window above the sink until I thought it would break the glass. I put my hand to the pane to test for stability. Suddenly, something reached up to meet my hand through the blur of white outside.

A face appeared at the window.

CHAPTER 24

I stared out into the huge, glowing eyes of a cat—definitely larger than a domestic cat. I removed my hand. It removed its paw. I put my hand back on the window. The paw came back to match exactly where I'd placed my hand. I moved my hand higher. The paw moved up. I moved my face closer to the window to get a better look. The cat moved its face to the window, pressing its nose against the glass.

This was no wild cat. And it would freeze if I left it outside on a night like this. I hurried to the door and opened it. The animal leaped inside and shook itself like a dog. Snow flew everywhere.

When are you going to stop being so impetuous and start thinking before you act, you impulsive moron? This was no domestic cat. It had to be the wild animal—the spotted cat—Clarence and his friend had talked about. I backed away, reaching along the counter for the bread knife in the drainer.

The graceful cat, sleek and lean with a body about three feet long, advanced toward me, watching me with those wonderful immense eyes. I touched the drainer behind me on the counter, felt for the knife handle, never taking my eyes from the cat. Tawny-colored, with dark spots and the tiger-striped face of a kitty, its rounded ears were in perfect proportion to its delicately shaped head. Its tail, about fifteen inches long, whipped back and forth as the cat moved slowly, almost curiously, toward me.

Wild animals smell blood. I had to protect Hildegard before the cat attacked her. Oh, why had I opened that door?

Suddenly the cat stopped, sat on the worn, braided rug in the middle of the kitchen floor, and began to clean itself with its long, pink tongue. I stared, not believing what I saw. Then I noticed a slender silver band around its neck. The cat had on a collar.

"What're you doing, opening the door on a night like this? What's going on in there?" Mrs. Piggett hollered from the living room.

"A cat was out in the storm. I let it in." I wasn't sure I wanted to tell her exactly what kind of cat I'd let in. I studied the animal as it deliberately ignored me. Too small to be a jaguar or cheetah, too delicate. Not a bobcat or a mountain lion.

Then it hit me. This was an ocelot! I'd seen one in California at the Exotic Feline Breeding Compound in Rosamond, in the Antelope Valley. Peaches, the ocelot, had been their mascot, their show and tell—actually their pride and joy, I thought. The cat had been raised on a yacht, potty-trained to use the toilet, and was a gentle, loving animal who enjoyed being petted and pampered. She also loved to suck on fingers. She was often taken to schools to educate children about exotic cats and their threatened extinction. When raised as such from young kittens, I'd learned, ocelots made excellent pets.

Apparently, this was someone's pet. It certainly hadn't threatened me, and it had exhibited the mannerisms of a well-trained feline at the window. I opened the fridge, figuring the vegetable beef soup that had satisfied me might do the same for the cat. A well-fed animal should be a happy animal, and I definitely wanted to keep this one happy.

I set the whole bowl on the floor in front of her and backed away. She looked at me with those exquisite eyes, sniffed the soup, then went back to the meticulous job of cleaning. I left her to her bath, wrapped some ice cubes in a towel, and went to the living room to apply them to Hildegard's leg.

"Where's the cat?" Mrs. Piggett demanded.

"Having a bath. I hope you don't mind, but I gave her the soup. I thought she might be hungry." Then a surprising thought hit me. "You don't happen to have a cat, do you?" It didn't seem logical that the beautiful, exotic animal in the other room could belong to this cantankerous old woman, who didn't seem to own one beautiful thing in the world. I honestly hadn't seen anything of beauty here, except the setting for her home and the horses in her barn.

"Can't keep 'em around," she grumped. "If the coyotes don't get 'em, the wolves do. Bring it in and let me take a look at it."

"I think she'll come when she's ready. Tell me about yourself, Mrs. Piggett. Have you lived here all your life?" I positioned the wooden rocking chair where Mrs. Piggett could see me without moving, and settled into the narrow, worn, cushionless seat.

"Darn near. Fifty years of it, at least."

"What about your family?"

"Husband left when the kids were in high school. Janet and George wanted to go with him, but he took off without 'em. George found him after graduation and lives with him now. Janet stuck around. Guess nobody'd have her. She kept to herself, her books, her computer. Smart girl."

That fit the pattern for questions forming in the back of my mind. "How often does she come out here?"

"Every weekend. Drives out on Friday after work and goes back Monday morning. Spends most of her time in there on the computer. Brings groceries and whatever I need from town."

"How do you contact her without a phone?"

Hildegard gave me a withering look. "E-mail." She might as well have called me a blithering idiot. It was no wonder her family had deserted her. Who could live with the constant rudeness from this cold, churlish old woman? Then I had another thought. Maybe their desertion had spawned her bitterness. Had her resentment and disappointment molded her into what she had become?

"Would you like me to e-mail her now and tell her what's happened? Cody said they'd send a helicopter for you as soon as anything could get in the air, but it probably wouldn't be for at least a day or two."

"No. No need to have her worrying, if that's what she'd do. When they get here is soon enough to let her know. She can meet us at the hospital. Where's the cat? I want to see what you've let into my house." Hildegard seemed uneasy. Why didn't she want her daughter to know? Because a stranger was in the house? I had to get to that computer.

Or was it as simple as she said? She just didn't want her daughter to worry. There was, indeed, reason to worry. I'd have to watch the leg carefully. In fact, I should probably cut the jeans away and examine it—not that I could do anything if something were drastically wrong, or get anyone here to take care of her. Talk about feeling inadequate!

The cat, whom I decided to call Peaches, strolled through the door at that moment. She paused, examined the room, and ambled directly to me. She stopped, eyed my lap, and jumped up on it, curling up in a big ball.

Hildegard's eyes grew immense. She opened her mouth, but no sound came out. Her hand went to her throat and I thought she was going to scream, but she didn't.

"Mrs. Piggett, meet Peaches, the ocelot. Well, I don't really know what her name is, and I don't really know if she's actually a she—all cats are 'she' to me, and all dogs are 'he'—but she's obviously someone's pet. This must be the 'wild' animal that's been spotted up here."

I rubbed the cat's head and under its chin, a touch all felines appreciated, from the smallest kitten to the biggest cat.

"Get it out of here." Fear tinged the command in Hildegard's voice. "It's a wild animal. It'll kill us."

"I don't think so. I named her Peaches after an ocelot I met in California." I told her about how the "goodwill ambassador" of the Exotic Feline Breeding Compound toured schools, shopping malls, everywhere they could get the word out about the endangered species of cats and what was being done about it at their facility and all over the world to protect them from extinction.

As I stroked the cat's incredible soft coat, I touched the silver chain and found hidden in the silky fur of her throat a metal plate with a phone number. And some disconnected letters: E Da Hah.

"E Da Hah. Any idea what that means?" I asked my dour hostess.

"Shoshone word. That's where the name Idaho came from. Describes the light forming sort of a crown on the tops of mountains at sunrise."

"Well, E Da Hah, I guess Peaches gets to keep her own name. And I'd better call your owners and let them know you're all right." I reached for my purse, dug out the old cell phone, and dialed the number.

"Cody." He answered immediately, on the first ring. Interesting. I'd pictured him with a wild animal instead of a domestic one, but the breed was a surprise.

"This is Allison Allan. Have you lost something?"

"E Da Hah. Did he show up there?"

So I was wrong on two counts. The ocelot was male. "Yes. He's presently curled up in my lap, putting my legs to sleep. Do you live near here?"

"Over the hill, at the top of the box canyon."

"Does he roam the hills a lot?"

"No. We run together, but I don't let him out alone. I must have left the door ajar when I went to Clarence's and he slipped out."

"Anything special I need to do for him tonight? I assume you'll want to come for him as soon as the storm lets up."

"Just leave the bathroom door open and the toilet seat up. He's trained to use that."

"That's a coincidence. I know of another ocelot in California also trained that way."

"Peaches? That's where I got the idea and the cat. E Da Hah is on loan from there for some special training." For the first time, I could hear a little humor in Cody's voice. Maybe he wasn't such a bad guy after all. Then he asked, "By the way, how did you come to let him in? Most people are terrified when they see him."

"When he pressed his nose against the kitchen window, I couldn't resist him. If the occasion ever arises, I'll tell you about a lion who became my best friend. But right now, I think my batteries are about gone. Later." I disconnected.

"Tell me about Cody," I said to the woman who remained stock still on the sled. It struck me then that she really was a diminutive person. Only the bulky coat gave the exaggerated impression of size. I'd noticed from the first that she wasn't much more than skin and bones, but it hadn't dawned on me that she was even shorter than my five feet four inches. She fit perfectly on the sled.

"After you tell me about the lion." She watched the ocelot with those icy blue eyes, as if expecting that at any minute it would pounce and devour her. I didn't think she'd make a very tasty meal, besides the fact that there was no meat on her bones.

I related the story of Kat, the pet lion of a man who'd kidnapped me and held me hostage on his island near Hawaii. Kat had helped me escape, kept me warm, and saved my life.

"A full-grown lion?"

I nodded. "Probably weighed three times what I weigh, stood nearly four feet tall. He was magnificent." And I had loved him dearly. "Now tell me about Cody."

"He and Janet went to school together. She had a crush on him the whole time. He was nice to her, but that's 'cause he was raised a gentleman. Never made fun of her or called her names like the others." Hildegard paused, then went on thoughtfully. "Something different about that boy. Lots of Indians around here, the reservation being just below Blackfoot, but Cody was different from his kin. Don't know whether it was knowing his ancestors were historical figures, or his upbringing, or just what."

"How was he different?" I'd certainly noticed it. But how do you put your finger on an enigma?

"Had his head in books, like my Janet, except for summers with his grandpa. He had a thirst for learning. When he wasn't studying, he roamed these hills. I'll bet there isn't a square inch up here that he hasn't tromped over with either a coyote pup or wolf cub. Didn't take much to human friends, though. Tried to tame a mountain lion once, but it turned on the livestock, so he took it up in the hills and let it loose."

"What did he do in the hills?"

"Studied nature. Looked for signs of his people. That was what turned him into an archeologist, I guess. Liked discovering stuff and working alone." Hildegard yawned.

"You should probably get some sleep. Can I get you anything?" *Besides a hospital, surgery, and an attitude transplant?*

"Put a couple more logs on the fire. We'll freeze to death if it goes out."

I stuffed three more split logs into the tiny stove, then checked Hildegard's leg. "I think I'd better cut your pants so I can look at that wound. I can't pull them up high enough to see it."

"Not on your life. Paid good money for these, and you won't go ruinin' 'em 'fore I've got 'em half wore out. I'll let you know if my leg starts gettin' bad. This isn't the first time this has happened. I know about gangrene. Just pack it again with ice, and then you can go sleep in Janet's bed. I wash the sheets every Monday morning when she leaves, so bedding's clean."

After I'd locked both doors and settled Hildegard in for the night, E Da Hah followed me into the bedroom. He curled up on the foot of the bed, as if that's where he belonged. I looked at the computer—the monitor was on. I touched the space bar and the menu came up, with a light that blinked "Mail."

"Mrs. Piggett, the mail delivery light on the computer is blinking. Do you want me to check it for you? Maybe Janet's worried about you."

"No. Don't bother it. She's always getting mail from somebody, but she can get it in town, so she just deletes the messages when she gets here. She won't be thinking about me."

I walked back into the living room. "I thought you said you didn't have a phone out here. You have a phone line for e-mail."

"I don't have a phone. Janet has a line for her computer." She shut her eyes and dismissed me by ignoring me.

I stood by her side for a minute. "Good night, Mrs. Piggett. Call if you need me."

"You can be sure I will."

Sweet dreams, you sweet-natured old thing. I fell into bed with my clothes on. Or Connie's clothes. Why did I always end up with somebody else's clothes? You'd think I didn't have a penny to my name, as frequently as I went home in someone else's wardrobe.

I closed my eyes, but the wind shook the house till I was afraid the roof would come off. E Da Hah didn't seem concerned. He rolled over on his back, paws in the air, and snored softly. Just like my cat when she was totally relaxed.

But I couldn't relax. I kept thinking of Bart in some cave, nursing a bullet wound. And Clarence. Poor Clarence. And Cody's question, "How did you find out about the bug?" Why did he phrase it that way if he didn't plant it? And there'd been no denial.

Was rustling cattle the only thing going down here? Could the noises and lights all be attributed to a huge plane landing and taking off loaded with stolen livestock? Then why the fires?

I sat up and looked at the computer. I'd never sleep unless I at least tried to see what Janet's books contained. I didn't have great hacking skills, but I wasn't exactly computer illiterate. As I sat down at the desk, I heard Hildegard.

I hurried in to see what she needed. Her eyes were closed, and she seemed to be talking either in her sleep or to herself. "'Tain't right," she said. "Clarence was a good man. They shouldn't have killed him."

I knelt by the sled and whispered, "Who shouldn't have killed him?"

"I knew those men were up to no good when they drove out here in their big, fancy SUV. Nobody pays that kind of legal money for something they could have dirt cheap."

I held my breath, then whispered again. "What did they buy?"

"Land. And they're still goin' after it—all they can get their hands on. What they can't buy, they'll steal or kill for. They're that kind. My Janet shouldn't be working for people like that."

Did I dare press my luck? "Who are they?" I said quietly into her ear.

Hildegard didn't answer. She didn't open her eyes. She didn't move anything but her lips. They pressed together in that little thin line and disappeared. I returned to the bedroom, sat on the edge of the bed, and pondered what had just transpired.

That had been a performance staged for my benefit. She wasn't talking in her sleep, and she wasn't talking to herself. She was giving me answers to questions I hadn't asked. Did she know how badly I wanted the answers? Had she overheard my phone conversations with Bart, and then with Cody? Of course she had. Did she suspect we were here to catch the very people her daughter worked for? I'd bet my inheritance she did. The wily old witch!

But she'd just involved her own daughter. Why? To warn me about the danger? I had no doubt the danger was very real. After all, they'd just killed a sweet, harmless old man and shot my husband.

As I thought about it, that was actually the only new information she'd given me. She hadn't told me who was involved, and we already suspected that people were grabbing land up here. Her little act required further pondering, but in the meantime, after her revelation I had no qualms about tackling the computer. I'd have to do it carefully. If Janet had set up a booby trap, it could shut down before I'd gotten into it. I needed Oz here. Oz! Of course.

CHAPTER 25

Bart said to be sure I called Anastasia. If they'd actually been able to land, they'd be worried sick by now. We'd left no word where we'd be. I tiptoed back out to the living room, hoping not to wake Hildegard if she'd been able to fall asleep. I'd left my purse by the rocking chair, which was next to the sled. Hildegard had been doing a little snooping herself.

That explained the play-acting.

I returned to the bedroom with my purse and called the Shilo Inn on the old cell phone. I had to save the batteries on the new one. That was my link to Bart—my only lifeline to my injured husband.

"This is Allison Allan. Have my parents checked in yet? Jack and Margaret Alexander?" I waited.

"No, not yet," the receptionist reported after a prolonged time away from the phone.

They must have been diverted by the storm. "How about anyone else in their party?" I listed everyone in Anastasia. No one had arrived yet, but the airport had been closed since late afternoon. I left a message: in case any of them called, we were snowed in.

If the fickle gods of fate were smiling on me tonight, I might luck out at the Control Center. David would have checked the weather before filing a flight plan, and hopefully had postponed their flight until the storm lifted. I dialed the Control Center in California. Bart's mom, Alma, answered. Oh, dear. Trouble.

"Hi, Alma. It's Allison. I've got to reach Oz immediately. Is he there?"

"Not right now. How are you? What are you two doing?" Alma wanted to talk. I'd known she would.

"We're in the middle of a blizzard—snowed in. Who's there? I've got a computer problem, and I need someone who's a whiz to handle it for me."

"At the moment, only Else and me."

"Great. Put her on—quickly, will you? The batteries on this phone won't last much longer, so I only have a few minutes, and this is really important."

The beautiful Else came on the line. "What's the problem, lady?"

Awed by her beauty in every way, I never thought of her as just Else. I briefly outlined the computer situation, and the brilliant beauty walked me through the steps to enable her to access Janet's computer from the Control Center in California.

"Can anyone hear me?" I needed to report what we'd learned, but didn't want Alma to know about Bart.

"No. I just sent Alma to bed. She's been here all day and is exhausted. What's going on?"

"Record this, but don't let Jim or Alma access it. They don't need to worry about Bart. They have their hands full, but I need Dad to know our situation." Watching the battery light, I quickly poured out everything I could remember from the time we'd arrived, adding information I'd gleaned from the brochures that I thought might be helpful. Else interrupted occasionally to ask questions, but otherwise listened and absorbed.

"Where is everyone?" I asked when I'd finished. "When are you arriving? I thought most of you would be here before noon today."

"Between the storm and some new information we've had to check out from McAffrey, it just didn't work out. But we're watching the weather. David picked up the Lear this afternoon, and we'll arrive en masse as soon as weather permits. How are you holding up?"

"I've almost been too busy to worry about Bart. But now that it's time for bed, or past time, my mind will overload. Gotta go. Better save what little battery's left. Oh, Else, wait. I hesitate to do this, but in case things get out of hand, copy our new cell phone numbers. Please don't let anyone use them until I give the okay. I'm keeping my phone clear for Bart to call, and if anyone calls his number, it will alert his captors to his phone. Say a prayer." I hung up.

Else's religion consisted of a combination of beliefs she'd gleaned from different sects, all of which believed in the power of prayer as deeply as we did. In fact, Anastasia represented quite an ecumenical group. All the major religions were represented, and several minor ones. Bart and I were the only Mormons.

Speaking of prayer, it was past time. I got on my knees and poured out my heart to a loving Father in Heaven who already knew all that was going on. Sometimes I wondered why it was necessary to tell Him about it when He was, after all, omniscient. Probably to remind me of my total dependency upon Him.

Then I asked for help. A lot of help. All my guardian angels and then some. In fact, how about a legion or two of angels who weren't too busy on some other project? That *might* be enough to get Bart out of his predicament. As far as I could see, it would be the *only* way we could make it happen.

I did snoop a little. My feet were freezing in my sandals, so I opened Janet's drawers until I found a pair of warm wool socks. She kept nothing unusual in her drawers, and very little clothing. Most of it must be in town where she lived. I checked her closet. Only a few ranch clothes. No office outfits. If she was in such demand, she must be making good money, but nothing I found indicated that. Could Hildegard be mistaken about Janet's abundance of clients, or was the plain Jane plain and understated in her dress, as well? This was an unusual family at the least, mysterious at the most.

E Da Hah managed to occupy the entire bed, sprawling from one side to the other. Whatever happened to curling up in the corner? I scooted him over, which he didn't appreciate, and tried to relax on top of the bed with my clothes on. For some reason, even with the dreadful storm howling outside and almost guaranteeing that no one would sneak up on us, the thought of getting undressed made me nervous.

With that in mind, I vacated Janet's room with my gun and phones tucked securely in my purse. I retrieved my coat, gloves, and boots from the living room and carried everything into Hildegard's bedroom. I checked the injured woman, sleeping soundly with her leg sufficiently iced, and added another couple of logs to the fire.

When my nerves tingled like this, it was time to make contingency plans. As careless as I'd been today, I had to accept the fact that I'd been spotted. And Cody knew where I was. I didn't have a great feeling about his part in all this. If anyone asked for a prime local suspect, he'd definitely top my list.

If Else had succeeded in downloading Janet's files without leaving telltale signs that they'd been tampered with, I'd be surprised. Janet could probably access everything here from her computer in town. If she discovered the break-in, she'd be here at first opportunity—or send the people she worked with. I didn't want to be around when that happened. Cody would show up first thing, too, to fetch E Da Hah, and someone would come for Hildegard. Way too much traffic for my liking. I needed to be gone, looking for Bart, before it all arrived. Hildegard would be fine until Cody came.

I set about exploring the place. I didn't know what I was looking for, may not have been looking *for* anything but certainly *at* everything. I didn't find a single thing of value or beauty. I'd been in places of abject poverty that contained more beauty than this plain, sad little house.

Behind the door I assumed was the pantry, I discovered a set of stairs leading to the fruit cellar and snowmobile garage. I thought I'd left the doors open, since I'd been in such a hurry to get Hildegard off the ground. They'd probably been blown closed by the gale forces that pummeled and pounded the house.

The area was cold, but not freezing as I'd expected, probably because it was underground. The wooden doors were heavy, so apparently it didn't freeze in here. That would explain why the snow machines weren't covered. Unfortunately, the one I'd left by the front steps would probably be frozen in the morning and unusable until it thawed. If the snow drifted too deep, I couldn't take Toby out in it. I'd have to borrow a Ski-Doo.

It surprised me to find no dust on the shiny surfaces or seats. They were fueled and ready to go. Someone took very good care of them. Hildegard or Janet? This was the first snowstorm of the season; they wouldn't have been used recently. Had they just been uncovered, or were they dusted frequently? Puzzling. What was the motivation? And who was motivated?

I started back up the stairs to the kitchen, then stopped. If I needed a quick exit, how fast could I get down here, open the doors, start a machine and escape? Not very. The heavy wooden doors would be the key. They closed with a metal bolt—when the doors were brought together, the bolt dropped into place. The latch had to be raised for it to open.

I maneuvered a Polaris snow machine in front of the doors, then searched for a piece of rope or string. Not finding any, I retrieved the red bandana Connie had given me and tore it into strips, which I tied together. Then I rigged the latch so as I mounted the snowmobile, one tug at the strips of cloth would release the catch and the doors should swing open. I didn't test my theory, but it looked perfectly feasible.

That done, I climbed the narrow wooden steps into the kitchen. I checked Mrs. Piggett, gently added a few more ice cubes to the plastic bag in the towel, put a log in the stove, and went to Mrs. Piggett's bedroom. E Da Hah could have Janet's bed all to himself.

What had I forgotten? From where would the danger come? Ski-Doos or helicopters approaching would be easily heard. Skis or snowshoes would be silent. If the front door opened, would I have time to escape to the fruit cellar before someone stopped me? And exactly who did I expect to come bursting into Mrs. Piggett's home, looking for me?

I pondered that question as I lay atop Hildegard Piggett's bed with a worn, faded quilt pulled over me. Bart's captors would come to collect the stray they'd left behind, but who were they? And had I done everything I could do to protect myself and my baby? That thought electrified me. I'd been so consumed with others' problems, I hadn't thought of the baby for hours. I wished I hadn't thought of her now. My eyes were suddenly wide open, all thought of sleep fled, and the dream, that vivid, clarifying dream, returned to torment me.

Why do choices have to be so hard? How could I possibly choose between my husband and my baby?

I had no choice. No one else was available. Bart could be dead before Anastasia even arrived in Idaho, much less appeared in the mountains to search for him. The consequences of the dream registered again. I could choose to have this baby, or I could choose to stay in Anastasia and work with Bart. That's what it all boiled down to.

Why, Father? Why did You bring us together against all the odds we've faced, if we'll be separated more than ever if I have a child? Why did You bring Bart back into my life if his lifestyle will keep us apart so much? I thought parents were supposed to raise their children together. A joint enterprise.

I tried not to blame God for all of this. I knew there had to be some grand plan here. I'd been obedient to every law and commandment I was aware of. I'd tried to be kind, loving, charitable, patient, virtuous, obedient, and truly Christlike in all my actions. I acknowledged that I often failed, but I kept trying.

Whoops. I had to repent of my uncharitable thoughts toward Mrs. Piggett.

In my heart, I knew God doesn't punish us by making bad things happen to us. He simply lets us be tested and tried during this mortal time, and learn how to overcome obstacles—with joy in the doing. Right now, I couldn't find much to be joyful about. I fell asleep trying.

I woke with a start. The silence in the house disconcerted, no, terrified me. I lay on the bed paralyzed with fear, straining to discover what had jarred me from sleep. I stood, listened, crept quietly through the kitchen into the living room. A red glow from the wood-burning stove provided enough light to see Hildegard still asleep on the sled, not looking like she'd moved at all. I slipped another log into the stove, checked her ice bag, and wandered the small house, trying to determine what had awakened me.

Suddenly I realized that the wind no longer blasted and rocked the house. The strange silence after the turbulent storm woke me. The blizzard had abated. From the kitchen window, I could see out the mouth of the box canyon into the valley beyond. The full moon we'd enjoyed briefly on the river the night before now peeked through the thick clouds, brilliantly lighting the snow-covered earth.

The moonlit world was as silent outside as it was inside. The quiet brought disquiet to my soul. With the storm gone, someone would come. How long did I have? When had the storm stopped? Was it a temporary respite and would the wind return with a vengeance, or had the storm blown itself out?

Trouble would come from Janet's employers if she'd discovered her computer had been hacked, or from the rustlers who'd taken Bart captive. Or were they one and the same? And where did the terrorists fit into this picture? Maybe three sets of trouble approached. Maybe Cody belonged to one of those groups. Or did he comprise the fourth on the list, and the trouble I needed to fear most? I didn't doubt his ability to track me wherever I went. And he was probably the closest—just over the hill at the top of the box canyon.

Father, guide me. Should I wait for morning or go now, leaving Hildegard? I desperately needed deliverance from this overwhelming stupor of thought.

There were too many what-ifs. What if the interstate had been kept open all night through the storm? It wouldn't take long to arrive on snow machines from the highway. What if the cave where they held Bart was nearby? Those men could be here in no time in the moonlight. What if Cody was the threat? He could ski silently down the mountain in minutes.

How did I fight an enemy when I didn't know who they were, where they were coming from, or when they would be here? I just knew someone would come. That certainty quickly grew into a sure knowledge that I had to act—now. But go where? To find Bart, of course. I just had no idea where to look, and wherever I went, the tracks would be obvious, making me an easy target.

Father, I'm stepping into the unknown darkness and depending on guidance. I know You won't do anything for me that I can do for myself. But I don't know what to do. Show me, and I'll do it. Gladly.

It would be dawn soon, although it couldn't be much lighter after sunup than with that full moon reflecting off the snow. I crept to the doors, unlocked front and back for rescue people, asked for a blessing on Hildegard since I was deserting her, and donned Clarence's sheepskin coat and my sandals inside the manure-covered boots. I used my penlight to find my way down the narrow stairs.

How I wished for a pair of skis, so I could quietly slip away! Once I started that engine, it would awaken the world, announcing my intentions and my whereabouts. With gun tucked in the waistband of my jeans and phones in my purse, which I'd wrapped around the handle of the Polaris, I reluctantly released the latch on the doors and tried to swing them open.

They wouldn't budge. We were literally snowed in. I looked around the cellar and found a snow shovel. I'd never used one in my life. Not part of our household equipment on the coast of Southern California.

I hurried upstairs, out the kitchen door, and worked at clearing the snow from in front of the big double doors. Drifts stood four feet deep in front of one, only a couple of feet in front of the other. That's the one I tackled. While I worked up a sweat moving the heavy white stuff so I could get one door open, the moon disappeared. Little puffs of snow kicked up around my boots as the wind picked up again.

If that's an answer to my prayers, thank You. If it's one more obstacle . . .

Finally I could tug the door open enough to wheel the Polaris out. I pulled the axe from the wall where it hung above a chopping block just inside the door, and relieved the closest tree of two full, wide branches. With the red bandana tied in strips, I secured them to the back of the snow machine. Hopefully they'd obliterate my tracks, or at least make them less noticeable.

Hildegard called as I started to push the door shut. Only for a second did I think of just jumping on the machine and taking off without finding out what she needed. I slipped back inside, left the boots at the top of the stairs, and entered the living room.

"You leaving?" One simple, curt question.

"Yes. Now that the storm's over, someone will come for you. I've got to find my husband. I'm afraid when they get around to questioning him about who he is and what he's doing here, if they haven't already, things could get very nasty."

"Little Miss Do-Good."

I ignored her sneering tone and tried to think Christlike thoughts about this poor, lonely woman who had to be in a world of hurt. I could empathize with her incredible pain. I'd taken a dive through an elevator hatch in San Francisco and suffered a compound fracture in my arm. I knew what she had to be going through.

"Before you go, I need three more painkillers."

I bit my tongue and went for the pills, doling them out one at a time as before. I'd bet she wouldn't even say thank you. Of course, I needed to thank her for my refuge for the night, so I guessed we were even.

"When Cody comes for E Da Hah, please ask him to take Toby back to Clarence's so his kids can do whatever they want with him. I'm going to borrow one of your snow machines. I'll make sure it gets back to you. Thanks for shelter from the storm. It probably saved my life."

"No probably about it." She paused and pursed her thin lips. "You saved mine. You're smart to leave. The best way would be north. If you . . ." She stopped at the unmistakable sound of a snow machine. We exchanged a quick glance and I raced back to the kitchen, slipped into the boots, and flew down the rickety stairs. I didn't know who it was, nor did I need to wait to find out. I wasn't worried about Hildegard. She'd been here forever and would probably outlast the troublemakers, especially since her daughter was involved with them.

She'd said to go north. That meant toward the end of the box canyon and in the direction of Cody's place. I jumped on the machine, started it, and headed up the hill behind the house. Was it smart to go north? Could I be trapped at the end of the canyon if it was too steep? I had no reason not to trust Hildegard, but it worried me to take off into the totally unknown on somebody else's say-so. That leap-of-faith thing again.

Clouds completely covered the moon now, and if it hadn't been for the simple brightness of the snow, I'd not have had a clue where I was going. I didn't turn my light on. Until they stopped their Ski-Doos, they'd never hear mine. Looking back as I reached the end of the rise on which the house was perched, I could see three lights. Two were closing in on the mouth of the box canyon, and one was far back in the valley.

I slipped into the trees and wound my way through the slender white trunks of the aspen. The hill steepened. I didn't dare slow down or stop for fear I wouldn't be able to get going again. I couldn't tell if it started snowing or if the wind blew the snow off the trees above me, but I could barely see in front of me. I desperately needed to turn on the light, but knew that would be a dead giveaway.

Finally I gained the top of the box canyon, and paused at the edge of a clearing. For a minute I could only see one light, probably the lone machine that had been in the valley behind the other two. It had just arrived at the house. Where were the others? Then I saw them, halfway down the hill behind me. They were on my trail, just entering the trees and the steep climb up the hill.

I panicked. Where could I go? Who were they? Hildegard said north. I pointed the Polaris north and throttled up. No sense trying to be quiet; apparently the branches dragging behind me hadn't fooled anyone. Or had Hildegard told them in which direction she'd sent me?

Father, now would be a good time to send those guardian angels.

I whipped through the fir trees, feeling like someone on a slalom run. The snow stung my face and teared up my eyes. I hoped I was keeping a northerly direction, but it was hard to tell in the trees, in the snow. I could be going in circles. When I saw a small clearing ahead, I glanced over my shoulder. They were gaining. The lights bobbed through the trees too close behind me.

I'd never outrun them. This wasn't my forte. Give me a jet ski on the water, or pull me behind a boat on a ski, and I might have a chance at some kind of contest. Not here. I was a novice, totally out of my element.

Suddenly, a light appeared, coming straight at me. Blinded, I swerved and nearly overturned the machine. It was another snowmobile, but the skilled rider was adept at maneuvering and veered in a circle around me, motioning for me to follow.

Cody! Out of the frying pan, into the fire.

Another leap of faith? I hadn't much choice when it came to trusting him. I didn't see people standing in line to help me. I hit the throttle and tried to keep up. At least I didn't have to worry about the direction; he definitely knew where he was going. And we were making much better time than I'd made as I tried to find a path among the trees.

We stopped abruptly at a huge rock. "Drive behind that tree," he shouted. "There's a hole in the rock big enough to hide you. I'll lead them away."

Without stopping to question, I maneuvered the Polaris into the little gap barely big enough to provide cover. Cody grabbed the branches I'd been trailing, swirled them in the snow to obliterate my tracks, and tossed them at me to plant in the snow to cover the opening. He did a couple of runs up the hill on either side of the boulder so there would be two sets of tracks leading from this point.

Had I been wrong about Cody, misjudging him completely? Or had I run from someone who'd come to help Hildegard, and she'd sent them to find me? Maybe the ones trailing us were the good guys, and Cody was actually the villain. I didn't know. My instincts currently were out to lunch. What had happened to the unfailing intuition that Bart had come to trust, and that I'd always relied so heavily upon? Trauma? Exhaustion? Worry? Any of those could mask it.

Suddenly the roar of engines echoed through the cavity in which I cowered, pausing at the tracks in front of the rock. I covered my ears to protect my eardrums from being shattered, and terror filled both body and soul. The men were so close I could have reached out and touched them.

CHAPTER 26

Would they fall for Cody's ruse? Did I want them to? What if I was hiding from my rescuers? How I wished I knew the players in this deadly game!

Whoever they were, they took off, one on each side of the rock. I breathed a sigh of relief and whispered a silent prayer of thanks as their noise dwindled and died out over the hill. Was that a clue I should pick up on—that I'd actually been relieved when they didn't find me? Probably. Dense as I was right now, I'd always believed in my intuition. It was time to start grasping those clues I usually caught the first time around.

I hadn't been clicking on all cylinders lately. Bart's captors would have checked his ID, discovered his identity, and figured anyone traveling with him presented a danger to them and their cause. They'd be anxious to get their hands on me. I remembered my carelessness yesterday. Any twelve-year-old would have done a better job of staying out of sight.

The Lord knew exactly what He was doing in telling me to get out of this dangerous spy game. I didn't think quickly enough, or I'd have realized yesterday that they knew I was trailing them. But with the storm approaching, they could also be sure I wasn't going any farther than the Piggett ranch. I'd have to stay there until they were ready to come and get me.

I waited. Surely Cody would come back. Or should I leave before he returned? Decision time. My little voices argued: *If you truly believe he's a bad guy, get your body out of this crevice and put some real distance between you. If you don't think he's a villain, or aren't sure, then his knowledge of this area could be a real help. After all, you did pray for guardian angels.*

True. I did.

Then I heard the roar of a snow machine approaching fast. So fast I thought it was going to fly right on by. It paused long enough for me to hear Cody's distinctly pronounced instructions. "Follow me. I've lost them, but they'll soon figure out they've been tricked."

Adrenalin pumping, I shoved the machine out of its tight parking spot and followed Cody. It must be about sunup. The world now had a gray cast. Cody flew through trees, down gullies, and over bumps that had me bouncing off the seat of my machine when I hit bottom. Then we came to a straight stretch that could have been a road or a field before being covered with snow.

He slowed so I could catch him. I envied his warm, padded, one-piece snowsuit. I could use one instead of jeans now caked with snow, freezing my legs.

He pointed ahead. "Keep going straight until this ends. I'll create a diversion behind us. Veer left at the end and wait for me in the trees."

I barreled ahead, finally able to enjoy the fun of the snow machine when I could actually see where I was going and felt in control. The world had no horizons. Snow-covered mountain and cloudy pre-dawn sky blended into one blue-gray background. Stands of trees created a darker tone in the monochromatic tapestry, with the entire scene softly veiled by lightly falling snow.

Glancing over my shoulder, I watched Cody whipping back and forth across my tracks, making what looked like a string of continuous dollar signs in the snow. Or like somebody had been out playing games early in the morning. It made me want to flop in the fluffy white stuff and make snow angels by waving my arms and legs up and down.

I got into the spirit of things in my own timid way by weaving back and forth within the confines of the flat surface until I reached the end of the trail. As instructed, I veered left, heading for some fir trees up the side of the hill. Just inside the tree line, I stopped and waited for Cody, watching as he continued his hijinks, zooming around boulders, in and out of trees, up and down the small rolling hills like a kamikaze pilot. In the seemingly reckless way he handled the Ski-Doo, he looked like an accident about to happen. I acknowledged, with great awe and respect, that it was skill and experience.

He joined me, motioning me to follow, and headed into the thick of the trees. His eagle eyes—or hawk eyes—may have been able to see clearly in the dim light and falling snow, but I wouldn't have dared speed through the evergreens with what seemed like an open throttle. I could barely keep up as it was.

Finally, just before we crested the hilltop and left the trees, he wheeled right, headed for some craggy rocks, whipped around them, and vanished. Even the sound of his snowmobile disappeared. I followed his tracks around the rocks—right into the gaping mouth of a black hole. I cut the engine.

"Good job." If I hadn't recognized Cody's distinctive voice next to me, I'd have jumped out of my skin. I almost did anyway. I reached into my purse for the penlight to see where we were, and remembered something else. As I turned on the light, I activated the phone. I should have done that sooner. The fact that I'd been a little too busy to think of it wouldn't make me feel any better if Bart had tried to call and hadn't been able to reach me.

"Turn off the light. What are you doing?"

"Turning on my cell phone. My husband has his, or did have last night when he called, and said he'd try to reach me again today to tell me where he is and who's holding him."

"Who are you? Why are you here?"

I didn't like being in the dark, not being able to see the eyes, the face, the person spitting out questions that I hesitated to answer.

"I could ask you the same thing," I countered. "Who are you? And how did you know I'd left Hildegard's? Where are we? Why are we here? I don't know whether to trust you or not. Can I please turn on the light? I prefer to see who I'm talking to."

"You mean read my face, see if I'm telling the truth."

Why did his astuteness surprise me? "It's nice to be able to do that. Since I haven't yet decided if you wear a white hat or a black hat, I need additional clues."

"I don't wear a hat. I'm an Indian."

"Good Indian or bad Indian? Am I safe with you? Did you rescue me from the bad guys, or were they coming to rescue me from you?"

I turned on the light. The smile on his face caught me off guard—a reaction I'd never have anticipated from a man I'd considered taciturn.

"If you insist on the light, we need to go farther back in the cave. It's still dark enough outside for the light to be seen from across the valley." He turned and headed deeper into the black cavity. I played the tiny beam ahead of him, but it became apparent that he was completely familiar with the cave and totally at ease in the darkness. Maybe I'd misjudged him. He was kin to cat, not wolf.

We turned a corner, and I felt the space around me diminish. When he stopped, I played the light on the small area. A few feet inside the entrance, the cave had opened to the size of a room, roughly ten by ten. This portion was intimate—maybe six feet by seven feet, with much of the room taken up by rocks that seemed to have been evenly spaced at the base of the stone walls.

"Looks like a meeting room." I flashed the light on Cody's face. "Or a council chamber."

He sat on one of the rocks and motioned to one opposite him. "Or Boy Scout powwow room. How about question for question?"

"How about answer for answer? I have far too many questions and not nearly enough answers." I placed the light on a rock so we were both illuminated as much as possible, considering the penlight's tiny output.

"Fair enough. Who are you?" Light and shadow created an interesting character study on Cody's handsome face.

Was it time to reveal myself—or play it cool until I knew more about this man?

"The truth," he said, reading my hesitation.

"We're with Interpol—anti-terrorist division."

Cody's face blanked, all expression carefully masked except for the hint of disbelief in his piercing black eyes.

"I have ID," I added.

"ID can be forged."

I shrugged. "You wanted the truth. Would that be easier to believe if I were a man, or if I said my husband was an agent and I just tagged along?"

A smiled played about his mouth. "Are you accusing me of discrimination?"

"If the shoe fits." I returned the smile. "I'm sure you're acquainted with the phenomenon."

He nodded. "Is that why you're reluctant to believe I'm a good guy? Indians are historically portrayed as villains."

"I don't usually come with preconceived notions about people. I can't afford to carry that kind of baggage around. It's too heavy. Can we quit parrying and get to the gist of this?"

Cody dipped his head as if in agreement, then tilted it to one side. "Which is what, as you see it?"

"Whether we can trust each other." I'd suddenly decided that I could, indeed, trust this mysterious man with a secret. And I now had an idea what that secret might be. The little pieces of puzzle I'd been pondering the last two days started falling into place.

"Step into the darkness with faith, believing that I will lead you, and I will take you safely where you need to go." Sister Ruiz had quoted that in Relief Society last month. I didn't remember where it came from, but it was true.

He looked at me across the three feet of space that separated us. "Aren't you afraid I'll scalp you when your back is turned?"

I smiled. "I'm not that paranoid. And I won't touch *your* apparent ethnic paranoia. I have much more urgent problems."

The taunting smile disappeared from his face. "Your husband. Is he Interpol, too?"

"Yes."

"What brought you to Idaho?"

I leaned toward him. "I think you already know the answer to that. I think if you shared what you know about these people who are causing the strange occurrences, we'd be a long way toward solving the problem that brought us here."

"Which is?"

"Sorry, Charlie. Your turn. You put the bug in Clarence's phone, didn't you?"

Surprise flashed momentarily across Cody's face before he smiled in acknowledgment. "How did you know?"

"To begin with, I was suspicious of the way you phrased the question about us finding it. I think you wanted to find out who might be behind these things. You were listening to see if anyone called

Clarence and offered to buy him out, weren't you? Did you tap everyone else's phone up here? Who are you working for?"

"Mrs. Allan, you surprise me. Where did you ever get that idea?"

"Your interrogation skills are too well-honed—and familiar. In the minutes we've been here, I've formulated several other ideas about you, too. What was your graduation date from Quantico, or was it some other police-type academy? Who are you with?"

Cody folded his arms, leaned against the stone wall behind him, and watched me without comment, though I'd label the look in his dark eyes curiosity.

"I graduated last Christmas," I volunteered. "While you're trying to decide if you can trust us, and if you'll help us by sharing your information, answer me this. How did you know I was coming up the mountain on the snow machine? That wasn't coincidence, your being there to guide me, was it?"

"I'd been watching the house all night. I figured if they had your husband, they'd want you, too. You sure didn't act like an agent out there when you left Clarence. They had you under surveillance the whole way up and down that mountain. Or was that a ruse to throw them off track, so they didn't think professionals were on to them?"

I smiled. "Whatever works." I hoped he believed that's what I'd done. I didn't want anyone to know how incredibly stupid I'd been. "There were three lights. Were they all together?"

"The third machine was Gary Dodson. I didn't know how soon the storm would break and they'd be able to get a chopper up here, so I called last night and asked him to come the minute he could get through and take Hildegard back to the highway. They can drive or fly her out from there without fear of wind shear from the mountains."

"Thanks. I'm glad she's on her way to the hospital. Having had a compound fracture, I know how painful they can be. She's quite a character." Then I had another thought. "I hope Gary knew about E Da Hah before he got there, or he might have gotten the surprise of his life."

"I told him. I didn't want anyone shooting first and asking questions later."

I paused, not sure how to broach my next question. "Janet's involved in what's going on up here. I'm not sure whether it's terrorists or rustlers, or if they're one and the same. What have you found out?"

This was the moment of truth, and I believed the quick disposition of this matter hinged on whether or not Cody chose to share what he'd learned thus far in his investigation. It didn't matter that he hadn't even admitted he was investigating anything. My intuition kicked back in, and I felt confident I was right about him on all counts. Amazing what a little faith can do.

I waited. Cody would have to make the next move. I could sit here all day, because until Bart called, I had no other clues to move on. Then I had an agonizing flash. What if the phones didn't work through all this rock? My old one hadn't been able to penetrate some buildings.

I had to get out of here and into the open, where there would be no question about receiving his call. I grabbed the light and headed out into the larger chamber.

"What's the matter? Where are you going?" Cody asked, following on my heels.

"I deal in what-ifs, and I just thought of a terrible one. What if my husband has been trying to reach me, and the cell phone doesn't work in this cave?"

"Good thought. It may not."

As I hurried toward the entrance to the cave, which was now clearly outlined by the pale blue light of dawn, something moved in the darkness to my left. At the same moment I whipped my light toward the movement, my nose connected with a smell potent enough to knock a weak person right off their feet. A smell even worse than that aftershave the terrorist had worn.

CHAPTER 27

"Get out of here. Fast!" Cody shoved me toward the entrance to the cave. I'd have stood frozen with fear if he hadn't. I couldn't believe what I'd just seen, but I wasn't about to stand and debate the existence or the identity of the creature revealed by the penlight.

In the split second it took me to propel myself out of the cave, I ruled out the possibility of using the Polaris to escape. I'd never get it turned around in time, and even if I'd had the foresight to leave it pointed out instead of in, I'd never have been able to mount, start, and get it out into the snow fast enough.

I burst from the cave and flew down the hill, hearing Cody chanting something behind me. I didn't dare turn around to see if he'd followed me and was praying, or if he'd stood his ground and was trying to hypnotize the creature. Or converse with it in some tongue common to denizens of this part of the wild. At this point, he was on his own.

I clutched the cell phone in one hand, the penlight in the other, and couldn't have dropped either to pull my gun if my life had depended on it. Besides, what good would my little pea shooter do against that behemoth that had to weigh six hundred pounds if he weighed an ounce?

I saw the trees coming, knew I had to act at this moment or be torn asunder by five-inch claws. Shoving my treasures into the jacket pockets, I fairly dove into the low-hanging branches of an evergreen tree and scrambled as far up as I could get, as fast as I could get there. Thank heaven I'd been a dedicated tomboy as a child, and had spent more than my fair share of time climbing trees. That practice probably saved my life now, notwithstanding the cumbersome boots, jacket, and leather gloves, all of which were several sizes too big.

Knowing safety wouldn't be guaranteed in the tree, I concentrated on attaining the highest branches, then secured myself by sitting on one fairly solid limb and wrapping my arms and legs tightly around the rough, pungent trunk of the evergreen. Then I hung on for dear life.

Ursus arctos horribilis had been known to push trees over or shake their quarry out of the treetop if they wanted it badly enough, if they couldn't just climb the tree and knock their prey to the ground. As I settled in, I saw movement on the pale-blue valley floor below. Two snow machines followed the tracks we'd made in the snow. Those tracks would lead them directly to the cave, and to Cody. And my tracks in the snow would lead them straight to me.

Where was Cody? I hadn't heard horrible screams of anguish, so I had to assume he'd safely eluded those deadly claws and powerful jaws. Not to mention mighty paws that could knock a man's head right off his shoulders. Killer Claws, Jaws, and Paws. Great title for a book. Somebody had probably already thought of it.

I watched the area around the cave's entrance. Nothing moved. I scanned the rocks to either side, and above it. Still nothing. What had happened to the animal? Was he at this moment devouring Cody? I couldn't bring myself to climb down and investigate. I was no match for a grizzly bear under any circumstances, and if I were branded a coward the rest of my life because I didn't go to his rescue, so be it.

Besides, the steady hum of the snowmobiles was getting closer by the second, so danger approached on another front.

Yes, Father. I got the message. I'm not cut out for this type of work. I promise I'll be happy leaving it to those members of Anastasia who live for the adrenalin rush and the danger. I acknowledge I'm not one of their breed. Please get me out of this in one unscathed piece, and I'll take the first flight to California and do my part from the Control Center.

Was I so stubborn and pig-headed that He had to go to such great lengths to prove His point? Probably.

The closer the snow machines came, the more worried I grew about Cody. Since the grizzly hadn't shown his black nose and silver-tipped fur outside the cave, I had to believe he was preoccupied with

Cody. If the resourceful Indian somehow managed to evade the bear, could he do the same with the two men now approaching the cave?

Suddenly the cell phone in my pocket beeped. My heart stopped. I tore the glove from my hand, and with fumbling fingers plucked the phone from my pocket. "Yes?" I breathed into the mouthpiece while I turned the volume down as low as I dared. I couldn't *not* take the call I'd been waiting for since last night. But I also couldn't let those two on the ground hear the radio beeps when they turned off their engines, which they most surely would do any minute.

"Where are you, Princess? Still at the ranch?"

"Later on my situation," I whispered. "Do you know where you are?" I slid the phone under the sheepskin jacket while I beeped off and Bart beeped on each time we changed speakers, never taking my eyes from the two men below me.

"I've overheard a couple of conversations that might give you some clues, especially if you can convince Cody to help. He probably knows this area well enough to identify where I am just from the description. Think you can get him to cooperate?"

"If he's still around, I'm sure he will."

The men below followed the tracks almost to the rocks and stopped. If they didn't know the area, they wouldn't know about the cave. They couldn't see the entrance from where they were. They conversed for a minute, then throttled their machines and roared around the corner of the rock. The sound was deafening as it resounded through the cave and echoed down the hill and across the valley.

That was their first mistake. The second proved fatal.

They stopped at the mouth of the cave, revved the engines one more time, and dismounted from their snowmobiles. Their guns might as well have been water pistols for all the good they did. U. A. Horribilis came roaring out of the cave, and moving faster than I could believe, slashed his way through those two unsuspecting men like Sherman through Atlanta. Or the Indians through Custer's army.

"What's that noise I hear?"

"A grizzly bear decapitating one of the men chasing me on a snowmobile."

I tried not to watch the R-rated slaughter occurring below me, but I couldn't take my eyes from the carnage. They'd reaped the anger of the bear we must have awakened from sleep. But I'd felt, as we had walked into the dark interior of the cave, that Cody knew the place intimately. Didn't he know the bear was in there? Or had we been more quiet than those two, who were noisy enough to wake the dead?

As the grizzly sniffed his handiwork, I looked away. Definitely nothing to view on an empty stomach.

"Allison, where are you?" When Bart called me by my given name, he was unusually upset or concerned. He'd be both if he could see me now.

"I'm in the top of a very tall pine tree, and I've just watched an enormous grizzly bear dispatch the two men who came for me at Hildegard's before dawn. Cody intercepted and led me on a merry chase away from them. Bart, have you got time for idle chitchat like this?"

"This is not idle chitchat. Are you safe?" My husband's anxiety fairly oozed from the phone, it was so apparent in his voice.

"I'm safe, but those two men no longer have a mortal care. As for Cody . . ."

I still hadn't seen any sign of him. Until that bear disappeared, I'd stay right here if I had to spend the next week in this tree. Some woman in California stayed in a tree for a whole year, protesting its removal. Guess I could handle a measly seven days, if it came to that.

"What about Cody?" Bart tried to be patient with me, but I had a hard time concentrating on our conversation while worrying about the missing agent of some as yet-unnamed agency whose help I needed very much at the moment, and who I'd decided was probably a nice guy after all. Besides, he'd saved my life. If there was any possibility he was still alive, maybe I ought to reciprocate, as soon as the monster tramping back and forth in front of the cave disappeared.

I brought my focus back to Bart. "We'll talk about Cody in a minute, right after you tell me about your bullet wound. Has it been taken care of? It's not getting infected, is it? How come you can talk? You don't seem afraid of being overheard."

Bart interrupted with a series of beeps, informing me that he wanted to say something. "Stop! One question at a time. Yes, I'm alone. No, I'm not getting infection in the wound. I told you, the bullet only grazed me, and I packed it with snow. Frostbite, maybe, but no infection. They tucked me in what I think must have been a guard post of this old mine, waiting for some big honcho to get here to interrogate me. Everyone is running around like there's no tomorrow, so they've sort of forgotten about me."

"Good. Tell me what might help me find you. Oh, wait. The bear is taking off up the hill. Hang on while I get down out of this tree and see what happened to Cody. I'll let you know when I get to the bottom."

I dropped the phone into my pocket, put my glove back on my nearly frozen hand, and descended the tree considerably slower than I'd ascended it. I beeped Bart back to report I was safely on the ground once again, that I'd determined the bear was well on its way up the hill, and that I was going back into the cave to look for Cody.

"Princess, I want you out of there."

"I want me out of here, too, but first I have to find Cody. Since he saved my life, I owe him. And second, I have to retrieve Hildegard's snow machine. I promised I'd return it. By the way, her daughter, Janet, seems to be the bookkeeper for either the rustlers or the terrorists. Have you found out who your captors are?"

"Yes. The white supremacists, formerly from northern Idaho. They've got an arsenal that could rival today's U.S. Army, and from the labels on some of these cartons, it looks like federal arms and supplies are being diverted here."

"Then we'd better get you out of there fast. If it's that big an operation, your life won't be worth two cents when they find out who you are." I stopped dead in my tracks, chills shivering through me from head to toe. "Oh, no! Mom said Osama bin Laden is coming to Idaho. Bart, that's probably the big honcho they're expecting. Let me find Cody. We've got to get you out of there! Tell me what you know." I made mental notes as Bart recited what he'd observed so I could repeat every word to Cody.

Suddenly, without warning, Bart beeped off right in the middle of a sentence. Had someone come, and he had to hide the phone? Or had he been caught, and they'd confiscated it?

Judiciously avoiding the red snow, I raced into the cave. My stomach lurched at the smell inside. Or was it the thought of Bart's obvious danger that set my midsection churning?

"Cody, where are you?" I stopped at the snow machines we'd parked a few feet inside the entrance, listening for a reply. Had I heard something?

"Cody? Are you in here?" Again I heard a faint sound in the dark. I fished my penlight from the depths of my pocket and, holding my breath against the stench and the fear roiling in the pit of my stomach, I headed straight back into the part of the cave we hadn't gone into, passing the little room around the corner in which we'd held our powwow.

"Cody?" I stopped and listened. Was the sound I heard an answer to my call? What if it wasn't Cody at all, but the mate of the bear, or its young? The faint, indistinguishable sound might even be an echo. I advanced deeper into the cave and called again.

"Here." This time I recognized not only the sound, but the voice.

"Where? I don't see you!" I'd been shining the light along the walls of the cave as I'd gone, but I'd found nothing.

"Up here, about ten feet farther."

I played the light along the rock, but still couldn't find Cody. "Okay, are we through playing hide and seek? I give up. I can't find you."

"Stop."

I stopped.

"Look right."

I looked right. A bare wall faced me.

"Higher."

I shined the light up to the ceiling of the cave, and there, snug as a bug, Cody nestled in a crevice against the top of the cave.

"Finally," he said. "I didn't think you were ever coming back for me. I figured you wouldn't stop running until you crossed the Montana border, as fast as you were going down that hill."

"Actually, I climbed a tree. Too bad there was no one around to record it. I'd have made the *Guinness Book of World Records* if I'd been timed. Are you going to stay up there all day, or what? The bear's gone."

"To use your word, 'actually,' I'm stuck. I've never been on this shelf with my snowsuit and boots on, and I'm wedged in so tight I can't get out."

"How did you get up there in the first place?"

"The same way you climbed that tree—adrenalin. It was the only place I could think of that was out of reach of Old Blue. I thought if I went one way and you went another, he'd have to choose between us. I figured I'd have a better chance of evading him than you would, and since I know this cave so well, I headed for this little niche where he couldn't reach me. I taunted him . . ."

"Was that the chant I heard?"

"Yes. Bear hunters use it to trap their chosen bear. But once I got in here, I couldn't get out. My boot's stuck, and if I try to get down I'll break my leg. Can you unzip my boot so I can slip my foot out of it and get off this shelf?"

"You sound a little desperate. You don't happen to suffer from claustrophobia, do you?" I shuddered, knowing I'd never have been able to spend more than five minutes in that tiny space.

"Why do you think my chosen profession keeps me outdoors most of the time? A little help, please?" His voice was pitched slightly higher this time.

"Ready to deal?"

"What do you mean, deal?"

"I know I owe you for my life, but I need a really big favor, and since you seemed a little reluctant to agree to help us . . ."

"You'll get me down if I'll cooperate."

"You are one smart Indian. Agreed?"

"I was going to help you anyway. I just wanted to see how much information I could get out of you. The boot?"

I shined the light on the shelf, saw the zipper, but I was too short to reach it. "Got a stepladder stashed in here anywhere?"

"You seem like a resourceful person. I'm sure you'll think of something."

"I probably could, but if you had any suggestions, it might speed things up a bit. My husband called. We need to get him out of wherever he is as fast as we can."

"There are rocks everywhere. Can't you roll one over to stand on? Just hurry. This feels more like a coffin every minute."

I focused the light on the floor of the cave, searching for something manageable to roll over and stand on. I suffered from the same horrible affliction, so I knew I couldn't leave Cody trapped in that tiny space any longer than necessary. Finally I spotted a boulder that would give me the height I needed, but was small enough to move and round enough to roll.

With the penlight between my teeth to illuminate what I was doing, I shoved with all my might to get the boulder started. Then it rolled into a small depression and wouldn't budge. I sat down and shoved with my feet, finally dislodging it.

"Are you carving it out of the wall yourself?" Cody called.

Finally I managed to muscle it into place, stood tiptoe on the rock, and unzipped the boot. "I'll never understand how you got that high without something to stand on. And in the dark, too. You must have cat eyes." I jumped off the rock and moved out of the way so Cody could escape his prison.

"A running jump, a burning desire to stay alive, and I've paced off every inch of this cave so many times I don't need lights to know where I am." Cody landed lightly on one foot, reached back up to dislodge his boot, and sat on the rock to replace it. "Okay. Where do we find your husband?"

CHAPTER 28

As we hurried to the snowmobiles at the entrance to the cave, I repeated Bart's words before he disconnected. "It's an old mine with the original timbers, like railroad ties, still at the entrance. There's a wrought-iron gate on the outside of the ties, and thick wooden doors on the inside, so the mine can be open to the air or closed against the elements. Ring a bell?"

"Mrs. Allan, . . ."

"Allison, please."

"Allison, do you know how many mines there are around here with that kind of opening? Not the gates or doors, of course, but the mine entrance? We're talking dozens, if not more. This used to be mining country. There are a dozen more that are simply caves, and that many, at least, that are open pits, like the opal mine you visited."

"How did you know we went to the opal mine?"

Cody shrugged off my question. "Up here, no one does anything without everybody knowing about it. What else did your husband say? We have to narrow this down."

I tried to remember exactly. "He thought it took them about an hour to get to the mine on horseback. They didn't break their necks to get there, but they didn't dawdle along the way, either. Does that help?"

"Some. Did he say what direction?"

We pushed our snowmobiles out into the subdued light of a cloudy day, where we were confronted by the human debris left by the grizzly.

"Whoa." Cody stopped abruptly and whistled. "Good thing you didn't fall. That could have been you. Who are these guys? Did you ID them?"

"No. It wasn't light enough to get a good look from my perch in the tree, and I was anxious to find you when I came down. I think it might be the two who broke into our hotel room and shredded my clothes, but I've no way of being sure. Oh, wait. I tore the gold chain off the neck of one. Can you tell if one of them has any marks around his neck? And one should have a broken wrist."

"Why don't you check, Allison?" Cody looked at me curiously. "You're supposed to be a professional. What happens when you don't have someone around to do the dirty work for you?"

"I really hate to toss my cookies in front of people. You want to watch me do that?"

Cody flashed me a look of disgust, then bent to the appalling task of checking necks. He shook his head. "Forensics can check after they've cleaned these guys up. Too messy to tell right now." He gingerly pulled back gloves and found one wrist in a slender cast.

"Guess that's a pretty good indication he's the one who nearly killed us in Tucson, and these are the two that broke into our room at the hotel." I shuddered. "Even for a couple of creeps who have given us major grief, this is a terrible way to die."

"You're right. I'll notify the authorities so they can come for them before the animals do." He straddled his snow machine, hooked a leg over the handle bars, and leaned one elbow back on the cushioned seat. "By the way, how did you know this guy had a broken wrist?"

"Cody, can we save the questions—and everything else—until later? I'm more concerned for my husband, who I hope is still alive, than I am for a couple of people who won't know the difference if someone comes for them today or tomorrow. Even an hour can make the difference for Bart. What else do you need to know to find that cave?"

I tried to be patient and diplomatic. I tried not to lose my cool. I didn't want to do anything to upset this man who had the knowledge to find Bart. Probably the only one who did. Silently I begged, I beseeched with my eyes, not trusting my voice to speak without betraying my raw feelings. Professionals don't cry, but I'd never felt less professional and more helpless in my life. What if he chose not to help? What if he didn't see this as the great priority I did?

Animosity charged the air as Cody studied me. Was he annoyed that his suggestion had been questioned? Or did he see it as an order being challenged? Was he trying to establish right from the start that he was in charge?

"I happen to love the guy," I said quietly. "And I need him more than I can tell you. Can we look for him first, and take care of less vital things later?"

Finally he shrugged. "You didn't say what direction they took. Where did they catch him?"

I breathed a quiet sigh of relief and reported my steps from the time I'd left Clarence, up the hill, into the trees, and described the rocks in which Bart hid to watch the valley—the rocks where he'd been shot.

"But you don't know where they went from there?"

"I followed the trail northeast, down the hill, toward Hildegard Piggett's ranch. It started snowing before I got even halfway down the hill, so I couldn't follow their tracks. They could have cut east, then gone south from there for all I know." A feeling of hopelessness descended as the breeze kicked up light, loose snow crystals and shifted them in new patterns, filling in the tracks of the snow machines and turning the red snow pink.

Cody shook his head. "Not south. That would take them over the mountain toward the opal mines. They'd probably head for the Divide. Fewer people, more open space, and old mines."

"And more snow." As I watched snowflakes dance through the air, I couldn't appreciate the beauty of the scene. If this man didn't know where Bart was, if there were many mines to be searched, most of them toward the high peaks of the Continental Divide, and snow continued to fall, the chances of finding my husband before something happened to him diminished by the minute.

I pulled the small radio/phone from my pocket and tucked it into the hood of the coat next to my ear, then tightened the strings and tied the hood around my face. If Bart called while we were riding, I wanted to be able to hear the beep over the roar of my machine.

Cody sat up on his snowmobile and nodded at me to get on mine. "They probably went up behind my place toward Lookout Point or Signal Mountain, but they could have gone farther up than that. We'll refuel, then check a couple of mines." He took off without looking back. If my Polaris hadn't started, I'd have been left alone on the hill with the gruesome remains.

I continually lagged behind the expert, not being as adept as he was at maneuvering the Ski-Doo. He flew over snow-covered hills with the grace and beauty of a seagull skimming white-capped waves, dodging obstacles I couldn't even see. I dogged his trail stubbornly, determined not to make him stop and wait for me.

What had happened to Bart? Why hadn't he called back? Had the "big honcho" arrived? Was it actually Osama bin Laden? A shiver raced through me, and I blocked out the monstrous stories I'd read in the files and newspapers about the terrorist. If they were interrogating Bart . . .

I offered still another prayer for my husband's safety and well-being, and turned my mind to other things. What could I do besides worry about Bart? Call and see if anyone from Anastasia had arrived. Find out what Else discovered in Janet's files. Should I tell Cody that Bart had found the suspect motorbike in the cave?

Something about Cody had changed. I couldn't put my finger on it, but for one thing, he wasn't as friendly. The bantering comradery we'd established in the cave vanished once we walked out and he discovered the grisly scene in the snow. Why? It upset me to see that horrible scene, but I wouldn't have expected the same response from a man.

Was his reaction a matter of sensitivity? Or a sudden acknowledgment of the seriousness of this business in his backyard? Or did he recognize the men? That possibility really chilled my blood. Had I been too quick to trust Cody? Had my intuition led me astray?

I don't know how long it took us to get to Cody's house. I'd stopped thinking about anything except staying in his tracks. Wind and snow froze my face, and my jeans, wet from our first trip, were collecting an ice pack that I'd have to knock off before I'd even be able to walk. Icy particles blew into my coat sleeves, freezing my arms. In short, I was miserably cold, starving, and worried. Not just about Bart, but suddenly about being alone with Cody.

I still felt he was a federal agent, and that we were basically on the same side, but I no longer felt we had the same goals. Did it have something to do with the secret he harbored? If he was with a federal agency, his allegiance should be to helping fellow agents accomplish their missions. Unless he felt that people with Interpol didn't fall into the "fellow agents" category.

Numb to everything except following the tracks in front of me, I hadn't noticed where we were until we plunged into a dense forest of evergreens. With snow falling again in huge, heavy flakes, I could barely see the tracks of Cody's Ski-Doo in front of me. I tried to hurry faster, to catch up and keep him in sight. It wouldn't do for me to lose him completely. I had no idea where we'd come from or in which direction we were headed.

The climb steepened, and as I crested the hill and followed the tracks into a small clearing, I could see the faint outline of a house through the blinding snow. Hopefully, it was Cody's. I didn't know how much more cold I could take. My blood was too thin for this kind of weather.

I still couldn't see the man, but I followed his tracks right up into his garage. He waited there for me and shut the doors as I cut the engine on the Polaris.

I pointed to his machine. "Poetry in motion." My cheeks were so cold my mouth would barely form the words. I rubbed them to restore feeling.

"Thanks. This your first time on a snow machine?"

I nodded, peeling the caked ice from my jeans.

"Not bad for a beginner. I take it you're a water baby instead of a snow bunny."

"Pegged."

"You're also frozen." He hung his discarded snowsuit on a hanger just inside the door to the house in what looked like a mud room. Or did they call it a snow room up here? There was a neat place for his boots to drip-dry just below the hanger where his quilted snowsuit could also dry if wet. Cody wasn't cold, dressed in those duds.

"Come on in. I'll heat some soup."

I followed Cody into the snow room, plopped my boots next to his in the tray, and hung my coat next to his. I wasn't sure I liked such a cozy arrangement, but I looked forward to that hot soup more than I dared think. That promise I made to the Lord to go home and do my share of Anastasia's work from the Control Center wouldn't be hard to keep. In fact, I couldn't wait to get on that plane back to sunny California. I couldn't stop shivering.

I grabbed my purse from the Polaris and checked the battery on the radio/phone. How many more hours would it last? The worry churning in my stomach now was stronger than the hunger gnawing there. Why hadn't Bart called? What kept him from giving me further instructions on how to find him? It frightened me to think of all the terrible things that could be going on right now—wherever he was.

Cody took one look at me and grabbed a woven Indian blanket from the back of his sofa, tossed it around my shoulders much as Dominic would have swirled a cape in front of a bull, and gently shoved me down in the chair nearest the wood-burning stove. My teeth were chattering so hard I had to press my lips together to keep from biting my tongue.

He left the room and returned with a pair of expensive-looking fleece-lined sweat pants and matching sweat shirt with a tiny gold crest on the front. "Get out of those wet jeans and put these on. I'll get that soup heated."

Unable to speak, I nodded. He left, and I immediately heard pots and pans banging in the kitchen. I looked for a place to change, saw the bathroom, and hurried to get out of my icy clothes. I draped the icy jeans over the towel rack to let them drip into the tub—or at least they would drip when they started to thaw. The sweats felt heavenly with their padded, quilted sleeves, and I hurried to huddle next to the stove and finish thawing out.

To save the charge still left in the old cell phone, I'd use Cody's to call the Shilo Inn to see if everyone had arrived. It would be nice to have some help out here. When Cody figured out the location of the cave, we'd need Anastasia to spirit Bart out of there without launching a major attack on the terrorists. Or rustlers.

Which was it?

"Soup's on," Cody called from the kitchen.

"You mean you're going to make me leave this wonderful fire?"

"No. But your soup's in here. I'm not a servant, so if you want it you'll have to come and get it." Reluctantly I left the warmth of the fire and joined Cody, hoping the soup would warm me from the inside out and I could finally find out what he knew.

I picked up my spoon, took a deep breath, and plunged into my questions before I'd even had one sip of steaming soup. "Bart and Clarence saw tire tracks from what they believe to be a very large plane. Have you seen or heard it land or take off from up here? I assume you do have a sweeping view, since you're up so high."

Cody shook his head, his black eyes narrowing as he bit off a chunk of cornbread.

"Does that mean you haven't seen anything, or you haven't heard anything, or both?" While he washed the cornbread down with half a glass of milk, I continued. "Hildegard Piggett's ranch house looks over the valley floor where Bart and Clarence saw the tracks and hoofprints. Hildegard swears rustlers are behind everything that's going on up here, and she figured the rustlers were using planes or helicopters. I'll bet she's seen them."

Cody put his glass down and leaned forward. "And what is 'everything that's going on up here'?"

The man must have frostbite of the brain. "The noises, lights, ground tremors, slaughtered sheep, stolen cattle. Don't tell me you don't know about any of those. I know you're aware of the fires. And your E Da Hah is the strange spotted wild animal that's been seen in the mountains."

"Where did you hear all this?" His black eyes were gleaming spots of obsidian in a face that suddenly didn't look so tanned.

"You just told me everyone up here knows everything that transpires. Now you're denying you're aware of what's occurred the past few weeks?" I sat back in my chair and glared at him. I knew I was gullible, but was it so obvious to others? Did he think I'd believe he didn't know about it when he kept telling me—when everyone kept telling me—that "everyone up here knows everything that happens"?

Cody went to the stove and filled his soup bowl again. When he sat down, he folded his napkin back in his lap and met my stare. "I've been gone to Hell's Canyon for over a month, studying pictographs discovered last year. The first phone call I had was from Clarence about the fires. I checked out a few, but nobody said anything about lights, noises, or anything else."

"Not even Clarence, when he called you?"

"We talked about the fires." Cody dug into his second bowl of soup.

Did I believe him? Why would he lie? To cover his participation in some of it? Was that his secret—that he was a major player in this whole mess? Why did it have to get harder instead of easier to tell the good guys from the bad guys?

CHAPTER 29

We finished the meal in silence. Maybe he needed time to sift through things he'd heard that hadn't meant anything at the time. Maybe he was planning how to get rid of me and restore peace to his mountaintop. There was no peace in this snug retreat at the moment. Tension was as thick as the soup I'd just enjoyed.

I carried my bowl to the sink and rinsed it out. Cody was a neatnik; his spotless kitchen and orderly living room attested to that, as well as the gleaming sink in his bathroom. Not even water splatters on the mirror.

Cody opened the door into the snow room. "I need to run down to Hildegard Piggett's and get E Da Hah before we leave to find your husband. Why don't you curl up on the sofa and catch a quick catnap while I'm gone? I shouldn't be more than thirty minutes, and you look like you could use the rest."

"How will you get him back? The snow's pretty deep now." I couldn't picture the ocelot leaping through snow twice as deep as he was long.

"He rides on my snow machine. Be right back."

"Can I use your phone while you're gone? I need to see if my parents have arrived yet with the rest of the Anastasia team." I hurried to the stove in the living room with its welcome, warmth-giving fire.

"Anastasia?" Cody peeked his head around the corner.

"The name of our Interpol unit."

"They're all coming here?" A frown wrinkled Cody's handsome face.

I nodded. "Dad pulled everyone back from whatever international case they were working on. Said the presence of foreign terrorists on American soil took precedence over everything else." I stopped, remembering the conversation I'd had with Cody a couple of hours earlier. "When we were in the cave, talking about trusting each other, I mentioned the strange occurrences up here, and you didn't even question it. In fact, I remember speaking about it twice."

"I thought you meant the fires."

I watched his face, watched those intense black eyes that revealed absolutely nothing, just as the blank expression on his face told me nothing about what went on in his mind. Would that I could ever be so unreadable!

"Cody, I know your mind is quick. You're observant. I'd place you very near the top on the intelligence totem pole. And I'd appreciate it if you didn't do both of us the disservice of placing me near the bottom of that icon. Contrary to your personal opinion at the moment, I don't belong there. Why are you playing dumb? What are you so afraid we'll find out? According to Clarence, these things have been happening for weeks, so even if you'd been gone a month, how could you have missed knowing about them?"

That brought Cody all the way back into the living room. "Whoa down a minute. Answer some questions before you set fire to my wigwam. When did this start?"

I snuggled down by the fire. "Clarence said a few weeks ago. Someone is buying property, anything anyone will sell. They figured the fires were an attempt to encourage a few more to sell, and the rest were scare tactics." I watched Cody's carefully masked face. Did he really not know? How would I tell? And how much *should* I tell if he insisted on playing dumb? "Hildegard Piggett said she'd been approached by some men in a big SUV offering a lot more money than she thought her property was worth. She didn't think it was legitimate money. She's not too happy about Janet working for them, especially when they killed Clarence."

Cody squinted at me. "Are you talking in circles here, or have I completely missed the thread of this conversation?"

"Personally, I think all that blood muddled your mind. Go get your pussycat. Maybe the cold air will clear your head. I need to use your phone."

"You are talking in circles. Now you're back to the phone." He shook his head and headed for the kitchen door.

"Don't get lost in a snowdrift. I'd never know where to come looking for you."

He turned at the door and pointed a finger at me. "Don't you leave the house. I might not be inclined to even try to find you."

Probably the truth. If I'd become a thorn in his side, how easy would it be for him to take a few more hours than necessary to begin searching if I became lost? "Have I disrupted your life that much?" I asked.

"If what you say is true, yes. A few rustlings, ranchers might handle. On a large scale, no. But international terrorists are a different story. That's hard to believe."

"Well, put this little item in your pipe and smoke it while you're going after E Da Hah. Osama bin Laden is known to be in the country, was seen leaving Denver, and is likely to show up in Idaho any minute. Bart said his captors were expecting a big honcho to come, so they hadn't bothered to interrogate him while they were getting ready. Add up those numbers and see what you come up with. Truth is truth, whether it's convenient or not. Now, I'm assuming I can use your phone, since you keep avoiding the issue. I promise to pay for all long-distance calls."

Cody stared blankly at me, then turned and left the house. With his portable phone in my hand, I stood by the window and watched the noisy snow machine disappear into the incredible whiteness outside. Even the snow-laden Douglas fir trees were simply slightly darker shades of the intense white that covered everything.

I called the Shilo Inn, but Dad's line was busy. They'd leave a message for him to return my call. While I waited impatiently for the phone call, and feeling anxious to begin the search for Bart, I explored Cody's house. Lots of windows, lots of light. I peeked in the only closed door and found a darkened spare bedroom with windows shuttered from the outside. It was on what I thought might be the north side of the house, the side that would get the most cold and wind. Cody's bedroom was also on that side, but his windows were curtainless. His claustrophobia must be worse than mine. The furnishings were modest, but nice. About what you'd expect from a bachelor pad.

The books on his shelves in the living room and his bedroom were also what I'd expected: volumes on Native American history, Lewis and Clark, and a couple of shelves full of geology and archeology.

I returned to the spare room to check the bookcase in there. The whole thing was devoted to police procedurals, suspense, mysteries, and every volume of the Navajo policeman series by Tony Hillerman. Plus a few biology, botanical, and art books. I closed the door behind me, then looked around the rooms again. Something didn't seem quite right. Something bothered me about Cody's beautifully neat house, but I couldn't put my finger on it.

As I prepared to search dresser drawers for some clue to Cody's identity, the phone rang.

"Alli, where are you?" The agitation in Dad's voice said volumes about the state of affairs at the Shilo Inn.

"Hi, Dad. I love you, too. What has you up in arms this morning?"

He took a deep breath. "Sorry, Bunny. You've had me worried. You're snowed in? Where? Are you okay?"

"I'm snug as a bug. I'm not sure about Bart, though. I talked with him early this morning, but we were cut off as he described where he's being held. He hasn't called back. He said they were expecting a big honcho to arrive, so they hadn't interrogated him yet. Dad, I think it's bin Laden himself they're expecting."

"Hmm. You didn't hear anything unusual before you were disconnected? Sounds in the background?"

"No. He just beeped off. We have new phones with direct connect if you're in the same calling area. I didn't dare call him back because his radio would have beeped. He could have seen someone coming, and if they moved him back into the cave, he couldn't receive the signal. So I'm sitting here watching the battery fade, waiting to hear from him."

"Where's here?"

"The mountaintop home of a Native American archeologist. Our new friend and informant, Clarence, felt he was trustworthy. I get the idea from our conversations—not what he's said, but how he says it—that he might be a federal agent of some kind. Or was." New thought. The home of a former agent could be a dangerous place to be, depending on his reason for being "former." "Would you run a check on the guy and see who he really is?"

I stopped. I had no earthly idea what this man's last name was. "Put that on hold a minute while I see if I can find out his full name. Clarence only called him Cody, and that's all I know him by. There must be some papers here somewhere with that information. While I'm looking, answer me this: what kind of huge airplane can land without a runway or landing strip, just flat valley floor, pick up a load of cattle, and take off again? Mountains are probably two to three thousand feet above the valley elevation of six thousand or more." I resumed looking for Cody's personal papers. Thank heaven for portable phones.

"C-130-J could handle that. That's the plane that flew into Guatemala, landed in an open field, and left tons of relief supplies for survivors after a hurricane devastated the area."

"Thanks. Next question. What did Else find in Janet Piggett's computer files?" I wasn't having much luck finding information on the elusive Cody. Where would the man keep his papers? Surely he had bills to pay, files to keep. Was that his secret—his identity?

"A treasure trove. She holds the purse strings for a major cell of terrorists. She's got records of numerous money-making operations, including mining of several different minerals, and rustling is big bucks. By the way, we've identified the leader—a fanatical ex-patriot gun runner and mercenary with a reputation for being a ruthless killer. Apparently he decided the military's in such a shambles that it's the perfect time to take over the government."

"What a terrifying thought." Then another terrifying thought struck. Cody could return at any moment, and I hadn't found a thing. I'd searched everywhere except his closet, so I headed there with the phone plastered to my ear.

Dad was just getting started. "Since the last military-hating administration cut what amounted to a superpower army, navy and air force from our services, those remaining in the military might just be disgusted enough to follow a charismatic leader who promises to rebuild America's power and glory. He's preaching that the United States is not only a shadow of what it was ten years ago, but it's become the laughingstock of the world with the former administration's political and sex scandals in the White House. Don't know if they'll wait to see what the new president will do or not."

"Frightening. What else do you know about him? Is he here? What's the strength of the cell?" Nothing in the huge closet. Wish I had one this big. Wait a minute. What does a man with so few clothes need with a closet this size?

"With what Dominic, Lionel, and Oz gleaned from interviews with map holders at Nellis, Mountain Home, and Hill AF bases, it looks like they're expecting to train upwards of five hundred people, who'll then become cell leaders all over the U.S., training their own cells of five hundred. Did you find a name for me to check?"

"Still looking." I pushed aside the clothes hanging neatly on evenly spaced hangers. Voilá! Cleverly concealed in the pinewood paneling of the end wall was a door. Being used to the hidden passages of the mansion on the estate where I'd grown up, I quickly located the switch that opened the door in what looked like a knot in the wood.

"Thanks, Dad, for all that experience in opening those secret passages you built into the mansion. I just found a door in Cody's closet. You wouldn't believe how clean this place is, and I don't just mean neat. There isn't a clue to his identity anywhere. What does that tell you about him?"

"He has secrets to hide. Bunny, are you sure you're safe there?" Dad didn't even try to hide the worry in his voice.

"As yet, I don't have any reason to believe I'm not. While I'm thinking about it, can you get someone up to the U. S. Experimental Sheep Station? We never had time to check it out, and the more I think about it, the more concerned I am about these people covertly taking it over. If the station's purpose is to eradicate anthrax and other diseases, who knows what possibilities exist for terrorists? Someone from the cell could have gone to work there, with plans to sabotage or steal the virus or bacteria."

"I'll get David on it. His assigned section seems to be uninhabited."

"The other thing that probably needs immediate attention is that chemical and non-chemical assessment system the INEL developed for the Army. Sounds like something terrorists might find handy if they're engaged in any kind of biological warfare. I know you've already thought of a zillion possibilities for the INEL, including sabotage and heisting the radioactive waste to use for nefarious purposes. Dad, give me a minute to see where this passage leads."

I hadn't found a light switch on the interior wall, so I ran for my purse and the invaluable penlight. I'd just entered Cody's bedroom when I heard the roar of a snow machine approaching. I flew to the closet, shut the secret panel, rearranged the clothes as I'd found them, and hurried back to the chair beside the wood-burning stove. The Ski-Doo raced toward the house, slowed briefly, then throttled up and roared away in the opposite direction, its sound soon smothered by the steadily falling snow.

What was that all about? I went to the window. Nothing moved in the Currier and Ives scene but snowflakes, falling so heavily that my fear of not being able to find Bart returned with a vengeance. Who'd been here? Why hadn't they stopped? Had Cody returned, then left again?

"I'm back, Dad. Strange thing just happened. A snowmobile raced up to the house, slowed, then took off again."

"Bunny, can you leave? I don't like the thought of you all alone up there with someone you can't trust completely."

"Physically, I could leave. I have a Polaris, but I don't think it would be smart to take off in all this snow without knowing exactly where I'm going. And I don't have a clue where we are in relation to anything else. My powers of observation were frozen on our way here, and I didn't watch for a way out. No lectures, please. I know it was stupid."

"No lectures. How about the closet? Are you going back in?"

"Yes, now, before he decides to come back, if it was Cody. Maybe he decided to check out the mines without me hindering him. He said he knew a couple of possibilities where Bart might be. Dad, I think Cody is the only person who can find Bart—one more reason I can't leave here. It's the overriding reason, in fact. I'm going into the closet. Hang on."

But before I reached the bedroom door, I heard something out in that white world of silence that curdled the blood in my veins and set my heart pounding violently against my ribs. Some sound that wasn't snow-laden branches breaking. Or the wind, which was completely still. Or a snow machine. Or a human voice.

CHAPTER 30

I hadn't turned on any lights, relying on the illumination from the uncurtained windows. The windows were the problem now. Anyone looking inside might see me unless I stayed below the windowsill. I shuddered. It wasn't any*one*. It was any*thing*. That sound hadn't been human.

Another bear? If it wanted to get inside, the glass wouldn't even slow it down. Timber wolves? Despite what I'd recently read about their mostly benevolent nature toward humans, a pack of hungry wolves might not have the same attitude as the writer of the article.

What else lurked in these hilltops? Mountain lions. Again, a mighty swat from a powerful paw, and the window—and my safety—would be history.

The classic Alfred Hitchcock horror movie, *The Birds,* suddenly came to mind. Clarence's description of the number of raptors inhabiting this wild place, plus my imagination, created an array of hawks, eagles, falcons, great horned owls, and other sharp-beaked and clawed carnivorous creatures skulking in the skies and trees, waiting to crash through the glass and devour my flesh.

I shuddered.

A human voice startled me out of my wild imaginings and returned me to the realm of reality, to the reasonable, the rational. "Bunny, what's going on? What did you find in the closet?"

"Oh, Dad." I put the phone, forgotten in my hand, back to my ear and breathed again. "I had an interruption and haven't made it to the closet yet." Should I tell him and have him worried beyond reason? Or stall, brave it, and investigate?

"What kind of interruption? Allison, what's going on up there? Where are you? I'm coming to get you the minute this fog lifts."

I straightened my shoulders and took a deep breath. I was, after all, my father's daughter. I would investigate. "You have fog?" I said lightly. "We have so much snow falling right now that if it keeps up like this, it'll reach the windows before day's end. Dad! That could be a good thing. If bin Laden hasn't arrived yet, hasn't been able to get up here because of the storm last night and the snow today, this may keep him away even longer. Maybe long enough to find Bart." If Cody ever returned.

The noise came again, this time accompanied by a sound emanating from the kitchen. I wished I wasn't my father's daughter. Or that he'd been an accountant. Or an architect. A farmer, a welder—anything but a persistent pursuer of terrorists. Then I wouldn't be in this isolated place, surrounded by creatures who didn't know people weren't menu items to be ingested or torn asunder.

I headed for the kitchen, not as fearlessly as I'd have liked, but going nevertheless. On the way, I grabbed the gun from my purse. "What else do you have to tell me, Father dear? You can't have given me all the information your tenacious troops have discovered."

"Bunny, you'll make me old before my time. What's happening? That cheery tone is as false as any I've ever heard."

"Sorry, Dad. Didn't want you to worry about your only child. I heard a noise outside, and I'm going to investigate."

"Don't you dare leave that house! That is an order, do you hear me?"

"I hope no one else did. You sound like an overprotective father, not the head of a group of highly trained and skilled, experienced agents." That didn't include me. I didn't consider myself anything more than just the junior member of the gang. Certainly not skilled or experienced. But I hoped the terminology would remind Dad that I had been trained. And I hoped it counted that I'd been experiencing the trials and tribulations of an agent for a year now.

Movement at the window behind the breakfast nook caught my eye. I took a deep breath, moved along the wall farthest from the glass, and approached the corner, hugging the refrigerator as I neared the window. Suddenly a spotted paw reached up and tapped the window—the noise I'd heard from the kitchen.

"Bunny . . ."

"It's okay. It's Cody's cat wanting back inside." I didn't tell him what kind of cat as I hurried to the door and allowed the snow-covered animal inside. E Da Hah performed the ritualistic shaking of moisture from his luxurious coat, then after a welcoming or thank-you rub against my legs, made a beeline for the kitchen stove. He smelled the leftover soup.

I tucked the gun in the pocket of the sweat suit, put the pan on the floor, and ran to Cody's bedroom. "Riddle solved about the mysterious snow machine that came and went. Cody dropped off his cat, then left again. I suspect he's gone to check out some caves solo—without my hindrance. I'm in the closet now." Penlight on. "There's a steep set of stairs. I'm at the top. Wow!"

"What did you find?"

"Dad, you won't believe it. It looks like a mini version of our Control Center. Computers, fax machines, I think there's even forensic equipment. And a wall full of files. Our Native American archeologist, expert guide, and tracker who prefers the moniker Cody, is really Joseph Jefferson Cody. See what you can find on him while I see if I can find who he's with. There must be something here that will connect him with some agency."

"Bunny, be careful. If he's a former agent, or a renegade, and he finds out you know who he is, you could be in great danger."

"Don't I know it." E Da Hah had joined me in the upper room and curled up in a corner on the carpet to perform his ablutions. He was apparently familiar with the place.

But before I'd discovered anything further, I heard the unmistakable sound of an approaching snow machine drift up the open stairway. "Dad, I'll call you back. Sounds like Cody's home. I've got to get me and the cat out of here. Later."

E Da Hah went limp and allowed me to carry him to the stairs. I grabbed the portable phone—almost left behind—and hurried downstairs, closed the secret door, and straightened the clothes back in their former carefully spaced manner.

I flew out of Cody's bedroom, dropped the phone in its cradle, and leaped into the chair by the fire, trying to look relaxed and lazy. E Da Hah promptly curled up at my feet and resumed his interrupted bath.

As the sound of the engine increased, it occurred to me there was a lot of noise for just one Ski-Doo. I peeked over the top of the windowsill and saw two lights bobbing through the trees, approaching from the direction Cody had originally taken when he left, and from whence he'd come on his brief return. It was not the direction he'd taken after dropping off E Da Hah.

My danger antennae went on full alert, quivering like a divining rod over an underground river. I crawled to the doors to make sure they were locked. Who would come calling on a day like this? As far as I knew, Mrs. Piggett was Cody's closest neighbor, and she'd still be in the hospital. But Janet and her employers might be searching for the houseguest who helped her mother. Not to be unneighborly, but these were people I definitely didn't want to meet.

The engines whined down next to the house and stopped. Someone knocked on the door. Silence. They banged loudly on the door. A short period of silence before the doorknob rattled. A long, unnerving, absolute quiet hung over the house. No engine noise. They weren't leaving. They were exploring, trying to find another door, another way in.

If they didn't know I was here, if they were just canvassing the neighborhood, hitting the nearest neighbor, and if they didn't find me, maybe they'd quickly continue the search elsewhere. I crawled back to the snow room, grabbed Clarence's coat and boots, scooped up my wet clothes from the bathroom, and raced into Cody's closet. I pressed the knot in the paneling and was about to disappear inside when I remembered my purse and the second bowl in the sink.

If they found any trace of my having been here, this wouldn't work. I certainly didn't need them hanging around, waiting for Cody to come back. As I hurried out of the closet, praying I could get to the kitchen and back without being seen, I heard the shattering of glass behind the closed door in the spare bedroom. Apparently they meant serious business. I darted into the kitchen, grabbed the second bowl, spoon, and glass, and shoved them under the kitchen sink, then raced back through the house, scooping up my purse where I'd tossed it by the chair.

All this activity aroused the curiosity of the ocelot. E Da Hah jumped up and raced with me to the bedroom and into the closet, ready to play. I faced two problems: silently closing the secret door, and getting E Da Hah just as silently up the stairs, which should share wall space with the spare bedroom. Anyone creeping quietly into the house would be able to hear squeaks or thumps made on those stairs.

I slid the clothes hangers back into place, and with my heart pounding loudly in my ears, held my breath and pressed the knot to conceal the staircase. The door slid closed as quietly as those marvels of engineering Dad and Jim had devised for the mansion. *Thank You, Father, for innumerable small blessings.*

Grateful to find the penlight still in my pocket, I illuminated the staircase to locate the cat and carry him upstairs. I found him curled comfortably on the stairs, snuggled into the sheepskin coat I'd tossed there. Maybe he had a good idea. I sat on the step next to him, turned off the light, leaned back on one elbow, and rubbed his head.

I wouldn't have thought to bring him with me, but if the intruders had seen what looked like an exotic wild animal staring at them with those enormous eyes, they'd probably have shot him. I listened, heard nothing. Either they were being totally quiet after breaking the window or this secret area was well insulated. Probably the latter.

The minutes stretched into an eternity. Had they gone? I hadn't heard a noise or movement in ages. Was this place so soundproof that I wouldn't even be able to hear the rumble of the snow machines leaving? Or were the intruders playing a waiting game to see who would eventually show up at this house at the top of the hill? I wasn't about to reveal myself just out of curiosity.

I slid to the foot of the stairs and curled up at the bottom next to the door, laying my head on the incredibly soft fur of the ocelot. Cody had said to take a nap, and I figured I had no other choice at the moment. Besides, I'd had very little sleep the night before.

The phone beeping in my pocket woke me. "Bart," I breathed into the little instrument. "Where have you been?"

"I got pressed into a chain gang this morning, moving a shipment of boxes that arrived just before the storm hit. Some genius finally figured out they had an able-bodied man lounging around, and they put me to work. You were right. Osama bin Laden is expected to come as soon as the snow stops and they can get him up here. The new cell leader is bringing him. I expect they must both be in Idaho Falls or nearby, ready to move as soon as weather permits. Has Anastasia arrived?"

"Yes. I talked to Dad. Can you give me more details about your location? Cody says there are dozens of mines around here, and he needs more information."

"It's near the top of a good-sized mountain. There are no roads leading in. Everything's been air-lifted by helicopter, or brought in by C-130s and hauled up the mountain on horseback. You can't believe the amount of stuff here, for the short amount of time they've had to bring it in and the difficulty of getting it here. There's big money behind this—funding from deep pockets. This is no penny ante operation."

"Anything else that will help us find you?"

"There must be a separate mine shaft or cave nearby where they keep the horses. We rode them up, and I haven't seen, heard, or smelled them since. There wasn't time to get them down the mountain before the blizzard hit, so they have to still be up here. I'm also hearing interesting sounds that aren't from the main shaft, but I haven't pinned them down."

"How's your bullet wound?"

"No problem. How are you?"

"Hiding with an ocelot in a secret room in Cody's mountaintop retreat. I think he's gone to scout some of the nearby mines, and someone broke into the house a while ago."

Bart was silent for a moment. Then, "Did you say ocelot? And someone's in the house with you?"

"Congratulations. You just passed two parts of your hearing test. Remember Peaches from the Exotic Feline Breeding Compound? Cody has what could pass for her twin."

"I can't believe how you attract danger and trouble. Please be careful."

"You missed a part of your test—the secret room. I guess the ocelot threw you. Our friend has a miniature version of Anastasia's Control Center. His name is Joseph Jefferson Cody, and I'm sure he's with—or was with—a federal agency. Just haven't learned which one, or his current status."

"Princess, can you get out?"

"No. I'm not abandoning the safety of this little nook until I know for sure the intruders have gone." I didn't tell him I had no idea how I'd find that out unless I opened the door and physically checked.

"Gotta go. Someone's bringing dinner. MREs, clearly labeled U.S. Army. There are tons of them here. I'll try to call again before they lock me up for the night. If you haven't heard from me by eight o'clock, turn off your radio and save the batteries. Take care of our daughter. Love you."

I sat in the dark with the instrument pressed against my cheek, grateful for his safety, at least for the moment. I hadn't thought about our daughter for a while. About her safety. I'd used Bart's trick of blocking everything from my mind that didn't pertain to the moment. Her safety was something I couldn't worry about until Bart was safe.

Creeping quietly up the stairs, I commenced a search of the upper room with the aid of the penlight, making as little sound as possible as I opened drawers and fingered through files. Nothing jumped out at me that seemed relevant to our case, nor did I find anything other than Joseph Jefferson Cody on any correspondence or files. No agency. No unit. No nothing.

Did I dare try the computers? Always iffy if you're not a whiz hacker. Not one of my current talents, but since I'd be consigned to Control Center duty from now on, I might develop into one.

I slid into the chair, and as I touched the computer, the room suddenly blazed with lights.

"Find what you were looking for?"

CHAPTER 31

I whirled to stare into Cody's hostile black eyes. His frigid tone left no doubt of his current opinion of me.

I took a deep breath and volleyed. "It's about time you got back. I was ready to send the Boy Scouts to find you. Did you locate the mine with the bars and wooden doors at the entrance? Did you see anyone there? Were your friends still here, or did they leave before you returned?"

From his taut, muscular shoulder leaning against the door frame, to his arms folded tightly in front of him, to the grim line of his lips, there wasn't a soft, forgiving angle on Cody's entire body.

I forged breathlessly ahead. "I'd have been at the front door to welcome you, but frankly I didn't think I'd like your house guests—the ones who broke the window in your spare room to get in—so I hid in your secret hideaway and was grateful to have it. Thanks for providing this safe haven. You didn't answer my question. Were they still here, or did they get tired and leave?"

"And you didn't answer my question. Did you find what you were looking for?" Icicles might well have dangled from his words, so cold was his voice.

"As a matter of fact, only partially. I did discover your name. I didn't discover who you're with, however. Or are you a free agent? Do you belong to the highest bidder? If so, I can beat the price anyone else will pay if you'll find my husband."

If Cody hadn't had such good training as a child, as Clarence had indicated, I think he would have hit me. His eyes scorched me, his muscles rippled with the effort of controlling himself. He was probably gritting his teeth to keep from screaming at me. Did I dare push the envelope further?

"You could thank me for saving E Da Hah's life. I expect the intruders would have shot him on sight, thinking he was a dangerous wild animal." No comment. I shrugged. "You're welcome. Nice setup you have here. I told Dad it was like a miniature version of our Control Center."

"You told someone about this room?" He came at me off the doorframe like a jack-in-the-box.

I held up both hands. "Remember, your mother taught you to be nice to girls and never hit the weaker sex."

"What do you know about my mother? You are a . . ."

I covered my ears, just in case he decided to finish the sentence.

He stopped like he'd run into a glass wall and glared at me. Then he spun on his heel and stalked down the stairs. I followed.

"Go. Leave now. Get out of my house," he growled.

"I can't."

"Why not?"

"I don't know which way to go."

He whirled to face me as we entered the living room, stabbing his finger toward me. "I'll tell you where to go."

I smiled sweetly. "Thank you, but I have no desire to go there. I'm trying to live my life in such a way that I'll go to heaven instead. Did you find the cave where they're holding my husband? I assume that's where you've been since you dropped off E Da Hah."

It was then I saw the house. Or what was left of it. I clamped my hand over my mouth to keep from screaming. Slowly I turned in a circle to view the damage. There couldn't have been a single thing in the entire house they missed tearing up, slashing, breaking, or covering with what looked like blood.

"Oh, Cody, no. No." Then, as the realization hit me of what they might have done to me—to my baby—my knees suddenly gave way. I sank to the littered floor, my arms wrapped tightly around me to keep from being sick, tears streaming down my face. All the ramifications of the dream and my choices assailed me, leaving me physically ill.

"You brought them here. You caused this. They would have left me alone if you hadn't come." Cody spat the accusing words with bitterness and rancor.

I looked up at him through tear-filled eyes. "No. That's not true. They did this to you because they thought you were hiding me, helping me. But they wouldn't have left you alone. Whoever you are, you're a threat to them." I wiped the moisture from my cheeks. "Unless you're one of them. Only then would they let you stay."

"You don't know that."

"Oh, but I do. I know these people. I know what they're capable of. They give no quarter. They take no prisoners unless there's a profit. They're not forgiving. They're not charitable. They don't give a fig if you promise to mind your own business and let them do whatever they please. Promises mean nothing to them. Did they offer to buy you out?"

Cody's jaw tightened. They had. First guess right.

"And you told them no thanks. You wanted to stay, but you had no interest in whatever they wanted to do. You wouldn't interfere with their enterprise."

Teeth grinding. Second guess right.

"And you thought that would be the end of it? Cody, I have a reputation for being gullible and naive, but even I know better than that. I may not know your history—yet—but you can bet they know everything about you, from what you wore the first day of school to your favorite food, your favorite vice, your greatest weakness."

As I watched the emotions he tried to mask, I suddenly had another flash of intuition. "But you knew that. You knew that all along. You *wanted* them to think you were gullible and naive. You wanted them to think that even though you'd been professionally trained, which you can be assured they know, you were still just a dumb Indian who didn't know the difference between land developers and international terrorists."

His wince told me my third guess had hit the mark, too.

"You tried that with me. Play dumb. Forget conversations. Strange occurrences up here were news to you. But you know what? You don't play dumb often enough to have the role down. You weren't convincing." I got to my feet. "Want some help cleaning this up?"

Cody didn't speak. For the first time since I'd met him, his piercing black eyes mirrored some uncertainty. He stepped to the window, running his hands through his thick blue-black hair.

Leaving him to think, I turned to see what might be done to the house to make it liveable. It looked hopeless. My inclination would be to sweep everything outside, set fire to it, and hose down the house. Or just burn it down and start over. It truly was that bad.

I went upstairs and gathered my belongings. E Da Hah didn't want to give up the sheepskin coat, and when I pulled it out from under him, he stalked out. Cody was still standing at the window when I returned.

"If you can't stand the sight of me, I'll leave," I said evenly. "You'll just have to loan me your sweat suit and point me in the direction to civilization. I'd prefer not to leave because I desperately need you to lead me to my husband. I was serious when I said I'd pay you any amount of money you wanted."

Cody turned and pointed at the chair disgorging its stuffing. "Sit." The uncertainty was gone from his eyes, but I wasn't sure what I saw there now, besides anger.

I sat.

E Da Hah took the opportunity to jump up and curl on my lap. A scowl crossed Cody's face when he saw it. Not good timing, cat.

Cody stepped toward me and pointed an accusatory finger. "You have just blundered into—and ruined—something that took me months to set up." He was so irate he couldn't seem to find the words he wanted. "I don't have any idea how I can recover this mission." He stalked back to the window and stared out at the falling snow.

"If you'll tell me what you were planning, I might be able to help," I offered quietly, not wanting to ignite his ire again.

He kept his back to me. "I think you've done enough already."

"I didn't mean just me. I meant Anastasia. Assuming, of course, that you were working against the terrorists and not for them."

This time he turned and looked at me. "Do you work at being obnoxious, or are you just naturally that way?"

I smiled. "My resumé says I'm naive, impetuous, imaginative, stubborn, despise being dirty, abhor terrorists and bad guys in general. I've been called a lot of things by a lot of people, but never obnoxious. That puts you in a class all by yourself." I watched Cody's intense eyes. "You like that, being in a class by yourself. You don't want to be like anyone else, to be tucked into someone's common cubbyhole classification."

"Anything else, Miss Know-it-all?"

"You're an expert at what you do, everything you do. You're incensed because this was going to be another perfect case on your record, and you think I botched it for you. News flash, Charlie. These are bigger boys than you thought. There's more at stake here than first appeared. It's going to take you and whatever agency you work for, Anastasia, the FBI, and who knows what other help we'll need, to contain this treason." I stood and looked him squarely in his beautiful dark eyes. "Now, do you want to share what you know, or send me back to Anastasia and we'll handle it our way?"

Cody turned back to the window without speaking. I figured this must be a guy thing, not wanting to lay all his carefully arranged cards on the table for a woman to see. The cards he'd been working so hard to get all in a row without anyone knowing what was in his hand.

"I'll tell you what. How about if you get on your incredible equipment upstairs and find out who Jack Alexander is, and get the skinny on Anastasia. Then I'll call Alexander, and you can discuss this with him instead of a lowly female employee. That should satisfy your macho mentality. Then maybe we can begin to make some progress. And get my husband out of the clutches of those fiends before the really bad guy shows up and kills him. Because you can bet your bottom dollar that Osama bin Laden knows all about Anastasia and Jack Alexander and Bartholomew James Allan."

With my crooked little nose bent out of shape even more by this stubborn mule of a male, I dumped E Da Hah off my lap and headed for the kitchen to find a garbage bag and start cleaning up the mess. E Da Hah followed and leaped atop the refrigerator by the door.

I had to do something until this stubborn man deigned to help me find Bart. Had to be busy. And even if Cody could stand the mess, I couldn't. The intruders had strewn everything from the cupboards over the floor, so finding the bags was easy. I took the box into the living room. Even a whole box of bags wouldn't make much headway with this destruction.

The books hurt me the most, so I began there, stacking in a pile the ones that were not fatally damaged, inserting torn pages in ones that could be salvaged. In one corner, books had been strewn from the bookcase without being totally vandalized. I sat on the floor, opened one with a Lewis and Clark cover to make sure it was intact, and discovered the book didn't match the cover. The next two were the same. Non-matching book and cover.

I leaned back against the wall and watched Cody, still facing the window. I caught his eye in the reflection of the glass.

"You are one cool customer. And I'm really slow on the uptake. You're not upset about the destruction here, because none of your special things were touched. That's what was strange about your house. I couldn't put my finger on it at first, but it lacked personality. No character-revealing 'stuff' sitting around or hanging on the walls. No little artifacts from your digs. No Native American art. Your house was sterile. You expected something like this, or to be burned out, didn't you?"

Cody silently inserted a couple of logs in the wood-burning stove before he plopped into the slashed chair. "Anything else you've observed, Mrs. Allan, that I should know about myself?"

"I charge a lot of money for my psychoanalysis sessions. I'm *very* expensive. I'm not sure you can afford me. But we could strike a deal. Help me find my husband, and I'll give you ten free sessions."

"You never give up, do you?" Cody seemed suddenly weary.

"Not where Bart is concerned. If I thought I had a prayer of finding him myself, I'd be out there right now. But you and I both know I can't do it alone. I think you're the only one who has any idea were he might be. In fact, I'll bet you could take me to him right now." I watched Cody's eyes. His face remained an unreadable mask, but his eyes betrayed him.

"You do know!" I was exultant. "You found the cave this afternoon, didn't you?"

Cody didn't even smile. He just wiped his hand over his eyes, as if to erase the scene before him. Probably hoped I wouldn't be there when he looked up again. He leaned an elbow on the arm of his chair and rested his chin against his fist. "Do you ever get tired of being right?"

"No, because it's so sweet when it does happen." I jumped to my feet. "Can we go there? Will you take me?"

"Do you ski?"

"On water, gracefully. On snow, I can stand up. We can't take the snow machines?"

"They make too much noise."

"But you just got back from there, didn't you?"

"I only took the Ski-Doo part of the way. I skied the rest of the way so they wouldn't hear me coming."

"Do you have extra skis? And boots? That would fit me?" I didn't relish the idea of trying to ski in boots my sandals would fit in—like Clarence's.

"I can outfit you, but I'm not sure it's a good idea. What kind of physical condition are you in? Can you ski cross-country for an hour? I won't carry you back if you get tired. You'll be under your own steam."

"I'll expect nothing from you but an expert, patient guide. No helping hand. No pampering." I had to add the patient part. I wasn't much more than a novice, and I knew Cody would be able to ski like he was born with slats on his feet.

"I'll get the gear. You wait here." He headed for the snow room.

"Can't I help?" I started to follow.

Cody turned. "I'm curious. How did you find my little hideaway?"

I smiled conspiratorially. "Why? Do you have another around here somewhere?" In an instant I knew he did. The look of disbelief that flashed across his face, then disappeared just as quickly, was like an outright confession.

"I have a sixth sense about these things," I teased, laughing at the look on his face. Then I got serious. "I was raised next door to a mansion built and designed by my father and my husband's father as the West Coast Control Center for Anastasia, then the brand-new anti-terrorist division of Interpol. There were secret passages in the house, and Bart and I played in them as children. I learned how to discover secret doors and find the hidden buttons or nails or bulges in the carpet, or knotholes that triggered the openings. You don't know how deliriously happy I was to have found yours when I did, and that it worked as silently as those in the mansion."

Cody had relaxed only a small degree.

"Would you like me to turn my back, or go lock myself in the bathroom so I don't see where you're going? I promise I won't peek.

Actually, I think it's incredibly wise of you to have done it. No one respects anyone's privacy anymore. You can't even lock your house and leave it secured without someone breaking the windows to get in."

At his continued silence, I turned to go, then whirled back around. "Now I'm curious. Did you build your home with the original intent of having the secret rooms because of your occupation, or did you add them later, when you started this mission?"

Cody sighed and threw up his hands. "I give up. How does your husband put up with you?"

I smiled. "He loves me. If you think I'm a pest now, think how it would have been to have grown up with me, and have me tag along after your every step because I adored you so much. So he's used to all my foibles and loves me anyway. Want some help with the equipment?"

"Want to find my storage room?" Cody challenged. He'd break some girl's heart someday with that gorgeous grin if she fell in love and he didn't.

"Sure." I stepped toward the snow room.

"Never mind. I believe you could. But we don't have time to get there and back before dark if we play games. Let's move." He stepped around me into the snow room. By the time I got there, the shelves had slid back, revealing a staircase leading down. Along one wall hung hooded white Arctic-wear snowsuits and camouflage suits. He thrust an Arctic suit at me. "Get into this while I get the ski stuff. What size shoe do you wear?"

"You mean you have a whole array of sizes?" I asked in disbelief.

"No. I wanted to know how many pairs of socks to bring so mine would fit you."

"Seven and a half."

"Thank you. Now get dressed." As I donned the one-piece suit, Cody moved swiftly down the stairs, returning with two pairs of white boots stuffed with socks. He closed the door to his upstairs room, which we'd left open, then shrugged into his whites.

"You know I'm doing this against my better judgment, don't you?" he said.

"I know. I promise you blessings in heaven for being such a good sport about it, and not booting me out on my ear in the snow."

"Oh, you have connections in heaven to make promises like that?" He'd beaten me getting dressed, even with the head start I had.

"Actually, I make such a pest of myself there, too, that my prayers are finally answered just to get rid of me." I smiled helplessly up at him, and he zipped the stuck boot zipper I'd struggled with.

"I believe you. I don't think for a minute you're joking."

I stashed the radio/phone in the hood again so I could hear Bart's beep if he had a chance to call. Then we donned white-framed infrared goggles and ventured into the snowy cosmos with our white gloves, skis, and poles. Even our faces were covered by white knit masks, making us as purely white as the world into which we were quickly assimilated.

I actually kept up with Cody as we started along the ridge of the mountain. Whipping through the trees filled me with unbelievable exhilaration, and I finally had a sense of why people lived in climates where there was so much of this incredibly beautiful, frosty stuff. It helped to be properly dressed for the occasion.

I kept a watchful eye out for landmarks, for some kind of trail Cody followed that I could repeat if I needed to go to the mine by myself, or if I needed to find my way back to his house. All I could see were snow-covered trees duplicating themselves again and again. Then we left the stand of Douglas fir and dropped toward a depression. On the opposite edge of the shallow valley loomed a unique outcropping of rocks. Finally, a landmark.

Cody flew by it and up the other side, heading again for the trees. I became more alert to what surrounded us, to who might be watching. With Osama bin Laden so close, his men wouldn't be lazy or lax. I couldn't afford to be, either.

The closer we got to the mine, to Bart, the faster my heart beat, and I knew it had nothing to do with the exercise. I could not imagine life without this man I loved so much. We had to reach him, to get him out before bin Laden arrived. Bart would become an object lesson in how to deal with the enemy when Bin Laden began his training. It would be ugly, painful, and fatal.

Suddenly I thought I glimpsed movement out of the corner of my eye—something besides the silent flakes of snow falling so thick that they nearly obliterated our tracks as we made them. Cody had seen it, too. He swerved into the dense stand of white-barked quaking aspen trees we paralleled and stopped. I followed suit.

I kept searching the area where I thought something should be, but the snow blended the horizon and the ridge so perfectly together that I couldn't tell where the earth stopped and the sky began. The infrared goggles should have sensed any warm-blooded animal or human. All remained white and cold.

Cody's white glove touched me. I read his silent question and shook my head. No, I couldn't see anything either. But the hair on the back of my neck prickled. I stopped Cody as he prepared to leave the safety of the trees and signaled "wait."

He searched the area again, as I did. Nothing moved. But something was out there. I felt it, just as I felt we must not leave the trees. It was the most ideal cover we could have behind the white bark of the aspen.

Cody touched my arm and silently questioned again. "What?"

How could I tell him that I didn't see anything, just that I felt it? He'd consign me to the looney bin. Suddenly he shifted at my side. I glanced at him and knew he'd seen what I knew was out there—but couldn't see.

I touched his arm and mouthed "where?" He shook his head. What did that mean? Then I knew. Clarence said Cody had a sixth sense about men and animals. He hadn't seen anything either. We were a pair of loonies. But neither of us moved. We watched.

Somewhere out there, something, someone, waited.

CHAPTER 32

I hardly dared breathe. Aware of the technology that Osama bin Laden employed in other countries, I knew his men could have parabolic microphones that caught whispers at a distance of hundreds of feet, not to mention infrared goggles or gun sights that revealed body heat, even if you were so well hidden the naked eye could never see you.

Sensors could alert them when anyone approached their hideout. There might be booby traps, mini-mines, lasers. Our hope for getting close to the mine lay in two possibilities: either such devices were not yet in place, or because of yesterday's storm, today's heavy snowfall, and their isolated location, bin Laden's men felt secure without them.

Whether sophisticated equipment had spotted us, or someone had inadvertently stumbled across us, the "how" didn't matter. Someone was out there.

Cody remained motionless, scanning the area in front of us, the open scoop of land between tree-covered hillsides. I turned ever so slowly and placed my back to the tree behind which I stood, watching in the opposite direction so no one could sneak up from the rear. What had we sensed that remained so well hidden?

Suddenly, in one smooth movement, Cody whirled and flew off through the trees behind us. If I hadn't already been pointed in that direction, I'd never have caught him. Then, instead of turning back toward the house, he veered in the direction we'd been going—straight for the mine.

If we'd been spotted, why on earth was Cody going for the mine? A quiver started in the pit of my stomach. Was I being gullible and following him right into a trap? "Mine is not to reason why, mine is but to do or die. Into the valley of death rode the . . ." I hated that last line. Why did that quotation always come to mind at the most inopportune moments?

Right now, I felt like I was on a collision course with the Grim Reaper. I was skiing faster than my meager skills safely permitted, and anything that appeared suddenly in my path would either be run over or would be my undoing. Cody zipped in and out of tight spots, between trees, over rocks. My reactions weren't as quick, nor my dexterity as highly developed as his.

Natural athlete I was not. Except in or on water. I was clearly out of my element in this country. And scared witless. One unexpected move, one unseen rock, one branch too low on a tree, one slight miscalculation, and I could wind up worse off than Hildegard Piggett. Then I thought of the baby. *Much* worse off than Mrs. Piggett. I said a silent prayer and plunged down the next slope, trying desperately not to lose Cody.

He never looked back. He skied like the legions of Satan sought his soul, and he was determined to outrun them. Did he even remember that I followed him? Sheer terror had my heart hammering my rib cage as I hurtled by trees, rocks, and bushes much faster than was safe or sane.

Keeping my eye on the almost invisible shape staying too far in front of me, while watching his tracks to make sure I stayed exactly where he'd been, began to wear on me. How long could I do this without a major mishap? Plunging headlong into unknown territory, I was an accident on its way to happening. Or had this become a suicide run for me—and my baby? A cold chill swept through me. If I called out, I could betray our location and bring the terrorists down on us. If I stopped or slowed, I'd lose Cody, which in itself could be a fatal mistake in this snow. *Where are my guardian angels, Father? Please don't let them take a Twinkie break right now.*

I didn't dare look back to see who, if anyone, followed us. I didn't even know whether Cody had actually seen someone, or if he'd simply decided to leave before someone saw us.

Then, without warning, Cody disappeared. I couldn't see him in front of me anymore. I hadn't heard a sound. A shot, even from a gun with a silencer, ought to make a slight pop that would carry in this vast silence. I whipped along the tree line and nearly ran into the man, standing still in the snow. I managed to stop without running over him, a minor miracle in itself. He didn't look at me, just stood as if he was listening to something. The snow falling? The cry of a hawk? I heard nothing but my heart pounding wildly in my ears. So loud, in fact, that Cody probably thought he was hearing war drums.

I let him do his thing while I caught my breath and offered a heartfelt prayer of gratitude for my safety. And while I was at it, added a plea for Bart's. He would be the one in desperate need of guardian angels if bin Laden arrived before we found a way to get him out of the mine.

Could Cody be lost? The intrepid tracker and guide who knew every inch of these hills? No. He must have skied them as much as he walked them. Winter lasted longer than summer at this altitude.

Then, as suddenly as he'd stopped, he took off again. Maybe he'd remembered that I was following him, had taken pity on me, and stopped so I could catch my breath. That being the case, I owed him one. I wouldn't have survived that breakneck speed much longer without a catastrophic calamity.

Cody set a more moderate pace this time, as if he'd outrun the devils and had time for a leisurely afternoon run in the snow. I assumed we were still headed for the mine. Now I could even enjoy the sound of skis shushing through the snow, the taste of the huge flakes on my tongue, the incredible beauty of this winter wonderland.

I wondered how far we'd come. He'd asked if I could ski cross-country for an hour; I'd assumed that meant thirty minutes out and thirty minutes back. Hadn't we been gone at least that long already? But the man just kept going. And going. We came to a steep incline that required tricky maneuvering to reach the top—tricky for me, not for Cody. But once on top, his strategy became clear. We leaned against the rocks and looked across the valley at another, higher mountaintop. A third of the way down the mountain, the upside down u-shaped dark timbers of the mine entrance were clearly outlined against the deep white snow.

Cody pulled a small telescope from his pocket and examined the entire area before handing me the glass. I zeroed in on my husband's prison. It looked so innocuous, so benign. An innocent old abandoned mine. But what secrets it held! Those secrets fell under the heading of treason.

Where had the helicopter dropped the supplies that were stashed in the mine? I swept the landscape again and spotted a good-sized flat spot to the right of the entrance. I wasn't sure a helicopter could land there, but one could certainly hover and lower a pallet full of boxes. It was hard to tell about the valley floor, because it was nothing more than a carpet of unbroken white. But it was certainly flat enough for a C-130-J to swoop down, deposit a cache of supplies or arms, take on a load of cattle or anything else, and disappear into the sky, largely unseen by the few inhabitants of this high country. That would explain the lights. And as the plane dropped into the deep valley, the sound of its engines wouldn't carry across the mountains.

Supposing we got near the mine, how would we get Bart out? I memorized every rock and ridge I could see through the snow, repeatedly examining the terrain around the entrance. I had to remember it well enough to describe to Dad. I handed the glass back to Cody.

"Ready?" he asked quietly.

I nodded. Silently we turned and headed back, this time by a different route. Even in the deepening dusk and the heavily falling snow, I knew we hadn't come this way before. Cody didn't break his neck to make time, nor did he seem concerned that we'd be trailed from the mine.

Suddenly we dropped into a box canyon, and I recognized Hildegard Piggett's ranch. "With all the snow, I'm sure no one's been here to feed her animals," Cody explained. "We'd better take care of them for her." It didn't take long with both of us working, and soon we were back on skis and headed up the canyon.

Night had fallen when we reached Cody's house, an early darkness caused by heavily falling snow. E Da Hah greeted Cody joyously when he opened the door, leaping into his arms and placing his paws affectionately around Cody's neck. We hung our ski togs in the snow room and stepped over the debris still covering the floor. Cody added some logs to the red coals glowing in the wood-burning stove, then settled in the slashed chair. I sat with my back to the wall next to the stove and stretched out my tired legs.

After several minutes, Cody broke the silence. "What happened to the chatterbox I found in my office? You're awfully quiet."

"Sorry. Thanks for taking me to the mine. I've been consumed with trying to figure out how to get in there and get Bart out as quickly as possible. Is there another way into the mine? A back entrance? I've got to call Dad—he'll be worried sick—but I wanted to have some kind of plan formulated before I did."

"Why will he be worried? Didn't you tell him you were here with me?"

I smiled. "That's why he was worried. Of course, I'm sure he has your full dossier by now, so that may alleviate his anxiety a little. But knowing Dad, since I haven't called back, he'll be pacing the floor." I shrugged apologetically. "I'm his only child."

"Then by all means, call. I don't want to bring the wrath of the great Jack Alexander down on my head."

"Are you being facetious, or do you know of my father?"

"Mrs. Allan, for someone who is so smart, you are so dumb. Or naive, as you put it. Anyone who's been to Quantico has been regaled with the exploits of the legendary OSI man who survived a car bombing, infiltrated the tightest bunch of rebels and terrorists the world had seen, and lived to establish Anastasia."

"I was wrong. You can play dumb. You had me fooled with your feigned ignorance of our identity. So who are you with?"

"Since you're such a whiz, I'll let you figure that out. Now if you'll excuse me, I need to check the answering machine. Want me to bring you the phone so you don't have to move your tired body?"

"Please do. I have very wobbly knees right now."

Cody threaded his way through the litter on the floor. I heard a familiar disembodied voice on the machine. "Cody, it's Dodson. It's about four o'clock, and I'm bringing a group of people to your house. They said you're expecting them. Should make it in a little over an hour unless the wind starts. Five machines loaded with equipment. Must be some party you're having up there. A little short on women, though. Have the soup hot."

I jumped to my feet and hurried to the kitchen. "Are you expecting someone?"

"No." Cody stared out into the darkness, then turned to me with a frown creasing his forehead. "Could it be your people?"

I held out my hand, and Cody tossed the phone to me. "It would be just like Dad to mount an exploratory mission and a search for his missing daughter at the same time. You can turn on the speaker if you'd like to hear the conversation." Cody punched the speaker button as I dialed the Shilo Inn.

"Hi, Mom."

"Allison, where are you? Are you all right?"

"I'm fine. Sorry I didn't call sooner. Cody took me to the mine to get an idea of what we're up against getting Bart out. We just got back. Where's Dad?"

I heard a deep sigh of relief. "He left a couple of hours ago with half the group to see if they could find someone to take them into the mountains where you said you were. He's been beside himself since you hung up and never called back."

"Things got a bit sticky here, then Bart called and gave me a little more information. When Cody returned, he consented to lead me to the mine. I was so excited I didn't think to let Dad know my plans—plus I figured he'd find out everything I couldn't tell him about Cody before I did."

"It's a good thing he discovered he could trust that man. I think he'd have called in the Special Forces if he hadn't. Alli, you've added more gray hairs to your father's head today than—"

"Message received," I interrupted. "I'm sorry. Who's with Dad?"

"Else, Lion, Dom, and Oz. David's still at the sheep station, but Jack wanted him to be near the plane in case they need it. Your father's set up computers—can't operate without them anymore—and Sky and Mai Li are helping me here."

"I assume someone bought snow machines and outfitted everyone with Arctic-wear this afternoon."

Mom sighed. "If your father keeps dipping into your inheritance to finance these expensive operations, you won't have anything left of it. I shudder to think what that bill came to—clothing, ski equipment, snow machines, trailers to transport them, renting a fleet of SUVs to pull them, not to mention the electronic stuff we needed that we didn't bring with us."

"It's to get Bart back. There's no better use for your money. As far as I'm concerned, he takes precedence over everything else, the ultimate bad guy included."

I'd settled back by the fire, the affectionate ocelot draped across my lap while I talked. Cody, still listening to the speaker phone in the kitchen, began the gargantuan task of restoring order to his kitchen.

"What kind of supplies is Dad bringing?"

"Food and bedding for an army, even tents in case they were needed. He's equipped to bivouac for a week if necessary."

"Sorry. We don't have that kind of time. We've got to get Bart out immediately, but it's a good thing Dad's coming prepared. A couple of hooligans vandalized Cody's house this afternoon and destroyed everything. They did leave the walls standing, so we're sheltered from the snow, which hasn't stopped all day. I'll bet it's snowed fifteen inches."

"Minimum twenty-four," Cody said around the corner. "Maybe thirty."

"Else will be in heaven. Right back in her element." Mom was quiet for a minute. "Where were you when they got in?"

"Hidden safely away in Cody's secret room. They never saw me, and I don't think they knew I was here."

"Do you know who it was? What they wanted?"

I glanced at Cody, leaning in the doorway watching me. "I think they were after me because I'd been in Hildegard Piggett's house. I think Janet sent them, or told them I'd been there. If Else's break-in of her computer was discovered, Janet would immediately suspect whoever had been near her computer on the ranch. Me."

"Are you safe now? Honey, what if they come back?"

"Cody will protect me."

Cody laughed and shook his head.

"And if he won't, I'll dog his heels while he protects himself." He shrugged as if to say, well, I can't stop that.

"What's he like?" Mom's voice dropped to a conspiratorial tone. "Your father had a hard time finding anything on him."

I looked at Cody brandishing the broom as I spoke. "Well, he's about six feet tall, thick blue-black hair, nicely trimmed. No braid. He has intense black eyes, a wonderful tan, and a disarming smile when he favors you with it, which is seldom. Usually he's silent and mysterious." Cody bowed. "Scratch that. That's what I thought before I spent the afternoon with him. A more accurate description would be grumpy."

Cody shook his head in disgust and went back to sweeping.

"He isn't married, probably because he looks down on our species from such a lofty macho level that he could never find anyone to measure up to his expectations. He hasn't scalped me yet, but I think he's considered it a couple of times. I actually haven't found his trophy room, but there's probably one here somewhere with all the white women's scalps he's collected."

Mom gasped. "Alli, the man sounds horrible." She paused, then said, "You're teasing me, right?"

"Right. Well, sort of. We have the speaker phone on, and he's been listening to every word I said—we said. I'm not in any kind of danger from Cody, except possibly being tossed out in the snow because I irritate him so. He absolutely can't understand how my husband can love me, much less live with me."

Mom laughed. "Hi, Joseph Jefferson Cody. I'm looking forward to meeting you and seeing if my daughter came anywhere near pegging you for what you really are."

"It will be a pleasure to meet you, Mrs. Alexander. I've been a great admirer of yours for several years, since my time at Quantico."

"They aren't still circulating those outdated stories, are they? All that happened so long ago." I could tell Mom was pleased by Cody's comments.

"Guess I'd better go help Cody with this colossal mess, in case anyone shows up. Right now there isn't a place to throw down a sleeping bag." I slid the sleeping ocelot from my numb legs and headed for the kitchen.

"Wait. Before you go, what's the number there?"

Cody recited his number into the phone.

"I assume it's a secured line," Mom added.

"Of course," I broke in. "Someone as intelligent as Cody wouldn't have an unsecured line." Cody shot me a look I couldn't read as he swept trash into a bag. "Got to go, Mom, before I'm scalped for insurrection. The Indians are looking decidedly hostile right now."

"Joseph, I hope you'll forgive my daughter's political incorrectness. She becomes absolutely unbearable when she's worried about Bart and separated from him. All the more reason to get him out of the terrorists' hands as quickly as possible. Before she drives us all to distraction."

"Love you, too, Mom."

I plopped the phone back in its cradle, and without a word plunged into the task of cleaning up the mess on the floor. As I picked through it, trying to salvage what hadn't been totally destroyed, I noted something interesting.

I straightened and looked at Cody. "You live a meager existence. If my pantry at home had been dumped on the floor, it would have taken a small bulldozer to clean up the mess—and we're gone frequently. This looks like a lot because it's scattered everywhere, but you actually have very little on hand for the kind of winters you get—unless you were caught by the unexpected storm and didn't have time to lay in supplies . . . which I don't believe happened. This is all part of the masquerade, isn't it? Where do you really live, Cody? Downstairs? Or do you keep everything important down there, and just bring up here what you need as you need it?"

"If I'm going to remain the man of mystery you thought I was, I'll let you keep guessing. Isn't that what women do—try to keep men guessing about them?"

"Some may. I don't believe in that. What if my husband guessed wrong about something that was important to me? I try to be very up-front with him about everything."

"Everything?" Cody looked suspicious.

"Well, almost everything." I smiled. "I guess everyone needs a little mystique about them to keep their mate intrigued."

We worked quickly to get the cans back on the shelves and sweep crackers, pasta, and cookies in the trash. I washed the plastic dishes that hadn't been broken and all the plastic containers, while Cody mopped spaghetti sauce, honey, cereal, and powdered cleansers from the floor.

We'd just restored some order to the living room when the thunderous roar of half a dozen snow machines shattered the comfortable silence in which we'd been working. The troops had arrived. At least I hoped it was Anastasia. I looked at Cody, suddenly fearful that we'd been too trusting and the terrorists might have returned en masse.

He motioned me into his bedroom with E Da Hah, flipped off the interior lights, and turned on floodlights that illuminated the snow-filled universe outside. I stood poised at the closet door, the ocelot draped across my arms like a luxurious heavy fur coat, waiting for the word to open the secret door and flee to the safety of the hidden room.

But what safety could I find there? Osama bin Laden's men wouldn't raid a second time. They wouldn't repeat what they'd done earlier. This time they'd be prepared to storm the place, tear it apart, and then burn it down.

CHAPTER 33

Multiple engines throttling up the steep hill created a deafening noise, rattling the windows and making the fur on the back of E Da Hah's neck stand up. He strained to get down. I tried to soothe him, to sweet-talk him into not leaping from my arms and running into the other room. "It's okay, beauty, it's okay," I murmured. "We'll know in a minute whether you're going to keep your lovely fur coat or somebody else will get to wear it. And whether I'll ever see my husband again."

That thought hit me in the pit of my stomach, and my knees almost gave way. *Father, again I promise that if you'll just get Bart free and me and our daughter home safely to California, I'll be perfectly content to stay there and give up this ridiculous, dangerous, terrifying lifestyle.*

Well, I acknowledged, maybe not *perfectly* content, but I'd do my share from the Control Center, and however else I could help without coming under fire from all the weirdos in the world bent on destroying my family. I knew one couldn't bargain with God, but I was desperate. Surely He'd understand and forgive me. Or simply ignore me if I was too far out of line.

I waited, holding my breath, burying my head in E Da Hah's lush fur and praying fervently that our visitors were not the terrorists. What would I do if they'd returned? It wouldn't be smart to hide in a room that was bound to go up in flames. What would Cody do? Flee to his underground room? Was it fireproof? Or would he head into the snow, hoping to elude them there?

My chances seemed a lot better with Cody than here. I left his closet and stepped out of his bedroom as the lights of the snow machines flashed across the darkened living room.

"Cody, it's me, Dodson," Gary called through the night. "Open your garage."

Thank you, Father, I breathed, and dropped the excited ocelot. E Da Hah raced to the window, stood on his hind paws, and pressed his nose against it to watch the lights as the snow machines bobbed across the yard and around the corner. He raced to the snow room and waited for Cody to open the garage door.

Cody hit the automatic opener and held the cat's collar while the snowmobiles pulled into the empty space on one side of the garage and lined up behind each other. At all the noise and commotion, E Da Hah retreated to his perch on the refrigerator.

I suddenly remembered Gary Dodson's message on the answering machine—have the soup hot. "Did you remember to heat the soup for Gary?" I asked, knowing he hadn't.

"Forgot about that. Will you . . . ?" He looked up hopefully at me for a moment, then went past me into the kitchen. I would have, if he'd asked. But I wasn't a volunteer in the kitchen of any man who had a problem with a woman being a government agent. He could heat his own soup.

The crew resembled a bunch of abominable snowmen in their white Arctic gear as they dismounted. Dad crossed the garage in three strides and took me in his snowy arms. "Bunny, I was so worried about you."

"And you're repaying me for that worry by turning me into a snowman." I pulled out of his freezing embrace and touched his rosy cheek. "Sorry, Dad. Cody took me to the mine, and I forgot to call you back. But I'm glad you're here, because we have a lot of work to do. Any word on bin Laden? Anybody seen him yet? It's probably too much to hope someone would capture the creep."

"Not yet. Where can we put these bunny suits?"

Gary knew the routine. He'd shed his snowsuit and headed for the snow room to hang it up.

"Cody has a mud room he probably only uses for snow stuff. Hang your things up there and come on in. We've almost got the place back to normal after our afternoon visitors. Else, how do you manage to look like you just stepped off the pages of *Vogue* after a trip like that?"

Elegant Else could wrestle in the mud and still be more beautiful than anyone else. If she wasn't so sweet, you'd have to hate her for it. She gave me a quick hug and hung her things. "I heard about the Native American poster boy you found up here and had to come and see him for myself."

"He's all yours, if you can get past his distrust of female agents. But if anyone could, it would be you." I walked with her into the kitchen.

The exuberant Lionel swept me off my feet in a grand hug. "You had us worried, little one. Glad you're okay."

"Just waiting for the cavalry to arrive. Whoops. Forgive the slip, Cody." I grinned at him when he glared over his shoulder at the comment. "Listen up, everyone. You need to know your host, and intrepid outdoorsman and guide. Ta Da! This is . . ." I'd been about to say Joseph Jefferson Cody, and he knew it.

"Cody," he interrupted.

"Cody," I repeated. "He graciously offered his luxurious accommodations." I stopped and looked at Cody. "Or did we just assume you would when Mom told us they were already on their way?"

Dad stepped forward and offered his hand to the piqued man stirring soup on the stove. "I see my daughter has managed to needle her way under your skin already. Thanks for intervening this morning and saving her life."

"He doesn't want your thanks, Dad. He's been sorry all day that he did. Next we have Lionel Brandt, our zealous Frenchman." Dom kissed my cheek as he moved into the room. "Dominic Vicente, Spanish ex-bullfighter. Then Oz Barlow, who is usually as irritated at me as you are." Oz ruffled my hair, kissed my cheek, and nodded at Cody, who was having a hard time keeping his eyes off Else. Her black turtleneck sweater and pants hugged a traffic-stopping figure. Radiant blonde hair brushed her shoulders, swaying with every movement of her graceful body.

"I've saved the best till last. Cody, meet our lovely Norwegian import, Else, who I'll match against you any day on skis. I'm sure you all know Gary Dodson. Good. That's all over—oh, no. There's one more member of the family you haven't met."

I stood on a chair and retrieved a slightly shaken ocelot from atop the fridge next to the back door. Else's attention immediately left

Cody and centered on the cat, much to Cody's apparent disappointment.

"He isn't fond of strangers," Cody explained. "I'll get Gary fed so he can get back to Spencer before bedtime in case the roads are open and he has to drive the school bus tomorrow. The rest of us will eat later. Make yourselves at home—what's left of it after our destructive visitors ransacked it."

Everyone migrated to the living room, leaving Gary and Cody alone in the kitchen. I wondered if Dad had explained to Gary what kind of expedition he headed—snow sports or war games—and why we needed Cody's help. Probably not.

We sat on the floor around the wood-burning stove, watching orange flames dance behind the smoky glass. I leaned my head on Dad's shoulder. "Sorry I had you so worried."

He slipped his arm around me and squeezed my shoulder. "Do it again, and I'll terminate your contract with Anastasia," he said sternly. That produced a snicker from the group. No one had contracts, and they knew my father's weakness for his only daughter. "So, what did you find at the mine? What does it look like?"

I described, in as much detail as I could remember, the distances involved, the hills, and the valley between the mountains. "Cody will be able to give you specifics. Apparently he's lived here all his life, and spent his childhood running the hills in the summer and skiing them in the winter. There probably isn't anyone alive who knows the area as well."

"When was the last time you heard from Bart?" Oz asked.

"This afternoon, while I hid from the vandals behind Cody's secret panel. He has a pretty sophisticated control center of his own here."

"What are our chances of a quick snatch-and-dash?" Lionel asked, fruitlessly trying to restore some order to his mane of tousled golden-blond hair.

"Again, Cody would be a better judge, but unless there's a back entrance, they'll see us coming. It appears to be well guarded. I think the Idaho term is 'loaded for bear.'" I looked at Dom and Lion. "You two are going to have to work some of your most incredible magic to penetrate this place."

Else nodded toward the kitchen. "Is he cooperating with us willingly?"

I shrugged. "Your guess is as good as mine. He's really enigmatic. He was so furious with me for blowing whatever he'd been working on for months up here that he would hardly speak to me. One minute I think he wants to go it on his own and do it himself, the next he seems cooperative. If he works with Dad, he may be fine. If I stay out of his way, he may be happy to do all he can to help us. He's the key—our only hope for getting Bart out before bin Laden gets to him."

Everyone watched the fire without speaking. Gary waved from the doorway. "You folks timed your ski party perfectly. Who'd have expected so much snow this time of year? Enjoy. Stop in at the store on your way back to the Falls."

They waved. Dad stood and went to shake his hand. "I appreciate your bringing us up here. Don't think we'd have found it in all that snow."

As the sound of his snowmobile disappeared, Cody emptied cans of soup into a pot to heat for our dinner. "I brought some fresh French bread," Else said, heading for her equipment in the garage. She helped Cody get the simple meal ready, then we ate on the floor around the fire.

Dad looked hopefully at Cody. "Would you be willing to take Dom, Lion, and Else to the mine tonight? I know you've had a long day, but we need to move on this ASAP."

"Sure. I'll give you access to every resource I have." Cody looked pointedly at me. "You won't have to break into the basement. I'll let you in." Then he turned back to Dad. "You can set up downstairs. It'll withstand anything but a direct nuclear hit." I couldn't tell whether his little smile indicated pride or a joke. What a puzzling, frustrating man.

"Good. I didn't relish the idea of posting guards all night. Thanks, Cody. If I'd been able to reach you, I would have asked if we could come before we descended on you. Oz and Allison can help me set up, and when you get back we'll be ready to formulate a plan."

I cleaned up our meal while Cody acquainted Dad with the house and showed him the alarms and lights and how to set and disconnect them. Oz toted equipment downstairs while everyone else donned snow gear and skis. They'd departed into the snowy night by the time I finished in the kitchen.

What a setup Cody had in the basement! These were the real living quarters with his personal treasures. Here were the Lewis and Clark books, probably everything ever written on the historic expedition, all well-worn from countless readings. On the outer walls, murals depicting the views upstairs replaced windows. It felt as open and airy as the ground floor. Must be Cody's clever way of coping with his claustrophobia. There was a wonderful master bedroom with more outdoor murals, a guest room which I commandeered for Else and me if we ever actually got a chance to use it, a huge, comfortable living room, and a large, fully stocked kitchen and pantry.

While Oz and Dad set up their electronic equipment, I luxuriated in a long, leisurely shower in Cody's champagne-colored bathroom, perfectly content to let Dad take charge of everything. A nice hot shower could wash away a multitude of sins, including exhaustion, exasperation, confusion, and accumulated emotions and impressions of the day, leaving my mind clear to tackle the next problem. The biggest, most important one. Rescuing my husband.

Unfortunately, I had to dress in the same too-large navy sweat suit Cody had loaned me. The radio/phone beeped as I towel-dried my hair. "Bart! I'm here."

"Wish I were. Any news from Anastasia?"

"They've arrived. Cody took Else, Dom, and Lion to see the mine. Dad and Oz are creating a sort of command post here. How are you?"

"Tired. I've been stacking crates all day. Most marked U.S. Military from a dozen different bases. The snow kept bin Laden and his cell leaders away, but they're helicoptering them in the minute it stops. According to someone here, that could be as early as first light. The snow's supposed to end and clouds clear away sometime tonight."

"Let me get Dad on the phone. If you end up back in the mine where we can't reach you, you won't have any idea what they plan to do." I hurried into the living room and handed Dad the phone. "Bart didn't say it, but he's wondering what the chances were we could get to him before morning. It seems that bin Laden's coming when the snow stops—possibly by dawn."

Dad took the phone. "How you holding up, son?"

"Managing, but I'll be a lot better if I get out of here before the big boss arrives. What does it look like?"

"Haven't had a chance to talk with Cody about the mine setup. Any ideas from your end?"

"Jack, there's a network of tunnels here, with more going on than storing supplies and arms. Every once in a while I get a whiff of chemicals. In one part of the shaft, I hear engines. In another part, mining sounds: mini-explosions, metal hitting rock. I'd say the old mine car railroad's working, from the rumbling I feel."

Dad paced as he talked. "Any idea how many men they've got up there?"

"Ten in my section. Another twelve that go back and forth. How many more I can't say, but from the sounds in the other shafts, at least double that number. They have bunks, a kitchen of sorts, and a latrine at the front of the mine. That's when I call—from the latrine. The phone doesn't work back in the tunnel."

"Have you been all the way to the end?" I followed Dad's train of thought. There could be another entry.

"I think so. Solid walls, top to bottom, except for one small shaft which must be for ventilation—too small for me to get through. I tried last night. Got stuck and almost didn't get out. It's near the bunk I sleep on."

"I'll ask Cody about it. How are they treating you?"

To this question I anxiously awaited the answer. Terrorists were not known for their humane treatment of prisoners.

"Osama bin Laden knows who I am and told everyone 'hands off.' He wants to personally administer the punishment that's my due. Other than a couple of guys spitting on me when they walk by, no one's disobeyed. No one dares. They're so awestruck by this creep, you'd think he walked on water. But they make sure I move twice as many crates as they do. Uh-oh . . . my guard's coming. I'll try to call before lights out."

He was gone, the slender thread of communication severed. I looked hopefully at Dad, silently asking if he'd had any epiphanies during the conversation.

He slowly shook his head. "We'll have to wait till they return. See what they think after they've seen the mine, and get Cody's input. He may know of another way in, though if he did I'm not sure why he hasn't mentioned it. You've discussed Bart's conversations with him?"

"Probably told him everything I know. If there's another way in or out, I'll bet he knows about it. And he likely wouldn't have told me. I have the same effect on him as I do on Oz." I reached over and punched Oz's shoulder. "Total irritation."

"Only because you deserve it, little sis," Oz laughed. After a brief episode of infatuation, Oz had decided that if he couldn't love me any other way, it would be as the big brother I never had.

I suddenly felt exhausted. The rejuvenation accomplished by the hot shower had dissolved with Bart's phone call and the realization that we had so little time to accomplish the impossible task before us. I'm sure Dad and the rest of Anastasia were thinking beyond Bart's rescue to the containment and eradication of the terrorist cell. I couldn't think beyond getting Bart out of Osama bin Laden's clutches.

"Bunny, why don't you go catch a few winks before everyone gets back. You look haggard. How long has it been since you've had a good night's sleep?" Dad rubbed his knuckles softly down my cheek.

"Six months."

"There's nothing you can do. I'll wake you when they come and we begin planning." He pushed me gently toward the bedroom door. I didn't object. I could do nothing except worry. If they came up with a viable plan, and I prayed they'd return with one, I'd need more energy than I could muster at the moment.

I fell asleep immediately, my weary body relaxing at once. And just as quickly, it seemed, the beautiful baby with azure eyes and black curly hair cried out for me. "Momma! Momma, don't you love me? Why don't you want me?"

"But I do, precious. I want you so much."

"If you wanted me, you'd leave. You'd go away from these bad men who want to kill you. If you loved me, you'd go home." My daughter cried, and I couldn't console her. She cried, and I couldn't get near enough to hold her and dry her tears. She faded slowly away, her forlorn cries rending my heart in two.

CHAPTER 34

I sat up with a start, my pillow wet with tears. My heart pounded, and I trembled from head to toe with a chill that had nothing to do with being cold. I didn't need that dreadful reminder that I shouldn't be here—that I should be safely at home in California, taking care of myself and my baby.

Did I have a choice I didn't have two days ago before Bart disappeared? Why couldn't I leave, now that Anastasia was here? Was there anything I could do that they couldn't do faster and easier and better? No. I could go home. I could leave as soon as they got Bart out of the mine. Certainly I wouldn't be able to leave tonight in the dark and snow. But first thing in the morning, when Bart was safely away, before Osama bin Laden arrived, I'd take the Polaris into Spencer and call Mom to come and get me. Then I'd catch the first plane to California.

That decision made, I joined the group as they settled in to brainstorm with steaming cups of hot chocolate. I scanned the faces of the just-returned foursome. Dominic and Lionel lacked their customary exuberance. Else's lovely features bore a glum expression, and Cody wore his usual emotionless mask. This did not bode good tidings.

"And the general consensus is?" I asked, jumping to the crucial business.

Lionel shook his head. "Did you ever see *The Guns of Navarrone?* Great old flick about an impregnable gun bunker in the rocks?" Most everyone nodded, and I could tell they agreed with his assessment. Impregnable.

"It can't be," I protested. "What about coming up over the top of the mountain and approaching the entrance from above?"

"Too much snow. Conditions are prime for an avalanche. Anything that disturbs the snow above the mine could cause those tons of snow to bury it," Dominic said quietly. "We wouldn't be able to get in until it melted."

I stared at Cody, who was concentrating on his fingernails, pointedly avoiding my eyes. "Cody, is there another entrance?"

Without looking up, he shook his head.

"There's got to be a way in. Bart said there's a network of tunnels. Surely there's more than one entrance. Think, Cody. You're my husband's only hope. If we don't get him out before Osama bin Laden arrives in the morning . . ." I choked back the tears. It would be too unprofessional to weep and wail. But that's what I felt like doing.

Dad spoke quietly. "Osama bin Laden knows Bart's identity—has a personal grudge against him. In May, Bart rescued a doctor and his formula to combat the Ebola virus and spirited them out of Africa. Osama planned to utilize that deadly virus to destroy the economy of a couple of nations so his rebels could seize what was left of government and country. He'll use Bart as an object lesson in torturing and dealing with infidels."

I didn't need to hear this, but I knew Dad had a reason for sticking the knife in my already aching heart and twisting it unmercifully. I watched his face, the muscles working in his jaw. His steel-gray eyes bored into Cody, who finally glanced up at him and winced involuntarily, then quickly resumed his emotionless expression and looked away.

"What about that ventilation tunnel, or air duct, or whatever it is? Bart said he tried to get through it, but it was too small. He almost got stuck. Does that lead anywhere? If there's one, surely there are more." I was pleading for my husband's life, and all Cody could do was sit and stare at his hands. I wanted to throttle the unfeeling man.

"Cody, please. Think. I'll bet you know that mine as well as you know the one Old Blue the grizzly was in this morning. Without a light, you vaulted into a crevice higher than my head with a huge, angry bear at your heels. You know these places. Clarence said—" I stopped, remembering the old man's final revelation. Suddenly the pieces slid neatly into place.

Cody looked up at my sudden silence.

I stared at him. "Do you know what Clarence's last words were? It was so important he couldn't wait for me to reach him. He gasped his message into my cell phone as I raced to him."

Cody turned away. He knew what I was talking about. "Clarence said Sacagawea's brother, Chief Cameahwait, showed Lewis and Clark a fabulous mine with a lode of gold and other valuable deposits. They never entered it in their journals because they didn't want anyone to know about it until they'd reported the discovery to President Jefferson. They wanted the treasure to belong to America, not to private individuals. Meriwether Lewis died on the Natchez Trace on his way to see President Jefferson. Historians are divided on whether it was suicide or murder."

Cody stood and began to pace the length of the living room.

"I'm betting on murder," I continued. "Lewis had the map in his possession. He was killed for it. Copies of a handmade map of some antiquity turn up around here from time to time, but no one's ever found that mine. No one—until you. All your books on Lewis and Clark were well read. You found the mine. There were enough clues in their writings, plus your Native American family's personal knowledge, for you to find the right cave."

Furious, I stood to face him, watching his broad shoulders sag. "It just happens to be in the mine the terrorists took over, doesn't it? If you take us in to get Bart, you'll have to take us to Lewis and Clark's treasure." I tried to swallow the rage that welled up in me. Tried to speak calmly and not scream at him. "That's why you were so irritated at me. You were afraid I'd discover your secret."

I hurled myself at Cody, pounding on his chest. "I don't want your stupid treasure! I want my husband. Keep your precious gold. A man's life is in your hands. You selfish . . ."

I felt Dad's arms around me, pulling me away, stopping me from pummeling Cody. He enfolded me in his arms, holding me so tightly against him that I could scarcely breathe. The room was totally silent except for my racking sobs.

"I'll take you in." Cody didn't concede that I'd guessed correctly. He simply agreed to do what I felt he should have done when he first discovered Bart was a prisoner there. If we didn't get Bart out because of this man's greed, I wasn't sure I'd be able to forgive him.

Cody retrieved a yellow pad from his desk and sat again in the circle on the floor. Dad pulled me down next to him, keeping his arm firmly around my shoulder.

Cody sketched the mine, showing the network of shafts, detailing their purpose. Bart had guessed right, except that there was more. Much more. "They've created new tunnels and concealed entries for easier escape. They've built a village in the mountain, and a chemical lab to experiment with bacteria and virus. They're pouring big money into biological warfare. One shaft's devoted to training in sabotage."

"How do you know all this?" Dad asked.

"I've been in periodically to check their progress," he stated matter-of-factly.

"Secretly, or as one of them?" I asked. Everyone looked away. Had they been wondering the same thing?

"At night, when everyone's asleep. I'll take you to the entrance I used. They haven't found it yet, or Cameahwait's treasure. No, I'm not one of them. I'm as anxious to get them out of there as you are, for obvious reasons." The look he flashed me was not one of brotherly love.

I ignored him and asked the obvious question. "So what's your plan, and how soon can we go?"

Suddenly the thud-thud-thud of a helicopter shattered the tense silence. Cody and Dominic jumped to their feet. That stirred everyone else. The two darted upstairs to see where it was headed, though we all knew. Osama bin Laden hadn't waited for dawn.

Everyone raced for the stairs but me. I couldn't move. I sat frozen to the spot, incapable of anything but fervent prayer. Every hope for Bart's rescue born in the last ten minutes dissipated. Every ounce of energy drained from me and I felt nothing but bleak, utter despair.

Then the ground shook as a terrible roar filled the air. It didn't take a rocket scientist to figure out what was happening. The vibrations from the helicopter had triggered the avalanche Dom and Cody feared. I suddenly had hope again. The helicopter shouldn't have had time to land. Osama bin Laden shouldn't have been able to reach the mine, to get to Bart. I flew up the stairs to join the rest at the windows.

The snow had stopped. A full moon peeked through the clouds, lighting the snow-covered landscape outside.

"Get into your gear," Cody ordered. "Let's see what we've got."

It took less than ten minutes to dress, load skis on snowmobiles (including an extra pair for Bart—just in case), and head for the mine. We'd take the machines partway for speed, then ski in silence the rest of the way. This time I had no problem following tracks or keeping up. With five machines in front of me, and Oz riding shotgun beside me, the way couldn't have been clearer, even without lights. When the moon dipped behind the clouds, it was still easy to follow their lead.

The helicopter zipped back and forth across the sky, darting up and down over the mountaintops, and even over the noise of the machines in front of me, I could occasionally hear the thunderous roar of still another snow slide reverberating into the valleys.

What was Osama thinking? Was he furious because he couldn't get in? Or had Cody and Dom overestimated the results of an avalanche? Maybe his landing spot had been disturbed, but he might still be able to drop from the chopper on a line and get in. If there was a way, I knew he'd find it. The leader of the terrorist world was not easily daunted. And he had a special incentive for getting to the mine. My husband.

About halfway, Cody pulled into a clump of trees, where we deserted our snow machines, donned our backpacks, and transferred to skis. Else kept pace with Cody, who maintained the same breakneck speed he had the first time I'd made this trek with him, even with the extra set of ski equipment strapped to his back. But I knew my limitations, and stayed at my own pace with Dad and Oz. As fast as the quartet in front of us were traveling, they still wouldn't beat us by more than a couple of minutes, and I had a much better chance of staying in one piece this way.

When we finally reached the rocks at the top of the mountain overlooking the valley and the mine on the other side, I didn't recognize the scene. The landscape had changed drastically from earlier today. First, there was no mine visible where it should have been. The dark u-shaped timbers had disappeared. No trees were discernible on the snow-swept slopes from the top of the mountain to the bottom, and where the landing zone for the helicopter should have been, a wall of solid white replaced the shelf.

The helicopter swept over the valley again, its spotlight revealing a ridge of snow piled halfway up the mountain on which we stood—evidence of the incredible power behind the avalanche to carry that immense amount of heavy snow so far and so high.

No one spoke. We were riveted by the silent scene before us. Then the helicopter returned and jolted me from contemplating the panorama to doing something before bin Laden did.

"Can we still use your secret entrance, or is it covered?" I asked.

Cody shook his head. "My entrance is covered. Their new ones are covered. There's no way in or out."

CHAPTER 35

"There's got to be a way." I wouldn't accept that answer. Then I had another thought. "If everything's sealed, what will happen in the mine? What about their air supply?"

"Their climate control system should work for a while, depending on how tightly sealed everything is." Cody paused. "Eventually, even it will shut down if it can't get enough air to operate on."

"What about the air shaft Bart found? Will it be blocked, too?"

"I can't tell from here."

"Then let's go find out. We've got to get there before bin Laden does." Cody might not understand the urgency, but Anastasia did, knowing that if we didn't get Bart out before bin Laden got in, it would be too late. Was he so unaccustomed to dealing with terrorism that he was ignorant of how they operated, of their cruelty, their disregard for human life, their disdain for all things not of their world view? Or was he simply unfeeling?

Cody and Else led the pack again, flying over snow sparkling like millions of diamonds strewn luxuriously in front of us. They were beautiful together, a synchronized duo dipping and swerving in perfect unison. They hugged the crest of the mountain as long as possible, then paralleled the tree line until they reached the valley floor, avoiding the avalanche area of possibly unstable snow. The rest of us followed in pairs, Dom and Lion almost keeping pace with the two skilled skiers, Dad and me a short distance behind, and Oz last as rear guard.

The helicopter returned as we congregated at the foot of the mountain. We remained motionless in the trees until it passed. Even in our Arctic whites, we'd be visible in the moonlight and the helicopter's high-intensity beam. Cody and Else led the way, racing across the barren valley floor, skirting the avalanche's path, and sailing up around the far side of the mountain.

We approached from a gradual incline that undulated to the top of the mountain in a series of shallow rises, each dotted with rock formations, some barely discernible under the snow, others rising dramatically toward the midnight blue sky. When the helicopter returned we crouched in the rocks, then crisscrossed up to the last stone formation near the top, the largest and most impressive on the mountainside. Billowing clouds swept across the silver moon, shrouding the snowy scene in mottled shades of darkness and moonlight. A blessing.

Cody slipped his skis off and began digging snow from the foot of a craggy rock. Dom and Lion immediately followed suit. We all silently shed our skis, buried them in the snow, and when Cody, satisfied with their work, discarded his backpack and disappeared into the dark abyss they'd uncovered, we did the same, dropping the backpacks into the hole before we joined the rest.

Someone turned on a small light from their pack, and we gazed around the cramped space into which we crowded. Cody motioned us closer and whispered, "This is the air vent. It's too small for any of us—except possibly Allison—to get through. I did as a skinny teenager. It slopes down about one hundred feet, opening into the shaft where Bart said his bunk is located."

We silently waited for the rest. There had to be more—a plan of some kind. Cody remained mute.

"And what do you propose?" I whispered.

"Nothing."

"Then why are we here?"

"You asked if the air vent was open. Yes, it is."

I was dumbstruck. I couldn't believe what I'd just heard.

"You must have had something in mind when you brought us here," Dad said quietly.

Cody waited for the roar of the helicopter to die away before he spoke. "You're the experts. I figured you'd think of something."

Oz spoke thoughtfully. "If we could get a message to Bart, is there any way he could get out from inside?"

"If we could get a map to him, he could follow it to another entrance that might not be totally buried. We might have time to burrow in to him by the time he made it there—and he could work at it from that direction."

"How do you suggest we get a message to him?" Else voiced the vital question.

"There's only one way," Cody said. "Hand carry it. It can't fall into the hands of anyone else."

Everyone looked at me. I closed my eyes. One hundred feet of very small tunnel. Everyone but Cody knew about my claustrophobia. Or did he? Had I mentioned it this morning? Was there really another way in, and had he chosen this as a way to punish me for all the trouble I'd caused him?

I took a deep breath. For Bart I could do this. For Bart I would do anything. "Okay. Draw your map, and explain to me where I'm going when I get there. And tell me how you survived going through this with your claustrophobia."

Cody smiled. "It was this air vent that caused my claustrophobia. I got stuck, thought I'd never get out. Spent the night. By morning, I was dehydrated enough to squeeze through. But we'll tie ropes around your ankles so we can lower you in, and if you get stuck, we'll pull you out. You'll have to shed that snowsuit. It will add too much bulk."

Did he know what he'd just done to me? My mouth went dry, and my stomach lurched into my throat. Never prone to panic attacks, I felt what must surely be one coming on now. My chest tightened and I couldn't breathe, couldn't get enough air into my lungs to make them work. I turned my back so no one could see the stricken expression on my face, and unzipped the snowsuit. Else helped me out of it, squeezing my trembling hand to give me courage. I needed an infusion of it, an IV full of courage to fill my system before I faced that terrifying tunnel.

Cody had been sketching a map with paper and pencil someone supplied from their backpack. "At the end of the vent, you'll be in an oval-shaped room filled with bunks. To your right is the entrance to the mine, to your left is the end of the shaft. That's the direction you'll take. When you reach the very end, there's a narrow cleft near the ceiling of the right wall, similar to the one you got me out of today."

I memorized the lines on the paper as he pointed them out.

"It's a shelf, about eighteen inches wide and eight feet long, that rises slightly then narrows and dips down. When you shine a light on it, it looks like it dead-ends there, but if you contort your body just right and stand up, there's a vertical shaft with finger grips carved into the rock."

"How far do we climb in the shaft before we get out?" I was glad we were whispering, because my voice trembled like my body. I didn't want Cody to know how panicked I felt.

"Fifty or sixty feet. Then it opens into a small room. There are three openings that lead away from that. Be sure you get the right one, because the other two are traps. In one, the floor drops away into a hole so deep I've never found the bottom. In the second, you wind for several hundred feet before it stops. But the tunnel is so narrow you have to back out. You can't turn around."

"And how do I determine which is the right one?" I shoved my shaking hands in my pockets to hide them.

"If you have a good sense of direction, it's the one on the north. If not, about ten feet in you'll feel some carvings on the top of the tunnel. That's the one you want."

"Who created this maze of tunnels and vents?" Else asked.

"Mother Nature did most of the work. My ancestors enlarged many of them. The mountain had special significance for them once. Miners searching for other lodes continued the network. The whole mountain is honeycombed with shafts and ducts."

I pictured each segment of our escape that Cody described. "You said the end of the tunnel might be blocked by snow, and we'll have to dig ourselves out."

"We'll start on that now, before dawn. By time you get there, with any luck we'll have the entrance cleared. Otherwise, just start digging and we'll find you."

That wasn't as encouraging as I hoped, but better than Bart being trapped inside the mine until Osama could get in, or being trapped and suffocating because no one could get in. I stuffed the paper with Cody's sketches into my pocket as Oz and Dom tied ropes around my ankles.

"Who's going to lower me in?" My heart was beating so wildly I could barely get the words out. I took several deep breaths, trying to calm myself, trying to dispel the awful fear that tight places always created in me.

"Else and I will stay here," Dad said. "Cody and the others will start digging. Any questions, Bunny?"

"Are these tunnels clear, or will they be filled with debris or snakes and spiders?"

Cody grinned. "Didn't I mention the second tunnel—that long, winding, wrong one? There used to be a nest of rattlers at the end. But don't worry. You'll find the right one. You're a smart girl. Besides, if you get that far in the wrong tunnel, the snakes will be hibernating, lethargic. Don't bother them, and they won't bother you." I didn't like the look on Cody's face when he delivered that encouraging bit of news. He enjoyed relaying it a bit too much. Then he turned and followed the three men out into the night to locate one certain spot on a hillside covered with deep snow, where they would commence digging.

That reminded me of something else. "If we have to dig ourselves out, we'll need gloves. Bart may not have any."

Else dug through the backpacks to see if someone had an extra pair. Lionel did. I put them on over my own gloves. At least my hands would be warm.

"One more thing. A light. It sounds like we'll be in a lot of dark spaces."

Else produced a four-inch mini-mag light from her bag. "Anything else?" she asked as I stuffed the light into my pocket.

"How about a clone to do this for me?" I tried to say it lightly, in jest, but my voice quavered when I spoke, betraying my fear.

Dad opened his arms and I went to him, closing my eyes tight to keep the tears back. He knew how scared I was. I couldn't keep that from him.

"Don't leave me in there," I pleaded. "If the rope stops moving, pull me out. Please."

"We will. I promise." Dad kissed my forehead and boosted me up to the opening, which was barely wide enough for my shoulders. I took a deep breath and wriggled into the tight-fitting tunnel that angled gently downward, praying mightily that I'd be able to do this—begging, pleading for power to overcome the claustrophobia that had afflicted me since childhood.

Cody might remember the exact experience that instigated his phobia, but I could not. I'd always had a fear of being enclosed in a small space and not having enough air to breathe. Of being trapped and not being able to get out. Of dying in some cramped spot where no one could find or rescue me.

This should have been a cinch. Just wriggle down this little tunnel and find my husband at the end, sleeping peacefully on his bunk. I didn't even have to climb up, which was a blessing. That would have been difficult enough for someone without claustrophobia. But the apprehension that overwhelmed me as I inched my way down toward Bart told me clearly it wouldn't be that easy. What could go wrong? The knot in the pit of my stomach indicated that whatever could go wrong, would.

And it did. Try as I might, I couldn't get past a narrow spot in the tunnel. I was stuck. I couldn't go forward or backward. I swallowed hard. Now was not the time to lose my cookies. Terror did that to me, and I was filled with terror. It rolled over and around me like giant waves on the sand, pulsed through me with each heartbeat. It paralyzed me, incapacitated my brain, immobilized my body.

Suddenly I felt a tentative tug at the ropes around my ankles. Nothing happened. My shoulders remained wedged in the tunnel. Then the ropes tightened again. This time the pull wasn't experimental. I felt my body stretch, pictured the torturous medieval rack, and wondered if this might add the extra inch to my height I'd always wanted.

Then I was free, being reeled back to the beginning of the suffocating tunnel. Dad caught me and lowered me to the floor in front of him.

"What happened, Bunny?"

"My shoulders got caught in a narrow spot. I couldn't go any farther."

Else grabbed my shoulders and felt the heavily padded quilting. "If you got rid of the sweat shirt, maybe you'd fit."

"Maybe I'd freeze, too. I'm none too warm as it is."

Else unzipped her snowsuit and peeled it down. "Turn your head, Jack. We're going to strip." She tossed him a backpack. "Dig out my jar of petroleum jelly. Alli, take off your shirt." She removed her thin black sweater and traded me for Cody's heavy sweat shirt. "We're decent. You can turn around now. Did you find the jelly?" Dad handed her the open jar of petroleum jelly, and she smeared it liberally on my shoulders.

"Your sweater! You just ruined it." I knew how much Else paid for her clothes. This probably cost her more than my entire clothing allowance for a month during school. Or now.

"It's just a sweater. You've got to get to Bart. Go!" She wiped her hands on my hips, and Dad boosted me to the tunnel.

I stretched my arms out in front and inched forward again, wiggling like a fish to gain forward movement. Slippery as a water slide it wasn't. It required effort to move, even with the downward slope. Encouraged by the successful rescue when I'd been stuck last time, I expended all the energy I had in getting through this part of the exercise, feeling, hoping it would be the worst. After all, I'd have Bart with me for the next phase.

When I reached the narrow portion, I stretched as tall and thin as I could, and managed to wriggle first one shoulder, then the other through, though my heart pounded so wildly in my chest I thought it would burst.

Another ludicrous thought flitted through my head as I continued working my way down the narrow, constricting space. How did a baby feel as it labored its way through the birth canal, having to scrunch its tiny head and shoulders through an amazingly small aperture? Maybe I got stuck during birth. Maybe that's where my claustrophobia originated. I'd have to remember to ask Mom.

How far had I come? The tunnel leveled out, but I couldn't see or hear anything ahead to indicate I neared the end. With no way to measure my progress, one hundred feet might as well be a mile.

Then the tunnel curved sharply, suddenly downward, and at the same time narrowed again. Narrowed even more than the first time. I heard voices—glimpsed light far ahead. But I couldn't move. I tried to back up. I couldn't get back over the hump. I tried to move forward, to dislodge my shoulders, but they were wedged tightly in the tunnel.

Suddenly a shudder shook the mountain, reverberating through my narrow little space, and an explosion echoed through the tunnel.

CHAPTER 36

Oh, Father, where is that legion of guardian angels? I need them. Desperately. Don't let them desert me now.

I had to get out of here. I tried scrunching one shoulder forward and one back. That didn't work. I tried to rotate my body, but my shoulders were wedged so tightly, so firmly that I couldn't even do that. I let out all my breath and tried each movement again. Nothing worked.

I fought the panic rising in me, fought the mind-numbing hysteria that would render me totally unable to think or act rationally. *Bart. Think of Bart.* I had to get out of here and find my husband. I didn't know what the explosion was, but if Osama bin Laden tried to blast the avalanche-packed snow from the mine entrance, he might just succeed.

Or if those trapped in the mine had tried that strategy to free themselves, they might be able to get out, which would give bin Laden access to Bart. I had to get to him first.

I concentrated on my shoulders, visualized shrinking my bones together, compressing them in as small a space as possible, then tucked my shoulder into my neck and stretched my right hand forward, my fingers reaching as far as they could.

Was there something down there?

I tugged the gloves off my right hand and reached again, felt the floor of the tunnel for what I'd thought might be an aberration. Yes. A small crack, possibly formed by water freezing and expanding in a tiny crevice. I didn't care how it got there. That it was there was miracle enough.

I stretched, got the ends of my fingers into the crack, and tried to pull myself forward. Had I felt a little give? I re-gripped, forcing my fingers deeper into the crevice, and tried again. Yes. I felt my right shoulder move the tiniest bit along the rough surface of the tunnel. It might work. I might be able to free myself.

Just as I felt confident I could do it, the ropes tightened around my ankles, and I felt the tug which would drag me backward and undo all I'd accomplished. *No! Not now. Please don't pull me back now!*

I kicked my feet frantically, hoping Dad would feel the movement and stop. Instead, he pulled harder. I kicked again, trying to draw my knees toward me so he could feel the torque from my end. He stopped.

Taking advantage of the momentary lull at the end of the rope, I concentrated, stretched once more, shoved my fingers into the crack, then strained with all my might to free my shoulders. My right shoulder slipped through, thanks to Else's petroleum jelly, then I rotated enough to get my left shoulder through. The spot was so small that I feared for a minute my hips wouldn't make it, but the rotation made it possible.

I was free. I was also ready to lose my cookies. I slipped the gloves back on my hand and wriggled forward as quickly as my body would move down the shaft. If only I could crawl. *If only I didn't have to be here.*

Suddenly I reached the end. The shaft widened slightly, but not enough to sit up or turn around. I'd have to go out on my head. I listened for close sounds, for people in the bunk room, but the voices and noises were farther away.

Inching to the opening, I peered around the edge. A single light on the wall dimly illuminated the area—light enough to get around, but not enough to interfere with sleep. The room seemed deserted. Of course. Just when I needed Bart to be in his bunk so we could quietly slip away, they'd probably pressed him into hard labor, digging them out of the snow. At the entrance to the mine. Why did there always have to be so many difficulties connected with everything I tried to do?

I'd have to go find him. But first I had to locate the ledge Cody told me about. I wanted to know exactly where it was when Bart and I headed for it, not have to stop and search.

Unbelievably, a bunk stood directly under the vent. Maybe Bart's bunk. If there was any possibility he'd turn up in the next few minutes, I'd plop down on his bed and wait for him. But there might not be a minute to waste before bin Laden gained entrance to the mine. We had to be gone before that happened.

I somersaulted down, untied the ropes from my ankles, and pulled them through the shaft. Probably wouldn't need them, but one never knew. Winding them up as I ran to the end of the tunnel, about sixty or seventy feet, I found the ledge Cody described behind some boxes. I moved a couple to make it easier to get up on the ledge, tossed the ropes up, then went to find my husband.

Since I couldn't just walk up to him in the middle of two dozen men and crook my little finger for him to follow me, I needed to blend in with the others. I shined the little light around the room and found a footlocker by each bunk.

The first contained bright orange coveralls. I found a stocking cap, and a baseball hat hanging on the post of one bed. I zipped into the coveralls, then pulled the stocking cap over my hair with the baseball hat on top, tilted low over my eyes. It might not fool anyone, but it would take a second look to determine that I was a woman. Were there women here? Bart hadn't mentioned any.

I breathed a quick prayer and headed for the entrance end of the tunnel. All the inhabitants seemed to be forward since the noise emanated from that direction. I tried to envision what I'd find, but didn't have any success.

Dad or other members of Anastasia probably would have planted explosives as they went, with the ultimate goal of destroying the place. I even spotted niches where they'd likely never be found until it was time to detonate them. But that was not my objective.

The nearer I drew to the voices, the harder my heart pounded. Surely they could hear it as I proceeded through the mine. Around a slight bend in the tunnel, I located the kitchen and the men. More than two dozen crowded around the entrance, cheering or urging someone on, while that many more sat at long tables drinking coffee, ignoring the chaos just beyond them.

I hugged the wall, trying to be inconspicuous in bright orange while I looked in vain for Bart. He was nowhere to be seen. My heart sank. Would I have to wade through that mass of men looking for him? There was no way I would avoid detection.

Noticing what appeared to be another shaft near the entrance, I shoved my hands in my pockets and, with my head down, made for that part of the mine. I watched out the corner of my eye to see if I'd been noticed, but no one paid me any attention.

Turning the corner quickly, hoping to avoid catching the eye of anyone at the entrance, I nearly fell over my husband, who was tied to a chair in full view of the crowd if they turned around. Bart looked up in surprise, then did a double-take as he recognized me. I crouched behind him and untied his hands.

"How did you get in here?" he whispered.

"Through the ventilator shaft. Too bad we can't go out the same way." I whipped off my hat and pulled the knit cap over Bart's blond hair, then tucked my hair up under the hat. "Let's go."

We strolled around the corner, walked by the men at the tables who were intent on conversation, and ran when we hit the empty shaft. I jumped on the boxes and climbed into the narrow shelf at the top, worming my way back as far as I could go. Cody was right. I'd never have expected to be able to get through here. Even with the light, it didn't look like anything but a dead end.

Suddenly we heard shouts from the entrance. Their prisoner was missing! The noisy search headed this way. *Please let the boxes hide us until we can get out of sight.*

Bart's wide shoulders hampered his progress, but he managed to catch me as I wriggled around and stood up in the vertical shaft. That would be a real challenge for him. I shined the light up, saw the finger grips, tucked the light back in my pocket and reached. Bart grabbed my legs and lifted me high enough to catch the higher holes, where I clung with one hand while reaching for the next one.

He'd managed to stand in the shaft, and with his hands on my ankles he boosted me above his head. I scrambled up, easily finding foot and hand holes big enough to slip the toe of my boots into. I climbed that stone ladder with the same fervor and adrenalin rush I'd used to ascend the pine tree and avoid the grizzly. Bart was right behind me.

I tumbled out onto the floor of the small room, and Bart nearly fell on top of me. With the mini-mag, I spotlighted the three arms leading in three different directions.

"North?" I whispered.

He shook his head. I pulled the paper from my pocket and showed him the sketch, not wanting to make any unnecessary sound. "Ceiling markings ten feet in on our escape shaft," I whispered.

We each took one. Not being an expert at marking off distance, I sprawled on the floor, put my hand where my head came, repeated that and figured I was in about ten feet eight inches. I felt backward on the roof of the shaft in huge two-foot circles and found nothing, then used the light to examine it. Still nothing. I came out to try another, expecting to find Bart waiting for me, but he was nowhere in sight.

I shined the light on the arm he'd taken. It was empty. I crawled to the third. Empty. I hadn't bothered to tell him about the rattlesnakes or the bottomless hole. I thought he'd come after me if he found the markings before I did. *Oh, please, don't let us get this close and lose each other.*

With the light between my teeth, I headed into the nearest shaft, watching the floor carefully for the bottomless pit Cody had described. Suddenly I felt something behind me in the small space and gasped, dropping the light.

"This way, Princess." Bart backed out, waited for me to retrieve the light and follow him, then headed into the second shaft.

"Where were you?" I whispered. "I didn't see you in here."

"Around the curve."

"You're sure this is the right one? The two wrong ones are traps."

He stopped. "Feel somewhere above your head. You should feel carvings about where you are."

I did, and wanted to cry with relief.

Bart wormed through the narrow shaft as fast as he could. I left space between us—breathing space. About ten feet of it. I was glad for the coveralls. I'd probably worn my elbows through Else's sweater. Blisters would come next. But we were on our way.

After an interminable amount of time, and innumerable twists and turns, I felt a crispness in the air that hadn't been there before. The end was near. Freedom!

Bart stopped abruptly. He didn't move, didn't speak. I finally couldn't stand it any longer, and crawled to where he was. "What's the matter?" I whispered.

"I can hear voices."

"It should be our guys, digging toward us."

"I'm not sure it is." Bart moved. "Slip up here and see what you think." He expected me to snuggle up next to him, to wedge myself beside him so I could hear? I didn't think so. What if we got stuck and couldn't get out?

"Come on," he urged quietly.

I'd already escaped once today. What I'd accomplished once, surely I could do again. At this point, if it got us out of here, I'd do just about anything. Even chance another bout of claustrophobia.

I wriggled up on one side until he could reach me, then he grasped my coveralls and pulled me forward. We were wedged in like sardines. Of course, having my husband pressed against me wasn't a bad thing, but the situation wasn't exactly conducive to romance.

I listened, heard nothing. "What did you hear?" I whispered.

"Voices."

"Four of them are supposed to be digging us out of here. Cody says the entrance will be buried in snow. All he had to do was find the right spot on a snow-covered hillside, and they'd clear it. I'm betting he hasn't found it. They should be looking or digging now. I think we need to start digging from this end."

Bart didn't say anything for a minute.

"Problem?" I asked.

"There's a spider web of tunnels. The men found dozens and explored them as far as they could. I don't want to bust out of here into the hands of those guys if they found a shorter way out than we did. Do you trust Cody?"

Good question. It was my turn for thoughtful silence. "He got me in to get you, and got us this far. I guess I do."

"You don't sound one hundred percent convinced."

"He doesn't like me much, but I don't think he'd sabotage the rescue—I don't think." Now Bart had planted doubts in my mind. I remembered Cody's glee at telling me about the rattlesnakes, and his obvious delight in my having to worm through the air vent. But would he intentionally let us be harmed? I didn't think so.

"It's got to be our guys," I said. "I'll go first."

"No, let me." Gallant Bart.

"Sorry, Charlie. You don't have claustrophobia. It's ladies before gentlemen." I wriggled ahead until I cleared Bart and could breathe again. The air was cold and fresh. As I put my arm out in front of me to pull myself along, it fell away into nothing. The shaft ended.

I twisted the top of the light to get the dimmest beam and shined it around. The cold air became a breeze when I poked my head over the edge.

"What can you see?" Bart asked.

"Nothing." I shined the high beam down the shaft. There was no bottom as far as I could see. I examined the three walls of the shaft that were visible. No shelves or shafts.

"Hang on to my feet." When I felt Bart grasp my ankles securely, I inched over the side to my waist and shined the light on the wall directly below. About six feet down, I could see a dark spot—another shaft.

"Pull me up." Bart dragged me back. "That jerk. He didn't bother to give me the rest of the directions. Looks like another shaft about six feet below us. I can't see anything else. Now what do we do?"

"Here. Tie this around your waist. I'll lower you down." He handed me one end of a rope. Bless the man. He'd picked up the rope I left on the ledge. I tied it securely around my waist, then looped it again under my arms and slid over the edge into the black void.

CHAPTER 37

With the flashlight, I investigated every angle I could see as Bart lowered me slowly into the cold shaft. There was nothing here except the hole I'd seen from above. Not anxious to enter something Cody hadn't told me about, especially in light of the rattlesnakes he'd mentioned, I let Bart lower me until I could get a good look before I swung in.

I'd discovered the origin of the cold wind. I shined the light as far into the shaft as I could see, and all it revealed was another curve downward. This looked like not just our best hope, but our only one. I crawled into the duct on my hands and knees and shined my light around the corner. "I think this is it," I said quietly to Bart as he peered over the edge. "Now, how are you going to get down here?"

"I'll lower myself over the edge, and you'll grab my legs and pull me in."

That terrified me. "Wait before you do that."

"Why?"

"I have to visualize this. If I can't hold you, you'll fall. Let me see if I can find some way to support myself so your weight won't pull us both over the edge." I examined the shaft. If I got around the corner and braced my feet against the wall, and Bart tied the rope around his waist, he could lower himself down, and when he reached the opening, which he should just be able to do with his six-foot-four-inch height and long arms, I could reel him in. At least that was the way it looked at the moment.

I recited my plan. He agreed it would work. I was glad he had so much confidence in me, because I certainly didn't right now. I hunkered down around the corner with my feet against the wall, said "Ready," and prayed.

As Bart's feet appeared, I pulled the rope tight, guiding his feet toward the ledge. He hung there for a long moment. "Letting go now." I jerked the rope with all my strength and fell backwards down the shaft, pulling Bart into the tunnel with me. I tumbled headfirst upside down in a corkscrew tube resembling a child's spiral playground slide, landing at the bottom seconds before Bart crashed on top of me.

We lay without moving for a second before we sorted out arms and legs and I turned on the light to see where we were. The bottom!

"How do we get out of here?" Bart asked.

I shined the light around the area, highlighting the patch of snow packed against a small opening at ground level. The way to freedom.

"We start digging."

Bart held up his bare hands. "Won't get very far this way."

"Not to worry, love. I came prepared." I pulled off Lionel's extra set of gloves and passed them to my husband. "However, maybe if we shine the light up through the snow and let them know where we are, there's a chance we won't have to dig ourselves completely out."

I crawled to the opening and thrust the mini-mag up through the snow, hoping the high beam could penetrate it. "Cody? Are you up there?" Not wanting to make a lot of noise, in case someone else happened to be there, I didn't yell. Yet. That might come if we didn't get out of here fast enough to suit me. I needed wide open spaces in a hurry.

"I'll take the first shift, Princess, and see how far I get." Bart crawled to the entrance, waiting for me to move so he could go to work. "By the way, thanks for coming in for me. They tried to start another avalanche by blasting to clear the entrance after bin Laden's helicopter caused the first one. I think all it did was shake up the place."

"And me. I was in that tiny little shaft, my shoulders wedged so tight I didn't think I'd ever get out."

Bart wrapped his arms around me and held me tight. "Knowing how small spaces affect you, it means that much more that you'd do it for me."

"I had very selfish motives. I want our baby to have a father to help raise her."

"Wouldn't miss it for the world." Bart kissed my cheek. "Now we'd better get busy and get out of here, so I can get my family safely back to California as soon as possible."

I seconded the motion. That dream had been too real, too vivid to dismiss—a warning I must not ignore a minute longer than necessary. While Bart scooped snow from the entrance into the little cave, I moved it back to make room for the next armful. Periodically I handed him the light to shine up through the snow, but we'd not heard voices since we hit the bottom of the cave. Had they moved away, thinking they weren't in the right place? Or had Cody quit trying to find us?

Cody might give up, but my father and the others would not. If they had to hogtie the man to keep him in place, I knew they'd do it.

Bart poked his head back in and whispered, "Come here. I have an idea." I joined him in the tiny white cosmos he'd created. "This snow is still pretty soft and fluffy. It hasn't had time to pack down. How about if I lift you, and you try to poke your head through?"

I sat on Bart's shoulders and he stood, shoving me up through the snow. I wriggled to make the space bigger, then stood on his shoulders. It worked. I thrust my arms above my head and saw a sliver of silver moon beaming through the clouds—and beautiful Else. She put her finger to her lips to signal silence, then grasped me by my arms and yanked me out.

The snow crumbled in on Bart, covering the hole I'd created. Digging with a frenzy, we were immediately joined by Dad and Oz, and in minutes, we pulled Bart from the snow. They pointed to armed guards standing on a pinnacle near the top of the mountain. Understanding the need for stealth, we saved the rejoicing. Dom, Lion, and Cody joined us, and without speaking, we silently crept through deep snow from one outcropping of rocks to the next, until we reached the starting place where we'd buried the skis.

As we put them on, Cody disappeared back into the hole where we'd found the air shaft I'd slithered through. He tossed up the backpacks, but didn't reappear right away. We were ready to leave before he finally signaled for someone to pull him up. With a wide grin of satisfaction and an exuberant thumbs-up signal, Cody tossed something to Dad. Whatever it was, it made Dad as happy to get it as it did Cody to give it.

Suddenly, the sound of an engine winding up and the distinctive thud-thud-thud of the helicopter shattered the silence. It wasn't returning from a flight; it had just taken off. Everyone dropped to the ground at the base of the rocks and curled into tight little balls as the helicopter rumbled overhead, passing so close that it kicked up the snow like a blizzard.

As the chopper climbed into the sky and swept around the back of the mountain, a deafening explosion reverberated through the night. Cody popped up and took off across the valley, the rest of us trailing behind as fast as we could move. He'd donned his skis while we mimicked rocks.

The explosion triggered a second avalanche. A wall of white thundered down the mountain and across the valley floor in the same path the first had taken. Cody avoided that area, leading us back into the safety of the tree line against the mountain on the opposite side.

We gathered there, waiting for the snow to settle so we could see the results of Osama bin Laden's attempts to get to the mine. He'd succeeded. The timbers at the entrance were once more visible against the white background.

My knees gave way, and I would have sunk to my skis if Bart hadn't grabbed me. "That was too close," I murmured, clinging to my husband as we watched the helicopter attempt to land near the entrance.

"Way too close," he replied. "Thanks, Princess. I don't even like to think what you just saved me from."

Dad signaled Cody and Else, and they took off in the direction of the house.

"We'll wait here," Dad said. "Yesterday before we came, we alerted the FBI and a Special Forces team to stand by in Spencer ready to strike. I called them when I knew you were through the shaft, and they're on their way. Cody and Else will guide them in."

Even from across the valley, we could see the doors open on the mine and dozens of little black and orange dots pour out into the snow. When the helicopter finally settled and the rotor blades wound down, the dots surrounded the machine.

Dad raised his hand, paused until no more men exited the tunnel, then pressed a button on the device Cody had tossed him. Seconds later another deafening explosion rocked the hillside. Then a series of muffled detonations, one after another, blew out portions of the mountain, sending rock and snow and trees careening to the valley below.

A smile of satisfaction lit Dad's face. "Cody planted a few explosives in the tunnels each time he entered over the last few weeks. That should end any hope of using that old mine for their activities."

The helicopter slid off its perch, tumbling end over end, disintegrating as it left pieces strewn down the snow-covered hillside.

As the echoes stopped reverberating through the night, the roar of snow machines, dozens of them, filled the valley. A formation of helicopters swarmed overhead, across the path of the avalanche to the ravaged mountaintop, disgorging hordes of Special Forces troops at the entrance of the mine, as well as above and around it.

Dad spoke into his phone, listened, argued, and hung up. "They insist they can handle this part without our help," he announced with more than a hint of frustration. "Let's get back to the house. We have some mopping up to do while they clean up this mess."

I had a million questions, all of which would have to wait until we reached Cody's house. I didn't understand how Dad could be so close to Osama bin Laden and not make sure he was apprehended. Who on earth had overridden Jack Alexander's authority? What if bin Laden slipped through the fingers of those on the mountain? I wanted him stopped. I wanted his career as the instigator of insidious acts of terrorism ended. I never wanted him to be a threat to Anastasia again. Or to anyone else in the world.

We skied silently to the snow machines, then Bart and I rode together on my Polaris to Cody's. We should all have been rejoicing; Bart had been rescued, Osama bin Laden captured, and the terrorists contained, but even the exuberance of Dominic and Lionel was subdued with disappointment at not being able to participate in the climactic events at the mine.

When we arrived at Cody's, he and Else were filling the table with heaping platters of bacon and eggs and pancakes and pitchers of orange juice. As we sat down to breakfast, physical fatigue and emotional exhaustion hit me with a double-barreled wallop. I didn't have the strength to even pick up my napkin.

Bart reached under the table and squeezed my hand. "Are you okay?" he asked quietly.

I nodded. The exertion of speaking was even too much.

Dad's cell phone rang. He listened, wasn't pleased at the message, and hung up. "I knew we should have insisted on being part of that group in the first chopper. During the last hour, they've scoured every cave and tunnel they can find. No bin Laden. He seems to have evaporated, slipped right through their fingers. You have five minutes to eat, then we're going back. Cody, you and Bart are the only ones familiar with the maze of shafts and tunnels. They've asked for both of you." He nodded at Oz, Dominic, and Lionel. "The four of us will go see if we can do some damage control. Else, I want you and Allison to stay here. Call Margaret. She's leading the roundup in town. Find out if anyone there has news of bin Laden. Get Mai Li and Sky on the airport and highways."

The plates of food disappeared before Dad's five-minute time limit expired, and Bart donned the snowsuit I'd worn. It fit him a lot better than it did me. He brushed a kiss across my nose. "Take a nap, Princess. We'll have some celebrating to do when I get back."

They left on the snow machines with a mighty din. The silence that followed their departure was eerie.

Else pulled me to my feet. "I'll clean up here. You lie down for a few minutes or you'll fall asleep at the table."

I didn't have the energy to argue with her. I didn't even have the energy to make it downstairs to the bedroom. I sank down on the carpet in front of the fire, stretching out next to E Da Hah. Else tossed me a pillow. "You did good, Alli. Made your dad real proud of you, especially knowing how hard it was for you to go into that tiny shaft. Rest for a while, then we'll talk."

"Thanks, Else. Call Mom now, and save the dishes for me to help with later." I fluffed the pillow under my head, but I couldn't sleep. Exhausted as I was, my eyes wouldn't close. Though my body was weary to the bone, my mind bounced from one idea to another like a Ping-Pong ball ricocheting from wall to wall.

Why hadn't they found bin Laden? He should have been in the

helicopter we watched slide down the hill. He didn't have time to get out, did he?

Unless he hadn't been in the chopper!

Unless he'd sent his cell leader to get the mine open and bring Bart out to him. No; he'd want to do his thing in front of the terrorists at the mine. But he could have sent someone to free the entrance while he waited somewhere else. Where would he wait? It couldn't be far. He'd want to stay close enough to get there immediately when the entrance was clear.

Hildegard Piggett's ranch. She wasn't home. Janet was involved with these people up to her earlobes, and it was the closest place besides this to the mine. And just down the hill from here. A ten- or fifteen-minute ski or snowmobile trip.

Else was unloading her backpack on the kitchen counter, an array of personal weapons that she was more than adept at using. If I had to be alone with anyone in the world right now, Else would have been my choice, even over Bart or Dad. I crawled to my feet, adrenalin alone giving me the strength to stand. E Da Hah followed me to the kitchen and leaped to his spot on top of the fridge.

"Else, I just had a thought. The Piggett ranch is just below here in the box canyon. Janet Piggett's the finance person for this group. They could have dropped bin Laden there while the entrance to the mine was cleared. I don't think he can ski since he walks with a cane, but he could send someone, or come on a Ski-Doo."

Else waved her hand over her collection, offering me my choice of weapons. "I thought of that. Cody gave us the layout up here when we went to the mine the first time. Said that's how you got involved." She smiled. "He thought you were quite a bungler until you kept coming up with all the right answers, uncovering the trail he'd kept hidden for so long."

"It took me a while to put all the pieces together in the right order," I admitted. "I should have been smarter and figured it out sooner."

"Seems to me you did pretty good. None of us had even heard of this operation four days ago, and you've been in Idaho only what, three days? The only glitch in the entire exercise was letting someone else take over the roundup. Jack and I discussed that while you were crawling through the tube, but he felt with the number of troops coming in, there wouldn't be a problem if they insisted we'd be in their way. They don't like to bring in someone who hasn't trained with them and isn't familiar with their mode of operation and signals." As she shook her head in exasperation, her blonde hair shimmered in the kitchen light.

I glanced out the window and quickly flipped the light off. With heavy clouds covering the post-dawn sun, lights inside uncurtained windows would shine like a spotlighted stage.

"Which one do you want?" Else asked, pointing at her arsenal.

"You choose for me. You know how I hate to use guns. Just because I can hit the bull's-eye at target practice doesn't mean I could shoot anyone."

"You won't have to. I'll take care of the shooting, Mrs. Allan. Put your hands on your heads and turn around very slowly."

The quiet voice behind us spoke Arabic, a language he'd know from my dossier that I understood and spoke. I didn't want to turn around. I didn't want to look into the eyes of this monster. I didn't want to have nightmares of him as I'd had of Raven.

With a sinking feeling, I remembered the dream. If I stayed, my baby would die. If my baby died, I would, too. An hour ago, I'd thought I'd beat it and was safe from the consequences. I'd thought: what could happen to me, now that Bart was safely out of this man's hands and we'd be on a plane to California before the day was over?

"Turn around," he commanded, all civility gone from his voice. "Since I can't have your husband, I'll take you. It will give me much pleasure, knowing what it will do to him to realize what happened to you, prior to your slow and painful death. Take their guns," he ordered someone I hadn't heard.

Slowly, ever so slowly, I began to swivel, raising my hands to my head at the same time. I heard footsteps coming toward us, then suddenly, in a movement so swift I didn't actually see her do it, Else scooped a gun off the counter, whirled, and fired. The man behind us crumpled to the floor.

E Da Hah, unseen just above them on the refrigerator, struck at the turbaned men with an outstretched paw, growling as he swatted again with the other, connecting with those long claws in both swipes.

Neither of the two men standing beside Osama bin Laden had seen the cat. They whirled toward their leader as he screamed in pain, grabbing his face. Else fired at the trio, and at a gun pointing around the corner as she shoved me into the living room. She tossed me a gun. "Stay down and watch those windows." I crawled behind the chair and kept my eye on the windows.

She paused at the kitchen door, listened to frantic voices in the snow room and garage, then whirled around the door casing, shooting as she went. The door slammed, splintering as her bullets raked it. Outside, I heard snow machines roar to life and disappear down the hill.

When it was all over, the body count was missing the one man I had hoped to see stretched out on the floor. Osama bin Laden had escaped. Again.

"I didn't hear them come in, did you?" I couldn't believe they'd been so quiet that we hadn't heard a door open.

"They must have been downstairs," Else replied. "They couldn't have come in through any of the doors, or we'd have heard them. They must have come here instead of the Piggett ranch and hidden in the basement, waiting for us to relax. Then they would have wiped out Anastasia. Can you get hold of Bart? I'll call Margaret."

I found my phone in my purse, while Else dialed her own to call Idaho Falls. I still had one tiny portion of the battery showing. I punched the radio. "Bart, can you hear me?"

It took a second for him to answer. "What's up, Princess?"

"Osama bin Laden was just here, but he escaped. Else got three of his men, but one was standing right in front of him when she shot, and that saved his miserable life."

"We'll be right there."

Else reported to Mom all that had happened. While she was on the phone, Mom got Sky and Mai Li organizing road blocks into Montana and out of Idaho Falls, and the FBI at airports all around the area. Wasted effort, I knew. He was too slippery. He would do the unexpected. Maybe take that snow machine into Yellowstone Park and spend the winter snowed in there.

E Da Hah watched from his perch atop the fridge as I prepared a special treat for him. Then he joined me by the fire, where I pampered and petted him until Bart, Dad, and the rest of the men returned.

"Come on, Princess. We're getting you out of here." Bart grabbed the snowsuit Else had left hanging in the snow room and thrust it at me. "Put this on." He turned to Else. "What's Margaret's number in Idaho Falls?"

Else dialed and handed Bart her phone. "Send Mai Li to the Spencer Merc right now. By the time she gets there, we should be there, too. Call this number and tell Bishop O'Hare that he and his wife have just won an all-expenses-paid vacation to Idaho for a week. Have him call President Dwyer and tell him he and his wife have won, too. They need to come prepared to go with us to the temple. Whatever they're doing, get them here immediately." Bart recited the bishop's number while I stood speechless.

"You're not moving, Princess," he observed.

"I can't. You amaze me."

Bart helped me into the snowsuit. "I'm not taking any chances on bin Laden's men coming back. Before they can regroup, we're leaving. Anastasia can handle anything else here. I've got to get you back to California—just as soon as we take care of this one very important detail. I figure it might take the bishop's entourage till tomorrow night to get here. In the meantime, we've got an appointment to make at the temple, and you need to go shopping."

"After a hot shower and a nap?" I asked hopefully.

"Affirmative." Bart tied the hood around my face and kissed me.

Oz and Lionel rode shotgun on snowmobiles to the Spencer Merc. Mom waited there for us instead of Mai Li. I should have known she couldn't stay away. I asked Gary to return Mrs. Piggett's Polaris, and to remind Cody to feed Clarence's animals until other arrangements could be made.

I fell asleep snuggled in my husband's arms on the drive to Idaho Falls, listening to Bart and Mom bring each other up to date. I don't remember much of anything until the next morning. When I opened my eyes, Bart was channel surfing, the TV muted, and sun streaming in the window.

"Good morning, Sleeping Beauty. Must be something in the air around here that knocks you out when you go to bed."

"It couldn't possibly be that I only get to bed about every other night."

"Naw. Couldn't have anything to do with that." Bart kissed me good morning, turned on the shower for me, and was shaving when I finished.

"You have our day all planned?" I asked as I stepped out of the shower.

"We have four hours to find you a new wardrobe, unless you're really thrilled with what your mom brought from your closet. At one o'clock we meet the O'Hare and Dwyer families at the airport, and we're scheduled to kneel cross the altar tomorrow morning in that long-awaited ceremony to seal us as husband and wife for eternity, if that meets with your approval."

"You've been a busy man."

"I didn't have anything else to do. My lovely wife was dead to the world for . . ." Our eyes met in the mirror, and I went into his arms.

"I don't much like your choice of words, cowboy." I shuddered, remembering just how close we'd both come yesterday to not making this important appointment.

"Sorry, Princess. I didn't think about it until it came out. It really was too close for both of us. That's why I decided, since you'd admired this lovely little temple by the river, that we'd better not postpone this a minute longer. Do you mind that I took the decision out of your hands?"

"No. It doesn't matter where we make this happen, just that we do." I looked up at him. "Are sure you can stand to be married to me for all eternity? That's a pretty long time."

"It will take me that long to figure out what makes you tick."

I kissed his hairy chest and went to find my clothes. When I'd glanced over the wardrobe Mom brought from home, I decided I didn't need to go shopping. "How about we do the tourist thing this morning instead of shopping? I'd like to see the river by day."

We knocked on Mom and Dad's suite and found they were just leaving for breakfast too, so we all went downstairs together to the hotel restaurant. I couldn't bear to go to Smitty's again. In my mind, that would always be associated with Clarence.

"Any word on the elusive Osama bin Laden?" I asked, hoping, praying he'd been caught.

"None. Seems the man's a regular Houdini," Dad said. "We followed the snowmobile tracks back to the Piggett ranch. While the Special Forces and FBI were busy at the mine, another helicopter landed and whisked him away. Since we didn't get him, I hope he's out of the country by now."

I had a lot of catching up to do, since I'd slept through all the mop-up operations. "What about the terrorist cell they were organizing?"

"Everyone's in custody. Charged with treason. The cell leader was killed when the helicopter rolled down the hill. Janet was apprehended for aiding and abetting the terrorists, and Hildegard Piggett, with her pleasant Pollyanna personality, is recovering in the hospital. I think she even admitted you may have saved her life. That must have been as painful as her fracture." Dad said it with a straight face, but he winked at me, then opened his menu and studied it intently.

I couldn't think of eating until I knew the rest of the story. "Cody really placed those explosives that destroyed the mine?"

Dad nodded. "It seems his treasure might also have been blasted into oblivion. You may owe him an apology, Bunny."

A thought occurred to me. "He'd already placed those explosives before he showed me the way in, hadn't he? If he was ready to blow the place up anyway, why was he so reluctant to help us get to Bart?"

Bart answered this one. "Cody's been working on this case since this faction began moving into the area over a year ago. He had a man on the inside and a timetable all worked out to capture the lot. He'd figured at some point it might be necessary to blow up the mine if he couldn't get the terrorists out any other way, so he'd prepared for that contingency. When we appeared on the scene and I ended up captive there, he thought his man could let him know when things got too dangerous and he could slip me out. He not only didn't want outside help, he didn't think he needed it, right up until Osama bid Laden suddenly appeared on the scene. Then the situation got out of hand fast."

"Guess he's a good guy after all," I conceded. "I'll have to apologize for my erroneous assumptions." I reached for Bart's hand and interlaced my fingers tightly with his. "He did show me how to get you out of there in time, so I'm grateful to him for that. But I was just so furious when I thought all he cared about was that stupid treasure, even when I realized he'd probably been looking for it all his life and discovered it—only to have the terrorists move in on top of it."

Mom looked up from her menu and smiled. "Actually, his treasure may be easier to get at now. The explosion uncovered a rich vein that looked like opal material in one of those three tunnels—the one with the rattlesnakes. He brought back a chunk of rock that contained the makings of an incredible pink opal." Then she leaned close to me and said quietly, "I met your Cody, and I liked him. He told me confidentially that he's been mining the area for years. He found the treasure on his nineteenth birthday while performing a traditional tribal ritual. He's given thousands of dollars to benefit Indian youth programs, but he'd rather no one else knew about that."

"Boy, was I wrong about him!"

"Not really," Mom said with an understanding smile. "You did manage to see beyond his carefully prepared facade. That probably irritated him more than anything. Almost everyone else respected his aloofness and left him alone. That's how he'd managed to keep his alter-ego secret all these years. When he was called away on a job with his agency, he dropped the hint he was off on another archeological dig. No one ever suspected he was anything but what he wanted them to see. Until he met you."

"Have you two made up your minds what you're going to order?" Dad asked, peering over the top of his menu. "Our waitress won't come back until we put these things down and look like we know what we want."

As I looked at my menu, the delicious aromas in the restaurant reminded me I hadn't eaten for a while. As usual. "What about the chemical lab they had? What did the explosion do to that? Wouldn't it have spread viruses and bacteria all over?"

"One of J. J. Cody's specialties was explosives and demolition. He sealed that shaft so it will never again see the light of day," Mom said. "You were right. He is an enigma, but a likeable one."

"Just what arm of the government is he with? And why wouldn't he tell me?" This was the final piece of my puzzle.

Everyone looked at each other, then ducked behind their menus, pretending to study them.

"What? What's going on? Surely you know."

Bart took my hand, looked me in the eye with those incredible azure orbs, and said with a mischievous smile, "He made us promise we wouldn't tell you. He said that would be sufficient payback for 'a curious snoop like you.' His words, not mine," he added quickly.

"That rat! Okay, I rescind my apology. Won't you even give me any hints?"

Mom took pity on me. "I'll give you one. It's a new sister agency that—"

Dad interrupted with a maddening grin. "Maggie, that's enough clues. Let's see how quickly our brilliant daughter can find the answer on her own."

Mom shrugged apologetically.

"That's okay, father of mine. Here's tit for tat. I made a discovery that I'm not going to share with you until I've learned Cody's secret. The longer it takes me to find out who he works for, the longer I'll take to share my tidbit. Let's see how you sleep wondering about that!"

Dad just smiled benignly and waved at the waitress.

Having received all the answers I'd apparently get, I ordered breakfast and stewed over Cody's final victory. There would be a way, and I'd find it, even if he covered his tracks very carefully. He might be an expert in the woods, but I was no slouch at solving puzzles.

After breakfast, Bart and I walked along the Snake River and stopped to read the Ten Commandments carved on a pink marble stone. "If everyone would live by these ten rules, you'd be out of business and I might have a full-time husband," I said wistfully.

"You'd probably get tired of having me around day after day."

"Try me and see."

Arm in arm, we walked a little farther to the war memorials. "Too bad we don't have memorials for the common, everyday heroes. I'll bet there wouldn't be enough room along this whole river to accommodate them all." I thought of Clarence and his choice to step away from his comfortable front porch and make a stand for freedom. A stand that had cost him his life. A reminder that not all battles for freedom were fought in foxholes, and not all soldiers wore uniforms.

"Should we commission one?" Was Bart just playing along, or was he serious?

"Maybe we should build one with no names, and dedicate it to the unsung heroes who quietly make a difference without anyone noticing. I'd like to think that would include just about everybody at one time or another."

"You are such an optimist, Princess. Maybe that's why I love you so much. You see so much good in this world, when there is so much evil."

"How can you not think there's more good than evil? Just count the people we've met in the last four days alone who have made a marked difference because they were inherently good, beginning with Sgt. Mike Saunders in Shreveport; Kay Sterling's friend, Lisa, in Abilene; JoDee and Brock in Tucson; Clarence, Cody, and Gary; not to mention Else saving my life. Even Hildegard Piggett, bless her cantankerous soul. And how many times have you bailed me out?"

"You win. Life is good." We stopped to gaze up at the temple and Bart took me in his arms. "I wasn't sure we were ever going to make it this far. A year ago, when we were baptized, it seemed like having to wait a whole year before we could be married for time and eternity . . . was an eternity. How many times in that last year have I come close to losing you? Now, if something does happen to one of us, at least we'll have the consolation that our separation is only temporary, and we will be together again after this life."

"And all you have to do is keep me in one piece for two more days, then get me on a plane home," I grinned. "Think you can handle it till then?"

As we walked arm in arm back toward the river to watch the rushing, rippling water disappear in a froth of white over the Falls, Bart smiled and shook his head. "I don't know, Princess. Forty-eight hours can be a long time when you have such an affinity for trouble. It may take all of Anastasia to see us safely through these next two days. But since there isn't anything more important to me in the whole world . . ."

"Including catching Osama bin Laden?" I interrupted.

"Especially catching Osama be Laden," Bart affirmed with conviction in his voice, "and every other terrorist in the world." He stopped and looked down at me. "I want you to know that I'd give up this line of work in a heartbeat if I thought that would protect you from danger. When you risked your life and the life of our baby for me, I saw how selfish I'd been in wanting you near me, in wanting to continue getting my thrills at the expense of your safety. Just say the word, Princess, and I'll find another line of work."

I was so overcome with a rush of emotion, I couldn't speak. The one thing I'd hoped for, every time I'd considered quitting Anastasia—and now he offered it as a gift. A gift I couldn't accept.

"No comment?" Bart asked quietly.

I reached up to touch his face. "You'll never know how many times I've yearned to hear you say that. And never more than now with a baby to look forward to. I've always been afraid you'd be on the far side of the world when I needed you most and you wouldn't be able to get home. But I can't ask you to change what you are for me. Fighting terrorism is your life's blood. If you gave it up for me, it wouldn't be long before you'd begin to resent me for taking you from what you love to do. Some men can sit behind a desk and find satisfaction. You can't. But I'm touched that you'd make that sacrifice for me. Thank you."

"Are you sure, Princess?" Bart took my face in both of his hands and tipped it up to search my eyes. "You made the most unselfish decision I've ever known when you missed that flight out of here to stay and find me, knowing there was every possibility you and the baby might not survive. Would you deny me the opportunity to reciprocate?"

"No. It's just not necessary right now. I'll tell you what, big guy. I'll keep the offer in mind, and if the time comes when I think we both could handle it, then I'll give you the opportunity. Okay?"

"Okay." Bart didn't quite succeed in keeping the relief from his voice. He planted a quick kiss on my lips. "If there's anything else you'd like to do before we leave Idaho, speak now. As soon as we're through at the temple tomorrow, I'm taking my two women home to California."

His two women. How wonderful that sounded.

ABOUT THE AUTHOR

Lynn Gardner is an avid storyteller who does careful research to back up the high-adventure romantic thrillers that have made her a popular writer in the LDS market. For her first novel, *Emeralds and Espionage,* she relied on her husband's expertise as a career officer in the Air Force, interviewed a friend in the FBI, and gathered extensive information on the countries in which her adventure took place. Additional extensive research in Hawaii, San Francisco, and New Mexico allowed her to create exciting stories with realistic settings for her other novels.

When Lynn's scheduled trip to Thailand and Sri Lanka was canceled because of raging fires in Southeast Asia, her son and daughter, who both work in the garment industry, were able to visit these countries. With specific instructions from Lynn on sites she'd researched, they gathered the information and took the pictures she needed to make her novel as vivid as all of her others have been.

For *Amethysts and Arson*, Lynn traveled solo 6,000 miles, from coast to coast, through sixteen states, to discover historical sites and other important targets in the major cities of the South for her villain arsonist to destroy.

Jade and Jeopardy takes place on her home ground in California, and also returns to the East coast, to a few favorite locations she fell in love with on previous research trips.

For *Opals and Outrage*, Lynn went all the way home to her roots in Idaho where she was born and raised, before getting married and beginning her travel adventures with her husband for the last forty-two years. She attended high school in Rigby and Blackfoot, and knows and loves the country in southeastern Idaho.

Lynn and her husband, Glenn, make their home in Quartz Hill, California, where they were awaiting their mission call when this book went to press. They are the parents of four children.

Among her many interests, Lynn enjoys reading, golfing with her husband, traveling, beachcombing, writing, family history, and spoiling her five granddaughters and four grandsons.

An excerpt from Clair M. Poulson's
thrilling LDS mystery novel

I'll Find You

PROLOGUE

June 13, 1984

 Squeals of little children's laughter mingled with a warm summer breeze before floating cheerfully through the second-story window of Mindy Egan's home. She smiled and looked up from her cleaning. Through the large window of her son's bedroom, she caught sight of an older model green car moving very slowly down the street toward their house. Her eyes lingered longer than seemed reasonable to Mindy; and for reasons she could not fathom, she felt a sharp twist in the pit of her stomach.
 Instinctively, she stepped closer to the window where she quickly spotted Rusty in the neighbor's front yard as he played with his constant playmate, Jeri Satch. Both almost six, both with tousled hair, both in blue shorts, and both barefoot, they squealed in delight as they chased a bright red ball across the lawn. Reassured, Mindy smiled and turned from the window as her infant daughter began to fuss in the room across the hall.
 Mindy spoke softly to the baby and as she rocked the crib, she thought about how close Rusty and Jeri were as friends; yet they

looked so different. Rusty was light-complexioned, with intensely blue eyes and sandy hair—and in spite of being constantly outside in the summer sunshine, he didn't tan easily. Jeri, on the other hand, had dark brown hair, and skin that seemed to tan instantly with the first appearance of the summer sun. Mindy sighed as she reached for the baby whose cries had intensified. But before her hands had touched her daughter, a terrifying scream from outside penetrated the house. Mindy whirled, and tore through the door, across the hall, and to the window of Rusty's room. Jeri was screaming, Rusty was nowhere to be seen, and an old green car was leaving a trail of blue smoke as it hurtled away from the curb.

"I'll find you!" Jeri screamed as Rusty's head popped up in the front seat of the old sedan and then was shoved roughly back down by the driver.

Mindy realized instantly what was happening, and fled in terror toward the stairs. She ran outside, stumbled, fell down the steps, picked herself up, and rushed across the lawn to where Jeri continued to scream and call Rusty's name.

"Mindy, what's happening?" Katherine Satch yelled from her porch.

"Call 911! He took Rusty!" she shouted.

"Who took . . . ?"

"Just call!" Mindy screamed.

Katherine dialed. Jeri cried. Mindy stared in horror as the green car carrying her son turned a corner two blocks away and disappeared. The mild breeze that only moments before had carried the laughter of children now dispersed the blue exhaust.

When the cops arrived minutes later, Mindy described the green car. She tried to describe the driver, but all she could recall was a black baseball cap.

Little Jeri finally calmed down enough to be of some help. "I told Rusty to stay away from the man in the car," she sobbed.

"What did he say to you kids when he stopped?" Officer Howard Gray asked.

"He wanted to know where somebody lived."

"Where who lived?"

"I don't remember." Jeri started to cry again.

"Mrs. Egan says he was wearing a black hat. Can you think of anything else about the man that will help us recognize him when we find him?" the officer asked.

"You've got to find him. You've got to get Rusty back," Jeri sobbed. "He's my best friend ever."

"We will, Jeri, but we need your help," he assured her. "What else can you remember?"

Jeri was thoughtful for a moment. "His hands were dirty," she said at last.

"Like with dirt from the ground, or spilled food, or maybe grease?" the officer asked.

Her face brightened momentarily. "Yeah. Like when Dad works on the car," she agreed.

"Good," Officer Green said. "He must be a mechanic."

"He wasn't a mechanic," Mindy said firmly.

The officer looked at her. "Why do you say that?"

"His car smoked. Mechanics have cars that run well," she reasoned.

"Maybe," the officer said, "but not necessarily. What else can either of you recall about either the man or the car? Did it have Utah plates?"

Mindy thought hard. She had no idea. Neither did little Jeri, but she remembered something else. Brightening, Jeri said, "He smokes."

"He smokes," the officer repeated. "And how do you know that?"

"A cigarette fell out of his mouth when he grabbed Rusty," she revealed.

A look from Officer Green to his partner sent the other officer scurrying across the yard. "Marlboro," he said when he returned a minute later carrying the partially burned cigarette in a plastic bag.

More police came. Mindy was assured that the department was doing everything that could be done to locate the suspect's car. Thirty tense minutes passed. Mindy's husband, Patrick, rushed in. He embraced his wife who started crying again. The terrible story of the kidnapping of his son was recounted for his benefit.

Jeri, whose eyes were red, sat tentatively on her mother's lap. "I'll find you, Rusty," she said softly and then, before her mother realized what was happening, Jeri was off her lap and racing for the door.

"Come back here, Jeri!" her mother ordered.

Jeri paid no attention, and in a moment she was outside and running up the street in the direction where the green car had taken her best friend forty minutes earlier. Her mother caught her and carried her kicking and screaming back to the Egans' house.

"The police will find him," she assured her daughter, but Jeri was not buying it. "It's my fault he's gone. I should have grabbed his hand," she agonized. "I've got to find him and tell him I'm sorry."

"It's not your fault," Officer Gray said. "It's the bad man's fault, and we will find him."

They found his car.

They did not find the man with greasy hands who wore a black baseball cap and smoked Marlboro cigarettes, or the little sandy-haired, barefoot boy wearing a bright yellow shirt and blue shorts.

The car had been stolen from a garage in Salt Lake City several weeks earlier. The plates on it were Utah plates but belonged to a 1998 Buick. They too were stolen. The car was only about a mile from town, abandoned in a small grove of trees beside the road. Tire tracks indicated another car had been parked in the grove as well. It appeared that the abductor had left another car there for the very purpose of switching. Now the police had no description to work from.

Rusty Egan, a sweet boy, a well-behaved boy—Jeri Satch's best friend—was in serious trouble. Rusty Egan was gone.